To Rupert – my wine-spiration

Summer at the Vineyard

Fliss Chester

ORION

First published in Great Britain in 2018 by Orion Books,
an imprint of The Orion Publishing Group Ltd
Carmelite House, 50 Victoria Embankment,
London EC4Y 0DZ

An Hachette UK company

1 3 5 7 9 10 8 6 4 2

A CIP catalogue record for this book is
available from the British Library.

ISBN 978 1 4091 7864 4

Typeset by Born Group

Pri   s plc

1

'Darlings!'

Jenna Jenkins heard the voice before she saw the person — but she knew full well from the 'not quite screech' timbre that it belonged to Sally Jones. A smile spread across her face as she saw her best friend — bosom buddies since they met at university; the college bar a far cry from the elevated establishment they found themselves in tonight. However, Jenna's smile wasn't just in recognition of her best friend, but also for the fact that 'darlings', plural, referred to the fact that she had turned up to this extraordinarily swanky wine tasting with her boyfriend (relish the word!) Angus.

'I knew you'd be late you naughty things.' Sally bustled up to them, squeezing past a couple of well-dressed gents in pin-stripe suits, to give them both a set of air kisses. Jenna smiled to herself as she leaned in for the greeting, wondering at what point to tell Sally quite *why* they were so late, and whether a rather fancy wine cellar in Piccadilly was quite the place to mention the words 'hanky-spanky' and 'bum cheeks'.

'Sorry, sweetie,' Jenna almost couldn't keep a straight face. 'We just paused for a little, er, lubrication, on the way.'

'Honestly, Jenna, you're invited to a wine tasting, you really shouldn't need to be drinking en route! Angus, I thought I could rely on you to drum some etiquette into this one over the last few months!'

'He's certainly drummed something into me.' Jenna couldn't keep a straight face and turned round to see

Angus reddening like the claret that was being decanted and tasted around the room.

Jenna had been with Angus since they — almost literally — fell into each other's arms on the ski slopes a few months ago, and having been single for so much of her post-university life (and, if she thought about it, bar a few drunken snogs and the odd dance-floor grope, her pre- and during university life, too) it was simply the best feeling in the world to finally have a boyfriend. And if that boyfriend happened to be way over six feet tall, with abs like rock and a head of sandy-coloured hair offset by the most brilliantly blue eyes, not to mention a rakish scar that ran down his left cheek, which to Jenna's mind just made the posh boy just that little bit more edgy — then more the better.

'Shall we get a glass?' Angus said, more to deflect attention from his blushing than to answer Sally's joking probe of a question.

'I'm not sure this one needs any more to drink.' Sally slipped her arm through Jenna's and started to lead her towards a group of familiar faces. 'Do remember, darling, this is one co-ed occasion where it is very much encouraged that you spit!'

Sally and her fiancé Hugo Portman had invited Jenna and Angus to the Peregrine Cellar at Carstairs & Co, London's oldest and most revered wine merchant. Royal warrants were practically spilling out of every bottle and it was the bastion of old-world sophistication and good old-fashioned poshness. Jenna accepted a glass from Angus. Though she was not one to shy away from new experiences — especially if they involved wine — she was more than a little overawed by the place, and its people. It reminded her of her first few days at Cambridge — walking in, thinking you're pretty well the smartest person you know, top of the heap in brains and birth and then, bam — you realise you were so wrong and there is another world out there, another red velvet rope to cross, another whole — and very much higher — level of toff. As if fate was listening in to her inner monologue a man with the reddest of trousers walked past her, his tweed jacket brushing her arm in all its traditional scratchy glory.

'Ah, Jenna!' Hugo bellowed, pulling her into a warm embrace as he made way for the red-trousered man to pass.

'Hello, Hugs,' Jenna replied. 'Sorry we're late, but wow — I had no idea places like this still existed!'

'Family owned since 1701 — and provider of all sorts of deliciousness to *la famille* Portman since 1945, when old grandpops staggered home from fighting the Hun and decided he needed a drink!'

'You do crack me up, Hugo.' Jenna stepped back and let Angus through for a manly handshake and back slap. The two of them — Hugo in his pin-stripe suit and her Angus in a smart blazer and chinos — looked so much more at home than she felt in this 'cellar', the name belying the fact that it looked far more like your average gentleman's club. The wooden linen-fold panelling was glossy from years of polishing — and hanging on it were portraits and landscapes in ornate gold frames, hunting scenes and pencil studies of spaniels and horses — all of which could have easily graced the walls of the National Gallery just down the road. Along three sides of these panelled walls were trestle tables, draped in starched white table cloths. To Jenna, it looked like an incredibly posh village hall all ready for a jumble sale, but instead of the smell of old plimsolls there was a hint of cedar wood and wine in the air, and instead of some grey-haired old dears elbowing you out of the way for that third-hand cardigan, smartly dressed men and women courteously side-stepped each other. On the tables were bottles, decanters, spittoons and neat little bowls of cream crackers there to act as palate cleansers so that those in the know could tell the difference between their merlots and pinots.

'Hugo.' Jenna looked back up towards her friend's fiancé, the huggable Hugo — another old friend from university who had been as keen on the college bar as his books. 'So, what's the deal here then, Mr Wino?'

'Ah, so.' Hugo kept hold of his glass in one hand as he used the other to remove a very official-looking catalogue from his clenched armpit. 'You see you get yourself one of these and it tells you what's on the tables. Then you find the corresponding number and pour yourself a bit and see what you think. If you're feeling very spodlike you can write down your thoughts — how it tastes, the texture—'

'Texture? It's liquid, isn't it? Won't I just end up writing "wet" next to everything?'

'Oh, Jenna,' Sally piped up, having turned around briefly to air kiss a svelte woman, dressed in a charcoal grey pencil skirt and black chiffon blouse.

'As I was saying,' Hugo carried on, winking at Jenna, 'sometimes the texture can tell you a lot. It's not just wet, is it? I mean, sometimes the wine is thick with fruit and sugars and sometimes it's raspy and thin.'

'I wish I was raspy and thin,' murmured Jenna, looking over towards Sally's terribly chic friend and thinking of her own post-getting-a-boyfriend diet that had been hindered by some delicious meals out at various high-end eateries around London. If music be the food of love, then steak and chips and salted caramel chocolate puddings were definitely the food of *lurve*.

'Good thing I like you fruity and, er. . .'

'You can stop right there, Angus!' Jenna glared at him, knowing full well that he was a massive fan of each and every one of her curves. 'And as punishment, go and get

4

me a nice glass of. . .' she took Hugo's catalogue from him and had a quick look through '. . . um, number 15, the Lafite.'

'Punchy start Jenks.' Hugo nodded to himself in appreciation.

Jenna chatted away to her friends while she waited for Angus to get back from the tasting tables, taking in the surroundings and soaking up the atmosphere — reminding herself that this really wasn't the occasion to soak up the wine too. Angus duly returned in a minute or so with a glass of the most exquisite French red wine — a Bordeaux of such distinction that even Jenna couldn't write it off as being just 'a nice winey wine' as she did with most of the plonk that sloshed around her life.

'Blimey, Sals,' Jenna looked towards her friend, 'why don't we get this sort of thing when we come to your house usually?'

'Probably because that's about a thousand pounds a bottle,' the voice was not Sally's, but that of a well-dressed fellow who'd been networking around the room.

'Ah, Jonty,' Hugo made the introductions. 'Chaps, this is my contact here at Carstairs, Jonty Palmer-Johnston. Jonty, you know Sally, the old soon-to-be ball and chain, and this is Jenna, a chum from looniversity, and Angus, her boyfriend.'

'Shame,' Jonty murmured as he surprised Jenna by winking at her and then taking her hand and whisking it up to his lips for the briefest of kisses. Laughing, he turned to Angus and shook him rather vigorously by the hand, while slapping him on the back. Finally, he turned to Sally and gave her a kiss on each cheek, ignoring her 'less of the old' telling off that she was giving Hugo.

'So,' Jonty stood back and addressed the four friends. 'Have you made the introductions yet, Sally?'

5

Jenna looked puzzled, and subconsciously cradled her recently kissed hand in the other one. 'I thought we'd just. . .?'

'No, silly.' Sally slipped her arm into the crook of Jenna's and wheeled her around so that her eyes came to rest on a group of wine tasters, all packed around one area of the trestles. There was a tall, older gentleman with silvery grey hair standing behind the table, talking animatedly with the group and pouring out small amounts into their proffered glasses. He was dressed smartly, but looked so effortlessly chic and so amazingly handsome, that even though he must have been a good forty years older than Jenna she found it hard, once she had noticed him, to take her eyes off him.

'That particular silver fox over there,' Sally explained to her, 'is Philippe Montmorency.'

If Jenna had any spare pennies to her name, one of them would have dropped at the mention of that aristocratic French *nom*. Ever since Sally and Hugo had got engaged they had talked about having their wedding in France. It was a country that they unconditionally loved and when Hugo had suggested that his friend in the wine trade could introduce them to a chateau owner, Sally had been onto it in a flash and arrangements had been made. It was due to Jonty (Jenna started to worry even more about her finances with all these dropping pennies — Sally had been mentioning his name for months!) and indeed Philippe himself, that the wonderfully thick card invitation inviting Jenna and Angus to the wedding of Mr Hugo Fitzwilliam Boniface Portman to Sarah Elizabeth Bronwen Jones — otherwise known as Sally, of course — had the most impressive venue address of Château Montmorency, Margaux, Bordeaux, France.

'Sals,' Jenna felt slightly ashamed at how hard it was to take her eyes off Philippe, 'you naughty thing, you. You never told me what an absolute dreamboat he is!'

6

'He's old enough to be your grandfather, sweetie!'

'I know, I know, I'm not suggesting *that*. He's just so, well, I can't put my finger on it, but so *French*.'

Sally chuckled and squeezed her best friend's arm before turning back to the conversation that Hugo was having with Jonty about his latest order of a few cases of rather nice Burgundy.

Angus replaced Sally at Jenna's side and she filled him in with who the attractive Frenchman was — although not exactly in those terms.

'Now I see why we got such a stiffy,' he said under his breath.

'A what?' Jenna looked at her boyfriend and raised her eyebrows.

'A stiffy. You know — a thick invitation — like the ones you get from Buckingham Palace when you get invited there for garden parties and what not.'

'Yes, dear.' Jenna shook her head and gave Angus a somewhat withering look. 'All those times I've been invited to have tea with the Queen. How could I not know what a stiffy is!' At that point she laughed as Angus raised his eyebrows right back at her.

'Oh, I think you know full well what a stiffy is. I'm just not sure I like the fact it's a rather attractive Frenchman who's given you one!'

Jenna and Angus re-joined Sally, Hugo and Jonty and finally got down to the business of properly tasting some wine. After Jenna's rather strong start, as Hugo had pointed out, she'd let Jonty guide her — and indeed all of them — around the tables, trying the most delicious wines from famous names such as Château Haut Brion and Château Margaux. Jonty eloquently told them about each wine and although Jenna got quite sidetracked when he spoke about the left bank (surely a shopping district in Paris?) and malolactic fermentation (shouldn't you see a doctor about that?) she did take on board that she was lucky enough to be tasting some of the very best wines in the world. He rhapsodised about the first growth wineries — those given a special status by Napoleon III back in 1855 — and Jenna's eyes widened at the cost of the bottles. She tried to concentrate on the socio-cultural lesson she was receiving but all she could think of was what she could do with that money instead. Dinner at La Gavroche. . . a new handbag. . . and probably still have change for a bag of Skittles and the bus ride home. When finally they made it round to the wines that were being presided over by the charismatic Philippe Montmorency, from the less well-known and 'only' *cru bourgeois superieur* estate of Château Montmorency, Jonty wasted no time in introducing them all and letting the older Frenchman take over.

'*Enchanté*,' he had begun by embracing Sally and Hugo warmly and greeting Jenna in that most sophisticated of French ways. She'd blushed as once again her hand had been brushed with the lightest of kisses. After Angus was introduced, he started to talk about his home and its wines in his gently accented English. 'My family have been at Château Montmorency since the 1500s, although the old house was burnt down in 1759 — a terrible thing, terrible. Still, the vineyards were undamaged and my family had a quick glass of wine and rebuilt — so there, that is now the new chateau.' He showed Jenna and Angus a picture on his smart phone of the most elegant stone building — honeyed in colour offset by the verdant green of the vines that grew almost up to the very front of the house.

'I recognise it, Philippe.' Jenna felt almost abashed using his first name — surely someone as princely as Philippe Montmorency should at least be addressed as Count or Le Comte or whatever? 'Sally has been showing me pictures of it — I'm one of her bridesmaids.'

'Of course, *mademoiselle*, she has spoken of her best friend and I have promised her that you shall have one of the finest bedrooms when you come to stay. A beautiful room − like that of a princess.'

Jenna was star struck. Never before had she been so utterly charmed by someone who wasn't trying to get into her knickers − or at least she assumed he wasn't as he just seemed to be the most wonderful, avuncular of gentlemen. She watched as his eyes crinkled into a smile as he told the group about his babies − the first and second wines of the chateau.

'You see, a winemaker has this choice to make,' he continued. 'Do you put all your eggs − or in our case, grapes − into one basket and make a nice wine, or do you split them − take only the very best and make the very best, but risk the second wine not being as good as the blend you could have made if you'd used all of the grapes?'

'Hmm. Like making a punch at a party,' Jenna piped up. Everyone turned to look at her, so she boldly carried on with her metaphor. 'You know, you're inspired by the gods or whatever and your first batch is dreamy-mcdreamface, but you know if you use the dregs later on in the evening to make another batch it'll never live up to the first. . .' she tailed off as her friends awkwardly shuffled their feet and looked anywhere but at her. She was saved by Philippe reaching across the table and gently squeezing her hand.

'*Exactement*, Jenna.' There was an almost audible sigh as Sally, Hugo and Angus relaxed back into the conversation. 'But luckily,' Philippe carried on, 'I think my dregs have made something that you might call "dreamy-mcdream-face", *mademoiselle*. Here, try some.'

Jenna gratefully took a tasting sample from Philippe and made sure she made all the right noises, which truly wasn't hard as the wine, albeit only the 'second' one of the estate was as delicious and well balanced between fruitiness and structure as any of the more well-known wines she'd had that night.

'Cheers, Philippe,' she toasted him. 'With your drink-making skills you can come to one of my parties anytime!'

Philippe chuckled, Sally rolled her eyes and Hugo and Angus creased up laughing, only recovering themselves when Jonty came back to the group, wondering what all the giggling had been about.

'Our dear friend Jenna here,' Hugo put his arm around her and began to explain, 'may not be taking her Master of Wine exams anytime soon, but she's still definitely my favourite mistress of wine, eh, Jenks?'

Jenna wasn't quite sure why what she'd said was so funny but laughed along too before turning back to chat wedmin with Sally.

Sally was about to launch into a varied and detailed description of the canvas covers that Philippe had promised them for the dining chairs at the wedding when she stopped in mid flow. The babble of voices quietened and the sea of red trousers became more like the Red Sea itself, and parted to reveal Bertie making her entrance. Roberta Mason-Hoare to her underlings, of which there were many (in fact, almost everyone else in the world counted as an underling), Bertie to her friends. And Dirty Bertie to her 'special friends', who Sally sometimes uncharitably thought were as numerous as her underlings. Bertie had knocked about with Jenna and Co at university, but ever since she'd inherited some of her grandfather's fortune she'd turned from a nice Suffolk girl to some hideous socialite — complete with transatlantic drawl. Or, as Jenna and Sally sometimes thought, from Pony Club to Private Members Club at the drop of a diamond-encrusted hat.

'Babes!' Bertie swooshed onto the pair. 'Fancy seeing you two here! I thought you'd be more at home with a bag-in-box from Lidl, sweetie.' This barb was directed at

Jenna, who scrunched up her mouth in the effort to keep from saying something very unladylike back to Bertie. Sally came to her aid, as only best friends can.

'Actually, Jenna has been perfecting her palate with this rather nice 2009 Margaux — I think even you'd agree that it's a good enough tipple, Roberta?'

'Oh, yah, quite. Anyways, mwah mwah, ladies, must go mingle, know what I mean?'

In her wake she towed Max, who gave a thumbs-up hello to the girls before eyeing up the tables brimming with the world's finest wines. Max Finch was the final piece in the friendship-group jigsaw. Tall, dark and handsome was the hackneyed phrase that in this case perfectly summed him up, and before she'd met Angus a few months ago, Jenna had thought herself head over heels in love with him. It had taken a recent ski trip — organised by Bertie and during which she snared him for herself — for Jenna to realise that her mostly unrequited love for Max had finally worn out, to be replaced by something much more real and genuine with Angus.

'Wow, she never fails to amaze me,' Jenna said before taking a much needed sip from her glass. She knew full well that Bertie didn't mean her caustic remarks; well, she *meant* them, it's just there was no filter between brain and lips.

'Just ignore her, sweetie,' Sally said. 'I wonder what she's doing here anyway? I know it's not our private party but Hugo said it was pretty exclusive, just those of us who regularly bought wines from Philippe and the other chateaux here tonight.'

'Lucky you — exclusive or not, I think I'm going to get serious wine-rack envy next time I come to your house.'

Sally ignored her friend, lost in her own musings. 'I guess Max buys some too? I wouldn't be surprised if he's been laying down wine since university.'

'I wouldn't be surprised if he's been laying down lots of things since university. . .'

Sally snorted with laughter into her glass, which in turn set Jenna off into giggles.

'I'm so glad you can laugh about him now, darling.'

'I know I wasted so many years crushing on him,' Jenna admitted with a little nostalgic sigh as she cradled her glass in both hands. 'But I couldn't be happier with Angus.'

Jenna looked over to where Angus was in deep conversation with his old friend Max, the latter obviously finally allowed to break free from Bertie's slipstream. Max — and lustful thoughts about him — had taken up so much of Jenna's life until Angus had come along, and seeing them both together like this, as she had done several times over the last few months since they'd got together, always left her with a bit of a tingle. A Jonty-shaped obstacle suddenly blocked her view of her boyfriend and her never-to-be-toyed-with friend and brought her back into the real world.

'Top up?' he said as he leaned in over her and proffered the half-full bottle he was carrying. 'It's a Saint-Emilion 2010 — top-notch stuff.'

'Thank you, yes.' Jenna had never been known to refuse a refill and quickly downed her last gulp.

'So, you're in the art world, I hear?' Jonty expertly poured the ruby-red liquid into her glass, courteously ignoring the fact that as he did so, Jenna was surreptitiously wiping away her accidental wine-moustache with a crumpled-up tissue. 'Must be awfully glamorous — Damien Hirsts all over the place and rich collectors shouting "show me the Monet!"?'

'Ha. Not really. I'm behind a desk most of the day, chasing invoices and ordering stationery. Really not terribly exciting.'

'You should come and join us then. Trips abroad, wine tastings in beautiful vineyards, high-end client entertaining here in London — it's great.'

Jenna couldn't work out if the offer was serious or just Jonty wanting to show off what an exciting business he happened to be in. She looked at him quizzically.

'Honestly, we could use a few nice "gels" round here. Trouble with the wine trade is it's all red-trousered toffs.' He looked down at his own *pantalon rouge* and winked at her. 'And we need a bit of a feminine touch.'

'So you're saying you're like the employment version of a bachelor pad — all black towels, seventy-two-inch TVs and terrible glass coffee tables, desperately in need of some throw cushions and a scented candle?'

'Ha, yes, although I like to think of it more as all leather armchairs and cigars desperately in need of some chintz.'

'Touché. If things go horribly wrong in the art world, I'll let you know.'

Jenna couldn't help but be a little bit buoyed by the whole conversation, especially when Jonty slipped her his business card. She only had time to notice the raised gold embossed type with a Royal Warrant stamped on it in heraldic reds and blues before she quickly slipped it into her handbag as Angus came over to join them.

2

The black cab pulled up outside Jenna's little flat in Battersea, an area of London that could pass for Chelsea if you squinted — or for Tooting if you didn't. As the engine ticked over, Angus handed Jenna out of the cab and then left her to fish around her extraordinarily cluttered handbag for her keys while he paid the driver. Jenna was getting used to these little luxuries — cabs rather than busses, meals out rather than another TV supper in on her own — yes, having a boyfriend with a little spare cash was definitely something she could get used to.

'Found it!' Jenna proudly thrust the bunch of keys in the air, narrowly missing Angus as he walked up the pathway behind her.

'Good-oh — get us in, then.' It wasn't a cold night but the April showers of last month had persisted and rain threatened the pair as they stood exposed on the front path. Angus hovered protectively behind her as she opened the main front door to the Victorian house, which had been converted into several 'bijou' flats. One of these small — some would say downright poky (and some would be right) — flats had come onto the rental market a couple of years ago — just as Jenna had started looking — and she'd leapt at it, loving the fact that she could just about afford to live on her own in London. The idea of sharing a large house with umpteen other flatmates — as so many of her friends did — had struck the fear of God into her, not to mention the fear of constant noise, damp laundry, fights over the TV, the hob, the washing up. . . no, she had left behind dormitory-style living at university. After sharing with a couple of mates for her first few years in London she had finally found this place and she relished having her little home to herself. Of course, it had its downsides. The size was one thing — Jenna could walk the entire length of her flat in under five seconds and barely used the full length of the vacuum cleaner cord to get around the whole place.

Once in through the main front door, Jenna and Angus climbed the narrow staircase up to Flat 3. Ever the optimist, Jenna had hung a little name plate saying 'The Old Vicarage' on the wall next to the door (nothing like a bit of positive visualisation she'd thought to herself, even if the leap from tiny flat to Georgian rectory was a big one). She tipsily traced the words on the plaque as Angus took over key duty and fetched his own set out of his pocket and battled with the three sturdy locks that Jenna insisted were needed, even in one of London's leafier neighbourhoods. The flat's front door led straight into her bedroom-cum-sitting room, which in turn had two doors leading from it, one into the tiny kitchen and one into an even smaller shower room. The whole place was no larger than most flat's front rooms, which in fact this had been before the chancer of a landlord had converted it.

Jenna gave a little sigh as she surveyed the mess. On her own she could just about cope with the lack of storage — coxing and boxing as her mother would say — to find spaces for her work clothes, shoes and handbags. Not to mention suitcases, wedding hats and some rather lovely fabric she had picked up at a vintage sale. All of these things had found a place, over the last couple of years under the bed and around the two little armchairs and coffee table that sat snugly in the bay window of the main living space. She loved to sit there on a Saturday afternoon and see the world go by under the dappled leaves of the London plane tree that stood majestically outside. She wasn't on a busy road, but at one end it ran into Battersea Square, a lovely little village-like market place edged by welcoming restaurants and independent shops. There were nights when she'd peer out of the bay window and look down the road to see the comforting sight of the bars' twinkling fairy lights and hear the laughter and chat of friends and lovers enjoying this little piece of heaven in London. And since Angus had become a fairly regular fixture in her flat they had more often than not been one of those couples — escaping the confines of the flat for an evening and heading down to the square for drinks and supper under the glittering lights. Tonight though, there was no escape from quite how small the flat suddenly felt. Angus's jeans lay across the armchair, his trainers kicked not quite under the bed and his gym bag blocking the bathroom door. Jenna felt rather guilty when the thought passed through her mind that perhaps, just perhaps, she would give up one or two of the little luxuries that being with Angus afforded her, just to get some bloody elbow room back.

'You OK, JJ?'

'Oh, it's just this flat is — well, it's verging on the chaotic.' She let her bag slump down from her shoulder onto the floor — or at least onto last Sunday's papers, which were doing a very good job of becoming a carpet. 'I feel like a battery hen.'

'Or a battery Jen?'

'Ha.' Jenna nudged one of Angus's brogues away from the kitchen door with her toe.

'Look, JJ, if it's getting you down I can always move back in with the 'rents.'

'No, I love having you here, really, it's just it's so small.' Of course Jenna wished Angus would just suggest they combine incomes and find somewhere together — although knowing that his parents had possibly one of the largest houses in the leafy London suburb of Barnes made Jenna question why he'd want to. Why would he ever spend money on renting when he had a parent-pad and a shag-pad at his disposal? Jenna was thinking this all through for the umpteenth time as she slipped into the kitchen. Spit (occasionally) she may have done, but with all the wine they ended up drinking she would definitely need to swallow a glass or two of water if she was going to be at all useful at work the next morning. As she stood at the sink she felt a touch on her arm. She turned round to see Angus looking down at her — his eyes met hers and she remembered why she had put up with the carnage for so many months. He gently took her in both his arms and held her close, kissing the top of her head before resting his cheek against it.

'I'm sorry,' he mumbled into her hair.

'You don't have to be sorry, Angus.' Jenna lifted her face up to look him in the eye. 'You just have to be tidy.' She winked at him and he took that as his cue to hold her tighter and lean down to kiss her, at first softly and then with more passion Barely letting each other go, they stumbled, still fully clothed, towards the bed.

'Oh, Angus,' Jenna sighed through the kisses, 'I'll take chaotic mess with you over *anywhere* with *anyone* else *any* day.'

'I should hope so, JJ. . .' he replied, while slowly starting to run his hand over her blouse, unbuttoning it to reveal her lacy bra. Gradually more clothes came off — his shirt fell victim to her wandering hands, while her skirt was ruched up and before very long tights and knickers were discarded on the ever messier floor. To Jenna's joy Angus brought her to such an exquisite orgasm with his kisses and licks that she barely heard him say '. . .because I love you.'

3

'Late again, Jenna?' Clive Hartley looked down the length of his beaky nose at her. 'Sorry,' she mouthed as she snuck in behind her desk and turned her ancient computer on. As the machine hummed into life and got itself together she did the human version and poured herself a stewed cup of coffee from the 1980s-style percolator that lived in the little kitchenette next to her desk. Her office was on the second floor of the private art gallery — Roach & Hartley — where she worked, itself housed in what would have once been a Georgian townhouse in the glamorous area of Mayfair in London. The gallery had been established in 1836. . . and almost de-established countless times thanks to the founding partners and generations of younger Roaches and Hartleys' gambling habits, luxury lifestyles and dubious business acumen. The one thing no one could say about Clive Hartley and Martin Roach, however, was that they didn't know their onions when it came to the art world. Jenna had started working with them a few years ago and although she could barely manage on her paltry pay packet she loved being at the heart of the art world, working with the best contemporary artists, mounting their exhibitions and dealing in fine art from the previous century, too. It always gave her a buzz to know that her little desk, tucked up on the top floor of the building with a view over the rooftops and their fire escapes, was only a few feet from works by some of the most famous artists in the world. Just last week they had taken possession of a particularly fine set of prints by Picasso and Jenna's task was to generate a hype around them, hopefully culminating in selling them on behalf of their client to the highest private bidder after the month-long exhibition in which they were the star exhibit.

'It's not that I mind, dear,' Clive said to her, crossing the few steps from his larger office across the stairwell and joining her in the cramped little kitchenette. 'I'm just jealous. Pablo and I haven't been out on the razz for months.'

Jenna loved hearing stories about the long-suffering Pablo — Clive's partner of about twenty years and the life and soul of the party when the gallery held its well-attended private view evenings.

'In fact, I think he might be having an affair.' Clive clasped his coffee mug to his chest. 'I caught him Snapchatting another man last night and it led to the most terrible row.'

'Oh, Clive.' Jenna placed the coffee jug back on the percolator's hot plate and faced her boss. As annoying as he could be with his histrionics and downright diva-ish behaviour, he was a gentle old soul really and definitely the more fun of the two managing partners. 'You know those apps only lead to headaches — and heartaches. Too much and they very much become *anti*-social media. . .'

'I know, Jens, I just can't un-see what I saw.'

'Which was?'

'A fully grown man's penis with dog ears and a sticky-out tongue.'

'Oh, Clive — please!' Jenna put her hand up in mock defence. 'Not before I've finished my coffee!' She ushered him out of the kitchenette and guided him back towards his desk. She knew he had as much work to do as she did to get these Picasso prints sold and she fussed around him for a few minutes, fetching him a mug of coffee and a couple of biscuits before settling down to her own computer.

An email pinged up and Jenna smiled as she saw the sender was Angus. As much as she loved her job, she

19

loved that she had Angus in her life even more, and even the sight of his name — Angus Linklater — in the email sender line sent a little tingle all over her body. Just as she was about to open it up and enjoy reading it while sipping her coffee, Martin Roach came huffing up the stairs from his desk in the gallery below. Large and sweaty, he was the polar opposite to the happy-to-indulge Clive. His *raison d'être* seemed to be bullying the staff — if it wasn't Jenna getting two barrels from him it was the interns and part-timers — all of whom were desperate to please and worked for free or for a pittance, just to get a foothold into the competitive art world.

'Jenna, you're fucking late.' His forthrightness took her by surprise, although after all the years she'd worked with him, it really shouldn't have done.

'I'm sorry, Martin. It was the trains—'

'Which one?' His interrogation put her on edge, their mutual distrust of each other widening like a canyon in an earthquake.

'The Battersea Park to Victoria one.'

'That's *one* fucking stop.'

'I'm sorry, Martin.' Jenna knew that no amount of slagging off Southern Rail was going to get her out of this one. The irony being, for once she wasn't late due to being hungover — and genuinely all the trains had been up the swanny that morning — but she could see spittle forming at the sides of his toad-like mouth and it was making her feel too queasy to carry on.

'Well, sort it out and if you're late again, then that's it.' He turned and walked into Clive's room, no doubt to continue his ego-enlarging by pushing his not-inconsiderable weight around.

'Reproached by Roach,' Jenna seethed. And trembled slightly. She hated confrontation and it annoyed her that her automatic reaction to these things was to quake in fear.

Roach was a bully. She wasn't even that late — ten minutes or so at the most — and if she hadn't spent another five hearing about Clive's sex life she could have. . . well, could have got on with her work. She turned back to her computer and shook the mouse to wake up the screen again. There was Angus's email, still unread and beckoning her to open it. She took a sip of her coffee — now lukewarm — and started to read it, smiling as her eyes darted to the bottom and saw three little Xs after his name. Dinner tonight? he suggested. Somewhere fancy. Suddenly Martin Bloody Roach and his bullying ways melted into insignificance and her mind wandered to where in the flat she had flung that little black dress that Angus had liked her in — and out of — so much the other night?

4

Jonty twisted the gold signet ring on his little finger as the tube trundled across West London on its way to Victoria. When he first got it, he'd had to check which hand it should go on. Right as a bachelor, left if you're married. Or was it always left? He'd held back from googling it, not wanting his search history as a stark reminder that he didn't inherently know. He'd settled for left in the end having flicked through the back pages of *Tatler* — the glossy photos of the glams and also-glams in the society-orientated Bystander section revealing so much of how the other half lived. And it was that 'other half' that he was pretty bloody keen to assimilate into. Jonty Palmer-Johnston had been plain old Jonathan Johnston until he got to university and had, by deed poll, inserted his mother's maiden name into the equation. He'd also spent his first term's student loan on the signet ring — finding a second-hand one in a backstreet jeweller, with who-knew-whose crest stamped into it. There had been no paternal back slaps, no ceremony, no coming of age, no fuss, no fanfare. He'd just handed over the cash to the jeweller and slipped it on his pinky. By the time he was meeting fellow cadets from other universities at the Officer Training Corps — the *de rigueur* club to join for those heading off to Sandhurst after formal education — he was introducing himself as Jonty PJ and the ring, along with the muddied Barbour wax-jacket and varying shades of coloured trouser, had become a de facto part of his new personality.

The train shuddered to a halt at Barons Court and the bloke sitting next to him lolled along with the motion and knocked into Jonty's shoulder. Mutual apologies were uttered and Jonty noticed this guy had a signet ring on too. Hell, it was West London, what did he expect? Even the station names were posh — Barons Court, Earl's Court — could it get any more aristocratic? Jonty knew he was halfway there to joining 'em, rather than beating 'em. His big failing though was cash, or rather the lack of it. As the train lurched out of the station he thought more about it and his mind wandered onto the tasting last night. That girl Bertie was something else, for a start. A cheeky glance at her family's account before he left the office last night showed that her family must be loaded. Her father's cellared collection would make any wine geek wet themselves — choice vintages from famous chateaux and more champagne than you could drink — or for that matter, bathe in — in a lifetime. He remembered seeing Bertie's face pop up in those Bystander pages time and again, pouting next to a minor royal or partying on the deck of a super yacht. As much as Jonty would have loved the chance to complete his metamorphosis from lower-middle-class caterpillar to upper-class social butterfly with the help of that trust fund, even the blindest of bats could see she was besotted with Max Finch. As the train clattered out of Gloucester Road station his mind turned to Jenna. Not as glamorous as Bertie, and definitely not as rich, judging by the scuffed suede of her boots and lack of bling. He absent-mindedly twisted his signet ring again, lost in thought as the train bundled along the tracks. Jenna seemed a nice sort of girl, though, who might not be astute enough herself to see through his carefully woven back story and plentiful amounts of rather new tweed and so, in her own way, might be rather perfect for him, rich or not. There was just the teensy problem of her boyfriend. Jonty pondered it as the train pulled into its next stop. A plan was forming in his mind and it blurred into clarity, just like the posters on the station platform did, as the train slowed to a stop.

Jonty got off the tube at Piccadilly Circus and was shoved along with the crowd to the top of the stairs that led from the platform up to street level. The early summer morning had improved since he'd got on the train at Hammersmith and the sun crept over the tops of the buildings that lined Piccadilly, dazzling Jonty as he watched out for puddles due to last night's rainfall. It gave him a buzz, walking down this famous street, heading in the direction of the Ritz, past Hatchards, the oldest book shop in London and the regally named Duke Street St James's. He turned left into the Piccadilly Arcade, a splendid example of *fin de siecle* style, lined with purveyors of stupidly expensive socks and poncy perfumes from Florence. At the other end he emerged into Jermyn Street, where not so long ago he'd steeled himself and forked out for a hand-made suit. The price had been eye-watering (not to mention when the tailor accidentally caught one of his testicles in a zip), but it was worth it to look the part of a gentleman. A few more steps and he came to the small alleyway that discreetly led to the courtyard that contained the head office — and indeed only office, if you didn't count the one in the Cayman Islands — of Carstairs & Co, Wine Merchants To The Filthy Rich. Okay, so he added the last bit himself, but that's certainly how it felt at times. He let himself in and the old-fashioned bell tinkled above the door. The receptionist looked up from behind her large antique desk and smiled at him. He liked it here. It made him feel very much part of the establishment. He just needed to make a bit more money, and if this summer went to plan, then he would certainly be doing just that.

5

Getting ready for a night out at speed should be an Olympic sport, thought Jenna as she hopped across her flat's bedroom-cum-entire-square-footage with one leg in a pair of sheer tights, the other trying to balance her on the way to the bathroom. She'd found the dress she wanted to wear lodged behind one of the little armchairs in the bay window and having dusted it off and given it a cursory sniff, she had hung it up in the shower room, with the water on full blast in order to get the creases out. This was supposed to work, but all it did for Jenna was create a terrible hair-frizzing, steamy atmosphere in which to do her make up. *Creases schmeases*, she thought and grabbed the crumpled LBD off the hanger and slipped it over her head. Its soft cashmere-blend fabric clung to just the right bits — a miracle in the eyes of Jenna and a feat that elevated it to film god status of The Glad-Rag-Iator (unlike The Lying Bitch In The Wardrobe which was a terrible dress that looked stunning on the hanger but made you look like Jabba The Hutt when on — and don't get her started on The Frocky Horror Show, an online purchase that pretended to be silk but made her fear for her life near any naked flame).

Grabbing her hair straighteners she tamed curls and creases in equal measure — although stopped when the slight burning smell from her dress started to overpower the Jo Malone perfume she'd liberally spritzed on it in lieu of a proper dry clean.

She glanced down at her watch — seven forty-five — she had about five more minutes if she was going to get back into the West End by eight thirty. Angus had booked a table at a newish steak and lobster place just off Carnaby Street. It had opened to considerable fanfare about three weeks ago, and now the celebs had stopped showing up the bookings were open to mere mortals. Needless to say, Bertie had regaled them all about it when they saw her last night at the wine tasting — *daaaarling* Cara and *soooper* Kate had been on her table for the opening night along with some 'hedgies' — the ghastly cutesy-sweet term she used to describe hedge-fund managers, who in Jenna's experience were usually neither cute nor sweet.

Five minutes later and she was half running, half hopping down the road to the station, simultaneously cursing and praising her choice of footwear — something this painful to walk in must look simply fabulous, right? Why the hell hadn't she just ordered a cab from one of the many apps stored on her smart phone? Still, the station was in sight and she knew she had a few minutes spare to get her breath back on the platform.

As the train rumbled into Victoria station Jenna mentally planned her route down to the tube — trying to work out which one would have the fewest steps. Step-free access may be for the much-deserving disabled, she thought to herself, but surely it should apply to her tonight too? She flexed her toes before popping them back into her shoes and then looked up and out of the carriage window to see the platform slowly appear next to her as the train slowed down. Something caught her eye. A familiar face. Where had she seen him before? Tall, but not Angus tall, stockier, and with a slightly receding hairline, but quite handsome nonetheless. . . with the train slowing she had just enough time to take in the fact he was well-dressed with a bright pair of red chinos. . . of course! Jonty from the wine tasting! *Avec les pantalons rouge*! Jenna smiled to herself; there was always a certain satisfaction in actually getting to the answer of the 'who's that?' game. With so many people in London it was almost impossible sometimes to work out if the familiar face was local, client, old friend, famous or just another same-ish face you passed every day. The train finally came to a stop and she scooped up her little evening bag from the seat next to her. When she — as elegantly as possible — got off the train she glanced up the platform to see if he was still there, but there was no sign of the roguishly handsome man, or his brilliant red trousers.

Angus waved as she entered the restaurant. Glad of a guide to help her navigate the packed bar and crammed canteen-style tables, she manoeuvred herself through the crowd. Every step in her deeply uncomfortable shoes now felt like an ordeal — *an ordeal through heels*, she thought to herself through gritted teeth as tipsy diners and coat-laden chairs drew out her final few steps painfully. Finally she almost fell into Angus's arms as he got up to greet her, a smile spreading across her face as he kissed her tenderly on the neck, before giving her a peck on the nose. He guided her into the chair opposite him — their little patch of table was at the end of a long trestle and couples and groups were sitting along it; chatting, eating, clinking glasses, picking their teeth, swigging wine, calling wait staff. Jenna turned back to face Angus and relaxed as she subtly flicked off her shoes under the table.

'Hello, gorgeous.' Angus took her hands in his across the table. 'You look stunning tonight, JJ.'

Jenna, who felt more sweaty than stunning, was silently cursing her choice of cashmere as being far too warm for the early summer evening, while thanking it for never showing any sweat marks.

'I just want to take my clothes off,' she blurted out before really realising what she'd said.

'I bet you do, you naughty thing.' Angus chuckled to himself. 'Better wait until we get home though.'

The waiter approached and Angus, who had already been studying the wine list as he waited, ordered a bottle of decent Malbec and asked for a few minutes so they could decide on food.

'And tap water,' a red-faced Jenna cried at the retreating back of the surly waiter who waved a hand in confirmation as he headed back toward the kitchen.

'So, how was your day?' Angus leaned in again and Jenna filled him in on Clive's Snapchat nightmare and grumpy old Martin Roach and his threats to sack her on the spot next time she was late.

'So for God's sake don't let me get too squiffy tonight,' she pleaded. 'I honestly think I'm this close to getting fired.'

'Would it be such a bad thing if you were?'

Jenna had been expecting a 'they'd never let go of you, star employee and borderline genius that you are', or at the very least a 'don't be silly, he's just bluffing the old fool' platitude.

'What do you mean?' She glared at him, losing eye contact only to acknowledge the glasses and bottle of wine that was put in between them. Angus poured them both a glass and ordered them both a steak with a side order of half a lobster each. Adding in a little 'and skinny fries please' Jenna softened again towards her boyfriend, although parked the analysis on how easily bought she could be in the back of her mind for later.

'I mean,' Angus clinked her glass with his, 'if you did lose your job, you could find another one – or come away with me. . .'

'Away? Angus. . . are you. . .?' Jenna's hand started to tremble a little bit, was he leaving London?

'No, no.' He put his glass down and soothed her with a hand over hers. 'It was just an idea. I could work abroad and you could join me.'

Jenna took a long sip and thought about it.

'Just an idea, huh?'

'Yes, honestly. Look, JJ, I'm sure they won't fire you. You'd have to do something pretty catastrophic for them to let you go.'

'Thank God. I can barely pay the bills as it is. . .'

'You know I can always help you out.'

Jenna bristled. She loved Angus and she was grateful that almost as soon as he'd moved in he'd started paying his share of the bills, but apart from being treated to nice meals out, she did not need someone to keep her. The problem was, her own morals were so muddled in her mind she couldn't really articulate them to Angus — especially not when he looked so genuinely caring, not to mention so utterly sexy. Luckily their steaks arrived — sizzling sirloins smothered in melting garlic butter. More glossy, salty butter was dripping down the shell of the half lobster they each had as a side dish, the sheer luxury of it almost making Jenna scared to tuck in. Angus broke the spell by gouging out a deliciously rich piece of white flesh from the lobster and forking it into his mouth. Jenna smiled as a small amount of hot butter dripped down his chin. She reached over and gently wiped it off with her finger before bringing it back to her lips and licking it off.

'Looks like I'm the one who needs to help you out right now.' Jenna's air of seduction was only stymied by the fact that she had leaned over and now got hot buttery sauce on her boobs — well, on her dress, The Glad-Rag-Iator potentially ruined by delicious dairy! Angus knew better than to laugh — or to offer his services as a bust-wiper.

'Bugger.'

'Butter.'

'Yes, bugger butter — I'm sure it'll rinse off later, though.' Jenna tried to console herself. 'I mean, if a sheep or perhaps some Nepalese cashmere-laden goat wandered into a dairy and accidentally wiped butter all over themselves, they wouldn't be stained for the rest of their lives, would they?'

'Not by the butter perhaps, but I can just imagine it now, a nasty internet slur starting, headlined Sexy Sheep In Dirty Dairy Buttery Buggery — well, that would be poor sheepy's reputation stained beyond return!'

Jenna looked quizzically at her boyfriend and then burst out laughing. 'Just wait until poor goaty gets Greedy Goat Is Licking Lobster Lothario then. . .'

Their eyes met as far too many scenarios played out between them both of quite what they might do to each other with all the delicious melted butter and aphrodisiac lobster, not to mention the luscious steaks that they now both tucked into with zeal, swigging back the wine with them. Conversation soon moved on from sheep and goats to Sally and Hugo, and with Jenna having dabbed her own chest to remove as much of the garlicky sauce as possible (it really wouldn't have been seemly to have Angus do it) they chatted about the forthcoming wedding and plans for getting across to France.

'I can't believe it's next weekend.' Jenna had been helping her best friend plan her wedding for ages, although even she would admit she had got a lot more enthusiastic about choosing chair covers and party favours once she was coupled-up.

'Matron of honour, eh?'

'Hey — maid of honour, thank you very much. Not so much of the matron.'

Angus laughed and chewed the last mouthful of his steak. Placing his knife and fork together on the plate he wiped a final French fry around the juices and popped it in his mouth with his fingers.

'Well, my very own maid — hopefully of dishonour — what say you I get the bill and then we can discuss on the way home quite why Sally hasn't given you a wonderfully feathery duster to go with the maid outfit I very much hope your position entitles you to?'

Roughly forty-five minutes and one very steamy cab journey later, Jenna and Angus were back in her little flat. Jenna had had to concentrate very hard on giving the cabbie directions while Angus slowly stroked her thigh, moving his hand further and further towards the moment when she was forced to yell, 'Just here, thanks!' to the bemused driver. As soon as the last lock on The Old Vicarage's door was opened, Angus started kissing Jenna's neck. Small electric sparks coursed through her body and she leaned her head over to one side, stretching out her neck to give Angus as much canvas as he needed to kiss her and kiss her and kiss her. Not missing the cue, he spun her around so he could kiss her cheeks, her forehead, her nose, her lips. . . and locked together they walked and stumbled and laughed their way the few steps from the front door to the bed. Falling back onto it together, the giggling (on Jenna's part, anyway) gave way to passion as they clawed at each other's clothing, kissing all the while. Jenna let her hands feel the taut and contoured muscles of Angus's back and chest through the expensively fine fabric of his shirt, as he let his hands slip under the cashmere of her dress, stroking her thighs, working his way closer and closer towards her most sensitive area. Jenna squealed in delight as his delicate strokes tickled her, her giggles hardening his already proud cock as he gently let her go and started loosening his belt buckle. Getting her breath back for one moment, Jenna lay on her bed, heart racing — pounding with the pleasure of not only what she could see in front of her — toned, sexy, handsome, and, slowly now, naked Angus — but the exquisite knowledge of what was to come. And Angus, as always, did not disappoint. Sure enough, his hands, his kisses, then his licks and nibbles all sent her to the very point of climax so that she felt as if she was on the edge of a cliff, the sea crashing in waves of pleasure below her and then a rush — the swan dive into those crashing waves as she gave herself to him again and again, utterly, fuckingly satisfied and once more giving silent thanks to the gods of orgasms that brought Angus into her life.

'Thank you, darling.' She always felt gratitude was due — especially when tonight really had been all about her, from the fancy meal out to the stupendous orgasm.

'My pleasure, JJ,' Angus lay back on the bed next to her, and turned to face her. 'Maids, even those of honour, need a bit of filth every now and again.'

6

As the plane touched down at Bordeaux airport one week later, Jenna gave a little prayer of thanks. Not only for the safe landing, but also for the fact that finally the debacle of the last couple of days of wedding planning was finally, hopefully, over. She wouldn't have called Sally a bridezilla exactly — more of a wedding-planner-saurus-rex — and Jenna definitely felt her role should be renamed 'made to' rather than 'maid of' honour, as she seemed to have spent the last forty-eight hours at Sally's beck and call being *made to* do everything, be it to double check that everyone had their flight times and outfits, or that the chateau was fully prepared and the fairy lights had been strung 'just so'. Jenna had made so many phone calls to the place she was starting to feel like she was stalking them; the only bonus being that on several occasions she had had the pleasure to actually speak to Philippe Montmorency himself, his dulcet voice reassuring her that all would be well as soon as the wedding party arrived.

'You can't trust the French, though,' Sally had countered with every solution that Jenna had presented her with over the last few days and said again now while on a hushed phone call in the office.

'I thought you loved the French? And France?' Jenna had known Sally for about ten years and at times she still completely mystified her.

'Yes, but, darling, when I'm not there to chivvy them on, who knows where those lovely little John Lewis fairy lights might be now? If they're in the greenhouses and not the orangery, I mean. . .'

Jenna had quickly made her excuses on the phone call at that point — partly because Sally was being a Class A Nightmare and partly because she'd heard Martin Roach huffing and puffing his way up the stairs towards her.

All this had happened earlier in the week — along with the 'quickie' civil ceremony that Sally and Hugo had legally had to do before the big white wedding in France, which in itself was fraught with who should be invited ('Not ghastly Bertie, though Hugo would love Max there I suppose. . .'), where they should go for lunch afterwards ('Oh Le Caprice surely? Or maybe just a few friends at Claridge's?') and what Sally and Jenna, as her witnesses, should both wear ('I'm going to sparkle like Markle in Erdem I think, sweetie!'). Finally, though, Jenna was now out of the office, out of London, landed in France to blue skies and no doubt glorious sunshine. The passengers around her unclunked their seat belts as the light pinged off and started to collect their hand luggage from the overhead lockers.

Jenna waited until she was at the luggage carousel to zip off a quick message to her mum to say she had landed safely, and a slightly longer one to Angus, who wasn't flying in until the next day, in time for the pre-wedding drinkies. She, of course, had to be there to help Sally with the pre-pre-wedding drinkies and suppers and decorating and. . . and. . . Jenna breathed a slight sigh as she waited for her suitcase, imagining the umpteen little chores and last-minute 'essentials' that she'd be doing for her friend. All that aside, there were benefits to being a bridesmaid, and one of them was that Jenna hadn't felt the need to lug a massive hat with her (although more than once at past weddings her choice of hat with the widest of brims had at least preserved her personal space from overly friendly uncles). As the conveyor belt lurched into action she looked around at her fellow passengers, a mix of stylish French, the men with their spotless shoes and jumpers loosely draped over their shoulders prep-school style, the women in huge, dark sunglasses and impossibly tight white jeans on equally impossibly thin legs. Then the Brits, all in all just a little more crumpled in appearance, paler of skin and duller in clothes. . . until she caught sight of a vibrant green pair of trousers. Like a peacock among pheasants he was standing there, a jacket tossed over one shoulder as he tapped his phone screen. Jonty. Jenna wasn't sure if he'd recognise her, so she decided to hang back at least until she had a suitcase to her name before making his acquaintance again. Just as she was looking back towards the luggage carousel he glanced up from his phone. His eyes met hers briefly — she was caught staring at him! Argh! He waved, at least she thought he might have done, but at that moment her suitcase trundled into view and she was caught in that awkward moment of wanting to look at him again and wave a hello, but not wanting to lose her elbow room at the belt. Prioritising the suitcase, she quickly lunged at it, but misjudged the whole thing terribly and ended up catching the handle of the case, but the force of her lunge and her case's awkward position on the conveyor meant her whole body weight was flung onto the belt.

'Fuuuuuu. . .' The embarrassment was almost too much to bear as she flailed around trying to unscramble herself from the moving belt and several other suitcases.

'Stupid English,' a Frenchman snarled at her as he effortlessly reached onto the conveyor and nipped his neat little bag away from her windmilling arms. Jenna felt tears welling up in her eyes as she realised *everyone* was looking at her — and *no one* was helping her. Biting down hard on her lip, she brought her focus away from the laughing and jeering crowd and steadied herself against her case. Just as she was working out how she was going to get off the moving belt with any vague sense of propriety, before the authorities no doubt came to take her away, a Jonty-shaped miracle happened.

'Take my hands.' He reached over to her on the belt — now at least she was facing forward with her arms the easiest thing for him to grab. Five seconds earlier and it would have been her ankles. Pulling her up and off the conveyor he let her hands go, only to grasp onto her again by the tops of her arms, holding her steady as she got her breath and balance back. Jenna was utterly dismayed, embarrassed, dirty, and on the verge of tears. Her lovely pale buttercup yellow jeans that she'd been so careful not to spill anything on during the flight (the temptation for a Bloody Mary had been strong, but she knew herself better than to be lured into having one of those in-flight stain-makers) were lined with greasy stripes from the conveyor and her lightweight blouse had ripped as each panel had turned around the end of the carousel. Clothes, however shredded and dirtied, could be replaced, but her dignity was mashed beyond all repair. She stood dazed, tears springing into the corners of her eyes as Jonty pulled her into a hug. She didn't fight back and wanted his checked-shirted shoulders to envelop her away from the judgmental French eyes.

'Thank you,' she managed to stutter out, as he released her in order to collect her suitcase that had come full circle round the belt again. Back at her side, he put his arm around her and it took almost all she could muster to remember that she hardly knew him, really. Hero to her he may be, but burying herself into his shoulder was perhaps not that seemly.

'Let's get you out of here, shall we?' Jonty gently moved away from her and pulled up the carry handles of both their suitcases. 'Nothing to declare?' he smiled at her as he moved towards the green aisle to exit the arrivals hall.

'Except my genius?' Jenna quoted, before picking up her broken sunglasses that had been going round and around the now almost empty belt. 'I doubt the French will even let me in. . .' she muttered as they headed out towards the main terminal entrance.

Jenna stared out of the window of the BMW hire car, her natural chattiness and politeness temporarily stunted as she ran through the last half hour or so in her mind. She could hardly bear to think back to the luggage lunge disaster — the belt of infamy, the carousel of shame — but after going through passport control Jonty had guided her through the airport and sat her down with a strong coffee while he went and sorted out his car. Gradually, she'd pulled herself together as the hot caffeine shot had coursed through her bloodstream, although she really could have done with that Bloody Mary — or three — now. She'd looked around at the constant flow of people through the airport arrivals hall. No one from their flight had still been around — so if anyone had glanced over they would have just seen a more-than-slightly grubby-looking woman with a bird's nest for hair (the frizz she constantly fought against had decided to pay her a visit just to add to her woes) looking warily back at them. Now, though, through the car window she saw the beginnings of fields of vines. Once past the industrial outskirts of Bordeaux itself, the country-side opened up into beautiful sweeping hillsides, each one hemmed by vines in dizzyingly straight rows. As they sped past row after row they blurred into one and Jenna had to look away to save herself from getting car sick — but hey, what would a patch of vom do to make her outfit look any worse? Still, she couldn't embarrass herself in front of Jonty any more and she looked away from the window and towards him. He'd rolled up the sleeves of his blue and white checked shirt and his aviator-style sunglasses hid his grey-blue eyes. His hair had started to creep back from the top of his forehead but it sort of suited him — it gave him a look of authority and experience, backed up by the solidity of his figure. His arms especially, she noticed, where he gripped the steering wheel with concentration, were muscled while not being ultra-defined — chunkier than Angus's, and slightly hairier.

'I'm so unbelievably grateful.' She felt the need to thank him for about the fifth time since they left the airport.

'Honestly, Jenna, it really was my pleasure. I'm just amazed that no one else leapt to your aid.'

'Froggy gits.'

'I mean, it's not like you weren't flapping around on there for quite some time before I stepped in. . .'

'Oi, don't remind me!' Jenna saw him smile over at her while not wanting to take his eyes too far off the road.

'Seriously though, Jenna, I'm glad I bumped into you.'

'Rescued me, more like!'

'Ha, yeah. All part of the service.'

'Speaking of which. . .' Jenna paused before asking the question that had been on her mind since she first spied the vibrant green trousers in the baggage reclaim hall. 'I know I was plucked from my bed at stupid o'clock this morning to get here so I could help Sally with the organising, but why are you here so early? I mean, you are a guest, aren't you?'

Jonty laughed, but Jenna saw him flex his arm muscles as he squeezed the steering wheel a little tighter. 'Yes, I'm very much a guest — but only from Friday at 5 p.m. onwards. Until then, I'm here on behalf of Carstairs & Co, doing a bit of a meet and greet with Philippe and checking the new vintage is up to what it should be before we take delivery in London, that sort of thing.'

It all sounded rather glamorous to Jenna who listened as Jonty told her all about the wines that the chateau produced and more about Philippe and the Montmorencys — including how some branches of the family were now well established in other typically French industries, such as fashion and foie gras production. As the only child, Philippe had inherited the estate from his father in the 1970s. He'd used his family connections to glean all he could about marketing and brand awareness. The thought of anyone so sophisticated as Philippe Montmorency — with cousins who were fashion designers, for God's sake — seeing her in her current state of *déshabille* sent a fresh wave of shame through Jenna's body.

'I wonder. . .' she started.

'. . . If I can sneak you in to get changed?'

How had he known exactly what she was thinking?

'Yes,' she whispered, knowing full well that their arrival was expected not only by their host but by Sally who would no doubt be on the lookout. 'You might as well chuck me straight in the laundry basket and take me round the back.'

'I'm sure taking you round the back is most guys' idea of heaven, Jenna,' Jonty glanced over at her again and she reddened, 'but I'm afraid I'm a front door kind of guy.'

'I. . . I mean. . . I didn't mean it like that!' she blustered, and Jonty laughed at her.

'I know, I know. I'm sorry, but I couldn't resist.' He kept chuckling at her as they drove along.

'The problem is,' Jenna had calmed down a bit and started picking at the ripped sleeves of her blouse, 'I actually really liked this shirt and now it's totally ruined. I mean, there's darning, and then there's darn well no bloody hope.' She folded her arms across her chest and stared out of the window again. 'I really loved this shirt,' she whispered to herself, but Jonty looked over and smiled at her briefly before concentrating on the road again.

7

Jonty carefully steered the car down the driveway, which was lined with very French-looking poplar trees. He couldn't believe his luck when Jenna had turned up — and around and around — at the airport. There were more than a few times recently when she'd popped into his head, especially when something else of his was in his hand, and being able to play the hero made him feel like a gentleman more than any pair of new Hunter wellies or a box at Ascot could. What's more, he'd enjoyed chatting to her on the drive from the airport and had felt a sense of pride as he pointed out local landmarks as they'd neared the entrance to the chateau itself. Although it was just on the edge of the village — in fact, from most of the front bedrooms you could see across a few acres of vines right into the windows of the little honey-coloured houses — the driveway curled around the estate and gave any guest arriving for the first (or indeed the hundredth) time the most glorious view of the chateau. It was low and wide, with a central portion dominated by stone steps that led up to the raised ground floor, flanked either side by massive stone urns filled with olive trees and roses. The front door itself stood under a stone portico and above that a row of windows echoed those of the ground floor — each one at least six foot tall, the height balanced out by the white shutters that opened like angel's wings beside each one. To the left and right the house rose up to three storeys, again the full-height windows and their white shutters seemed to sparkle in the French sunshine, the whole place glowing like a golden palace surrounded by the lush green of vines and formal terracing. Jonty let Jenna take it all in as he brought the car to a stop in front of the stone staircase.

'Not a bad pad, huh?'

'It's beautiful.'

'The perfect place for a *liaison dangereuse*, wouldn't you say?' Perhaps he'd gone too far. Jenna narrowed her eyes while she looked at him and tilted her head before huffing out a sort of raspberry and turning to open the car door.

'JJ! Darling!' Sally swooped down the stairs towards her, clutching a fistful of papers in one hand and trailing ivy from the other. 'Just in time to help me decorate the orangery, sweetie.'

'Oh good,' whispered Jenna, aware now that a moment to herself over the next few days was going to be as rare as rocking horse poo.

'What on earth happened to you?' Sally had finally noticed Jenna's less than pristine look once she'd kissed hello to Jonty, who had been busy in the background sorting out their cases.

'Honestly, don't ask, Sals. It was terrible.'

'Oh, Jenna. . . you poor thing. Here's me all trailing ivy and seating plans. . .' She passed the crumpled-up papers to Jonty and let the ivy fall from her hand so she could give her old friend a proper hug hello. 'Honestly, sweetie, what happened to you?'

Jenna filled her in on the horror in the arrivals hall and accepted another hug as she was gently mocked by her best friend.

'It's not that I'm not sympathetic. . .' Sally chuckled a bit. 'It's just, well, who else could this have possibly happened to?'

Jenna rolled her eyes. 'Calamity Jane?'

'Calamity Jenna more like, sweetie. Now, come with me, I must take you over to the orangery. Jonty,' she turned to him, 'would you be a darling and take Jenna's bag to her room?' Without waiting for a yay or nay, she bundled Jenna up the steps and into the cool, dark hallway of the house. Beautiful encaustic tiles covered the floor, while the walls — there were six making up a large hexagon — were painted in the most ethereal and romantic *trompe l'œil*; chubby cherubs sat upon popcorn-puffed clouds, looking down with their lyres and flutes to figures in a pastoral landscape who were obviously enjoying some bacchanalian delights as they feasted on meats and grapes while wine was poured by buxom serving wenches into their goblets and mouths.

'Inspiration for the wedding reception?' Jenna asked her friend, winking at her as she did.

'It's rather fun, isn't it? Hugo would have loved that — in fact, please don't remind him, sweetie, or he'll have us all in togas and sandals, feasting on haunches of venison before you can say "where's the orgy" — and as fun as that could be, Mummy would *not* be impressed!'

The girls laughed and for the first time since arriving in Bordeaux, Jenna started having fun. Sally showed her round to the back of the chateau, although it was no less grand for that. The 'back door' of the house led straight onto a terrace — the same width as the house and deep too. A grey-and-white cat sat looking at them from atop a stone balustrade as Sally showed her over the edge. The view was unreal and Jenna pinched herself. The gravelled terrace had two sweeping staircases that led to a lower terrace with formal lawns and a pond, edged by box trees. Beyond that, the vineyards started and never seemed to stop as they followed the contours of the hilly land.

'The slopes make for the best grapes,' the voice was low and kind and Jenna turned round to see Philippe, in all his silver foxy glory. Sally made the re-introductions and Jenna had to hold back from telling her friend quite how many times she had spoken to Philippe on the phone in the course of the last few days of wedmin.

'A pleasure, as always.' He deftly leaned in to kiss her on each cheek, his aftershave a musky mix of cedar wood and figs.

'And for me, Philippe,' Jenna blushed, knowing that his next glance would be to see how terribly dirty and messy she looked. But he serenely moved on, bowing his apologies that he couldn't stay longer chatting and reassuring Sally that the orangery, the main venue for both the wedding and the wedding eve supper party, was looking *magnifique*.

And *magnifique* it was. Sally showed Jenna round the side of the chateau to the orangery — a room that the palace of Versailles wouldn't deem too shabby. Double height doors and windows flooded light into the pale stone interior and in between every window or door there was an enormous terracotta pot with a hugely mature orange or lemon tree in it. The whole room was fizzing with the aromas of pinched citrus peel, like the final spritz a bartender puts on a Cosmopolitan. Jenna whirled, her arms full-stretched as she took in the grandeur of the building.

'Of course, the long table will take up about half the length,' Sally told her, pointing out other bits of decorating that the two girls would put themselves to for the rest of the afternoon. 'Lights up there and ivy swags across the tops of the windows.'

'It'll be glorious, Sals, you lucky, lucky thing.'

'I am lucky, aren't I?' Sally seemed to take a moment of genuine reflection on her life. 'Hugo's been so good about all of this — as have Mummy and Daddy. I know they dreamt of my wedding being at home in Suffolk, but when the chance to be here turned up. . . I, well, *we* couldn't say no.'

'Now I can definitely see why!' Jenna gawped up at the swags, and not just the few ivy ones already in place but the old, softly hewn stone ones too. 'I mean if I. . .'

'You, darling, and Angus will have to have the big English country wedding so we don't miss out!'

The mention of Angus made Jenna automatically reach for her phone. He'd seen her message, the two little blue ticks showed her that, but there was no reply.

A few hours later and Jenna finally felt thankful for her pre-ruined clothes, as she'd been shimmying up and down old wooden ladders ('Well, if you're dirty anyway, darling, saves my Jigsaw troos!) hoisting up more swags of fresh ivy dotted with fairy lights ('I knew Jonny Lewis wouldn't let me down — these tiny flower lights from Peter Jones are spot on!') and lugging in gold-painted wooden chairs, newly delivered by the catering company.

'Ten down each side for tomorrow night,' Sally brusquely ordered, forgetting she was talking to her best friend and not a minion. 'And then a space and then the rest for the wedding breakfast.'

'I still can never understand why it's called that.' Jenna tried to bring Sally back to normal chat — it was that or snap back at her orders.

'Oh, sweetie, me neither, but tradition is tradition.'

'Maybe it's because in the old days, when you were marrying your smelly, pox-ridden cousin, you had to be still drunk from the night before to go through with it. Then you could sober up over breakfast.'

'Whereas we prefer a nice sober ceremony and a boozy feast — oh, how times have changed.'

'And with that lesson on the history of weddings, I am done.' Jenna wiped her hands down her once yellow, more now sort of *greige* jeans and picked the worst of the dirt out from under her fingernails. With thanks and hugs

44

exchanged, Jenna and Sally closed the door on the orangery and wandered out back towards the lower terrace. The last traces of afternoon light fell softly across the lawns and gravel paths and the friends took deep breaths of the warm early evening air, suffused as it was with the heady aroma of jasmine and honeysuckle. All in all it was a relief from the heat that had been building up in the orangery as they worked. Jenna saw the grey-and-white cat again, and without thinking walked over to go and pet it. What she had failed to notice was the cat was sitting the other side of a low channel that fed water down into the ornamental pond with its trickling fountain. In broad daylight you could clearly see it, but now in the gloaming it seemed to be just another part of the pathway and before she could save herself Jenna had splashed down into it, one foot tearing through a layer of protective netting while the rest of her body followed suit and slid and skidded into the narrow channel.

'Fuuuuuu. . .' For the second time that day, Jenna couldn't quite believe what was happening to her. As her arse struck the bottom of the channel she gave some thanks that it was only a few centimetres deep, something that was highlighted as the terrace spotlights suddenly turned on and she was captured in the full glare of them, like a starlet on the stage about to debut her first song. . . but all she wanted to do was disappear into the ground and she cursed and splashed and flailed as she tried to disentangle herself from the netting that she was now practically a living part of.

Alongside Sally's gasps and giggles, she heard voices and a fast pace of steps down the stone stairs coming towards her. Jonty, her knight in shining armour — or at least in dry clothing — ran towards her, narrowly missing the slippery stones of the channel himself.

'Jenna!' he yelled, but realised the drama was all but over as he took in the scene — Jenna slapping her hands down into the water in disgust while Sally took a quick photo — holding her phone as stable as she could while still in hoots of laughter.

'Just one more,' Sally snapped away, 'then you can rescue her again Jonty!'

At that Jenna said some words that need not be repeated and once again offered her arms up to Jonty to be helped out of her little mess. As he pulled her out, her foot became even more tangled in the netting and she skipped about on the path on one leg, clasping onto Jonty while Sally carefully unpicked her from it.

'Let's get you inside, shall we?' Jonty suggested as he gently let her go. 'And out of these wet clothes.'

'Yes,' said Jenna and then after a pause. 'And preferably straight into a dry martini.'

8

Beyond exhausted, beyond dignified. . . beyond wanting to be sober any more, Jenna climbed the grand staircase that swooped up from the hexagonal hallway with its orgytastic walls, careful not to let her sodden shoes, which she cradled to her chest, drip on the pristine steps. Not that her blouse and trousers weren't as wet as a bilge pump (in fact, she could just about pass herself off in Portsmouth as the prow of a ship at the moment) but she thought she should at least try to do what she could to preserve the chateau's interiors — if not her long-lost dignity. She followed Jonty, who led her along the first-floor corridor, past several large, wide, wooden doors to the room at the far end of the east wing. She knew it was the east wing as Jonty pointed out the figure of a puff-cheeked cherub who was apparently the west wind, blowing them down the ornately painted corridor towards the east — but Jenna, who usually fell over backwards to see wonderful works of art in situ, was just plain done with falling over at all and could barely contain her relief as she was shown into her room.

'Thank you, Jonty — I mean, for showing me up here. And of course for just now. And earlier. Oh God — you must think I'm the most terrible klutz.' Jenna bowed her head but raised it up as she waited for him to answer.

'I think it's quite endearing, actually.' His voice was soft and Jenna felt like he really meant it. As she looked up at him she felt the leaden weight of all her daily traumas fall away. She had just began to smile at him when he suddenly turned on his heel and walked briskly down the hall, calling back that she should relax and have a bath but be down in time for drinks at eight thirty.

Usually one to overthink every single action, Jenna uncharacteristically simply turned into her room and took it in, finally, in all of its rococo glory. It was beautiful, with white painted panels covering the walls, the panels themselves wide enough to hold portraits of haughty-looking comtesses; at least six of them looked down on Jenna who stood dripping onto the wide wooden floorboards. 'Sorry!' she whispered to them as she moved towards the other side of the room, past the elegant four-poster bed hung with swags of silk so that it looked like a ship in flight to Neverland. *There must be some mistake*, she thought, *this must be the bridal suite*. . . but no, for there hanging against the wardrobe door was the soft peach-coloured bridesmaid dress that she'd spent so long with Sally choosing, and her suitcase was neatly placed on a rack at the end of the bed.

Bridal suite or not, she was relieved as hell to find a massive en-suite bathroom. It too was panelled, this time painted a soft duck-egg blue, with the ceiling decorated to represent clouds, again with cheeky little cherubs looking down on her. She turned on the hot tap of the deep roll-top bath and heard the reassuring gurgle of ancient plumbing clanking into action. Surprisingly quickly, steam started to rise up from the gushing tap and she added a little splash of bath oil that had been thoughtfully put out on a side table next to the bath. Pulling off her damp and dirtied jeans she half walked and half hopped back to the bedroom, realising catastrophically late that her mobile phone had been as drenched as she had been. *That bloody cat*, she thought as she stared into the black, dead screen of her phone. Annoyingly, she'd thought she felt a reassuring buzz just before pond-gate and felt sure that must have been Angus texting her back — but now, without help from a tech whizz or a very large bag of rice, she wouldn't know. A tear welled up at the side of her eye, but she brushed it away and headed back into the bathroom for a well-earned soak.

'JJ!' Hugo's voice boomed across the drawing room as Jenna entered. Refreshed in some part by the bath, and in others by the little decanter of brandy she found on a side table in her bedroom, she felt more able to take on the crowd.

'Hello, Hugs — groom-to-be!' She let him fold her up into one of his signature bear hugs.

'You remember mater and pater, don't you, Jenna? Mum, Pops, this is Jenna, Sals' best pal and maid of honour *extraordinaire*.' Jenna embraced Hugo's parents and was about to start explaining that the only extraordinary thing about her so far was how many things she'd managed to fall into today when she was tapped on the shoulder by Sally who then whisked her off to say hello to her parents, who in turn greeted her with genuine warmth and chattiness.

The quick bath-time brandy aside, Jenna was gasping for a drink and made a beeline for the waitress who had just entered the room bearing a tray of chilled white wine in elegant, tall-stemmed glasses. Just as she was taking one off the tray, Jenna paused — this was no local French girl earning a few euros on the side. . .

'Izzy!' Jenna was shocked to see the chalet girl from her holiday just a few months ago now here in the chateau. Izzy had made quite an impression on most of the chalet guests in one way or the other. She'd slept with Max even while he'd been coming on to both her and Bertie, Jenna was pretty much sure of that. Sally and Hugo, though, had been so impressed by her catering skills that they'd stayed true to their word and got her quite a few private dining gigs in London since the ski season had officially finished, barely a month ago. And now, as Jenna took a glass of blissfully chilled white wine from her tray, she filled her in on why she was here.

'Yah, so like, my gap-year internship at Daddy's company just seemed so dull and I realised that I just really, really like cooking and stuff. So basically Sally has been awesome — I mean props to her totally — and got me a few jobs.'

'Gosh, so you're doing the catering for the whole wedding?'

'Yah, well, no, I mean, I'm helping Menou and his team, which is increds. He's amaze and this will totes help my CV look dookie fresh.'

Jenna could only bear to talk to Izzy in short bursts as it was quite a mental strain to understand her through all the lingo and abbreviations she used. Still, she was relieved when Izzy said she was sure there was some rice in the kitchen and she could take her damp phone there and give drying it out a go. Jenna smiled a farewell and turned back towards the room where Jonty suddenly caught her eye. Jenna looked at him. He'd smartened up his look since rescuing her from the water — the poor man hadn't had a choice really as she was sure her splashing had probably covered him in almost as much pond weed as her. He stood there now in smart burgundy-coloured corduroy trousers with a soft blue shirt tucked into them, the sleeves neatly rolled up to his elbows. She noticed his very smart leather-strapped watch and gold signet ring, both highlighting his lightly tanned arms.

'Feeling better?' He chinked glasses with her as she started about the fortieth thanks of the day. Waving it away he continued, 'So where is Angus tonight? He's invited right?'

'Of course.' Jenna seemed a little affronted at the thought that he wouldn't be. They were an established couple after all. 'He had to work, but he flies in tomorrow. But obviously, idiot-brain here has soaked her phone.' She gestured loosely towards herself. 'I'm sure he's probably sending me tracts of love poetry over text right now that I'll never receive!'

'Or dick picks.' Jonty raised his eyebrows at her. Jenna hadn't failed to notice that this was the second naughty reference since they arrived and logged it in her mind to be cross-examined later.

'I hope not. I gave him Sally's number as an emergency contact before I left and I think that's the last thing the bride-to-be needs!'

Almost on cue, Sally interrupted them and showed Jenna her phone. 'It's Angus, darling, a message.' Jenna hoped it wasn't a picture of his manhood, as much as she'd grown to love it, and was relieved when there were words and not willies on the screen. She read it and her heart almost swelled to cardiac arresting proportions. It said, 'Tell that fruit loop of mine I'll be there with a new phone for her tomorrow.' Those simple words made up for all the crappiness the day had flung at her and she beamed through drinkies and supper, making light conversation with the parents and the ever charming Philippe, and then headed up to her fairy-tale suite, thoughts of her lovely boyfriend and his super-thoughtful and generous ways brimming over in her mind. It was only when she got to her room and found, on the neatly turned-back duvet on her four-poster bed, a beautiful creamy silk blouse delicately embroidered with little flowers, that she stopped thinking of him. Because next to the beautiful blouse was a note that said;

'I may just be a replacement, but I hope you love me too. J x'

51

9

'He did what?' Sally looked incredulous as she buttered another chunk of croissant. The girls were the last down to breakfast and were mopping up what was left of the classic continental spread. Jenna had packed a piece of French baguette with cheese and ham because, well, just because, and she had a mouthful of it to get through before she could answer Sally, who from all appearances had thrown the pre-wedding diet to the four winds. 'He knows you have a boyfriend, right? And a silk blouse, I mean where the hell did he find that in those few hours?' The same thought had been going through Jenna's mind, along with 'what the actual hell?' and 'what does this mean?' since approximately 11.30 p.m. the night before.

Finally swallowing her chunk of sandwich, she replied, 'I have absolutely no idea. I mean, does he carry ladies' clothing around with him? Or does this village have a small boutique lurking in the vines?'

'To be fair, it might. . .' Sally mused on the point. 'But no matter *how* he got it, *why* he got it is far more interesting!'

'Bloody hell, yeah.' Jenna paused to slurp some rapidly cooling coffee. 'Do you think he likes me?'

'I can't see why not, but he does know about Angus. He met him!'

'Speaking of Angus, I can't tell him where it came from! I mean, I can't, can I? And with him staying in my snug little pad as often as he does, like all the time, he pretty much knows all my shirts.'

'I see your problem, sweetie. Hey — tell him it's mine. Or even better, from me. As a present. There you go, bridesmaid!' Sally pretended to hand a package across the table to Jenna.

'Ha! Thanks, Sals, so generous, very kind.' Jenna clinked her wide-brimmed coffee cup against Sally's and carried on chewing her massive cheese and ham sandwich, thoughts of Jonty and exquisite shirts whizzing around her head.

Izzy pushed the kitchen door open with her bum and put the tray down on the large refectory table. It reminded her of the one they had at home and that in turn reminded her of how disappointed her dad had been when she said she didn't want to go to Oxford. After all the post-school crammers she'd got into one of the best colleges there and there'd been tears as her parents had pleaded with her to think of her education and put it to good use. But she had rebelled because ever since she'd worked in that chalet this winter she'd enjoyed hostessing — it wasn't exactly hard (although to be fair, some pleasantly hard things had come into it — and her) and she was certain learning how to make delicious canapés and mingle among the upper classes was actually a much better continuation of her education than going to a fusty old uni or filling up photocopiers at Daddy's boring bank. Plus, there were some other benefits to working in this chateau.

'I'll tell Jenna to head downstairs,' she purred at Jonty, who was perched on the edge of the table, eating a plum from the earthenware bowl she had artfully arranged earlier that morning.

'Thanks, Iz, you're the best.' He leaned over and kissed her on the cheek — a kiss that although a hair's breadth from her lips was far too chaste for Izzy's liking. He might not be a Max, that roguishly handsome and ridiculously rich dickhead from the chalet, but she could see how someone like Jonty Palmer-Johnston could prove her darling daddy oh so wrong when he realised she could end up doing just as well by bonking rather than banking.

'Morning all!' Hugo burst into the room and greeted his fiancée and Jenna with such gusto it was hard not to laugh along with him. 'We're getting married in the morning. . .' he sang, 'ding dong the bells are gonna chime!' he flung his arms up as he scaled the high note, then stopped and deadpanned, 'which gives you about twenty-four hours to change your mind and skidaddle.' At that he planted a kiss on Sally's head and squeezed her shoulders.

'Oh, Hugo, you big silly.' Sally covered his hands with hers and hummed along with the tune. Jenna looked over at them and smiled, the thought occurring to her that now she was 'boyfriended-up', as it were, it might not be so out of the realms of reality to start thinking that this may well be her in a year or so. The happy three-some were interrupted by Izzy clattering in with a tray and a message for Jenna. Could she meet Jonty down in the cellar? Jenna looked over to Sally who raised her eyebrows at her, that one movement basically saying 'For God's sake go, I'm desperate to know what he's up to and if it means sacrificing yourself to the altar of boyfriend trouble, then so be it'.

Why on earth did Jonty want to see her? Instead of cheese and ham, her stomach seemed to be filled with wriggling bugs and as she searched around the ground floor trying to find the door to the cellar, the bugs wriggled more and more in anticipation of seeing him for the first time since *that* blouse had made its mysterious appearance. She once again found herself in the hexagonal hallway having walked back along the corridor from the breakfast room. One of the doors leading off it was ajar and through it she glanced a large study or library perhaps — its walls lined with bookcases and a large partner's desk in the middle. She was about to nose her way in when she saw that Philippe himself was sitting at the desk. She paused, not wanting to make a sound and disturb him but she lingered two moments more and noticed that his shoulders seemed a little more rounded than usual, a little less poised and his head, cradled in his hands was looking down at sheets and sheets of paperwork. Jenna edged away from the door and turned back into the decorated hallway, noticing then the almost imperceptible door under the staircase, painted to match the panelling all around it. It, too, was slightly ajar and as she pulled it open she knew she'd found the cellar as an unmistakable smell of damp and dust hit her. The door opened to reveal a staircase that steeply descended to the right. In front of her, as the top step turned into the staircase, she noticed harsh black brush strokes along the bare plaster wall spelling out, 'Ici on parle français'. She pondered the odd phrase, 'here we speak French' and thought she'd ask poor old Philippe about it later. She turned and followed the steps down, lit as they were by a single bulb hanging from a cord that looked like it hadn't been replaced since the First World War.

'Hello? Jonty?' she called out, really hoping that the lightbulb wasn't about to pop and plunge her into darkness — there were so many cobwebs down here she'd need rescuing by Spider-Man — or at the very least The-Thing-Most-Likely-To-Eat-Spiders-Man. She suddenly remembered the black, scrawled command painted onto the wall. 'I mean, um, *bonjour*? *Monsieur Jonty*?'

'Hi!' His voice rang out from below and Jenna followed it down the creaking stairs to where row upon row of bottles were neatly stacked on the old stone shelves. '*Bonjour* yourself. You can ignore that though, I do.'

'Um, right.' Jenna wrapped her arms around herself, as much to stop them flailing around in her usual way and accidentally touching any of the creepily dusty walls and bottles as to keep the chill from the cellar off her. 'Um, you wanted to see me?'

'Yeah. Cool, isn't it. Some of this is Philippe's personal collection. Of course the winery has a separate vinotech and *caves*. . .'

'A what and a what?' Jenna had clocked that he hadn't exactly answered her question, but her natural curiosity had taken over. Jonty had pronounced *caves* like 'carves' and she was running this odd word through her mind as he carried on.

'A vinotech is a library of wines and *caves*, well — that's what we're in right now,' Jonty explained and moved closer to where Jenna was standing. He pulled out a wine bottle, so completely covered in cobwebby dust that Jenna almost shied away in automatic repulsion. 'A 1989 bottle of this chateau's finest — any idea what that would be worth?'

'Well, I'm not sure I'd give it house room,' Jenna replied as she eyed the bottle suspiciously in case any creepy crawlies made their way out of the dust.

'At about £200 a bottle you might.'

'Blimey — why would anyone spend that much on wine? I mean, that's halfway towards a Kate Spade handbag right there. An investment piece.'

'Some might say this is an investment.'

'Not once it's in you, it isn't.'

'I can see I'm going to have to do a bit more work with you on this one.' He slipped the bottle back onto the shelf with the others and moved a little closer to Jenna. Feeling the tension in the air, she turned back to the shelves and looked studiously at the bottles. 'I hope you liked it?' Jonty's voice was soft and earnest.

'Oh yes,' Jenna stumbled over her words, realising straightaway that he was talking about The Blouse, which since breakfast had taken on capitals due to its importance. 'I mean, thank you so much. It's just so thoughtful and, I mean, you really shouldn't have. . .'

'I wanted to. You had a bloody crappy day yesterday.'

'But you did so much for me then anyway,' she interrupted, not wanting him to carry on as she was beginning to feel more than a little awkward.

'Well, I'm sure you'll look gorgeous in it later. You will wear it, won't you?'

'Um, yes, of course. I mean, it is lovely and I don't think even darling Philippe would like me to turn up to supper in a ripped shirt.'

'He might think it very *avant garde*.' Jonty was smiling at her, his eyes not moving from hers throughout the whole conversation.

'Very 'aving a laugh, more like.' Jenna scuffed her shoe into the dust on the cellar floor as she tried desperately to look anywhere but into the soft grey-blue eyes of her, well, her admirer?

'Hello?' a voice called down the stairs.

'Angus!' Jenna flushed pink as if she'd just been caught in some naughty act. She hadn't, had she? She had to almost mentally check. She heard his steps, confidently taking the rickety wooden staircase with ease, and turned to meet him as he galumphed into the dusty cellar. He wrapped his arms around her and gave her a kiss on the top of her head before kissing her properly on the lips. The awkwardness and tension eased from Jenna's body as she squeezed him just a little tighter before letting go. 'Angus, you remember Jonty from the wine tasting?'

'Yeah, hi, mate. Sals said I'd find you two down here. Up to no good, I should imagine?' He winked at Jenna, who coloured further at the innocent insinuation and didn't know whether to curse or thank her friend for sending her boyfriend straight down to find her here.

Jonty answered first. 'Just showing young Jenna here the secret stash for when we need it later. I mean,' he turned to face her again, 'that is the maid of honour's duty, isn't it, to keep the bride well oiled throughout the whole wedding?'

Relieved to finally know what she had been called down to the cellar for, apart from an awkward chat with a huge amount of sexual tension, she smiled at Jonty and nodded along. Still, desperate to bring this whole episode to its dusty end, she looked up at Angus and, batting a cobweb away from her face, suggested she show him up to their room. She turned to say bye to Jonty and found his cool, blue eyes locked onto her again. Then, without warning, he once more turned on his heel and went deeper into the cellar where empty bottles lay stacked up against barrels, barely visible in the edges of the single bulb's light.

10

The orangery looked divine — literally heavenly. Lights twinkled among the swags of ivy that traced the arches of the double height windows and tiny white rosebuds hung like angels from them. Candles lined the long table, which was covered in a hessian runner, with each place setting marked by what seemed to Jenna to be dozens of knives and forks — how many courses were they having? She and Angus were among the last to descend the chateau's grand staircase and join the other guests in the delightful orangery. After Angus had arrived and caught Jenna down in the cellar, really doing nothing wrong, she had felt the need to overcompensate. Showing him up to their palatial room, she pointed out the friendly west wind on the walls and tried to explain something about the context and art historical relevance of the harvest scenes and celestial trumpeters, but something in his eyes told her he was not thinking about murals at all and the only naked cherub he was interested in was her.

Still, even Angus had been taken aback by the grandeur of the room, its four-poster dominating the space that was otherwise filled with exquisite furniture and art work. Seeing it afresh, as if through Angus's eyes, Jenna noticed the beautiful Persian rugs, the highly polished furniture and then for quite some time the details on the silk on the underside of the bed canopy as Angus went down on her, making sure she was pleasured beyond belief. Slowly rising up her body, he had kissed her all over and Jenna had squirmed in delight as he made sure she was totally and utterly ravished before easing himself inside her, each thrust bringing her closer and closer to another amazing orgasm. She clasped his back, holding him tight to her as he brought them both to climax.

'Oh, Angus,' she sighed as he held onto her, before slowly releasing himself from her still shuddering thighs. 'If that's what they call a French connection, then I am more than happy to be FCUK'ed by you anytime.'

So, it was with rosy cheeks that Jenna and Angus entered the party and took their glass of champagne from the tray that Izzy was holding. Her simple white shirt and black skirt uniform was accessorised with a moody pout and Jenna wondered again why Sally gave the girl so much credit, as she seemed to Jenna to be on one long pre-pubescent sulk — however the sulk became more understandable when Jenna followed Izzy's glare to the most glamorous person in the room. Bertie had arrived. She may not have been on the top of Sally and Hugo's invitation list — the word 'frenemies' had been used more than once by Sally about her — but she was very much an item with their old friend Max and it was he who came over and welcomed Jenna and Angus into the group.

'Jenks!' Max threw a muscly arm around her and pulled her into his harder-than-ever chest. After years of lusting after Max, it was so hard for Jenna not to breathe in his familiar aftershave and let it open up all the emotions that years of friendship and unrequited love had built up. But, now she had met Angus she was finally over him and happy for him to be partnered up with the glamorous Bertie (at least it wasn't like he'd traded in Jenna for a similar model; that would have smarted). She pulled away and kissed him on the cheek and then dutifully 'mwah mwah'ed Bertie too.

'Simpl-o marvelloso to be here,' she drawled in her usual transatlantic accent, so different from the soft vowels of her native East Anglia. 'Jenna, doll, love the blouse, amazing to see you in something so nice for a change.'

Jenna was used to Bertie's barbs, and pressed her lips into a thin smile, waiting for the onslaught of the Bertie show. And she wasn't disappointed, as Bertie went on to tell the friends as they sipped champagne all about her last few days.

'When Sir Dickie invites you, you just say yah, right? So, that's how Maxie and I ended up in Monaco on Monday,' she explained. 'Luckily, Maxie's bank were totally understanding about him taking some last-min time off. I mean, think of the clients he could woo in Monte Carlo rather than Monte Bloody Boring Londono. I always feel more inclined to say yes to anything when I'm on the deck of a yacht, don't you?' She looked quizzically at Jenna as if she really was expecting a yes.

'The closest I've been to a super yacht,' replied Jenna, 'was a swan-shaped pedalo in Southsea.'

Bertie sighed. 'Oh, Jenna, sweetie, we really must do something about that.'

'About what?' Jonty — who had donned a rather impressive pair of vibrantly red trousers for the occasion — joined in the group and shook hands with Max and courteously kissed Bertie hello. Jenna couldn't help but colour as he leaned in to kiss her hello too. Surely, with Angus right next to her, that wasn't a linger, was it?

'Jonty, darling.' Bertie ran a manicured hand up and down his arm. 'I was just telling these heathens about the boats we played on in Monaco this week. Now, you would love this, they had some super wines on board, not to mention some super winos! Have you ever seen a supermodel fall overboard?'

Max carried on from Bertie in telling Jonty all about the fine wines they'd been treated to and Jenna and Angus listened to more of Bertie's super yacht chat. 'Darlings, you just have to come to the boat show with me in September. I met this super broker this week and he's going to design me something Neptune himself would be proud of!'

'I don't know about Neptune, but I'd like a trident through the brain at the moment please,' Angus whispered to a giggling Jenna who had kept nodding along to Bertie's outrageous boasts. Coping with Bertie aside, she was actually getting quite excited about the prospect of having some yacht-based fun when a resounding gong was struck and the guests were all called into supper. Hugo directed them to their places and as Jenna saw the weird and wonderful cutlery around the plates she wondered out loud about quite what they would be eating when the first set of dishes were brought through by a team of waiters.

'Aha,' Hugo held court at the end of the long banqueting table and clinked one of his many knives against his champagne glass. 'Girls and *garçons — escargot!*'

The guests all murmured and gasped as the waiters placed earthenware dishes in front of them — each one with six little holes in it, and in each hole a snail's shell with a little garlicky slug-like thing inside.

'I'm not sure I'm quite ready for this,' whispered Jenna to Angus as he gleefully pounced on the first snail with the special tongs that came with the dish.

'Hmm, they do sort of remind me of something. . .' Angus had pierced one of the snails with his two-pronged fork and jokingly zoomed it in front of her face, laughing at her reaction.

'Eew!' Jenna nudged him in the ribs and cautiously approached the molluscs with her own tongs and prongs. Anticipating a *Pretty Woman* moment she carefully scooped up a shell and tried to pick out the snail as daintily as possible. She was also very much aware of a certain pair of cool greyish-blue eyes on her, and she felt doubly worried as she realised that she really mustn't do anything to stain

The Blouse with the hot, garlicky sauce. The six snails eventually and carefully made it from plate to mouth with no slip ups, although the whole table had had a good laugh at Bertie as a snail that had escaped from Sally's clasp had ended up in her champagne glass.

'Slippery little fucker,' Sally misquoted the film scene while Bertie rolled her eyes and held her glass up for a passing waiter to dispose of it for her.

Courses and their matching wines kept flowing and Jenna was loving every minute of it. Angus was by her side. Her best friends were happy and their families were around them. Philippe once again looked as dapper as could be, and was being the most charming of hosts, clicking his fingers for more wine whenever the table looked like it was even vaguely running short. And Jenna was relieved that Jonty, despite his previous attentions, seemed to pretty much ignore her for the rest of the night, chatting away to Bertie and Max about the haves and have-yachts down in the very south of the country.

Hovering in the background wasn't usually her thing, but tonight Izzy knew her place. She was also quite impressed at herself and her schoolgirl French for managing the team of local workers — more used to vine pruning than fine dining — getting them to seamlessly serve the courses that Menou, the chateau chef, was creating in the kitchen. She looked over to Jonty every so often — studiously ignoring Max and Bertie who had had nothing but stink-eye from her since they arrived, not that either of them had noticed. Bertie had tried to buy her off from screwing Max when they'd stayed in the chalet she was working in earlier this year. Max had been a zingingly hot shag — all hard muscle and alpha grunts, and she had to admit, it'd been fun showing off to her 'gap yah' friends — none of them had shagged hot, rich bankers on their travels. In the end though, she'd taken Bertie's fifty-pound notes and left them to it. They deserved one another — her snobbish sneers and his jock-like jokes. No, Jonty was far more her cup of Earl Grey. More reserved and far less on-trend fashionable, and, slight age-gap aside, he would definitely pass muster if she brought him home to meet the parents.

Subtly swooping in to pick up the empty bottles of claret from the table — some of the best vintages of the chateau's own wine — she caught Jonty's eye. He winked at her and she tried her absolute hardest not to break into a massive grin. Holding it in, and holding one, two, three bottles to her chest, she quietly left the orangery and headed towards the kitchen. Why Jonty had asked her to leave the bottles for him at the top of the stairs to the cellar, she didn't know, but nor did she care. She was just happy to be in cahoots with the man she was rapidly developing quite a serious crush on.

11

Sun poured in through the huge window in Jenna and Angus's bedroom. Jenna had failed to grasp the whole shutters thing and anyway, she'd been too wrapped up in, well, Angus, to bear it much thought last night. She'd barely managed to sweep the huge velvet curtain halfway across the window before he had swept her up and plopped her on the bed and they'd done all sorts of naughty things to each other. Smiling at the thought of it, she glanced over to the travel alarm clock that Angus had sensibly brought with him: 8.30. *Bugger*, she thought, flinging the quilt off her and heading towards the bathroom. With titles come responsibility, and she knew it was her bridesmaid-y duty, let alone her absolute joy really, to go and help Sally get ready for her big day. And to be fair, the sheer grandeur of the chateau and her beautiful room helped her feel much more noblesse obliging to everyone around her. Teeth and hair brushed and a light jumper thrown over her strappy pyjama top, she lightly kissed Angus good morning and goodbye and let herself out of their room. Seeing the painted walls and all the heavenly figures on them, blowing wind or not, reminded Jenna to offer a small prayer to the hangover gods who had let her off lightly this morning, especially after all the delicious wines she'd enjoyed at dinner last night. She'd enjoyed talking to Philippe and Jonty about them too. Hearing Philippe speak about them as if each one was a child to him, she had almost welled up, which was a ridiculous thing to do in response to a middle-aged man talking about booze, but it just went to show how passionate Philippe was about his wines and how easily he could convey that passion to an enthralled Jenna. She cleared her mind and knocked on the door to Sally's suite, Hugo doing as tradition dictated and sleeping elsewhere.

Nothing in Jenna's room could prepare her for the sheer elegance and beauty of Sally's. It was huge, for a start, with three of the massive windows that dominated the entire west wing of the chateau. Each window was hung with golden silk curtains, their tassels gently swinging in the soft summer breeze that was wafting through from outside, bringing with it light aromas of lavender and rosemary from the terrace below. The room itself was painted a pale blue, and the ceiling was completely covered in a large fresco that depicted ring upon ring of angels all looking towards the central ceiling rose, which was decorated to represent the sun. From it hung a chandelier, its chain disguised by a creamy silk ribbon that flowed through the golden links.

'Quite something, isn't it?' Sally was sitting up in bed — not a four-poster but massive all the same, with a high headboard in cream and gold rococo scrolls. Her mother was busying herself around her daughter, urging her to get up and get bathed while also trying to floof out the long train of her dress to avoid any pre-ceremony crinkles. 'Mummy, please stop fussing,' Sally scolded her, and then in a much less harassed tone asked her if she'd mind popping down to the kitchen for a cup of tea. Glad of something to do, Mrs Jones agreed but made sure in no uncertain terms that when she came back she wanted to see Miss Jones in the bath and Miss Jenkins, well, Miss Jenkins doing some floofing or something. As soon as she left and had closed the door behind her, Sally fell back into the plumped pillows on her bed and patted the duvet next to her. Jenna scrambled on and lay looking up at the magnificent ceiling with her friend.

'Apparently Louis XIV came here before the original chateau burned down and so when they rebuilt they created this suite in his honour,' Sally explained.

'They must have sold a barrel-load of wine to pay for this,' Jenna wondered out loud, receiving a biff from Sally in response.

'You of all people shouldn't be such a capitalist philistine, darling. That's my job.' But even Sally had to admit that as ceilings go, she was more used to the glass variety, having bumped her head against it as much as she could.

'Philistine or not, I'm not going to risk the wrath of Mummy Jones by not having you on track and on time. Miss Jones — get thee to a bathery!'

'Slave driver,' Sally sighed, but there was no doubt that Sally really was incredibly excited about what lay ahead, that day and indeed in life. As she ran a bath, Jenna meandered around the room, looking at the exquisite decorations and pulling open random drawers out of decorative chests. Realising she may be about to find a wedding night treat in one of them, she stopped and instead stood next to one of the windows and looked out at the scene below. Like a movie set there was action everywhere. Trays full of glasses and cutlery were being carried to the orangery, two men lugged a heavy-looking black and silver case over to the lower terrace where coloured spotlights and a DJ stand were already being set up. Gardeners busied themselves cutting flowers and finding greenery to spruce up the already decorated orangery and among them all Philippe himself was picking a buttonhole, slipping it into his very neat morning suit and securing it with a pin.

'Ready?'

'Ready.'

Jenna looked at her friend and smiled. Sally's soft blonde curls fell around her shoulders, and the beautiful duchesse satin dress swept to the floor and pooled around her like a puddle of spilt cream. The dress was accessorised with a lacy bolero jacket that modestly covered her shoulders while ropes of her grandmother's pearls sat opulently around her neck. Sally kept reaching up to touch them, her nerves starting to show through her sub-conscious movements. She looked absolutely beautiful though and even Jenna herself felt a million dollars — or should that be euros? The pale peachy chiffon gown she had been given by Sally as her bridesmaid dress more than made up for all of the hectic pre-wedding planning. Sally's father took his daughter's arm in his and together they processed down the grand staircase of the chateau, the Parisian photographer snapping away from every angle, capturing Sally's special moments and her irrepressible smile, which lit up the whole house more than any southern French sunshine could.

The bridal party paused at the door that led to the terrace and Jenna stepped to one side to allow the photographer to frame just Sally and her dad against the golden stone-work and climbing honeysuckle. Jenna took a moment to check her own dress wasn't having some terrible wardrobe malfunction and as she hoiked up the bodice she glanced across to where an expectant Hugo and the rest of the wedding guests were waiting on the lower terrace. What she didn't expect to see was Angus, not in his seat, specially reserved for him next to hers in the pew-like front row, but leaning against the balustrade of the terrace — on his phone of all things!

Jenna waved across at him, trying to catch his eye, but the phone was clamped against his cheek and he was shading his eyes from the bright sunlight with the other hand. He didn't notice her and Jenna's waves became slightly more frantic, as she was desperate for him to stop talking on the bloody phone and go and sit down. . . as much as she'd love to one day walk down the aisle with him, here and now wasn't the time to do it and he was in danger of very much cramping Sally's style unless he vamoosed down those terrace steps and into his seat pretty pronto. Jenna was about to stalk across the terrace and physically go and yank the phone from his ear when he turned and waved to her, phone simultaneously slipping into his breast pocket. She made exaggerated shoo-ing motions with her hands, bouquet of peach roses and all, and he thumbs-upped back to her and trotted down the steps to his seat. Jenna breathed a sigh of relief and took her place behind Sally and her father as the Trumpet Voluntary played and they started the stately procession across the terrace and down the steps, towards Hugo and the wedding guests.

'I do,' Sally beamed and looked behind her at her friends and family who all spontaneously cheered. Jenna wiped a tear away from her eye and clasped Angus's hand as it lay on her knee. The celebrant carried on with the service — allowing Sally and Hugo to say their own vows to each other, something that had been missing in the register office ceremony back in London a few days ago.

'I promise,' Sally tearily began, 'to love and honour you and obey you as long as you don't ask me to do any blue jobs. . .'

'Did she just say blow jobs?' Bertie theatrically whispered to Max.

'. . . And I shall remind you every day that you are loved.'

Jenna welled up again and looked across to Angus. *He probably has no idea*, she thought, *how much I really, really want this too*. As Hugo galloped through his promises to love and honour Sally, including when she nagged him about unballing his dirty socks before he put them in the laundry basket, Jenna reached over and clasped Angus's hand in hers. Turning to look at him again, Jenna thought her boyfriend looked a bit distracted. He kept moving his sunglasses from his eyes to his forehead and his hand absent-mindedly kept moving up to his inside pocket as if to check his phone wasn't vibrating or something. Before Jenna could dwell on his state of mind much more, the opening chords of the recessional sounded and the glowing couple grinned their way back down the aisle, to much applause and cheering.

'Cheers.' Angus seemed back to his old, romantic self and clinked his glass of champagne with hers before giving her the quickest of little kisses. 'Here's to our friends,' he toasted and then turned to shake hands with Max and air kiss Bertie.

'I'm sure she said blow job,' Bertie repeated, while poking a canapé with a red-painted fingernail before turning her nose up at it and shooing the waiter away. Max smirked at her and took another refill from a waiter who was passing round the bubbles.

'Honestly, Berts, your mind is in the gutter,' Jenna said, wanting to sound more admonishing but actually quite liking *this* version of Dirty Bertie.

'As long as my body is in heaven, I don't see the problem,' Bertie replied before giving her boyfriend a meaningful look.

'Oh, get a room you two,' Jenna turned her back in mock disgust at her old friends as they fell into a proper snogfest. 'Angus. . .' but Angus wasn't next to her any more. She looked around and caught sight of him. He'd sauntered over to the edge of the terrace and had placed his glass down on the stone balustrade. His fingers still held the stem and he seemed to be fidgeting with it. She was about to approach him when she saw that his free hand was holding his mobile again. He squinted at it and then pushed it hard against his ear, obviously having trouble with reception. Jenna hung back, her curiosity giving way to her manners, which dictated that she gave him some privacy.

As she hovered she felt a light touch on her shoulder as Jonty appeared beside her.

'You look stunning today, Jenna,' he said, and Jenna went a shade of pink that almost matched the dusky peach of her gown. 'Problem is, Jenna, I had you pinned down as a traditionalist and it seems you're breaking rank by massively out-doing the bride.'

'Oh, I, um, no, you see she chose it. . .' She was flustered and found it hard to try and express herself while keeping half an eye on Angus. It was difficult to make small talk with someone who had such an intense look about him, albeit in a dashing *Four Weddings and a Funeral* way (it was a fact universally acknowledged that the plainest of men looked handsome in a morning suit, so how could she help it if her pulse raced when an already rather handsome man got the Hugh Grant treatment?), and so she was rather relieved when the dinner gong sounded. Jenna made her excuses and went to check on her best friend — the bride she thought she definitely wasn't outshining, except in the sweaty forehead stakes — armed with her bridesmaid's arsenal of pressed powder and lip gloss. By the time she'd made matte what once was shiny ('Thank you, sweetie, I was glowing buckets!') she felt a nudge at her elbow and Angus was there, ready to lead her in to their place at the long banqueting table.

12

The candles flickered on the table and the soft evening light was about to give way to night. The meal had been sumptuous with course after course of delicious French food, inspired by their surroundings, with a few Briticisms thrown in too. Foie gras with sauternes wine from a neighbouring vineyard had led onto miniature Scotch eggs served with a little shot glass of real ale, then sublime beef fillet had been followed by a cheese course (Hugo had insisted they did it the French way round — cheese before pudding — in a Frenchman's house). As they'd tucked into a final showstopper of a towering pile of profiteroles the speeches had started, and they were as heartfelt and funny as you could wish for. Philippe had welcomed them all to the chateau and said some lovely things about his English house guests, reminiscing about his youth, misspent or otherwise, in London. Jenna was touched by the beautiful Tiffany bracelet she'd been given as thanks for all her help and of course for being maid of honour, and clipped it onto her wrist straight away, leaving the tantalising little turquoise box on the table. If she squinted it could almost be a ring box. . .

Hugo had finished off the speeches with about ten minutes of quite out-of-character gushiness about his beautiful bride, and the moment he'd introduced her as 'my wife' had seen the guests almost raise the roof with applause, foot stamping and whoops. He'd finished with the generous line, 'Now go forth friends and have fun, it's all on the house, and when the house is as fine as this one, I'd say drink up!'

'Shall we?' Angus had stood up and was offering to help her up too. 'I think I need to stretch my legs after that feast.'

'Oof, yes.' Jenna accepted his hand and hauled herself to her feet, grateful for the flattering empire-line style bridesmaid dress that hid any post-prandial potbelly.

Angus led her through the chattering guests and they both seemed to relax a little when they hit the cooler outside air. 'Shall we go for a wander?' Jenna felt like it was high time she had Angus to herself. Apart from some very nice cuddles when she was getting ready for the ceremony earlier this afternoon, she'd barely had time to catch up with him since he'd arrived the day before, with a new phone as promised. And speaking of phones, she was keen to know all about these clandestine calls that he'd been getting. She let him lead her down along the terrace, and they each took a fresh glass of champagne from a passing waiter.

'I could get very used to this.' She took a sip of the delightfully sparkling wine and picked up the hem of her dress as she followed Angus carefully down one of the sweeping staircases to the lower terrace. Fully aware of her stunt the other night, she clocked the danger zone of the ornamental pond and its water channel and swore under her breath when she saw the grey-and-white cat again, in the same spot, but this time head down, ignoring them, cleaning itself.

Letting her long dress flow again she reached out and took Angus's hand in hers, slowing him down a bit.

'Sorry, Jenks.' He took the hint. 'I guess I'm not the one in heels.'

'Where are you leading me anyway? Got to check it's worth the walk, you know.' She winked at him.

'When you were helping Sal earlier I went for a walk down this way. Ah ha.' Angus had led her off the terrace and along a path that led to a little wooden door, almost concealed by the trailing ivy around it. Pushing it open, Angus revealed a perfectly laid out walled garden, the interior a perfect knot of garden herbs and vegetables. 'You see,' he turned to her, 'a proper garden full of useful things — none of this lavender and jasmine nonsense.' He winked and Jenna smiled at him, happy to breathe in the evening air laced with sage, rosemary and warm earth. They both meandered through the rows and squares of neat planting, occasionally leaning over to pinch a herb leaf between their fingers and breathe in the release of aromas. When they reached the middle of the maze-like garden they found a bench under a honeysuckle-covered archway and Angus suggested they sit down.

'I feel naughty leaving the party,' Jenna sighed while taking a deep breath, full of the herb and floral aromatics of the garden.

'How naughty?' Angus raised his eyebrows and, while taking a sip from his glass, with one hand he used the other to move Jenna's hand over his rather bulging crotch.

'Oh!' Jenna was taken aback, but then warmed to the idea. If telling the interns back at the gallery that she'd given someone a blow job on a chair lift a few months ago had caused gasps over the percolator, then saying she'd done it in a bloody chateau's walled garden would really get those Monday morning pulses racing. Plus, she really did feel quite saucy and probably took Angus a little by surprise at how wholeheartedly she took on his suggestion. Pausing only to take off his morning coat to act as cushion on the sharp garden gravel (*comfort was all-important to a successful blowie*, thought Jenna), she helped him release his rather substantial cock from his trousers. Taking a sip of the champagne she kept a little in her mouth before moving her lips slowly and purposefully over his massive erection. Teasingly, Jenna stopped just at the tip of his orgasm, letting him finish himself off while she gulped down another slug of champagne.

'Sorry, darling, it's just after all that supper I couldn't manage another mouthful,' she winked at him.

'I shall try not to be too upset that you preferred a profiterole to me.'

'Angus, you know you can squirt your cream into my buns all you like usually, but as Bertie would no doubt remind me, "a moment on the lips is a lifetime on the hips" and I hate to say it, but your crème anglaise isn't worth the calories!'

'Cheeky.'

'What's cheeky, Gus, is how long we've been gone,' Jenna straightened out her dress, patted her hair and added to herself *and how long you were on the phone for earlier*. Not wanting any sort of confrontation to spoil the delicious naughtiness of their little clinch she decided not to say anything about that and instead flirtily continued with, 'we better go back before Sally realises her *maid of dishonour* is well and truly, well, just *that*!'

Jonty, on the other hand, couldn't give two hoots if he was missed. Like Angus and Jenna just minutes earlier, he took a couple of glasses of champagne from a passing waitress, but instead of finding delights in the walled garden, he headed into the chateau. He'd had enough of watching Jenna and her loping boyfriend, and was starting to question whether he could ever win her over. He *needed* her to fall for him instead, and he was blowed if the expensive blouse he'd had couriered from Bordeaux two nights ago was going to go to waste. He pursed his lips and continued towards the kitchen. If he couldn't pull it off with Jenna, it was always good to nurture a back up and he was pretty sure he'd have more no-strings-attached luck with a certain someone, judging by the eyelash-fluttering looks he'd been receiving since she arrived. And his luck was certainly in, as when he entered the chateau's kitchen it was as if fifty or so people had never been catered for — the French chef in a show of uncharacteristic organisation had already cleared down the surfaces and Jonty's quarry for the night was on her own, wiping up the last few espresso cups and putting them back in the large dresser ready for the morning.

'Thought you might need this.' Jonty placed the glasses down on the refectory-style table and was more than a little gratified that Izzy turned round to greet him with a look of absolute adoration. *This could be easier than I thought. . .* Loosening his tie Jonty took his morning coat off and hung it over the back of one of the old wooden wheel-back chairs. He had barely started rolling up his shirt sleeves, in an attempt to look more casual next to Izzy's waitress outfit, before she had crossed the room and picked up one of the glasses.

'Thank you, Jonty. You don't know how hard it is being in here, when you lot are out there.'

'It's really no great shakes out there. I'd rather be here with you.' Had he gone too far? She'd almost choked on the champagne as he'd said it. . .

'Do you really mean that?'

He suddenly felt a little abashed, as no, he did not really mean it, but he took the glass out of her hand and locked eyes with her. Slowly he moved closer to her and leaned down to kiss her. Almost to his surprise, the ardour with which she returned the kiss was quite something and he was starting to wonder if he'd closed the kitchen door behind him.

Pulling away, he had a sly look — yes, the door was firmly shut — and then he began the full-on charm offensive. 'You know, the other good thing about being in here with you is that you're in that rather natty little waitress outfit.'

'I'd rather be in something slinkier. . .'

Jonty couldn't believe his luck as the ballsy girl started sliding her hands over his chest, fingering the buttons of his waistcoat. 'I think that little black skirt is just fine, from where I'm standing anyway.'

'Too much standing, I think,' Izzy really was getting into the spirit of it now, 'and not enough pushing me onto that table and ravishing me.'

Jonty did not need asking twice and in one rather slick move, even if he thought so himself, had picked up the nubile young waitress and slid her onto the polished oak top of the table. To be fair, at approximately 200 years old, the table probably had seen its fair share of comings and goings, but tonight it was treated to more *comings* than usual — with Izzy squealing out in pleasure as Jonty could be described as *going* for it.

'Who knew catering could be such fun,' giggled Izzy as she raised herself up on her elbows, her legs still hanging over the edge of the table. 'You certainly just put the cock into my coq au vin.'

'And hopefully the British beef into your bourguignon.'

'British boffing, more like,' she snickered as she pushed herself up to standing and straightened out her blouse and skirt, both of which had suffered a sartorial mishap.

With no comfy bed to snuggle into, Jonty felt less of a bastard as he rolled his sleeves back down and put his morning coat back on. He then kissed her goodbye and headed back towards the kitchen door.

'Maybe see you later?' she called after him.

Yeah, maybe, maybe, he thought to himself as he winked at her before heading back to the wedding party.

'Ladies! Ready?'

A chorus of yeses and wolf whistles heralded the fact that the small group of ladies, and the men who viewed this as a spectator sport, were indeed ready.

'Ok, then.' Sally turned her back to the balustrade on the terrace and prepared to throw her bouquet to the waiting women below. Jenna jostled for position, having just got back from the walled garden — and its delights — moments before Philippe had corralled the single female guests down onto the lower terrace.

'Hurry up!' Various men watched on, some in trepidation, as Sally (who was obviously enjoying every moment of her big day) finally counted down from three and hurled the bouquet over her head. As one, the bundle of girls raised their arms, their hands waving in unison like the tendrils of a sea urchin.

'It's mine, it's mine!' A squawk and a scrabble.

'Ouch!'

'My foot!'

Then victoriously the now battered bouquet was raised aloft.

'Damn.'

'Bugger.'

Slighted singles gradually pulled away from the triumphant winner.

'Well done, Bertie.' Jenna conceded defeat while nursing a bash to her upper arm that must have come from one of the sharpest elbows known to womankind. Bertie flashed a smile at her, then seemed to take control of herself. Jenna followed her gaze to the group of men standing to one side and saw that Max had raised a glass to her. Seconds later and Bertie was back to her usual resting bitch face and flicked a few upset curls out of her eyes before stalking away from the scene, distancing herself from anything as base as actually having to fight for something.

'Never mind, sausage.' Angus put his arm around Jenna's shoulder. 'Better luck next time.'

'If it hadn't been for *your* sausage, I might have been nearer the front.'

'It's just a second-hand bunch of flowers — I'll buy you a lovely new bunch when we get back to London.'

'I don't think that's quite how this works. . .' But Angus had wandered off towards a waiter who had appeared on the steps and helped himself to a large glass of red wine. Jenna sighed and followed after him, risking a glance over to where Bertie was now entwined around Max, the bouquet discarded on the balustrade now its fortune-telling duties were done.

13

There were plusses and minuses to being almost teetotal, thought
Bertie, who of course didn't count champagne. Or very, very
good wine. Minuses were that just once or twice she felt
like she missed out on the bonding experience that getting
royally shitfaced with a group of friends was, and of course
even super-rich, glamorous 'it' girls felt the need for a large
glass of bitch diesel after a hard day at the coal face of social
media updates and lifestyle photo shoots; but the plusses,
well one of them was having the mornings to yourself as
the house around you slept on in hazy ignorance.

Bertie slipped out of bed and left a lightly snoring Max
rolled up in the crumpled mess of Egyptian cotton and
pillows. He'd tried, bless him, last night to be all romantic,
but although absinthe might make the heart grow fonder,
it definitely didn't make Little Max any more useful, and
she'd had a wonderfully undisturbed night going over in
her head all the parts of the wedding that had made it
so special. Forget the bride and groom (Bertie still hadn't
quite forgiven Hugo for dumping her during their college
years — and what's worse, for Sally, who she took great
efforts to try to be nice to, but somehow always found
it easier to bitch about) — but the venue, the decor, the
lights. . . it had made her realise that with her thirtieth
birthday (shudder, she'll make sure *OK!* Magazine got the
message that she would *always* be twenty-nine) coming up
she needed a very swanky and very large place to party.
Her friend Dubious Dominic, who had leant her his ski
chalet earlier in the year, had said the Blake-Howard's
super yacht would be moored in Monaco at the end of the

summer and he was sure she could borrow it. She'd loved the idea. Who wouldn't want to see out their twenties on a yacht, swimming in crystal blue Mediterranean waters and dancing till dawn on the deck? But as yachts go, and she mustn't let it slip to Monty BH that she thought this, she regarded his floating gin palace as more super-saver than super-swish and it just wouldn't be big enough. Not to mention the finishing touches. . . could you even release doves from a boat? She'd be sure to check, but in the meantime she thought she might just sound out the absolutely charming Philippe about hiring this gorgeous chateau for the occasion. Of course she'd have to blow last night's celebrations out of the water — something a yacht literally would have helped with — *but*, she thought, *with a few Bertie-esque tweaks this divine maison would be just the place for her infinitely better party.*

She slipped her silky dressing gown over her nightie and flicked her hair over its collar before letting herself quietly out of the bedroom and along the corridor to the main staircase. Following the smell of freshly brewed coffee she crept downstairs.

'Philippe, *bonjour!*' She pushed open the study door that had been left ajar.

'Good morning, *mademoiselle*.' Philippe, who had been writing at his desk stood up and welcomed her in. 'It's Roberta, isn't it, *mais non*?'

'Darling man, yes, that's right.' She swooped around the desk, the silk of her dressing gown sweeping out behind her, and accepted a kiss on each cheek from him.

'How can I help you this morning. I hope everything was *d'accord*, OK, for you and your friends last night. You slept well? Some coffee, perhaps?' He indicated the cafétière on his desk.

'Terrible for the skin, darling, so no. But yes, *absolutement* to everything being so much more than just *d'accord*. In

81

fact, it was so lovely. . .' Bertie continued to sketch out her plans for her party and made sure that Philippe was quite aware that money would be no object to throwing the best birthday bash Bordeaux had ever seen. 'I'm talking swans in the fountains, miniature ponies in the grounds, as much of your delicious '09 as my friends can drink, and of course doves. Plenty of white doves that can resemble both my beauty, my serenity and my rebirth into a new decade.'

'It sounds quite the occasion,' a rather baffled Philippe countered, 'but I cannot see why not. The only problem, a little one perhaps, is that we will be harvesting the grapes in August or September, but the chateau itself is free — and looking at this summer's weather it's going to be hot and dry. Who knows, harvest could be done by August.'

'Well, that's settled then.' Bertie gave a girlish twirl and kissed Philippe on each cheek again. 'I shall have my people contact you when I'm home and they can talk moolah. Mwah!' At that she left and wafted back up the stairs to tell a very hungover Max the good news.

Philippe Montmorency couldn't understand it. His family had been making wine — and good wine at that — for hundreds of years. Château Montmorency was world renowned for its complexity and balance, ranking up there with its more expensive Bordeaux neighbours in quality and selling well and solidly for years. His family had poured their wealth into this chateau and its vine-yards and in return, for generations, it had literally poured wealth back to them — but since signing up to Carstairs & Co the bottom line had suffered. He had been too proud to admit to his old *negociants* — the local agents as it were — that he had been beaten down in price, and even since then he had seen little by way of return. *Merde*, he swore under his breath. Perhaps I'm being punished for my lack of loyalty. If my pride hadn't demanded I go for the prestigious Carstairs & Co. . . He tutted to himself. If I don't do something about this then I will be the last of the Montmorencys making wine and I might as well become a glorified clothes horse like my cousin Claude. He twitched the starched white cuffs of his shirt − mock his fashion-designer cousin he might, but he too knew the importance of looking as elegant and wealthy as you could.

To be accosted so early in the morning with the answer to his current problems had been a multi-faceted joy. Not only would any red-blooded Frenchman welcome a visit from a beauty like mademoiselle Roberta, and in her night gown no less, but to come offering *un cheque en blanc*. . . suddenly things were looking more *bon viveur* than *sacre bleu*. He put his paperwork to one side and decided to worry about the cash flow, sales and accounts a little later when Jonty was able to go through the books with him.

'Oh, byeeee, Sals!' Jenna hugged her best friend as she and Hugo prepared to leave the chateau. 'Or should I now say Mrs Portman?'

'It's going to take some getting used to,' Sally mouthed 'Mrs Portman' to herself a few times and then pulled a face at Jenna and whispered, 'I know it's a cliché, but it makes me sound like Hugo's mum. . .'

'I wouldn't worry about that. Judging by her gyrations round the dance floor last night, the name Mrs Portman is shorthand for "will do just about anything fun after a glass or two".' The pair burst out laughing and Jenna then turned to hug her old friend Hugo.

'Thanks for everything, Jenks,' he said as he pulled away. 'As for you, Mrs Portman. . .'

'Yes, dear?'

'No, not you, Mother. When have I ever called you Mrs Portman?'

'You never call at all, darling, but that's sons for you,' Hugo's mum raised her eyebrows to Jenna and Sally before getting back to sorting out the suitcases in the back of her and Mr P's car.

'Anyway, darling, as I was saying, are you ready to head to the Orient?'

'You two are so un-PC.' Jenna gave them a withering look. 'Have you got your pith helmet and colony-conquering plus-fours too, Hugo?'

'No, silly.' Sally clicked her tongue. 'We're off to the Orient, via the Orient Express. One of Hugsie's little word games made flesh, as it were. So, the most glamorous train in the world, a few nights in Venice and then off to Hong Kong and down to Bali. Bliss.'

'Oh I know, you lucky, lucky things.' Jenna pulled her best friend into another hug and then let Angus say his goodbyes. Jonty appeared from the front door of the chateau with Philippe, who to Jenna's mind looked a lot more relaxed than she'd seen him in days.

'*Au revoir, mes amis!*'

'Cheerio, chaps!'

'Have fun, darlings!'

'If you can't be good, be careful. . .'

A chorus of groans and cheers and then a rev of an engine and Sally and Hugo were off. Jenna waved until the car was out of sight and just a cloud of dry dust lingered by the gates of the chateau.

Jenna trailed her fingers down one of the ornate posts of the bed as Angus did a final check of the room just in case they'd left anything. Having told him about the time she'd left not one, but two socks, annoyingly of different pairs, at the home of her school French exchange buddy, meant Angus wasn't that confident in Jenna's packing capabilities and he triumphantly returned from the bathroom with her shampoo and conditioner, which she'd left by the tub.

'Thanks, Gus. Perhaps just a little part of me wanted to stay here. . .' she let her hand drift over the patterned bedspread that she'd pulled back over the bed in an attempt to leave it looking tidy.

'I'll go and put the bags by the front door, JJ. Our taxi will be here in five minutes or so.' He stooped to give her a kiss on the forehead, leave a few euros housekeeping tip on the bedside table, and then picked up both of their bags and headed out of the room.

Jenna sat still for a minute or two, taking in the beautiful room one more time. Letting out a little sigh she got up, knowing full well that by tonight they'd both be back in her little flat — a space so small that it could probably fit twice over in this generously proportioned room. Living together had seemed less claustrophobic here — but then that would happen when your bathroom is more like a ballroom than a bijou cupboard and you don't have to trip over your boyfriend to get to the kitchen. Just as she was about to turn and head towards the door she saw it slowly open and Jonty poked his head around it.

'Ah, hello there. Sorry to bother you, Jenna, but Angus says your taxi is downstairs.'

'Thanks, Jonty. And thanks again for all the help you gave me when I arrived, not to mention that lovely blouse. You really shouldn't have.'

'Again, it's my pleasure. I'm just sorry I can't give you both a lift back to the airport. I've got to stay on for a day and help Philippe with some paperwork. Perhaps I'll see you back in London, though?'

Jenna felt like she was betraying Angus by even making eye contact with Jonty at this moment but she managed a thin smile and a nod.

Jonty continued as he opened the door for her to slip out. 'You know, the offer still stands, if you ever need a job, that is. . .'

'Thank you, Jonty.' Jenna was relieved to be back on more neutral ground. She felt she could put on the mask of professionalism, which would hopefully hide the blushing in her cheeks. 'Now I've had a little peep into the glamorous world of wine, I can see the appeal, but I'm sure it's not all chateaux and parties.'

'You've got my card, though?'

'Yes, I think so. Goodbye again, and thank you.' At that Jenna descended the stairs and met Angus in the hallway. As Philippe warmly bid them goodbye and handed her into the waiting taxi she had the briefest of feelings that she might be back, but then the car door closed and the air con swept her up into the journey that would take her and Angus back to London and their normal lives.

14

By 10 p.m. on the Monday after the wedding, Jenna could count nothing about her 'London life' as normal. The day had started well — she'd bounded into the gallery, her steps lightened by the weight of gossip and news she had to tell Clive and the work-experience girl of the week. The current one, Arabella, though massively entitled, was a sweetie really and desperate to please, knowing that a glowing reference from the gallery would set her up for a career in the art world — plus Jenna had enjoyed sitting on the edge of her desk, nursing a coffee, and telling her all about the chateau and its, well, its environs, until Martin Roach had shooed her back upstairs to get some real work done.

It had been at about 11 a.m. that her world had begun to unravel. Analysing it in detail, as Jenna now did with the luxury and devastation of hindsight, it was really darling old Clive's fault. If he hadn't needed help at the morning's auction he would have been in the gallery and stopped the disaster, somehow, from happening. But he hadn't been, and at about 11 a.m. Jenna got a call on the intercom from Martin telling her that things were all going pear-shaped at an important art sale just down the road at Bonham's and Clive needed him to go and help. All par for the course in the Roach & Hartley world. Clive might have an eye, but he was the one that was useless with money — always spending too much on unknown artists and then conversely not bidding enough when an important painting came along that could really shine in the gallery and bring in the punters.

Jenna had sighed at what would probably mean a crabby Martin later and a terrible atmosphere all afternoon. If Clive had lost them the key piece they wanted to get for the gallery at this sale — a charcoal by Braque to go alongside the Picasso prints — who knew when and at what price it would come back to market. She confirmed to Martin that she and Arabella could easily manage the gallery for a bit while he was gone, and after checking that Arabella was at her desk on the ground floor she turned her attention back to her computer and its spreadsheets and marketing plans with only the odd glance over to the CCTV monitor on her desk to check the poor girl wasn't inundated downstairs.

If the unravelling of her day had started at around 11 a.m., then by midday it was spooling all over the floor. Arabella, unimpressed by the lack of payment she received for her bum-on-seat time at the gallery, called up to Jenna that she was leaving for a few moments to get a sandwich before the lunch rush. Before Jenna could lay down the law the young intern had put the phone down and all Jenna could do was rather hopelessly look at the CCTV monitor and watch Arabella pop her handbag over her shoulder and leave her desk. Jenna had rolled her eyes and saved her spreadsheet before heading downstairs to keep an eye on the main gallery until someone deigned to come back and relieve her. By 1 p.m. she was still alone and the couple of coffees she'd had that morning, not to mention the cleansing juice (Jenna had been inspired by at least some of Bertie's words over the weekend and had ventured into the realms of wheatgrass this morning) had been sitting in her bladder for quite long enough. She was desperate for a pee. The problem was, the loo was up on the top floor of the gallery — nicely convenient for when she was working at her desk, not so good now — and the longer she waited the longer those staircases would take to climb — arse cheeks and thighs clenched together may be highly effective for strengthening the core, but not for getting to the loo on time. As the desperation got more and more severe she finally, and, in hindsight, rather thoughtlessly, made a dash for it.

'It was only a quick pee. . .' was what she told the police officer, and before her the fiercely red face of Martin Roach and the crushingly upset Clive. The police officer, it had to be said, had a far better manner about her and a far greater belief in the powers of the Metropolitan Police and their network of coppers and cameras than Martin had, and Jenna had almost clung to the nice constable for dear life, knowing that as soon as she left to call in the theft of the Picasso prints she would be at Martin and Clive's mercy.

'You stupid, stupid girl,' Martin rounded on her as soon as the police officer had left. 'Why didn't you lock the fucking door before you deserted your post?' He spat the words out at her and didn't wait for an answer before continuing. 'Even an imbecile intern would have locked the fucking door.'

Jenna thought Clive had tried to poor oil over the troubled waters, although those waters might as well have been flames and the oil a rather effective accelerant. 'Martin, we're insured — we can sort this out.'

'Insured? For a bloody walk in? We're insured against breaking and entering and theft where we have done everything possible to secure the assets. Not left the fucking door wide open.'

'I'm so, so sorry, Martin.' Jenna couldn't think of anything else to say. There was no one else to blame. She had done something incredibly silly but usually it wouldn't have mattered, not really. Generally, only four or five punters a day came in to browse, the other potential buyers all had appointments. Her train of thought led to an idea. 'He must have been waiting for an opportunity, I mean, there was no one in sight outside when I dashed upstairs. . .'

'Hiding behind the bins?' Clive made a nervous little joke.

'I don't bloody care. She's out.' Jenna saw the clenched jaw through Martin's jowls and knew there was no arguing with him. His hands were balled into fists and she thought that if she tried to fight her corner she might end up on the receiving end of one of them.

'Martin, can we? I mean, we should talk this through. . .' Clive seemed oddly calm in the face of the tragedy. 'An on-the-spot firing could lead to an HR nightmare.'

'This is the grossest of misconducts,' Martin's gaze levelled at his business partner, 'and I for one can't stand the sight of her any more. Get out!' he shouted the last words directly at Jenna who fled upstairs to her desk, as much to grab her handbag as to regroup and think if there was anything she could do. Clive was right, could they fire her straight off? Before she could think on it any more she heard a bellowing shout from the ox-like man downstairs. 'Jenna!'

She quickly looked about her desk. It had been her home for the last few years — in fact, she'd probably spent more time here in this office — nicely tucked away above the buzz of Mayfair below, having fun little chats with Clive, sharing stories with the interns and plugging away at her career, aiming to one day manage a gallery of her own — than in her own little flat. Through her now freely flowing tears she picked up a couple of her favourite pens, her personal notebooks, some old auction catalogues with turned-down pages and her spare pair of 'going out' shoes that she kept under the desk for those last minute, unplanned nights out; she then clicked on her mouse and lit up her computer screen and started deleting personal files, all the while listening to the increasingly aggressive shouts coming from downstairs. She clicked delete on the last file and picked up her bag. A photo of her mum and dad and the family spaniel had been Blu-Tacked to the edge of her screen and she peeled it away and slipped it into one of the notebooks. 'Sorry, folks,' she whispered as she heaved her bag over her shoulder and headed down the narrow little staircase to the gallery below.

Martin didn't even look at her — his face was almost white with anger, the colour drained from it as he rested his whole weight on the wall where the Picasso prints had once hung. Jenna looked over at Clive, who was tapping a number into his phone, but he looked up and smiled at her, which at that moment meant the world to Jenna and made her tears flow even faster. She mouthed a 'sorry' to him and slipped out of the open door — no point in having it closed now — and made it to the end of the road before the first real sobs racked through her body.

Jenna walked down Bond Street in a sort of daze. She replayed the events over and over again in her head. She couldn't blame Clive for needing help at the auction. She couldn't blame Arabella for wanting an early lunch and the best of the Pret sandwiches. She couldn't even blame Martin for firing her. She had been a total numpty. Art gallery management one-oh-one — you don't leave Picassos unprotected. She hovered at the end of the road, where Bond Street met Piccadilly, and the crowds swarmed around her, the tail end of the lunchtime rush going back to offices and desks in lovely non-shouty environments. Jenna wiped her cheeks again and ignored the one or two odd looks she got from passers-by. She wondered why, in a city the size of London, you didn't see more people in tears on a daily basis. Or was it just her life going down the pan at the moment? Still, at least she had Angus and although the little nagging voice inside her head did remind her that he hadn't been all that supportive last time she mooted the possibility of losing her job, she rooted around in her bag and found her phone inside one of her shoes that had been unceremoniously shoved in there and gave Angus a quick call. Thankfully, his words were like a balm and his idea of getting herself home and curling up with an old favourite book was a sensible, if rather dull one, especially compared to her initial idea of getting herself into a bar with a rather large glass of wine and a deluxe box of Kleenex. Why not combine them both? She headed down to Green Park tube and to the mini supermarket in the station where she plucked the cheapest sauvignon blanc off the shelves and paid for it alongside a family pack of Dairy Milk.

By the time she'd got back to her flat, the screw top of the wine had 'mysteriously' worked its way loose and she was beyond caring if anyone saw her take a surreptitious swig from the carrier bag. She generally held a dim view of afternoon drinking, unless you were on holiday or at a wedding, of course, and an even dimmer view of drinking *a la* tramp — but hey ho, needs must and all that. After letting herself into her flat, battling with the locks and keys while balancing bags and bottle and ripping 'The Old Vicarage' name plate off in a harrumph of ill-temper, she spent the rest of the afternoon in between swigs phoning her parents ('Oh dear, darling, were they terribly expensive?'), approaching job agencies ('can we rely on a good reference from your last job?') and texting friends ('OMG, WTF? U ok babes?). It had all passed in a bit of a maelstrom of tears, exasperated conversations and quite a lot of self-recrimination.

And then Angus had come home and that's when Jenna, now very much with the benefit of hindsight, realised that the threads of her life that had begun unravelling that morning, and then spooled on the floor around lunchtime, had now rolled out of the house, across the pavement and probably under a passing bus. Angus *had* been lovely and held her and said he was shocked and that it wasn't her fault and she just cried and cried and cried into his shoulder. But then the argument started.

'I just don't know how I can pay the bills without a job,' Jenna had said, before blowing her nose again on a fresh tissue. 'I don't have any savings and I can barely afford this place and life and everything as it is!' The pile of red-edged statements scattered on the floor on her side of the bed were testament to that.

'Look, JJ, let me help. I can pay more towards the bills and you can rely on me as the entertainment fund.'

'You pay your share already, Angus, and I can't have you pay for *everything* when we go out, I just can't.'

'Your parents, then? Can they help you out?'

'And admit to them that I haven't managed to save a penny? They told me not to take on a flat I could barely afford and I lied to them and said I was earning more than I did so Dad would get off my case.'

'Oh, Jenna, why. . .?'

'Why? Because we're not all blessed with trust funds, that's why!'

'That's not what I meant, JJ.'

Jenna's mood had gone from 'woe is me' to 'come and have a go' aided, no doubt, by the bottle of wine.

Angus continued, 'Then let me help — more than just paying my bills and taking you out. Jenna, I love you and I can afford to keep you. . .'

'Keep me? *Keep me?* Like a mistress? Or a servant?' Without realising it, Angus had hit a raw nerve and in Jenna's heightened state of tipsiness and anxiety that nerve was fighting right back. Her parents had never been rich and they'd taught her the importance of being independent and earning her own money. In fact — that was it, now she could identify it — it was *shame* that flooded her body as well as anger at Angus's insinuation.

'No, Jenna.' Angus flopped down onto the bed and tried to catch her hand and guide her down next to him, but she swished it away. 'Not keep you like a servant, for God's sake. Keep you in a manner you might like to become accustomed to, is what I was going to say if you'd let me finish.'

'Finish or not, it's the same thing and, Angus, I do not need to be kept. I just need another job.'

'Maybe one you take more seriously this time?' Angus smiled but Jenna couldn't see the funny side.

'What?'

'I mean, you want to be taken seriously, I get that, but you didn't really take that job seriously, did you?'

'Yes I bloody did!'

'Really? Like that time you said you were going to view an auction and you met Sally for chips in Green Park?'

'That was. . . well, that was my lunch break.'

'At three in the afternoon?'

'You don't understand, Angus,' Jenna poured herself another generous slug of wine and mumbled, 'working at Roach & Hartley might not have been everyone's idea of a "proper job",' she emphasised the words with her fingers, 'but it was my gateway to getting on in the art world. I want my own gallery one day and now I'm fucked. No one will ever employ me again!'

'Look.' Angus splayed his fingers out on his knees as he gathered his thoughts. 'I can help support you, you know, if you want to go back to basics. Start as an intern again.'

Jenna felt the rage rising inside her once more, not so much at Angus's repeated and unwanted offers to bail her out, but he'd just unwittingly confirmed to her what she already feared — she was finished in the art world unless she went right back to the bottom rung. And possibly changed her name. She slammed her glass down on the bedside table and threw herself into her pillow.

'Well, I'm not offering permanent support, if that helps?'

'Oh.' Jenna looked back up at him. So Angus didn't want to things to be permanent. 'No, that doesn't help.' She pulled herself back up to sitting, but Angus got up and suddenly the whole scenario seemed to be reversed. It was Angus's turn to get frustrated at her.

'Jenna, everything I say seems to be wrong. I don't get it. I offer help and I'm told it won't be accepted, I then say it needn't be forever and I get this.' Jenna could tell he was exasperated, but so was she. She'd gone from abject despair to self-righteous independence to rejection. And her head was starting to ache like something else, damn that afternoon drinking. 'Look, perhaps it's best if I go and leave you to your sulk.'

'Wouldn't you be sulking too if you'd just been shouted at, fired, made to feel like the fool you are and then have your boyfriend tell you he'll treat you like a kept woman but only until he decides not to. . .' Jenna's fire was lit again and she was almost yelling at Angus as she listed off her day's troubles.

'Jenna, I'm finding it really hard to talk to you right now, you're being totally irrational.' Angus went to the small side table beside the bed and picked up his phone and wallet. He paused there, deep in thought.

'Where are you going?'

'Home.'

Home, she thought. Because at the end of the day my little flat and I haven't been 'home'. We've been had. We've been used as a slightly more central London doss-house by someone who would never think of us as 'home'.

'Fine.'

'Fine.'

At that Angus left and Jenna fell back onto the bed, sobs racking through her body as she tried to work out what had just happened.

15

Jenna woke up the next morning feeling more than a little sorry for herself. There was no Angus in bed next to her and her flat, although cramped when they were in it together, suddenly felt as if its heart had been ripped out. She felt a little like that too, and as she watched the minutes of her might-as-well lie-in tick by on the clock that Angus had left on the bedside table, she reminded herself why she was in this lonely mess. They'd never argued before and this felt horrible. Through her hangover haze she reached over to find her phone and message him, but something held her back. Her mind waded through the swamp weed of her hangover. He can't have been that into her, not if he was bandying around phrases like 'it's not permanent' and 'this isn't home' — or at least she thought that's what he'd said. But he did say he loved her. She reached across for the phone again, then stopped. But then he left. If he really loved her, would he have done that? She wished she could call Sally but she couldn't bring herself to offload all her woes onto her pal who should be having the happiest time of her life. There was nothing like a sobbing friend, after all, to murder the atmosphere on the Orient Express. There would be plenty of time for Sally's analysis and no doubt rousing pep talk when she was back from her honeymoon. So Jenna had got herself up and showered and then pottered around the flat — although that in itself got too much to bear as she tried to avoid all of Angus's stuff. His jeans were still folded on one of the chairs in the bay window and his shaving kit still occupied a space by the basin in the little shower room. There was an angry and hurt part of Jenna who wanted to throw them all into a cardboard box and toss it out of her window into the street, as if she was a star in a Brooklyn-based rom-com. 'Take yer filthy rubbish, yer filthy piece of crap,' she said out loud to herself before wiping away a tear. Because of course there was a very hurt part of Jenna, too, who couldn't help but think that she'd just lost the love of her life.

Jenna was staring out of the window down onto the street below, absent-mindedly fondling one of Angus's socks, when her phone rang. Angus! She turned to locate the buzzing but couldn't immediately see the slim metal case of her iPhone. There — spotted — she pounced on it and caught it just in time to accept the call while seeing who was calling. To her bitter disappointment she had just answered the phone to Bertie rather than Angus and had no choice now but to chat to her.

'Morning, darling!'

'Hi, Berts.' Jenna couldn't quite match the other girl's enthusiasm.

'So, many lolz were had this weekend, yes? I super-loved that chateau. And Philippe was such a dream boat — *ooh la la*, I thought, if Maxie and I were not so hot to foxtrot I would deffo let him *palm* my *d'or* down in St-Tropez one summer.'

'Can I help you with anything, Bertie?' Jenna felt rude cutting her so-called friend off mid flow, but she was in no mood for listening to Bertie wax lyrical about her and bloody Max or her and bloody anyone really.

'Oh, right, chills, sweetie. What's up with you?'

Jenna bit her lip. She really didn't think Bertie would make the best confidante but Jenna was so consumed by the grief and upset of what had happened last night that she just blurted it all out, starting with Angus leaving her and finishing off with the added whammy of losing her job.

'Shit, dolls, you have had a terrible twenty-four, yes?'

'Shitter than a port-a-loo at a curry festival.'

'Ew. But poor you. Soz, honey. Look, why don't you come out with me tonight. Dry those eyes and get back on the wagon.'

'I don't think so, Bertie. I look a mess, I feel a mess. Oh God, what am I going to do?' Jenna broke down into sobs again.

'Right, no, stop.' Bertie wasn't consoling her as such, more just trying to get a word in through the tears. 'Look, I'll send a car round later, don't say no. . .'

'But I can't go *out!*' Jenna sniffed before giving in and trying to blow her nose with her spare hand and the edge of the duvet cover. 'My eyes are so puffy from crying they look like two piss holes in the snow and my nose is as red as a monkey's arse.'

'Delightful.'

'So thanks, but no thanks.'

'Well, you definitely can't stay in alone.'

'Alone. . .' The thought echoed through Jenna's head and thought how much nicer it might actually be not to stay at home and mope, so she begrudgingly agreed to Bertie's car being sent and hung up the phone, not having found out why Bertie had rung her in the first place.

Jenna had spent the hours after Bertie's phone call oscillating between getting ready to go out and collapsing on the bed in a heap of snot, tears and tissues. Her poor old duvet cover was definitely due a wash as it now looked like a face wipe from back stage at a panto — smeared as it was with running mascara and smudged attempts at putting on lipstick. If only a decent 40-degree wash could get rid of all her problems, not just the smeary, greasy, make-uppy ones. Still, as promised, the car had arrived and scooped Jenna up and only a few minutes later dropped her off outside a chichi little bar in South Kensington.

'Sweetie, you came,' Bertie purred at her as she slid off a bar stool and approached her friend. She was wearing a micro-mini leather skirt with matching thigh high boots and a billowing cream silk blouse with a pussy bow collar. Jenna thought she looked like a hybrid between Dick Whittington and Margaret Thatcher, but at least it was a hell of a lot more fashionable than her skinny jeans and faithful black glittery cardigan.

'Gawd, darling, you look like you're in mourning.' Bertie stood with Jenna literally at arm's length. 'Still nothing from Gus, I take it? Shame on him I say, for if he's the cause of this fashion travesty,' she winked as she rubbed a hand down one of Jenna's arms but then couldn't help but recoil as a loose sequin snagged on one of her nails, 'I shall have a bone to pick with him next time I see him.'

Bertie wasn't one to fuss or cluck around a friend, however much in need of a bit of love that friend was. Instead she flicked a fifty pound note over to the barman and told him to bring over some cocktails — 'And for heaven's sake, barkeep, not those fattening creamy ones, that's the last thing this girl needs — just make them strong' — and she pushed Jenna towards a little booth-like table in the corner of the bar.

When the cocktails came over they were indeed strong. And although Jenna winced at the first few sips she soon got into the soothing alcohol of the dirty martini and let all her woes tumble over Bertie again.

'Dolls,' said Bertie while she stirred the cocktail stick of olives around her glass (she knew enough about friendships to know that ordering strong drinks was required. . . but actually drinking? She didn't like Jenna *that* much), 'sounds like you need a full-on change of scene. I could make some enquiries?'

'Oh, could you?' Jenna didn't want to sound too desperate — and then remembered this was Bertie she was talking to and added, 'Into what exactly?'

'Oh, you know, see if anyone needs a galley slave on their yacht this summer, or perhaps some sort of hostessing in the south of France?'

Jenna ignored Bertie's suggestion that she was, in class terms, a mere 'galley slave' but she couldn't help feeling that a spark of an idea had just caught light.

'Say that again, Berts. . .' she wagged her finger in the air and took another slug of the gin martini.

Bertie looked a bit confused, then quickly remembered that furrowing one's brow was not good for the wrinkles so relaxed and repeated what she'd just said.

'That's it!' Jenna exclaimed as Bertie had listed off her ideas, 'The south of France!'

'Oh, *bon idée*, sweet cheeks — but where? Let me see.' Bertie whipped out her smartphone and started scrolling through her contacts. 'Monty Blake-Howard has a little place in Antibes, but I think he gets staff solely from agencies, um. . . there's Jacinta and Jolyon, they might need a nanny for little Horatio. . .'

'No, no. . .' Jenna waved a dismissive hand at Bertie, who pulled a very good 'affronted' face before remembering about the wrinkles thing again. 'You got me thinking. Where have we just been? France! And who did I meet, who offered me a job?'

'Not darling Philippe? Oh bravo, sweetie, well played.'

'No, not exactly, but Jonty did ask if I wanted to join him at, oh, what was it called — where we went for the wine tasting. . . gah, it will come to me. . . Carpark & Son? No. Um. . .'

'Carstairs & Co?'

'Yes! There! That's what I'll do!' Jenna suddenly turned from triumphant to sad again. And in a much lower voice whispered, 'Job sorted. Now just a heart to heal.'

'Oh tish-tosh, sweetie.' Bertie jabbed the now empty cocktail stick at Jenna (she had relented and at least eaten the olives, even if not a drop of gin had been drunk). 'You're doing the right thing. And fingers crossed they'll send you over to France and you can have a lovely time swanning around vineyards — though please, for my sake, do not over-imbibe, sweetie, empty calories, am I right?'

Sobering up slightly, Jenna grimaced at Bertie and hovered her hand over the last dregs of her martini, 'Of course, it's not set in stone, Jonty might be rather shocked at my sudden change of heart.'

'Darling, he'll be recruiting with his pants — and I must say you're not looking too shabby at the moment, little tubby, perhaps, and still betrothed to that terrible cardigan, but nothing a few hours down the gym and a trip to Selfridges won't sort out. I'm sure he'll take you on.'

'Thanks, I think.'

'I say go tomorrow and see him. Strike while the iron — and the man in the ironed shirt — is hot.'

'Okay.' Jenna paused and then thought out loud, 'What about references though? I'll never get those from Roach & Hartley now. . .'

'Oh references-schmeferences.' Bertie flicked her dead cocktail stick away from her. 'He won't ask for them. And if he does, I'll give you some — say you've been my private art consultant or something.'

'Would you, Berts? God, thank you.'

'And,' Bertie seemed to read Jenna's mind and passed her cocktail over to her, 'tell me all about it tomorrow when you've been to see him.'

After that the conversation descended into Bertie going on about some amazing party in Morocco she'd been invited to and quite how ridiculously rich some of the other guests were and Jenna stifled both sobs and yawns as she tried desperately not to think about Angus. The glimmer of a new job was the only light guiding her through the dark cloak of her sadness.

16

Jonty rolled up the sleeves of his shirt. France it may not be, but the upstairs office at Carstairs & Co was sweltering on this rather fine early summer's day. He hoped it wouldn't be a hot one this year, as the seventeenth-century buildings that housed London's oldest wine merchant were hardly adaptable to adding air con. His office had a lovely, if slightly shabby and stiff, sash window that looked over the roof tops of St James's, with their fire escapes, chimney pots and makeshift urban mini-gardens. None of them, he noticed, had an air con unit either. He'd be spending most of the summer back in France, though, which was pretty much guaranteed to be roasting, especially if he was going to be showing people round the vineyard. Jonty had a rather loose job description at Carstairs & Co and he liked it that way. If pushed he'd say he was an account manager, but he was more of a facilitator and when a client was someone like Philippe Montmorency then his bosses would allow him free rein to manage the account how he saw fit. And right now Jonty saw fit to have a rather cushty summer in the sun — or at least the shade of a decently thick-walled chateau and more specifically the nicely chilled cellar.

Jonty sipped his coffee. He'd flown back from France that morning, having stayed for a couple of days after Hugo and Sally's wedding weekend in order to go through the Carstairs contracts with Philippe and have a nose around the chateau's winery and bottling plant. He'd felt uncomfortable earlier that year when he'd been on the negotiating team — hammering down Philippe's wholesale prices so that they could make a decent margin in the UK market.

But Philippe was by no means unhappy with the coupling — he may be a semi-prestigious winemaker, but Carstairs & Co and its heritage was the last word in wine world chic. Jonty's official job now was to get the word out that Philippe Montmorency, and his eponymous chateau, was open for business, so he fired off a few emails to industry PRs, and newspaper columnists aiming to get some coverage from them while he was there to do show-and-tells this summer. And on a purely personal basis, the more he bigged-up Château Montmorency, the better it was for him. He was just writing an email to Andrew Bradstock, a famous wine journalist, inviting him to come and stay and review the chateau and its wines for *Decanter* magazine, when he had a buzz on the intercom from reception. To say the message he received from the receptionist was pleasing was an understatement and he ran his fingers through his sandy-blond hair before taking the narrow stairs two at a time down to the public reception area of the old building.

Jenna ran a finger over one of the bottles that was on display in the fusty old reception area of Carstairs & Co. A 2010 Bordeaux and a snip at £300 a bottle. *Blimey, that could pay my gas and leckie for a year.* Jenna had woken up that morning with one of those gin hangovers — not in pain, not ill, just foggy and groggy. She thought back to last night and how she'd made full use of Bertie's uncharacteristic generosity and had had two of those super-strong martinis. Plus a cheeky Cosmopolitan (the barman assured her it was more like a soft drink compared to the martinis. Oops). Still, gin was her friend and the morning fog cleared by elevensies (or second breakfast as she liked to call it) and she'd started to put her plan into action. Angus, of course, flooded her thoughts again and again, especially as she had to hunt around various belongings of his to find the gold embossed business card with Jonty's details on it. Jonty — and his ridiculous red trousers, but rather handsome everything else — might just be her saviour from the bailiffs, and so here she was, in the reception area of London's oldest wine merchant, ready to beg for a job.

'Well, hello there.' Jonty caught Jenna by surprise by coming up behind her as she was stroking the bottles of wine, which made her feel like an idiot for the twenty-zillionth time in the last forty-eight hours.

'Oh, Jonty, hi.' She desperately tried to read his signals as to whether a handshake or a kiss was appropriate. Jonty took the lead, thank God, and leaned down to give her a gentle kiss on each cheek while holding the tops of her arms.

'Great to see you, Jenna. Nice shirt,' he winked at her. That morning, she'd found the beautiful silk blouse he'd given her hanging half in and half out of her suitcase and it had seemed the most appropriate choice, after a quick spritz and iron. Good old Jo Malone, always there when she needed her.

'I guess it's the female version of looking pretty dapper?' She straightened the blouse as she spoke.

'Isn't that just called looking pretty?'

Jenna blushed, which seemed to be a fairly common occurrence whenever she was around Jonty. He continued, 'Pretty or not, looks like you might need a coffee. Happens I've got a pot on the go upstairs — shall we go up there to chat?' He gestured for her to go in front of him, then gently placed his hand on the small of her back to guide her in the direction of the staff-only stairs. 'Just follow your nose up to the top — sorry, it's a bit stuffy up there, seems it never got above twelve degrees in the seventeen-hundreds.'

His small talk helped to calm Jenna down a bit, and although a huge amount of her concentration was spent trying not to trip up on the rickety staircase, she did take in quite a bit of the building around her. Like her gallery — her *old* gallery, she self-corrected — the main offices of

Carstairs & Co cosily inhabited an old London merchant's house. Various doors and half-landings marked turns and twists in the staircase, which was narrow much like the one in her old office, but unlike the rest of the gallery that had been whitewashed (well, some sort of very well-chosen Farrow & Ball off-whitewashed in any case) and was sparsely hung with paintings with plenty of white space around them, this building was chock-a-block with portraits of generations of wine merchants and all their ephemera. The walls had paintings on them, but you might call it crazy paving rather than exhibition-quality hanging, with Holbein etchings alongside Stubbs-esque horses and old *Punch* magazine cartoons alongside framed cigarette cards. The whole effect was like a Dickensian curiosity shop.

At the top of the stairs was a little landing that was home to a hotch-potch collection of dusty old bottles. Jonty opened the door to his ramshackle office and ushered her inside, moving one of the old bottles into position as a door stop.

'Good to get the air flowing through,' he said as he wedged the huge bottle in place. The focal point to the cluttered office was an old mahogany partner's desk and although it had a relatively modern computer and screen on it, the rest was piled high with papers, journals and thick hardback books with names such as *Wines of the Alsace* and *Classic Bordeaux: The Greatest Vintages*. Jonty moved a few books off a chair and brought it round to face his on the other side of the desk. Jenna sat herself down and tried not to let Jonty see how much her hands were shaking as she accepted a chipped mug filled with steaming black coffee straight from the cafétière.

'No milk, sorry. I can never be bothered to go three flights down to the kitchen so I've got rather used to it.'

'Don't worry.' Jenna sipped the steaming liquid before coming out with the intro she'd been practising on the Tube on the way here. 'Thank you so much for seeing me without an appointment, Jonty.' She put the mug down on the desk, careful to find a patch not covered in paperwork or books. She looked down at her hands and then looked him in the eye, 'It seems it might be that I, er, could possibly be in the, um, position to take you up on the offer of a, um, position, er, I mean role.' *Oh dear*, she thought, this *really isn't going as seamlessly as planned*. Plus every time she said 'position' she felt a bit like a starlet in a porn film.

'That's brilliant, Jenna! Awesome!' Jonty alleviated any of her worries about her presentation skills as he jumped up from his chair and came round to her side of the desk. Jenna got up and did a little jumpy dance thing to mimic his excitement.

'Oh yay! I mean, brilliant!'

'You have no idea how much I really think this is going to be out-of-the-park amazing, Jenna.'

'I don't suppose you could tell me what the job might entail?' Jenna was suddenly worried at Jonty's enthusiasm and was a little circumspect about taking on a job that, for all she knew, could involve pouring champagne into the naked tummy buttons of rich businessmen, or sitting in a cluttered office with an ancient abacus working out profit margins. Neither of which she'd be much good at, although on second thoughts she'd at least give the former a go.

Jonty sat back down and took a hasty sip of his coffee. 'Yes, of course. You're going to love this. At least I hope you will. It'll be a bugger if you don't as I'm pretty stuck otherwise. I wasn't joking when I offered you a job here — I really do need some help.' Jenna shuffled in her chair, her body automatically reacting to the news that she would be working so closely with the charismatic Jonty. 'Plus, Philippe really liked you from the off so I hope you won't mind working with him too.'

'Oh, of course not. He was charm itself. But he's in France?'

'And so will we be, if that's OK with you? Basically, I'm going to spend the summer at the chateau helping Philippe with journalists and private tours, and overseeing the harvest when that comes in. So from now, until, say mid September?' Jonty was flicking through his desk diary as he spoke. 'Bloody annoying, actually, as I'll miss the start of the grouse season, but hey ho.'

'Oh, is that a week that you take off with your mates and complain about things a lot?'

'I'm sorry?' Jonty looked a bit perplexed.

Jenna faltered a little. This was exactly the kind of joke that she used to make with Clive, but it seemed to have fallen flat with Jonty, who was looking at her with a bemused expression on his face. 'You know, grouse, when you grumble about things.'

'No, Jenna, it's sport, you know, shooting. Birds.'

'Sorry, yes, I know. It was a joke.'

'Oh I see! A joke! Very good.' He cleared his throat. 'So how about it, Jenna. Do those dates work for you?'

Jenna still wasn't entirely sure what the job out in France would entail but she was happy to play along because right now going back to that glorious chateau in the summer sun, far away from her cramped little flat with all of Angus's stuff in it, seemed pretty bloody perfect.

'That sounds great, Jonty. Thank you.'

'We'll work out cash and stuff but you won't be disappointed, I promise. The problem is, how early can you start?'

'How about tomorrow?'

'Tomorrow?' The upper-class squawk almost deafened Jenna down the phone line. 'You do not hang about, do you, chick?'

'It just seemed to snowball, one moment we were having coffee and the next. . . well, the thing is, Bertie, it's just as we, I mean, I, hoped — I'm off to France!'

'You know what, doll, I consulted my astrotherapist about you this morning and, don't laugh — stop laughing — it was very expensive you know? Anyway, she said you were about to get some good fortune as Venus was rising into Uranus.'

Jenna tuned out Bertie as her mind whirred. Accepting a job so quickly was one thing, but she still had to think of a way to sublet her flat, Jonty said not to worry about money, but until she had her first paycheque in her sticky mitts she couldn't take it for granted. And if she was going to be in France for most of the summer then she really should cash in on her only asset, which was her tiny flat.

'Bertie,' she interrupted her friend mid-flow. 'Can I ask a favour?'

'Depends, sweets — if it involves fried food and wearing a onesie I'm not your gal.'

'Ha, no. Do you know anyone who might want to rent my flat from me — you know, as a short-term sublet?'

'Hmm. . . let me think. I'm sure I'll know someone. Hang tight, Jens, and I'll call you back.'

Jenna disconnected the call and dropped down into the underground station, her journey back to Battersea filled with hope, rather than just anguish and nerves.

She'd only been back in her flat for about twenty minutes — twenty pretty bloody horrible minutes as she carefully started folding up Angus's clothes and putting them in a carrier bag, every item another stab to her heart — when her phone rang again.

'It's me, chicks. All sorted. You can mwah mwah me laters, but for now, start packing.'

'Hi, Bertie,' Jenna reluctantly put down one of Angus's cufflinks as she tried to concentrate on the call. She so hoped that the call had been from him. 'Sorry, start again, what have you sorted?'

'Sublet your, well, your apartment if that's the right word for that little hermit cell you rent.'

'Thanks, Bertie, I think. . .'

'I'll text the deets to you, but basically there's this wonderful friend of a friend, a true royal, if you know what I mean?'

'If by royal you mean someone with a penchant for crowns and living in palaces?'

'Quite. She's a Saudi princess — so chic, can you imagine — anyway she's interested in your place.'

'Wow!' Jenna was completely taken aback. Not only were her financial worries taken care of, but her much-dented ego had suddenly received one hell of a boost. 'I'd be honoured, I mean, wow. But isn't it a bit small here for a, you know, real princess?'

Bertie guffawed down the phone. 'Gawd! No! I mean, yes, she wants your micro-home, but it's for her cleaner, silly! Her Royal Chicness has an amazing flat in the new Chelsea apartments down the road from you and she needs somewhere for her cleaner to do the ironing that's not too far, *capiche*? And I thought of your place — perfect as a little laundry, don't you think?'

'Oh. Yes, I suppose.' Jenna's ego withered as it took another sly kick to the back of its knees.

'Bright side, babes, no one is going to look after your shag-pad better than a cleaner.'

'I guess.'

'And it'll smell of fresh linen — dreamy. Better than whatever cheapo candles you can afford, yes?'

'Hmm. Okay, then.'

'So get packing, dolls, she's ready to move in asap!'

Jenna looked at the blank screen of her phone after the call was over and wondered quite how her life had changed so much in such a short time. She picked up Angus's cufflink again and popped it into her jeans pocket — there were some things she wasn't ready to rinse and clean out of her life quite yet.

17

Jenna squinted through her Gucci sunglasses (an eBay special, slightly scratched) against the hot, white sun that beat down through the car windows as she and Jonty sped through the French countryside towards the chateau. Jenna fiddled with the digital radio in the hire car trying to find something other than tinny euro-pop. She couldn't help but remember the last time they'd been in a car together and she almost crossed herself in gratitude that this time she hadn't fallen onto the luggage carousel in front of a plane-load of glamorous Frenchies. Jonty, in a subtle, yet decisive way, had leant over and picked up their cases to avoid any chance of it happening again. In fact, Jenna had to keep reminding herself that she was now on a work trip as she'd barely lifted a finger since she'd met Jonty at the airport a few hours ago.

'So can you tell me more as to what I'm going to be doing?' Jenna had settled on a classical channel, hoping that it would impress Jonty in some way and also because she was at the limit of her hire-car-radio technical knowledge.

'Basically follow me around with a clipboard as I follow Philippe around with a clipboard,' said Jonty, who laughed at Jenna's raised eyebrow and quizzical expression. 'Ha, okay, okay, there is more to it than that. I'm cataloguing his cellar, which will be one major chore, but don't worry, I won't expect you to miss out on the sunshine and join me down there. But while I'm doing that I need you to be the eyes and ears, and, if I may say so, very pretty face, of Carstairs & Co — greeting journalists, entertaining them with your sparkling repartee during dinner parties, showing them around the estate, that sort of thing. And then there's the wine buyers, too, who we'll be selling all the wines on to — again, guided tours, wine tastings, dinners. It's not rocket science but it needs a fun bubbly fluffy to charm the old boys.'

'Ah.' She parked how miffed she was about being referred to as a 'fluffy' while she mentally dealt with a more urgent issue.

'Problem?'

'No, no. I mean, it's just not what I packed for exactly.'

'What do you mean?'

Jenna thought back to the last-minute packing she'd done as she'd cleared out her little flat before the Saudi princess's cleaner arrived. She'd spent the last few days ferrying belongings back to her parents' house, telling them it was just a good clear out and nothing to worry about. She may have admitted to them that her career in the art world was over and that she was off to France, but she couldn't bring herself to tell the truth to them about her flat. 'Well, I thought you said I'd be helping with the harvest so I mostly packed dungarees and my old Doc Martens. I had no idea I'd be so, well, you know, on show.'

Jonty burst out laughing.

'I'm sorry,' Jenna said again. It seemed Jonty was constantly laughing at her and she was always apologising. She started to worry about blotting her copybook so early on in the working relationship.

'It's almost as if you expect me to buy all your clothes for you all the time, Jenna. . .'

'Oh no, honestly. I should have enough to get me through — I might be down the old *auto-lavage* in the village a bit though!'

'Or making a fashion statement with dungarees at dinner?'

'Or canapés and coveralls?' They both giggled and Jenna was once again lulled into the belief that this really was more of a holiday than a new job. Angus's admonishment rung in her ears, though — *you have to take this job more seriously,* she thought to herself.

'Oh, and you'll be chief organiser of your pal Bertie's party at the end of the summer.'

'What?' Now things had just got serious.

'Yes, Philippe is having kittens. He agreed to it when we were all there but she's already sent him forty emails with "suggestions", demands in other words. I think thirty white doves were mentioned at one point and swapping the fountain water for the house white. Anyway, he's far too nice to say anything to her now he's taken her dosh but he's going greyer by the minute so I said you'd take over the party planning. That's OK, isn't it? I need him fighting fit to sell the wine to the journos and punters.'

'Yeah, I guess. . .' Jenna could well believe that Bertie was pushing her luck along with her ideas and even with her recent uncharacteristic helpfulness it would test the very limits of their tenuous friendship to help organise the Bertie bash — without giving into violence and just bashing Bertie.

'*Mademoiselle* — it is so wonderful to see you again.' Either Philippe really was an old charmer or someone had told him that Jenna was now on Bertie duty. 'I hope Carstairs & Co realise that you cannot possibly work today as you have travelled a *grande distance*, to come and join us. I will ask Jonty to show you to your room.'

Jenna thanked Philippe and took in the sight of the chateau again. Had it only been a week since she was last here? So much in her life had changed that it hardly seemed possible that the chateau remained the same, its warm stone glowing gold in the afternoon sunshine. Her life, of course, had changed so much in just a week and so the building took on a sort of gentle familiarity and Jenna could at least look forward to being a guest, albeit a working one, in that gorgeous east wing room again.

'Follow me.' Jonty carried her suitcase for her as they headed into the chateau and mounted the stairs. But Jenna was surprised when he didn't follow the wind-blowing cherub and turn along the beautifully decorated corridor towards her old room.

'Oh,'

'Ah, yes, sorry. The *piano nobile*, as the Italians would call it, is for guests only, I'm afraid. You're bunking up here with us plebs in the old servants' quarters.' Jonty revealed a second staircase neatly hidden behind a secret door. The *trompe l'œil* was quite a masterpiece as Jenna hadn't noticed it the last time she was here. The staircase itself had none of the sweeping grandeur of the main one, which wasn't surprising for one lurking behind a hidden door, but it did emerge into a light-filled landing, which although less lofty than the highly decorated hall below, seemed more homely and relaxed. Jonty showed Jenna to her room, which was far more austere than the opulent one she'd had last time. The walls were plain with not much in the way of decoration save for a crucifix hanging above the single bed and a small landscape etching framed in thin dark wood that hung above a grey-painted chest of drawers. The bed had a prettily stitched quilt on it, though, and something that looked like a long sausage instead of a pillow.

'Sorry, Jenna, not quite the Versailles treatment this time, but if it makes you feel any better I'm just along the hall in very similar circumstances.'

'Reduced.'

'Quite.'

Just like my life, thought Jenna as she placed her suitcase up on the small side table next to the door. If there was a better metaphor for what had happened to her last week she couldn't think of one. She'd gone from having it all, from roll-top baths and four-posters, to spartan walls and a lonely single bed. However, Jenna felt that this garret, was the perfect place to lick her wounds and regroup. Jonty mentioned something about drinks on the terrace later and then closed the door behind him as he left. Jenna plonked herself down on the bed. She looked over at her suitcase, packed to the gills with almost all of her clothes. She'd find some suitable outfits in there somewhere. She leaned over and unzipped a little side pocket and fished around inside it. Her fingers clasped around the small golden cufflink that she'd found when she'd been tidying up her flat. *Oh Angus. . .* Jenna held it tight in her fist as she curled up into the foetal position on the bed. *Regrouping could start later*, she thought, as the fresh linen of the pillow case absorbed the first of her tears.

18

Jenna on a bike in Hyde Park, her legs akimbo as she flew along; Jenna eating a massive ice cream, her spoon about to crack through the chocolate sauce; Jenna and him in selfie mode up the Shard; Jenna and Sally smiling at the wine tasting. . . Angus's phone was full of pictures of Jenna. He was even greeted every five minutes as he activated the screen looking for a text message alert with a picture of Jenna and him at the Natural History Museum pretending to be scared of a dinosaur. A few flicks of a finger and these could all be gone. The screen saver could go back to a picture of mists over the Singapore skyscrapers, the pictures relegated to an archive folder or simply deleted. But he couldn't do it, any more than he could just delete the real Jenna from his life. On that Monday when she had been fired and after they'd had that massive bust up, Angus had roamed the streets of Battersea until common sense told him to grab a taxi back to his parents. He'd not really understood what had happened, Jenna might as well have been speaking in tongues, but the overriding feeling was that he'd been pretty much told to foxtrot oscar.

The problem was, Angus had had a rather interesting day too last Monday. Not a pinching-Picassos-while-you-pee-type day, but definitely one that he would have liked to discuss with his usually more level-headed girlfriend. He'd been offered a temporary, but exceedingly lucrative, secondment back to China. It had been brewing for a while and he'd felt bad having to keep his phone almost physically attached to his body while they were in France the weekend of the wedding. Pei Ling, his old boss from the architectural firm Stafford Ling in Singapore, had returned to her native Hong Kong after the gangster-led bar fight that had left him with the jagged scar across his left cheek and her hankering after retirement. She had one last project to do, and she wanted Angus to help her, if he was willing? And no, he had not really been willing when he thought he would miss a summer of fun with his gorgeous girlfriend — someone who, he thought, not only didn't mind the scar on his face but actively liked it; the result of a heroic action. Since that fight a few years ago, he'd covered the white welt with a thick beard, but one night on a ski trip earlier this year, the same trip where he'd got together with Jenna, his friends — ha, he didn't think much of them that night — had pressured him to shave it off. Jenna had been kind though and just a few days after that they'd been an item. And that had been about three months ago now. Three months of a pretty bloody brilliant relationship. Perhaps he'd come on too strong though? Maybe she really was feeling cramped in her little flat. It had seemed so cute and chaotic — so her — when she'd brought him home, injured and frostbitten after his accident on the slopes, but perhaps he'd just added to the chaos and tipped her over the edge? She'd never brought up the topic of them getting a bigger place together. Perhaps she really did love her little flat and own space more than she did him?

Pei Ling had emailed him again the day after his and Jenna's cataclysmic fight. Would he reconsider his initial no? *Yes*. He had typed it before he let himself overthink it, and now with his company's blessing he was sitting in the first-class lounge at London Heathrow, waiting for his gate number to appear, and flicking through his phone photos wandering what had gone wrong.

He scrolled down his messages inbox — in the past week or so other messages had bumped Jenna's stream down a bit. He'd wanted to text her so many times since they'd fought. A simple one-word 'sorry' or an essay of apology, but the problem was he still didn't know what he was meant to be apologising for, and why hadn't she texted him? More proof perhaps that she didn't want to take things further with him. He'd heard somewhere that you need to give women space, so he had. And then that space became a void and the void became almost unbearable until he found himself now hovering over the send button of a simple message: Leaving London today for a bit. Love you.

19

Jonty closed the door of his bedroom behind him. He, like Jenna had a small, garret-like single room — their only creature comforts were the pretty eiderdown and a small — and his room's case, pink — basin attached to the wall, above it a plain mirror screwed in directly to the old, Band-Aid-coloured plaster. He splashed some water on his face and thought about his next move. He couldn't believe that it had been that easy to get Jenna to accompany him to the chateau. And more so, that his bosses back in London had signed off on his request for an assistant quite so readily. They hadn't even queried it, although it might have helped that he'd asked for a signature after one of their very long and very boozy lunches. It seemed to Jonty that if there was a God then he was definitely moving a few chess pieces around in his favour.

The other bloody amazing thing was that Jenna hadn't mentioned her boyfriend once since they'd met at Gatwick airport that morning. If he wasn't on the scene any more it would make things so much easier. Jonty had felt his pride grow a little more as she'd smiled at him when they met up at the airport gate. He'd booked their airline tickets and had checked them both in in advance so he knew he had the short flight to Bordeaux sitting next to her — the perfect time to probe her on how much she knew about the wine trade, wine making and the importing business in general. In between her almost braining them both as she put her carry-on luggage in the overhead bin, and then accidentally calling the flight attendant about three times by stretching out her arms to pull a jumper on and off during the flight, he'd gathered that she knew just about zero about any of those things. However, he also now knew all about some great pubs in Battersea and how much one day she'd love to be able to afford to buy her own flat. Oh, and that if he ever needed fluffy handcuffs, L-plates, comedy bananas and penis-shaped straws at short notice, she was his girl, having overstocked on all of them for Sally's hen do. So, all in all, an interesting fact-finding mission about his new friend and one that had also led him to notice how gently her golden hair fell around her face, the dimples that creased into her cheeks when she smiled, and the quite frankly awesome pair of tits that strained out of her tight little T-shirt.

'Concentrate on the job in hand, mate,' he told himself into the mirror as he wiped his face with the hand towel that hung beside the basin. His eyes flicked over to a ledger that sat on his bedside table with a corkscrew lying on top of it. The contents would mean nothing to anyone else, but to him. . . he picked it up and pocketed the corkscrew too before heading down stairs to the main hexagonal hall-way and from there down to the cellar.

20

Jenna's new job was unlike any she had ever taken on before. Although, to be fair, she'd never worked in the wine trade and she'd certainly never set her alarm clock for 6 a.m., just so that she could see the sunrise over the vineyards.

The first day she'd seen it was by pure accident. She'd been worried about dehydrating in the heat and so had drunk so much water the evening before, she woke up with a bladder the size of a rugby ball, and although her little single bed was at that ideal morning temperature she had forced herself to get up to go to the shared bathroom down the corridor. The clanking of the old pull-chain cistern couldn't dispel the peace and calm she saw out of the window as the gentle mist that hung above the neat rows of vines dissipated as the golden glowing sun rose up over the village. She'd crept back to her bedroom and opened her curtains, then slipped back in under the eiderdown, pulled her knees up to her chest and gazed out of the window. She let a few tears fall down her cheeks as she looked out over the vines. It had been over a week now since their fight and she'd heard nothing from Angus. Nothing. As the milky light woke up the world around her, and a cock crowed out in the village somewhere, she flicked her finger across her phone screen. Still nothing. She herself had drafted text upon text to Angus, yet none of them had been sent as she still mulled over in her mind what he had meant. His words still hurt though — she was 'irrational' he'd said, not 'serious' about her career and worst of all, he didn't regard their relationship as permanent. She placed the phone carefully back on the bedside table and turned away from it and back towards the window in disgust, as if the phone itself had betrayed her and was the one to blame for the lack of messages, the lack of love.

Every morning since that first accidental early start she did this now. The alarm would go off at just past six and she'd lazily stretch and yawn and bring herself round to sitting upright, hugging her knees to her chest and staring out of the window. The morning ritual was a reward in itself, but she was fully aware it was these early starts over the last fortnight that were helping her drop off to sleep so quickly every night too; if she were any less tired then her mind wandered too far in the direction of her — she hated to say it — *ex*-boyfriend.

Brrrrring. The old-fashioned telephone bell on her smart phone broke the morning's quiet and Jenna scrambled to stop the noise as much as to answer the phone.

'Sweetie! You're up!' It was Sally.

'Yes, impressive, huh?' Jenna checked her watch and did a mental calculation. It would be about 5.30 a.m. in the UK. 'Why on earth are you, though?'

'Oh, jetlagged to buggery, darling. We just got home! I was going to leave you a message, but since you're awake. . .' Sally started to tell Jenna about how amazing the honeymoon had been and how much she and Hugo wanted to thank Jenna personally for all the help she'd given them at the wedding. 'Which reminds me, darling, what the bloody hell happened?'

'How much do you know exactly?' Jenna hadn't wanted to spoil her best friend's honeymoon with her dramas, but she felt bad that Sally was so out of the loop.

'Well, I know you're not in bloody England! And I know Angus isn't either as we saw him in Hong Kong!'

Jenna's body tensed up. Hong Kong? What on earth was he doing there?

'Oh, Sally. . .' Jenna didn't know where to start. She took a deep breath. 'Angus and I, we're. . . well, we had a. . . a fight.'

'So?' Sally's bluntness wasn't quite what Jenna was expecting.

'So. . . so we broke up. I had no idea he was in Hong Kong, though. What did he say? Was he okay? Did he mention me?'

'Slow down, sweetie, first things first, why are you not in the UK?' Jenna filled her friend in with the disaster that was The Firing, but how she'd luckily managed to land on her feet here in France, with no little thanks to Bertie. 'So when did the fight with Angus happen and why on earth didn't you tell me, sweetie?'

'It happened that night. He was offering me money but he didn't understand that I couldn't take any more from him, he already paid for so much, you know, dinners and drinks. . .'

'So you argued because he wanted to be even nicer to you and even more perfect?'

'It wasn't like that, Sal!' Jenna wanted to make her friend understand how the argument had gone, but even she had to admit that it was slightly foggy due to the bottle of lady petrol she'd sunk on the way home. 'He told me things had never been permanent between us and he didn't feel like my flat was his home. I think. Anyway, he hasn't been in contact *at all* since, so he must have meant those nasty things.'

'Darling, before you start blubbing, let me tell you what he told us.'

'Oh yes, what?'

'Well, he looked like death, I'll tell you that. Huggie and I barely recognised him. I was in Chanel at the airport actually and it was Hugo who nudged me away from the handbags as he wasn't a hundred per cent sure *it was* Gus.'

'And. . .?'

'Oh well, he said this opportunity had come up for a secondment to a project and it might take him into rural China but would be mostly based in HK and I just remember thinking, blimey, I don't think you'll last past the first bowl of chow mein, sweetie.'

'China. . .'

'Yes. Anyway, we asked him what you had said about it and wondered why it was all so sudden — I half expected you to pop up from behind the duty-free display, bottle of Gordon's in hand, too actually — anyway he mumbled something about opportunities and then made a dash for it. Very odd. So I thought to myself, as soon as I come home, I'll check on Jenks and here you are, buggered off too!'

Jenna burst out crying at that point and moaned to her friend about how shitty things had been.

'But, sweetie, what a place to mend a broken heart. I bet darling Philippe is as charming as ever and Jonty — well, I don't think Gus noticed but I certainly did — he had a real soft spot for you.'

'I don't know how I would have got through these last couple of weeks without him, Sals.' She hiccoughed a bit and told Sally all about her new job. 'So I basically organise these press trips and make sure journalists have all the right info before they arrive — propaganda before their "proper gander", as it were. Or at least I will be when Bertie releases me from party organising.'

'What?'

'Apparently Bertie loved your wedding so much, Sals, that she wants a re-run at the end of the summer. Except with swans. And a thirty-foot-tall, inflatable golden elephant.' Jenna paused expecting at least a snort of derision, but there was none so she continued. 'Apparently, she's offered Philippe a vast sum of money to take over the chateau like you did, but he was getting understandably flabbergasted so now I'm on Bertie duty, or Booty, as I call it.'

'Ugh. Don't.'

'Sorry.'

There was a pause before Sally could verbalise how she was feeling. 'I don't know whether to be flattered or as annoyed as Catherine of Aragon was when that bloody Boleyn girl turned up at court. Usurper!'

Jenna laughed at her friend. 'Don't worry, Sals, I have the feeling that due to the amount of Swarovski crystals that are being flown over to scatter everywhere, her party will be nowhere as subtly sophisticated as your wedding.'

'Did you say thirty-foot-tall, inflatable golden elephant?'

'Yes. And thirty doves. Plus two alpacas to help — and these are her words — "take away the negative energy built up by our modern urban lives".'

'What?'

'Exactly.'

The girls nattered on for a few more minutes before the clanking of the plumbing alerted Jenna that the household, or at least the 'servants' of the household, were waking up. They said their goodbyes and sent kisses down the phone to each other. But Jenna didn't get up. It was still early, and she wanted to process what Sally had just told her. Angus was in China. It annoyed her that she had been wrong in her make-believe scenarios — the ones in her head that had played over and over since the argument, ones like bumping into him in the local Little Waitrose or friends sitting round a pub table telling him that she was with the handsome Jonty at the chateau (she had imagined Angus breaking down into tears in that one. Satisfying to say the least) — but those, although slim-chanced at best, could *never* have happened with him hot-footing it off to China. Hong Kong, China. So many miles away. Did he really have to go that far to get away from her? And had it been so sudden or had he really been planning it for months? Well — she clasped her knees close and gave herself one more hug — she was glad he looked like a dog's dinner at the airport; maybe he should just jolly well stay in China.

21

'So, Andrew Bradstock and his wife Tessa will be here by midday.' Jonty was reading off an itinerary that he'd typed up and put onto clipboards for them both, as he and Jenna perched on the edges of their desks. This was the first major journalist to visit the chateau since Jenna had arrived, the first British one at least; several local reporters and Paris foodies had been on day trips and had mostly ignored Jenna as her faltering French failed to keep their interest. At least she had taken the 'Booty' off Philippe so he could do his charming thing. This English couple, however, was a different kettle of the proverbial.

'You should be here at the chateau to welcome them — they're in the east wing room, I'm afraid — and then lunch at one o'clock.'

Jenna nodded and tried to suppress her envy at the mention of her old room. 'Any points of reference I need to know, anything I shouldn't mention?'

She knew that whatever industry you were in there would be some clangers you could drop. There used to be an artist she'd worked with who resented any questions being asked about his paintings — not great when his work was totally unintelligible, even to the trained eye. A simple 'what is it?' had once cost her bosses three dinners out and a promise of a glossy catalogue to accompany his exhibition to placate him. Nothing quite prepared her for Jonty's answer though.

'Not really. Genuinely nice couple. Just don't follow them out to the vines later — that's scheduled in for three o'clock — they'll be having sex.'

'What?'

'Yeah. Well known in the trade. We need to look out for his review of the chateau and our wines, not so much for what scores he gives the claret, but as to how he refers to his wife.'

Jenna's shock had turned to puzzlement. She cocked her head to one side.

'His reviews always mention a visit to the vines, wherever he's staying — Italy, France, Argentina — wherever. And if Tessa has come with him he'll mention her in the review too. If it's the long-suffering Tessa who has been marched through the vineyard, it means she gave him a blow job. If it's the gorgeous Tessa by his side as he looked at the grapes then it was full-blown sex. And if it's the *bum*ptious Tessa who. . .'

'Stop! I get it. Yuk.' Jenna waved her hand in front of Jonty who was laughing to himself now. 'You were joking, weren't you?'

'No. Honestly. I bet you ten euros they'll leave after lunch with a picnic blanket under their arms "in case they get tired".'

'Wow. Just wow.' Jenna scribbled a note on her piece of paper — *don't follow* — next to the 3 p.m. slot in the itinerary, less as an *aide memoire* and more as something to do as her blush subsided.

'Still, you can't blame them. I mean it's rather nice work this, but poor old Tessa must get bored rigid by all this wine chat.'

'Something rigid anyway,' murmured Jenna as she bit her pen.

'You have to stop doing that.' Jonty gently took the pen out of her mouth. Jenna suddenly looked down hoping she hadn't unexpectedly been chewing on one of Philippe's incredibly expensive Mont Blanc heirlooms. 'Not for the pen's sake, but you saying "rigid" as you suck on that. . .'

126

He turned away from her and Jenna saw him close his eyes and sort of try to restrain himself. 'Sorry.' He turned back. 'I have to remember we're colleagues now and that really wasn't appropriate.'

'It's okay,' Jenna clutched the clipboard to her chest, 'I really don't mind. I mean, yes, let's keep it professional though.' She wanted to be more upset — demand an apology or threaten a visit from her very tall boyfriend — but Jonty's attempts at flirting were quite a comfort to her, bearing in mind she didn't have a boyfriend any more, very tall or otherwise. With Angus's words still ringing in her ears though, she vowed to take her work more seriously and so put on her 'business' face and stared at her clipboard.

Finally Jonty broke the silence. 'Right, well, it's time for a coffee I think. I'll see if Madame Lefort has put the pot on.'

Jonty left the little room next to the kitchen that they shared as an office. Once a butler's pantry, it was a little on the small side, but the reward was the aromas that often wafted through from the kitchens — freshly baked bread some days (the days when it wasn't a quick cycle into the village for an impromptu baguette) and on others the savoury smells of roasting meat. And this was summer when most of the meals were salads with cheeses, vast boards of charcuterie and delicious little pickles; think what it must be like in winter? Jenna often fell into little day dreams as she sat at her desk muddling through the vineyard's diary. The first few days had been quite full-on as she found her feet and she began to get to know her way around and what she was meant to be doing. Jonty would leave her there in the office on her own for hours at a time while he catalogued the cellar — something she almost volunteered to join him in as just sometimes the office seemed a little empty without him. She had begun to get used to a few of their morning rituals. By 8.30 a.m., she and Jonty were in the office having sat round the kitchen table with Menou the cook — a vast man of Angolan origin, who laughed like a pirate and had an odd habit of rolling his eyeballs back in his head, but if the catering at Sally and Hugo's wedding had been anything to go by — and indeed the kitchen suppers she'd been treated to — he was a very accomplished chef. Also at breakfast was Coco, the gardener-cum-maintenance man, who sat in silence at the table reading a copy of *Le Figaro* and occasionally snorting to himself and letting out the occasional 'boff' to the piece on European economics, a 'prrfff' to the announcement of a general strike among the postal workers. How such a grumpy and seemingly characterless man could be called something so charming as Coco bothered Jenna. It was a name that would have suited the adorable Madame Lefort who was the housekeeper and general mother of the household staff. She was an elegant woman, her long auburn hair always swept up into a chignon, and her clothes, though not flashy, always looked so stylish and eminently presentable — no mean feat when you considered how much work she did around the house; changing bedding, cleaning the fire grates, polishing the silver. . . She did all of this with such love and passion for the house that, most of the time at least, her dutiful nature rubbed off on the other staff. No one else could tell Coco to take his muddy boots right back to the garden, *s'il te plaît*, in such a way that not only did it not offend but led to one of Coco's rare smiles. And Menou would summon her over to his stove and consult in some rapid French that Jenna had no hope of deciphering, only for the conversation to end with Madame Lefort swatting Menou on his large backside with a tea towel as he boomed with laughter.

Madame Lefort seemed to spot straight away that Jenna was recovering from some sort of *affaire d'amour* and always made sure there was a pot of the best coffee brewing at elevenish, and if Jenna was alone in the office while Jonty was on one of his cellar missions, she'd as often as not bring her in a steaming cup with a little sponge madeleine cake.

'I know what it's like,' she'd said a few mornings ago as she made space on Jenna's ever-more-cluttered desk for the little plate of cakes and the mug of coffee, 'to love someone you cannot reach.'

Jenna looked up at her. 'How did you. . .?'

But the older lady had just smiled at her and swept a loose tendril of hair away from her face before heading back to the kitchen and her next chore of the day.

22

'Welcome to Château Montmorency, my dear Andrew and Tessa.'

While Philippe greeted them, Jenna tried to spot any evidence of a picnic blanket peeking out from their luggage.

'Let me take that for you.' Jonty was the perfect host, carrying their luggage inside, and leaving Jenna standing rather idly on the steps in front of the chateau, hovering at Philippe's shoulder in case he should need her to do anything.

'And you are?' Tessa turned to Jenna and floated a hand out towards her in greeting. She was older than Jenna had imagined from Jonty's description of their vineyard shenanigans, and more eccentrically dressed; her floral kimono wafted over vastly wide palazzo pants, and her hair was so neatly bobbed that she looked like an extra from a nineteen thirties whodunit. Tessa seemed to be one of those wives who had heard her dear husband's witticisms so many times before that she immediately stopped listening to him as soon as she found someone else to talk to.

'Jenna, Jenna Jenkins, ma'am.' Jenna took Tessa's hand and shook it lightly while cursing herself for treating the whole affair like a royal visit. Ma'am? She might have well as curtseyed! Luckily, Tessa laughed.

'No need for such formality, although I assume that you are the Carstairs girl? I wouldn't put it past them to have you all trained in cap doffing and regimental saluting.'

'I only wish I had been,' sighed Jenna as Tessa fell in line with her as they climbed the steps of the chateau and went into the marvellously decorated hallway.

'Oh, this is sublime!' Tessa clasped her hands together as she took in the grand staircase that wound its way up around the hexagonal hallway and its intricately painted bacchanalian scenes. 'Just the thing!'

'My wife,' Andrew took a pause from his conversation with Philippe to lean in to whisper to Jenna in a most conspiratorial way, 'has a thing for photography, or at least for modelling in photographs.'

'Oh.' Jenna didn't quite know what to say.

'Don't worry, just tasteful arty shots. I'm sure she'd love your help.'

'Jenna has a background in art, actually.' Jonty's voice echoed in the hallway as he made his way down the stone staircase, having deposited the bags in the couple's room.

'Oh, I don't know, not really,' Jenna wished she could make throat-slitting actions to Jonty as he descended but all eyes were on her.

'Oh really?'

'Yes, Carstairs & Co are very lucky to have her — she used to work in Mayfair, for one of the oldest galleries there, for years.' Jenna wanted to die inside at Jonty's words. What if anyone started quizzing her on her old job. . . and why she left it?

'Oh, that's simply wonderful.' Tessa pressed her hands against the tops of Jenna's arms. 'You can be my muse, my aide. . .'

'Your tripod, more like,' Andrew interrupted his wife before turning back to his conversation with Philippe.

'Well,' Tessa retorted, 'at least this young thing might be able to hold the camera steady. Those nudes we did in Sassicaia were terribly blurry thanks to your delirium tremens and I do really want to capture the spirit of this wonderful bacchanalian scene later this afternoon.'

Before Tessa could illuminate her new audience any further, Philippe invited them all into the dining room for lunch. Much to Jenna's embarrassment, as the men talked about wine and traded industry news, Tessa decided her new muse needed to know all about the effects of diffused light on the naked bottom and then launched into a lecture on representations of the female nipple in Modern British art. Jenna fervently wished she could disappear back into the kitchen with Madame Lefort as she carried terrines, salads and bread back and forth. It wasn't that Jenna was a prude, far from it, but the combination of being reminded of her old — and much loved — career in the art world and the fact that Tessa started mentioning her total lack of feminine grooming, well, Jenna thought she'd pretty much reached peak awkwardness. Unable to escape, she could at least exact her revenge on Jonty for volunteering her for what was sounding more and more like a late afternoon of sheer embarrassment.

'I'm sure Jonty, on behalf of Carstairs & Co, would love to accompany you both into the vines after lunch. I hear there are some merlot grapes just beginning to ripen in the south field.'

Jonty glared at her.

'No need for that, my dear,' Andrew cut in. 'I prefer to see them *au naturel* if you know what I mean.'

Jenna blushed. Was the trade secret about what Andrew and Tessa did in the vines about to spill out over the *salade niçoise*?

Luckily, he continued, 'I find if a representative of the vineyard, or its agent, is present you only ever get the marketing guff spouted to you. No offence, of course, to you, Jonty, or you, Philippe, but I like to take my time, Tessa by my side, to really admire the firmness of the fruit, the juiciness of the grapes; unrushed, unhindered.'

'We quite understand.' Jonty kicked Jenna under the table, but couldn't help sending a little smirk of 'I told you so' her way too.

Unable to conjure up any other suggestions for Jonty that could rival her imminent foray into the world of who-knew-what, Jenna just raised a silent prayer asking that at least some of his afternoon would involve long boring chats about fermentation tanks or degree-level analysis of the pH levels of the soil. As Tessa continued to impress the importance onto her of selecting the correct photographic filter for the exact amount of flesh on show, Jenna gradually came to terms with the fact that whatever wine-geekery Jonty would have to put up after Andrew got back from the vines, it would be ten times easier to cope with than the artistic whims of a recently ravished Mrs Bradstock.

23

'I think we both deserve this.' Jonty poured a generous slug of brandy into a crystal balloon glass and handed it to Jenna. They were in the drawing room of the chateau, its rich decorations echoing the style of the rest of the house — rococo furniture with its elegant golden scroll designs sat alongside intricate Persian carpets. Lights from hundreds of small bulbs in the chandelier above glittered across mirrors and their ornate frames and gave the room an air of magical elegance. Jenna gratefully took the glass from Jonty's hand. They had just finished supper and Philippe and the Bradstocks had bid them goodnight in favour of going up to bed early.

'So, how was the photoshoot?'

'I have no words.' Jenna, who had slumped herself into one of the silk-upholstered chairs, stared into her glass.

'Go on, try.' Jonty was smiling at her, leaning forward in his chair, his elbows resting on his knees cupping his glass in his hand. A conspiratorial atmosphere brewed between the two colleagues. As the ormolu clock delicately struck the hour, Jenna gave way to her natural good-natured giggles.

'Okay then. But I can't believe I'm about to say this out loud.'

'Go on. . .'

'Today marks the first, and I really hope the last, time that I assist a middle-aged woman in positioning her breast at the correct angle to receive the light, which I also had to position, to make it look like she is feeding a cherub — a cherub that only exists in two dimensions on the wall, no less — and then try to find somewhere to rest my eyes while she recites Sappho — in the original ancient Greek, of course — and then uses her remote control shutter release to take the photo when she is basically sort of climaxing. It was all very, very odd.'

Jonty couldn't contain his laughter and stood up and rested against the marble mantelpiece.

'That is hilarious, Jenna. Did you see the finished shot?'

'No, but hey — don't feel like any of us will miss out. . . the coffee table book entitled *At My Breast* will be gifted unto us for our help!' Jenna gave as theatrical as bow as she could in the chair. She had to admit, she was enjoying herself, through it all. And the yearning she felt for Angus, although not lessening, was certainly being numbed by the daily adventures at Château Montmorency. She still hadn't heard a thing from him — and it was over two weeks since she'd been in France, and almost three since their fight and his rather sudden departure from her life. And now he was in Hong Kong.

'I'm sure it's not the sort of souvenir you thought you'd be bringing back from your time here?' Jonty's low, masculine voice brought her round from her reverie. Making him laugh made her feel better, she couldn't explain it, but it empowered her, and she couldn't deny that he really was quite handsome, in a worn-out teddy bear way. His mustard-coloured cords were paired with an old burgundy-red cashmere jumper and he seemed so at ease with himself, almost as if he owned the place.

'No, I'd reckoned on a couple of bottles and some hard-to-shift wine stains, but no, a coffee table tome on Mrs Bradstock's Boobs was not one I would have guessed at.' She leaned back in her seat. 'Tell me, how was Andrew this afternoon? Please say he was at least boring and analytical and you're exhausted from high-level wine chat.'

'Ha, no, but he did mention the word *bum*ptious several times — it must be fresh in his mind—'

'Ew!' Jenna reached behind her for a small silk-covered cushion and lobbed it at Jonty, missing his head and only just sparing a porcelain shepherdess on the mantelpiece.

'Oops, watch out, Jenkins, destroying the Delft is bonus deductible.'

Jenna suddenly felt terribly embarrassed — the brandy was making her act so childishly. And Jonty's words — although quite possibly the kindest telling-off ever — reminded her of the shame she felt at being responsible for the loss of the Picasso prints. No wonder Angus said she couldn't be taken seriously. She knocked back the last of the throat-burning liquid and got up.

'Sorry, Jonty, time for bed for me.' She took the cushion that he'd retrieved from beside the fireplace and popped it back on the chair, giving it an extra pat for good measure. Turning back with a professional look, she hoped, on her face, she caught him studying her earnestly.

'Probably not a bad idea. Early start in the vines tomorrow — I'm due to give you the "marketing guff" that Bradstock refused this afternoon. I need you to accompany a group of wine merchants round in a couple of days and they'll know their stuff so you need to know yours.'

Jenna couldn't work out if she felt more at ease now that they were talking about work again, or a little sad that the happy camaraderie had ended. Maybe she shouldn't have finished her drink so quickly, maybe a little more tête-à-tête with Jonty would have been quite nice? Still, she could take her cue.

'Right you are, boss.' She gave him a mock salute, but he took her wrist and held it.

'I'm. . . I'm not your boss, not really. I'd rather we were friends.'

Shocked, Jenna looked up into his face. An electric pulse seemed to be flowing from his grip up her arm.

'Yes, I mean, that would be nice.' She wriggled her arm away although instantly missed his touch when she was free. 'Right though, off to Bedfordshire!' Jenna knew she was in trouble when she slipped into using posho euphemisms. She gave him a quick smile and turned away from their little tableau by the fireplace.

Running up the stairs, thoughts poured through her mind. Sally had said that Jonty seemed keen on her, yet *she* really wasn't interested, was she?

24

'Darling Jenna,' the honeyed transatlantic — by way of Suffolk — voice purred down the phone. It was 6.30 a.m. and even after last night's brandy, Jenna had been observing her morning ritual of watching the day break over the vines. She still found solace in the sheer beauty of the sun rise, the golden light climbing up the warm stone of the village houses, and most mornings let out a little tear as she remembered the circumstances that got her here. Yet this morning's solace had been rather rudely broken by the phone call from London. 'Apols for comms-ing so early, sweetie. I'm at morning doggie yoga and Sebastien has just taken Lola out for a chew-chew as she was not getting down with my downward dog at all.'

'Right.' Jenna was used to speaking to Bertie while the latter was engaged in doing something else that by all rights should be taking up all her concentration — yesterday morning before the Bradstocks arrived she'd phoned to speak about party favours while she was apparently having some Botox and fillers done. Jenna couldn't work out if her request for 'heartier halflings' was real or just a result of her face slowly paralysing. Jenna had jotted down Cartier cufflinks just in case.

'So, I was thinking — go with this, stay with me — a yacht theme with Mediterranean mermaids who would actually become waitresses and then showgirls for the finale.'

'I'm not sure there are many mermaids in Bordeaux, Bertie.' It was too early for Jenna to sugarcoat her sarcasm.

'I said stay with me, JJ, I do not need this negativity in my life. I'm working on my throat chakra and I'm feeling very emotional this morning.'

'Oh, Berts, what's wrong?' Despite herself, Jenna felt a pang of sympathy.

'Oh it's Max. He's being exceedingly sneaky and I'm sure he's hiding something from me. If it isn't ten carats and in a turquoise Tiffany box I'll be very, very cross.'

'Bertie, really? Do you think he's about to propose?' Jenna thought back to the bouquet toss and how she'd wished she could have caught it. . . the thought of Angus in his morning coat at the wedding pricked tears to her eyes again. No ring for her any time soon, especially not a 10 carat-er.

'Well, I mean, why wouldn't he be? Men don't just go out with people like me. We make connections. You know what I mean?' Jenna didn't really but nodded silently down the phone to her. 'Anyway, back to the par-tay. So, yeah, mermaids would bring in the nautical feel I think I've lost by not having the party on the Blake-Howard's yacht, which although small would have been super chic. And pearls. Find me pearls somewhere, doll.'

'Right, so mermaids, fish—'

'Arg! No, not fish! Wrong wrong wrong. I'm thinking giant clams as drink coolers, abalone trays filled with sand, and shells with glasses filled with edible pearls bouncing in the champagne. Honestly, Jenna, do I have to do all the thinking myself?'

'Nope, right.' Jenna scrawled words on the notepad she had by her bed. 'Mermaids, pearls, conches, clams, um, deck shoes—'

Bertie sighed down the phone. 'I have obviously not caught you firing on all — or any — cylinders, darling. If you were my PA you'd be caput by now. So, comms later when you're more with it and we'll go over guest list and planograms. Namaste.'

At that she put the phone down and Jenna was left in silence again, as if a force of nature, which truly Bertie was, had just whipped through the room. She was wide awake now, at least, although she would definitely not recommend the Roberta reveille to anyone as an everyday alarm. She pushed the eiderdown off her and got out of bed. Shrugging on an over-sized cardigan she ventured out to the corridor and the shared bathroom and started to get ready for her morning lesson on viticulture with Jonty.

25

'So.' Jonty pushed his rolled-up sleeves further up his lightly tanned arms.

'So.' Jenna stood next to him, clipboard in hand and pen at the ready.

'Here beginneth the lesson. This patch of land is called a *clos*. That's because, surprise surprise, if you look at that lovely old wall over there, you'll see we're *closed* in. All the best vineyards have these ultra-good *terroirs* — there's another word for your new lexicon — and some are small like this one, with barely enough vines in it to make a case or two, and some are vast.'

'How can they be *clos* if they're so vast they can't be closed in?' This was not the first piece of technical wine lingo that had threatened to aeroplane right over her head. In fact, since she'd been at the chateau she'd had so many new terms do a fly past that she was starting to feel a little bit like Gatwick airport.

'That's not really the point. We happen to have a nice wall here, but some don't.'

'And this *terroir* thing?' Jenna was trying to catch up but the sunshine was addling her normally more switched-on brain. 'How does that work?'

'Well, *terroir* is the term for the land, the type of soil, what sort of stones are in it, the minerals — they all affect how the grapes taste.'

'Wow.'

'Some estates are so protective of their *terroir* that generations of winemakers and owners have fought legal battles over their boundaries — even down to a few feet.'

'But surely one decent field is much like another, isn't it? I mean, I can understand how chalky soil might be different to sandy soil, but once you're in one area, isn't it all much of a muchness?'

Jonty coloured slightly. 'If I tell you something, will you promise you won't blush?'

With her recent track record, she couldn't promise that at all but she nodded anyway.

'There was once a producer, from around here, actually, who rather crudely spelt out the difference "a few feet" could make.'

'Go on. . .' Jenna was intrigued.

'Well, simply put, a journalist asked him why his wine was so expensive compared to his neighbour as they only had a few feet between them and he said, "There's a difference between the taste of your wife's front and rear bottoms, and they are only a couple of inches apart — so don't tell me how important a few feet can be!"'

Jenna's eyes went wide with incredulity at the filthy story.

Jonty smiled at her. 'Now, enough of that, follow me.'

He led her down between two rows of vines, the shade a welcome respite from the glaring sun on her blushing cheeks. It was only just past nine, but the sun was high and hot and Jenna was starting to wish she'd worn something cooler — both temperature-wise and sartorially — than her jeans and a long-sleeved GAP T-shirt. Jonty never seemed to change what he wore, referring to his red trousers as his 'action slacks' and rolling his sleeves up on the warmest of days. He always seemed to have the air of an off-duty army officer, and never more so than now as he held a vine leaf in one hand and carried on the lesson.

'So here we have your common-or-garden cabernet grape vine. It's ripening nicely and you can tell the visiting merchants that the soil has been rigorously tested for any non-organic compounds and found to be tip-top cow-poo-only grade. They can ask for a breakdown if they like.'

'Of the results, I hope, not the cow poo.'

'Quite. And if they like the subject of manure, then you can bring them onto our biodynamism.'

'Your what?' Jenna thought she was at a vineyard not the secret lair of some mad scientist.

'Biodynamics. To organics what vegans are to vegetarians — except a lot more interesting than your average vegan. The idea goes that if you plant your vineyard, and maintain it and harvest it according to moon calendars and things, your grapes will grow healthier and better — more naturally, as it were.'

'Surely that's a bunch of tosh?' Jenna might not have the professional nose of a sommelier but she thought she could smell bullshit.

'You'd think, but some of the most famous vineyards in the world practise biodynamism. I might have you out here under the full moon before too long, helping me with my horn.' His double entendre hung in the air and Jenna could think of nothing else to do but grab a vine leaf and study it intently.

'Horn?' As intense a student she was of that vine leaf she just wanted to check that Jonty was as red and blushing as she was.

'Cow horns.'

'First their poo, now their horns. I'm not sure the vegans would approve.' She raised an eyebrow at him, and Jonty laughed.

'In fact, it's poo and horns, I'm afraid, the former in the latter. Planted in between vines it's all part of biodynamics. But,' he let go of the vine and beckoned her to follow him along the row a bit more, 'now for something completely different. . .'

143

'*Bonjour*, Leo.' Jonty stretched out his hand in greeting to the short man who when they had come across him, had been standing on a bucket, secateurs in hand, his head lost among the vines. He'd jumped off his make-shift height-extender and rattled off some guttural French to Jonty as he pumped his hand. He paused to wipe his perspiring brow and then stuck his podgy little arm out towards Jenna. She shook his hand and then felt bad that her initial thought was how long it would be before she could wash it.

'Leo here is in charge of our vine team.' Jonty clapped his hand on the small man's back, and Leo smiled, which sent the crinkles at the corners of his eyes racing almost to his hairline. 'Leo makes sure the rest of the field workers are doing the right thing at the right time. They're not all as, how can I put this, conscientious as Leo.' Jonty exchanged a few more words with Leo and then said goodbye to the little man, who hopped onto his bucket to continue pruning the vine.

'What are they doing?' Jenna realised that far from being the only three people in the vineyards there was a general murmur and chatter of at least thirty workers, all working their way up and down the rows; most in dungarees, shirtless underneath to combat the fiery heat of the sun, others in old-fashioned smocks as if the farming garb of a nineteenth-century West Country yeoman was now *en vogue*.

'They're leaf-pulling, which means taking off the larger, under leaves so that the sun can get to the grapes. It's essential this time of year to give the grapes a chance to ripen. It's not like no one else does this, all the vineyards do, but it can be a bit touch and go.'

'If they don't ripen, what will happen?'

'The rivers will run dry, the locusts will come. . .' Jenna batted Jonty with her clipboard and he took on his teacherly role again. 'Okay, sorry. So, the grapes will eventually ripen, but the longer you leave it the more chance you have that it'll get to autumn and frosts and bird strike and boom, no harvest. If they're ripe by the end of August, because you've let them have all the sun it's possible to give them, then it's harvest time and money in the bag. Every week that goes past might be okay, but it might not, you just never know these days.'

'Indian summers do seem to be more frequent though.' Jenna thought September in France could be jolly lovely, still warm and definitely sun-bathing temperature.

'It's just the not knowing. Do you want Philippe to be even more grey?'

'Oh, I don't know, he's quite the silver fox. Perhaps a little more wouldn't hurt. . .'

Jenna expected Jonty to smile in response but he seemed pensive and shook his head.

'No, we need Philippe very much this side of a heart attack, at least I do.'

Jenna put Jonty's concern for the old boy down to his career and Carstairs & Co's relationship with the chateau. She changed the subject.

'Well, I feel very much more enlightened on viticulture, thank you, Jonty. I reckon I can wax lyrical on the joys of cow muck while introducing our guests to the Napoleon of the vineyard, although I might recommend they bring hand sanitiser with them.'

'Yes, he is a bit earthy, isn't he?' Jonty chuckled and, in much the same way as he had clapped Leo on the back earlier, he put his arm around Jenna and led her back up towards the house through the rows of vines. Jenna felt oddly comforted by his arm around her, even if she was worried that the extra body heat might make her sweat even more through her thick cotton T-shirt. As Jonty made small talk she tried desperately not to fixate on his arm around her and tried even harder to not think about Angus and what he might or might not feel if he saw her, here in this idyllic rural setting, with a man who, if she hadn't fallen so heavily in love with Angus a few months ago, would have been high on her 'let's have a fruity-frolicky good time' hit list. She decided another chat with Sally may not go amiss.

Unknown to Jenna and Jonty, another pair of eyes followed their progress back towards the chateau. *Who the fuck does he think he is?* The eyes blinked against the sun and dust and were wiped with the dirty sleeve of an old denim shirt. This only made them sting more and Dave White — Whitey to his mates, and most of his enemies too — cursed as he tried to find a less dirty bit of cloth to wipe his face with. Whitey — the irony being that a few years now of working as a casual labourer in shockingly hot vineyards had made him as tanned as a pirate — blinked again but had lost the couple in his sights.

Nice fucking welcome, he chuntered to himself. He was sure he'd just seen Jon Boy, his old mate from the estate. Jon Boy, who'd got the grades and left them all for some poncey university. Jon Boy, who had had a nifty way with a skeleton key and a gab on him that could wheedle his way into — and out of — everything. *So what was Jon Boy doing here, all toffee-nosed and lord of the fucking manor?*

Whitey wiped his brow again. He thought *he'd* done well to leave the estate, labouring his way around Europe, even picking up the lingo every now and again — *bonjour,* ladies, *auf wiedersehen,* pet, and all that. This spring he'd hitched a ride on a freight transporter that was destined for Dover, but he'd jumped off at Bordeaux, reckoning a season in the sunshine might make heading back to the UK a little sweeter — especially if he'd managed to come back with a picker's purse of cash and a topped-up tan to boot. And the life here wasn't so bad. The French midget who'd given him the job had let him sleep on his sofa until he, along with a couple of lads from Romania, found a caravan at the far edge of the vineyard to kip in. The nights were dull, but when the card games, played in stilted English, finished, he headed down to the village *tabac* and took a shot or two of absinthe with the local pickers and town drunks. His French was better than his Romanian and he'd grasped that a summer season here would be no worse than anywhere else, so had decided to stay. Eyeing up his old crony — Jon Boy — well, this could make things a lot more interesting all round.

26

As they climbed the front steps of the house Jonty raised his hand to shade his eyes from the sun and looked back out over the vines.

'I love this sunshine. It just doesn't get better than this, does it?'

'No, I guess not.' Jenna sighed and looked over the driveway to the fields of vines that they'd just walked through. Beyond that the village glowed in the mid-morning sun, the warm sandstone soaking up the rays. She wanted to say, 'Yes, yes it does get better. It was better when I had a boyfriend who loved me, hell, who even spoke to me. . .'

'Cheer up.' Jonty put his arm around her again. 'Tell me to bugger off if it's none of my business, but I haven't heard you talk about Angus since we got here. Is everything okay?'

The combination of someone being so nice to her, and thoughts of Angus so fresh in her mind, was enough to tip her over and Jenna burst out crying. Through the sobs she felt Jonty's arms fold around her some more and he brought her into his chest and gently rocked her as she wept. She had tried to be so strong, so focused on doing something else and forgetting all about Angus, that she hadn't realised quite how much she had bottled up all her feelings — a cellar's worth or so it seemed.

'I. . . he. . .' Jenna hiccoughed through her sobs.

'Hey, take your time, it's okay.' Jonty stroked her hair and the intimacy of it was almost too much for Jenna to take. She pulled away from his arms and wiped her eyes with her sleeve.

'I'm fine, I'm fine.' She reassured herself as much as him. 'Angus and I are no longer together.' There, she'd said it. It was over.

'Really?'

Uh-oh. Jenna needed none of this 'will he, won't he' chat; her resolve was weak enough and it had taken all her emotional strength to admit out loud that it was over.

'Yes, really. He walked out on me just before I left London and I haven't heard from him since.'

'What a shit.'

'I know, right?' Jenna finally felt some sort of release, vindication even! Before, when she'd spoken to Sally, she'd still wondered if she'd done the right thing, if she'd over-reacted, but now it was said so simply it seemed bang to rights. He had been a shit.

'You didn't deserve that. And hey, I don't know what went down between you two, but from what I can see, you're a pretty special lady and he's mad to let you go.'

'Thanks, Jonty.' Jenna wiped her eyes and running nose again with her sleeve. She couldn't work out if he was flirting with her or just being plain old-fashioned nice. He took her into his arms again and gave her another squeeze. She didn't instantly pull away and instead just enjoyed the physical contact. The fact that it was with someone who really wasn't bad-looking added to the pleasure she got from resting her head against the soft cotton of his shirt. It almost came as no surprise that she felt the softest of touches on her forehead, the brushing of his lips against her skin made her raise her eyes up to meet his. Still in his arms, she could barely move but she found that she didn't really want to and looking up into his grey-blue eyes, their intensity almost overwhelming her, made it easy to accept the kiss that he gave her. As their lips found each other's he stroked her hair, her back, his hands moving slowly over her body, giving her the briefest of tingles as his fingers gently brushed against the edge of her breast. It all became too much and Jenna pulled away. Embarrassed by how she must look, her tatty top and old jeans not a match to the romantic surroundings, she stepped back away from him and caught her breath.

'Jonty, I'm. . .' she was too flustered for words. How could she say she felt both elated and destroyed all at once? His kiss could be the start of a new adventure, but it was also the resounding strike of a nail being hammered into the coffin of another.

'I'm sorry, Jenna, I shouldn't have done that. Please forgive me.' In his military-style way he dismissed himself from her company and headed into the dark of the house, leaving her blinking away tears in the sunshine.

Jenna had feared someone would see her on the steps, grubby and teary, so she followed Jonty into the house — the dark of the hallway needing some getting used to after the brightness of the light outside. Thank God, Jenna thought as she found it deserted, and she scurried up the stone staircase to the first-floor landing and through the hidden door to the top of the house. As she got to the top of the stairs she listened out, just in case Jonty had done the exact same thing, but the only sound was the distant hum of a vacuum cleaner from the floor below; Madame Lefort no doubt already cleaning the Bradstocks' — her old — room.

'Damn it.' That had reminded her. She was needed downstairs in a few minutes to do the official goodbyes to Andrew and Tessa, and she was far from shipshape. She dashed into her room and stripped down to her bra and knickers and then grabbed the towel that hung from the back of her bedroom door. Loosely wrapping it around herself she hopped across the hallway and into the bathroom.

A few splashes later and a quick change into something a little less grotty — a pleated pale pink skirt and smarter black T-shirt — she deemed herself slightly more presentable, if a little red around the eyes. A spritz of her eau de cologne and a brush through her hair and she was done, closing her bedroom door behind her before she ran downstairs. Voices in the main hall below told her that she was just in time to form part of the farewell committee. Jonty was nowhere to be seen.

'Darling girl, your help was so appreciated.' Tessa kissed her on both cheeks and gave her a big hug.

'My pleasure,' Jenna lied as she realised she would never be able to scratch from her memory the sight of that woman doing weird things in the buff with the murals.

Andrew shook her hand too and having bade Philippe and Madame Lefort goodbye, tried to usher his wife towards the car.

'Don't rush me, Andrew.' Tessa fussed around, picking up her bags and photographic equipment.

'Have you got the picnic blanket, darling?' he said, and Jenna almost snorted with suppressed laughter, thinking back to Jonty's bet. She owed him ten euros, that was for sure. And perhaps a little more for putting, finally, a proper smile back on her face.

After they left, the hire car creating its own mini galaxy of dust as it hurtled down the drive and into the road beyond, Jenna headed down the hallway to the little office. The now-familiar smell of old stone mixed with cooking aromas calmed her down. Poking her head round the door, she wasn't sure if she was relieved or not when she saw that Jonty wasn't there. She plonked herself down at her desk and opened her organiser. Tomorrow would be the start of another round of visits. Wine merchants from all over the UK — Cheshire, Oxford, Sussex, London — would be arriving by midday and would expect the full chateau treatment. If the Bradstocks had been hard work for their fleeting visit then a night of entertaining wine merchants would be something else.

Jenna took a deep breath and opened her laptop. She then spent a good couple of hours (with a welcome sandwich courtesy of the ever wonderful Madame Lefort) genning up on the chateau from its Wikipedia page and learning more about leaf axils, phylloxera — a nasty disease that ripped through the Bordeaux vines in the nineteenth century — and fermentation techniques. She had yet to properly visit the actual wine-making part of the chateau and knew that instigating that would involve Jonty. She braced herself and went to go and find him.

27

'Found you,' the gruff voice caught Jonty by surprise. He was in the cellar — he'd headed down there after what had just happened with Jenna, his mind and body buzzing with the new level their relationship had just reached. To have those thoughts, those calculations and plans so rudely interrupted by, by. . . *Whitey?*

'David—' Jonty had barely turned on the single electric bulb in the cellar when the voice of his old friend had echoed through the room.

'Ooh la la, *David*, is it now. Too posh for your old mates?'

'Nah, Whitey, I mean. . . c'mon.' Jonty dropped his adopted upper-class accent, but rankled as he noticed Whitey chuckled as he did so.

'Thought so. Not so fuckin' fancy now, are you, Jon Boy?'

The use of his old nickname hit Jonty like a thousand pins. He thought he'd left all of that behind, on the wrong side of the tracks, when he'd left the estate and moved away. He subconsciously fiddled with his signet ring as the atmosphere — already damp and shadowy in the cool of the cellar — grew ever thicker and more tense.

'Gonna give your old mate an 'ello?' Jonty instinctively thrust out his right hand as if to shake but he'd massively misjudged it and Whitey was coming in for a manly hug — the whole thing jarred and the awkwardness of the situation was enough for Jonty just to blurt out what he was feeling.

'What are you doing here?' He couldn't help it, his vowels had lengthened again — too many nights out with the red trouser brigade had long ago laid to rest Jon Boy and his estuary drawl.

'Fine fucking welcome that was.'

Jonty paused. He had to think. He was nervous of Whitey. His way with a knife had earned him kudos on the estate — 'doing a Whitey' was shorthand for marking someone, pretty permanently. *What the fuck was he doing here?*

'Whitey, mate, look. Long time no see and all that. You took me by surprise.'

'Me an' all, mate. Look atcha!'

Jonty's relief — a chatty Whitey was better than a fighty Whitey — was short-lived as his old friend's countenance suddenly changed again.

'Look at you,' he repeated, more slowly. 'All smart like, aren't cha? Must be earning a pretty penny if you can fool these geezers with your hoity-toity voice and. . .' he waved his hand towards Jonty, and indicated his smarter clothes. Indeed, the difference between the two men was shocking. There was Jonty in his chinos and blue 'smart casual' shirt, the sleeves still rolled up since his trip into the vines. Jonty not only had his signet ring on, fake crest as it might be, but also a smart leather-strapped watch and the most middle-class of male footwear — the deck shoe. By contrast, Whitey was short and stocky. His denim shirt and old pair of dirty and baggy jeans were torn and greasy from outdoor work and lack of regular washing. His hair was shaved, a buzz cut, nothing for him to run his fingers through as Jonty was now rather nervously doing.

'Hey, it's still me underneath,' he tried a jokey tone.

'What's underneath is what I'm on about.' Whitey moved a few inches further towards him, both men now fully illuminated by the glare of the bulb. Jonty wasn't sure if he preferred it when Whitey was half hidden in the shadows, now fully lit he was as real a nightmare as Jonty could imagine.

'I, look, Whitey. . .' Jonty stammered as Whitey moved closer towards him, his thick denim-clad arm going behind his back. What was in his back pocket? Jonty thought he could see a glint of silver. A flick knife? Jonty moved back and thought wildly as to what was around him. Bottles. Could he glass this guy? How would he explain that to Philippe?

'You see.' Whitey brought his hand forward. The silver glint, much to Jonty's relief, was not a knife, but the clasp of a tacky wallet — Texas-style with studs and a great silver longhorn on the front. Jonty deflated slightly, which he hoped Whitey didn't notice as he carried on talking. 'Funds have been hard to come by these last few years and it seems more so for me than for you.' As if to illustrate his point he opened his wallet and showed the empty notes section.

'Ah.' Jonty got the game straight away. 'How much?'

'To keep my mouth shut about your 'istory?'

'How much?'

'Well, we got several years of adolescent behaviour — shall we say juvenile delinquency — to erase from my memory. Let's make that a thousand euros a year for seven years.'

Jonty almost choked as he tried not to laugh. 'Seven grand? Fucking kidding me.'

'Not much when you think of what I need to forget. Those bikes didn't nick themselves, did they, and that corner shop never did find out how that fire started, did it?'

'Two grand.'

'Six.'

'Two and a half.'

'Come on, Jon Boy, I wasn't born yesterday. Your fucking watch cost more than that.'

'Three.'

'Five.'

'Four — and that's it, you're gone.'

'Five and I'm gone. . . four and you just watch out behind your back, sunshine, to see if old Whitey isn't there

155

to remind you — and your bosses — about the half kilo of coke you mugged off from the local dealer.'

'We were kids!' Jonty was exasperated. That wasn't who he was any more, a petty thief, an arsonist, a drug dealer. Whitey could have been describing a stranger, yet the memories were all there.

'Four and a half and I'll get it to you by the end of the week — then you're gone.'

'I'll keep schtum for four and a half, but I'm keeping my job here till harvest. Then I'm done.'

He spat on his hand and offered it to Jonty, who looked at it with the disdain such a crude piece of contract-making deserved.

'Done.'

28

'Zhonty! A ha ha! *Non.*' Menou confirmed with his usual flair that he hadn't seen Jonty recently. So, kitchen, upstairs, terrace. . . everywhere she'd looked around the chateau there had been no sign of him. Jenna knew the only other possible place was in the dank cellar, unless he'd buggered off to the winery. She knew he was down there though, it really did seem his second home, which was odd for someone so sun-kissed. You'd expect a vampire-like person to emerge each evening from the cataloguing, but Jonty was the polar opposite of that drawn, ethereal, death-like look so beloved by the Camden Market goths. He was strapping and tanned and more than a little bit handsome and if he was no fan of KISS, then she could certainly become a fan of his kiss. She paused at the cellar door. *Ici on parle Francais.* She remembered the words that were scrawled in black paint down the crumbling plaster wall of the cellar steps. *Here we speak French.* She'd found out from Philippe over supper one night it was because the cellar had been used to hide several British airmen during the Second World War and they really did have to be reminded to speak French at all times in case the invading Nazis caught a whiff of any *rosbif* in the house. For now, Jenna was bracing herself to speak some English to another thoroughly English person, even if that English was a bit flustered, awkward and full of hesitations.

'Hello!' she called out as she descended the steps. There was no answer. The single bulb created its halo glow through the cobwebs and she could hear a faint clanking from further in. She shivered a little bit, the temperature and atmosphere was so different down here to the house above and a world away from the brilliant sunshine outside. 'Hello!' she tried again as she wrapped her arms around herself and bravely followed the pools of light from the bulbs that lit up each room. Jenna tried not to look either side of her, the bottles were so covered in cobwebs and dust that the grey veils over them hung like tapestries. These bottles can't have been moved for decades, yet occasionally she noticed a section of shelving with bottles gleamingly clean, not a speck of dust on them. *Ha*, she thought, *spiders your dominion diminsheth!*

She found Jonty about five rooms in. He had a massive ledger open on a picnic table next to him, and he was bent over it, writing. Odd items were scattered around him; funnels, corks, pens, towels, old labels and he seemed to be so fixated on carefully recording whatever it was that he had been doing that Jenna felt bad interrupting him.

'Hi, there.' She forced the words out and hoped they didn't sound as awkward as she felt saying them.

'Fuck!' Jonty jumped and gripped the sides of the ledger picking it up and holding it to his chest. 'Fuck, Jenna, sorry.'

'Sorry, I didn't mean to scare you.' *Of course he wasn't scared*, she thought. Way to go to insult the guy's ego.

'Yeah, no problem. Ah,' he put the ledger back down on the table, 'how long have you been there exactly?'

'A second, no more.'

'Great.' He seemed relieved and came over to greet her, though Jenna stiffened and then awkwardly turned it into a dramatic shiver.

'Brrrr. So cold down here, I don't know how you do it!' *Top marks for breeziness*, she thought.

'Ah, you get used to it, spiders and all.'

'I'm A Wine Merchant, Get Me Out Of Here!' Jenna tried out her best Geordie accent, mimicking her Saturday night faves, and Jonty chuckled. He was standing in front of her now, blocking her view of the room behind him.

'What can I do for you?'

'Actually, I was rather hoping you'd take me over to the winery. I thought I could complete my diploma in Montmorency studies over there so I can field questions from the merchants tomorrow.'

'Excellent plan. Tell you what, you skidaddle back upstairs and I'll meet you in the hallway in five mins.'

At that he gently pushed her out of the poorly lit room, but this time his touch was welcome against the cold of the cellar. She didn't flinch at all and missed it when he withdrew, and went back upstairs, into the warmth.

Jenna wandered out into the sunlight again, waiting for Jonty to finish whatever it was he was doing in the cellar. She ran her hand over the large wooden front door of the chateau, its soft green paint flaking due to the sun that hammered down on it, day in, day out. She idly picked at a loose bit then quickly stopped when she realised she could quite easily end up peeling off a huge chunk of the cracked paintwork and in so doing be arrested for defacing a heritage building or something. Perhaps Philippe really did need the money from Bertie's party to keep the place looking its best? She thought about that party. Who would Bertie invite? She seemed to be planning for well over a hundred people. . . or mermaids; in fact by the next phone call it would probably be turned on its head and be circus freaks and space odyssey themed.

'Daydreaming?' Jonty's voice was soft and gentle. Jenna really had to pinch herself sometimes to remember she was technically at work and he was her boss, whatever he'd said over brandies last night.

'This old door. . .' Jenna rubbed her hand over it one more time and then without thinking wiped her hand down her skirt. 'Oh.' She'd left a rather noticeable dust mark along the side of it. 'One more for the wash!'

'How is the clothing sitch, by the way?' Jonty asked. 'I must admit, I haven't noticed too many evening gowns cleverly crafted from overalls yet. . .'

Jenna punched him playfully on the shoulder. 'I'm doing fine, thanks very much — seems I packed more useful stuff than I feared.' She thought, however, about the suitcase she'd stuffed full of almost all her wardrobe from her flat and how it was worryingly starting to look a bit empty.

'Shall we?' Jonty gently pressed his hand into the small of her back and guided her down the chateau's main steps. 'The winery is a bit of a trek, which I'm not sure those slippers will deal with.' He indicated her very best French Sole slip-ons, the only decent shoe she'd managed to pop into her case.

'Ah, sorry. Shall I go and get my clod-hoppers on again?'

'Nope, not to worry, we'll take the Moke.'

Jonty led them down the driveway, fully dusty enough for her nice little ballet pumps, and then off at a spur that Jenna hadn't really noticed before. This part of the driveway carried on, lined on each side by poplar trees until it reached a group of old sheds and garages.

'Don't expect the Rolls,' Jonty said as he walked into the shade of one of the open-sided barns and grabbed a set of keys off a row of hooks on the wall. It spoke volumes for the safety and general sleepiness of the surrounding villages that the estate's various car keys could be left with such a *laissez-faire* attitude. Jonty led her round to the next bay of the barn and in it was the cutest little jeep-like thing Jenna had ever seen. It was red, but dulled by dust and could only seat two people, but its jaunty little headlights and white front grille gave it much more character than your usual run-about.

'The Mini Moke in all its glory,' Jonty explained as he helped Jenna climb in. There were no doors, just low sides so that you could hop in and out, well, if you weren't wearing a skirt anyway. Jenna tried to be ladylike and remember those finishing school tips that she'd read in the *Daily Mail* online. *Bottom first, knees together, then swing. . .* Buckled in, she watched Jonty slip in effortlessly and start the motor. The little jeep spluttered into life and after one or two revs Jonty got it into gear and started off down the road towards the winery.

God, Jonty thought. *What a difference an hour makes.* Having Jenna next to him in the little Moke was the tonic he needed after the run in with Whitey. The speed of the blackmailing still had him in shock and he glanced across the vines as they drove, wondering if he'd see his adversary's balding head glinting among the grapes. As he quickly worked his way through the gear box and picked up speed along the estate's perimeter road on their way to the winery he brought his attention back to the present, and noticed how the breeze caught Jenna's hair and sent tendrils dancing over her face and shoulders. He turned back to concentrate on the road, but images of glinting knives and Whitey's grimacing face kept flashing up in his mind. He put his foot down and accelerated, the stronger breeze now catching Jenna's skirt and ruffling it up her thighs, a pleasant distraction from the horrors of the cellar just an hour earlier.

'Wow.' Jenna had never seen so many barrels. They lay on their sides, one, two, sometimes three high stacked up along the walls and along the middle of the vast barrel room. Men worked with a crane to hoist barrels up on top of each other and another worker carefully chalked information onto the ends. The room itself was modern, like an airplane hangar, and smart enough to show off to journalists and merchants, if you could hear yourself speak above the rattle of the crane and the chains that hoisted the barrels up to the rafters.

'It's quite impressive, isn't it? And we're only a small winery here.'

'You always refer to this place as "we" and "us",' Jenna observed before Jonty could explain any more to her about the barrels. 'It's nice.'

'I've been working with Philippe quite closely since earlier this year, so I guess I do feel part of the Montmorency clan.'

'Would be lovely to really be part of the clan though, wouldn't it?'

'Ah, now I know what you were dreaming about by the front door earlier.' Jonty laughed. 'Do I have competition in the form of a wealthy, older, silver-haired Frenchman?'

Jenna smiled and awkwardly looked away. *Did he have competition?* So earlier wasn't just a one-off kiss? 'I can't think what you mean,' she managed before staring intently at a barrel end again. Jonty touched her on the shoulder and she turned to face him.

'You know exactly what I mean.' He bowed his head down close to hers but stopped short of touching her. Instead he leaned behind her and reached in between a couple of barrels where a pipette was lying. 'This is called a wine thief.'

'Ooh, sounds naughty.' Jenna was still buzzing from how close Jonty had just seemed to kissing her.

'Depends what you use it for?'

'Testing out your semillon?' Jenna's look of flirty innocence echoed the fact she'd emphasised how similar the grape variety sounded to 'semi on'.

'Or my ch-*hard-on*-ay?' Jonty countered .

'Well, I won't say you're *malbec*king up the wrong tree. . .' Jenna dissolved into a fit of giggles.

'Love the wine you're with, that's what I say.' Jonty left her briefly by the barrel to fetch a couple of glasses from a cupboard by the entrance. 'Fancy a taste?' he asked Jenna when he got back to her.

'Now you're talking.'

'Don't pull a face when you try it, this is what we call a cask sample and it isn't at all how it will taste once it's had its bottle age too.'

Jonty removed the bung from the nearest barrel and Jenna immediately smelt the warm, spicy notes of a red wine, its grapiness still showing through, but with the unmistakable notes of cigar smoke and vanilla too.

'Hmmm, even without tasting it I can get some flavours.'

'Try this, then.' Jonty dipped the pipette into the barrel and pulled out a sample of the rich, ruby-red wine. He squirted it into a glass and handed it over to her.

'When you get used to tasting cask samples you can tell what the wine will be like.' He took a sip, sucked it through his teeth and swirled it around his mouth before shooting the liquid out fast into a spittoon. 'Typical cabernet, spiced from the oak. Yeah, I reckon this one will mature nicely and age well in the bottle and when we're drinking it in, say in ten years' time, you can tell me I was right.' He winked at her.

Jenna raised an eyebrow at him and took a sip from her glass, but couldn't disguise her grimace at the astringency of the wine.

'Does madam want to spit?' Jonty offered up the spittoon. It took all of Jenna's will power to not splutter the wine out everywhere as she suppressed another giggle, and somehow managed to obediently spit out her mouthful into the waiting vessel.

'I think I need to work on my technique.' A dribble of wine dripped down her chin. Jenna was about to wipe it away with the back of hand when Jonty got in there first and gently wiped the drip away with his thumb.

'Sometimes it's just easier to swallow.'

Jenna gulped as she noticed the sexual tension build between them again and she looked up at Jonty who just creased up into laughter. She stuck her tongue out at him — and didn't resist as he stopped laughing and pulled her into a hug. 'Spit or swallow, Jenna Jenkins, you are the star who will be getting all of those grumpy merchants shouting from the rooftops about Château Montmorency wines!'

'Oh God, they'll just laugh at me.' She pulled away from Jonty and put on a serious face. 'You have to help me — back to the barrels!' She dramatically gesticulated towards the rows and rows of them in the room and Jonty laughed again.

'Not before I show you just how grateful I am to you for helping me out'

At that he leaned down towards her again and this time cupped her face and kissed her properly and deeply. His hands slowly moved down to her back and he pulled her closer in towards him. Jenna softened in his arms, her initial surprise turning to excitement, the same feeling she'd had when Angus had kissed her on that cold, dark night when they'd first got together in the blizzard. Angus, the snow, the chill of the barrel room; her thoughts all came crashing together and she pulled away from Jonty, rubbing her hands up and down her bare arms to get rid of the guilty goose bumps.

'I'm sorry Jonty, I. . .' she paused and looked into his grey eyes. 'I just need a little bit more time to get over. . . well, to move on from Angus. You know, properly.'

Jonty moved towards her again, but this time his hands just rested on her shoulders, his thumbs gently stroking her. 'No, I'm sorry. It's totally unprofessional of me. I promise, nothing more until you're ready.'

'Thank you.'

Jenna was utterly conflicted. Inside her a civil war raged between the upset she felt at losing Angus and the hope and happiness that these rather flirty moments with Jonty were bringing her. Jonty was true to his word, however, and for the rest of the afternoon he showed her around the different fermentation tanks, explained the system, pointed out the pallets stacked high with wooden cases of wine ready for export and then when there was nothing more to interest her in the industrial shed of a winery, he chauffeured her back to the chateau in the Mini Moke. He dropped her off at the main front door, coming up with some excuse about getting some fuel for the cars before the local pumps closed, and disappeared off in a cloud of dust down the driveway. Jenna stood on the steps and looked out at the billowing dirt and back of the little jeep. Jonty was everything she would have wanted if only she hadn't met Angus first. Angus. The thought of him, his ocean-blue eyes and scarred face, that exquisite mix of posh boy and scruffy adventurer, her first true love. . . she definitely needed more time to get over him, but she had an inkling that Jonty might be pressing the fast-forward button on that one.

29

Jenna had only been back in the chateau for a few minutes when she heard the phone ringing in her office. She dashed along the corridor and skidded to a halt on the flagstones outside the door, almost overshooting and ending up in the kitchen.

'Bonjour, Château Montmorency. . .' she gasped down the phone line, just catching it before it rang off.

'Jenna, you sound positively shagged out,' Bertie drawled. 'Anything I should know? *Anyone* I should know?' she laughed to herself before Jenna could answer her.

'Just out of breath, Bertie, you know how it is in these mahoosive houses.'

'Oh God, yah. I mean like I practically broke a sweat when Maxie and I went house-hunting the other day and this fabulous-o villa in Holland Park had, like, so many rooms.'

'Wow, house-hunting. That's a big step. Guess the diamond debate has been answered?' Jenna tried to sound bright and breezy, but the thought of *one more* couple having their 'happy ever after' while she was back to square minus one million did smart a bit.

'Gawd yes, in the bag, totes. I'm sure.'.

'Anyway, Bertie, what can I do for you?' Jenna had settled into her chair and was poised with a pen and pad of paper.

'Yah, right, so. New idea. Keeping the swans, doves and alpacas. Out with the merpeople — I mean, really? How could you have let me make such a fool of myself with that idea, Jenna? Darling Shabooti, my spiritual healer, said bringing so much sealife into the equation would definitely alter the humours in all of our bodies and the party would quite literally be a damp squib.'

'Right.'

'So out with the merpeople.'

'Inflatable gold elephant?'

'In.'

'Wine in the fountain?'

'Don't be silly.'

'I know, right, I'm sure your healer would be aghast at the negativity that house white can promote.'

'Absolutely, Jenna, I finally feel like we're on the same page here. Make it champagne, sweetie. And not that prosecco crap, real champagne. You know I can't bear anything else.'

Jenna was dying to text Sally with a live update of what was being said and wished she had some sort of record function on the chateau's old phone system.

'Anything else, Bertie, before I start instructing the gardeners to clean the fountain, because it really is quite icky.'

'Hmm. Good point. No point polluting the 'poo with algae. Tell you what. Get a new fountain installed on the upper terrace and we'll start afresh.'

'Right. New fountain. Got it.'

'And the new theme. Definitely and definitively it's going to be a good old-fashioned masquerade ball.'

'Ooh. That actually sounds quite fun, Bertie. Good shout. Much easier to arrange than merpeople.'

'Oh. Not too dull then? I mean if it's easy, is it worth it?'

'Bertie, I can tell you now, nothing about this party has been, or will be, easy.'

'Good. Brilliant. Can't have the Blake-Howards and darling Kate thinking I've lost my touch!'

At that she rang off and Jenna set about scribbling down all the new ideas that had flowed from Bertie like the crap out of a flooding sewer.

After Bertie's brain dump, Jenna had been quite relieved just to sit in the kitchen and see what Menou served up for supper. She was knackered. She'd been up so early for the tour of the vines — yet that seemed an age ago, even though it was just this morning. Since then she'd been kissed not once, but twice, by Jonty (what would her mother say!) and her mind was buzzing with thoughts and feelings. *Was Jonty really interested? Was she interested in him? What about Angus?* Menou placed a plate of *coq au vin* and new potatoes in front of her and carried on serving up the dish for the others. Madame Lefort sung a little tune as she loaded up a tray for Philippe and another one, she guessed for Jonty. Jenna wished she could escape up to her little room with a tray, as although she liked the gentle domesticity of Menou and Madame Lefort bustling around her, she was desperate to clear her head and just be on her own. Heartbreak, or indeed heart intrigue, had sadly done nothing to diminish her appetite (*her tears alone must have lost her a pound or two, though*, she optimistically thought) and she found herself using her fingers to nibble the last of the meat from the chicken bones. Madame Lefort clucked and tutted but gave Jenna's shoulder a little squeeze as she picked up her plate for her.

'I see you liked it, Jenna, that's good. Very healthy appetite you English girls always have.'

'I wish I wasn't so greedy.' Jenna forced a smile out for the middle-aged housekeeper, as much as a thank you for clearing away her plate as anything.

'*Bof*, I would not worry, *ma chere*, these slips of things these days that think they are so chic with their quinoa and their, how you say, spiralizers and spirulina. *Tcsh*, these are not foods. These are not healthy.'

Jenna could have hugged Madame Lefort at that moment, or at least made a lucrative living by kidnapping her and ransoming her off to private girls' schools to give all their young charges a sensible take on life.

'I totally agree, madame.'

'I mean,' Madame Lefort continued, she was on a roll now (in fact, a roll that she would probably have slathered in proper French salted butter), 'they say their bodies, they are temples, but blah blah blah. Temples are for dirty old monks, bodies are for pleasure!'

'I'd say my body is a temple,' Jenna joined Madame Lefort in her musings, 'but I will happily accept all food offerings my worshippers bring me.'

'*Exactement*! Now, I must go and see if my Philippe needs any more. Whoever said the way to man's heart was through his, how you say, stomach? Well they were definitely talking about the French!' Madame Lefort giggled to herself and Menou let out a huge bellowing laugh. Jenna caught the infection and laughed too and then bade them both goodnight as she headed up to bed, happy to end the day with a full stomach and the satisfaction in knowing she wasn't the only one in the chateau with a complicated love life.

30

'Bugger. Bugger.' Jenna swore under her breath as she searched around for something decent to wear. After breakfast, Jonty was driving to the airport to bring back four representatives of some of the best independent wine merchants in England. These were the men and women for whom she'd been busting a gut to learn about the chateau and wine making in general. She had tannins and vine training coming out of her ears, although she was less confident on getting phrases like 'methoxypyrazine levels' and 'phenolic ripening' out without spitting all over everybody. Which would be terribly embarrassing, which is saying something for an industry where spitting was generally seen as a good thing.

'Shit.' She rummaged through her clean, but un-ironed clothes, having finally found the washing machine a few days ago. She had, however, had a mini-disaster when she'd put the wash on only to spend the next hour and a half wondering where her red biro had gone. Finding a load of semi-pink, tie-dye-esque clothing greet her as the wash ended had resulted in language more blue than red, and also halved the amount of nice tops she had to wear. Luckily, deep in the bottom of her still vaguely unpacked suitcase was a pair of pristine white jeans and she paired them with her French Sole ballet pumps and a nice, not too pink, floaty blouse.

Running a final brush through her freshly washed and blow-dried hair — tamed at last with about a handful of hair serum (whoever suggested a 5p coin-sized of the stuff would work must have been barking) she dashed downstairs and headed into the kitchen for breakfast and a morning debrief.

When she pushed the door open she was greeted by a scene that involved Jonty wolfing down about half a baguette, thickly covered in Nutella, Philippe eating a more elegant breakfast of just a croissant, Madame Lafort fussing around Philippe dusting crumbs from beside his plate and Menou busying himself at the stove.

'I've got five minutes, Philippe, don't panic,' Jonty told the older man as he pushed the last of the baguette into his mouth.

'If you weren't up so late in that cellar you wouldn't be so tired and rushed this morning, that is all I'm saying,' Philippe soothed Jonty, who was clearly stressed. 'It's not good for you to be down there so much, I'm sure the cataloguing must almost be done.'

'It is, of course.' Jonty seemed annoyed to be asked about his time down in the depths of the house and nimbly changed the subject as Jenna joined them. 'Anyway, the next twenty-four hours will be cellar-free for me as Jenna and I work our magic on the merchants.'

'Good morning, all,' Jenna finally felt there was a polite enough gap in the conversation to get her morning hellos in. 'Ooh thank you,' she said as a cup of steaming coffee was brought over to her from the pot on the stove by a grinning Menou.

'Ha, is good go-go juice!' His voice had all the melody and subtlety of a honking hippo. If Jenna wasn't quite yet awake, after tasting Menou's coffee she certainly was. She'd foregone her early morning ritual of watching the sunrise over the vines today as she thought she needed maximum sleeping time in preparation for the wine merchants, whose reputations came before them.

'Can I ask something?' she interrupted Jonty and Philippe as they discussed which wines were going to be served for dinner.

'Of course, my dear.' Philippe was all charm as always.

'Can you tell me a little more about these guys, I mean the merchants. It's just, I know which companies they come from, but have you met them? Are they nice?'

'Jonty, I think this is your domain. I will bid you *au revoir* and see you both when we officially welcome the merchants to the chateau.' At that he took a last sip from his coffee and smiled at Madame Lefort as she dusted more non-existent crumbs from around his plate and left them to it.

Jonty turned to Jenna and she was a little upset when it seemed that he could look at her so dispassionately and so matter-of-factly, especially after yesterday's clinches. 'Right so, yeah, we have quite a mix really. Ladies first, there's Ginevra Smith from Perfect Pour in Hackney. She's very, you know. . .'

'What?'

'Hipster.' He said the word with the derogation he obviously felt it deserved. 'Oh and a, you know. . .'

'No. . .' Jenna was still chuckling to herself about his hipster comment.

'Well, anyway, then there's Richard Sitwell, he's a good bloke, in his forties but still likes a drink. . .'

'Obviously,'

'Actually, you'd be surprised at how many people in the trade give up the sauce. You go in looking twenty and come out five years later looking about sixty if you don't keep a lid on it.'

Jonty really was being a fun-killer this morning and Jenna started to miss the flirty, more carefree and less boss-like Jonty of the previous days.

'Then there's Spike Spooner, he's a wide boy from Cheshire. I think the wife made loads of money in women's boutiques or something. She subsidises his retail trade and he then gets to ponce around on these trips. Still, with three shops and most of the Waitrose-free market share in the north-west, he's not to be sniffed at. And finally there's Fat Fergus from Sussex who has been in the business man and boy, as they say; his family have owned Fitzpatrick & Sons in Chichester for about three generations.'

'Wow. Quite a lot to take in.'

'Well, get it all into that pretty little head of yours and I'll see you back here in about two hours with the whole rum lot of them.'

If Jonty hadn't smiled at her when he left she might have thought the last few days of flirting had never happened. When he did, though, it was only a thinly drawn line and she noticed the dark rings under his eyes that Philippe must have been commenting on earlier. After he left she tucked into her croissant and sipped on her go-go-juice coffee. Perhaps he was just giving her time and keeping things professional? She couldn't really argue with that, she had, after all, told him to do just that. She chided herself though for feeling just a little bit disappointed that he had taken her request so much to heart.

'Sals. . .' Jenna whispered down the phone. She had snuck in a call while Jonty was on his way to the airport and Philippe was tucked away back in his study.

'Hello, gorge, how's it going?'

'Um. Confusingly. If you know what I mean?'

'No, sweetie, not a clue, what are you on about?'

'Oh, Sals. I don't know where to begin. Have you heard any more from Angus?'

She couldn't deny that even with Jonty now in the picture, or so she thought before this morning's breakfast brush off, she still thought of Angus about a hundred times a day.

'Not a monkey's, sorry. I assume he's in deepest darkest and all that. Are you okay, lovely?'

'Oh, I just don't know how to feel and what to do.' She filled her friend in on the last couple of days at the chateau. 'So you see, it's been a bit interesting, if you know what I mean.'

'Blimey, sweetie, hasn't it just. But be careful, you know, don't burn too many bridges before you know how things stand.'

'Oh, Sals, don't say that. Jonty has been the only good thing to come out of the whole Angus drama!'

'I know, I know. I just can't shake the feeling that you two are perfect for each other, I mean you really had the real thing. I just don't know how one fight could have ended it. If Hugo and I broke up every time we fought I'd be a ten-tonne-Tessie, what with all the Häagen-Dazs and booze.'

Jenna ignored her friend. 'It's just if I'd never met Angus, and I might as well have not now, then Jonty would be right up my alley.'

'Sounds like he's about to be whether you'd met Angus or not, JJ.'

'Charming.'

'Look, sweetie, just be careful, that's all I'm saying. You've known Angus far longer than Jonty, and although I wouldn't chuck him out of bed for dropping crumbs either, well, just see what happens. Got to dash, honey, boss is coming back. Mwah mwah.'

'Bye, Sals. Love you.'

31

The rest of the day passed in a blur. Soon after midday, Jonty was back with a car full of laughing, stretching, crumpled and tired wine merchants. Jenna was so grateful for the quick precis she'd had over breakfast. *Spike from Cheshire*, she thought, *had sized up her bust, waist and hip measurements almost as soon as he got out of the car.* Ginevra had asked her awkward questions all the way through the vineyard tour and didn't crack a smile once, even at Jenna's quip 'Let's start with the vines and we'll end with the wines.' Jenna sensed Ginevra had taken an instant dislike to her and her white jeans as she herself was wearing a heavy wool tunic, totally inappropriate for the glorious sunshine of the region, although she did relent and take off her thick grey tights halfway through the swelteringly hot day. Richard and Fergus had asked more questions about pallet rates and marketing budgets than she knew how to answer, but Jonty and Philippe had taken over the general hosting at lunch and she'd had a bit of respite from the intensity of the merchants' questions and opinions.

'So, Jenna.' Spike brought her back into the conversation and she tried to ignore the fact that his eyes were focused on her boobs. 'How did a nice girl like you end up in a place like this?'

'Well, Spike,' she lowered her head a little to catch his eyes and bring them back up to face level, 'I used to work in the art world but fancied a change and as the socio-economic crossover of the two trades isn't that different, I've found it both enlightening and relatively straightforward making the switch.'

Ha, she thought, *that'll show you there's more to me than boobs*. She couldn't stand this slimy little man and his leering gaze.

'Flogging luxury goods to people with more money than sense. Yeah, I can see how you gravitated to Carstairs & Co.' He winked at Jonty who looked awkwardly down at his plate. 'Shame, could have really shown you what the wine trade is like if you'd come and worked with me.' He winked lasciviously and Jenna recoiled, wanting to put more than just a few inches between herself and the sleazy man. How did someone like him convince people to buy anything more than a pinot grigio for a fiver? She found it hard to believe, when, after lunch, she accessed the company's intranet and went over his buying history with Carstairs & Co. She saw that he took a lot of what was entered as 'private client wines'. Jonty had been his account manager for a year or so and it seemed that he managed to push Spike into all sorts of top-end purchases. Cases for well over £3,000, in some instances. Sitting in the little office after lunch — everyone was having a siesta before Jenna and Jonty were due to take the merchants down to the winery — she pulled out one of the Château Montmorency ledgers from the bookcase behind Jonty's desk and tried to cross-reference the purchases. She couldn't put her finger on it, but something didn't tie up and it intrigued her. Why would a ruffian like Spike Spooner buy so much top-class claret if he himself seemed to think it was all la-di-da and for the 'more money than sense' crowd. She skimmed her finger down the columns of the accounts book — grateful that Roach & Hartley had kept their accounts in the same archaic manner so she knew vaguely what all the rows and columns meant.

She hadn't got very far when the phone rang and Bertie's shrill tones distracted her completely from her forensic accounting.

'Jenna, massive problemo with the party-o.'

'Oh dear, what?' Jenna could hardly muster the excitement.

'I've just realised that the party date clashes with the start of the shooting season. . .'

'Oh please don't change the theme now to pheasants and peasants, I don't think I could cope!'

'No — but love the idea, saving that one for future, JJ. But I think I will have to bring the party forward — much earlier in August or even end of July — as I just have to accept the Blake-Howard's invitation to their Glorious Twelfth party.'

'Those poor little grouse.' Jenna decided against trying to make another joke about those unfortunately named birds. 'If Philippe is okay with it being brought forward I suppose that would be fine, in fact, it's better really as it'll miss the harvest by a few weeks hopefully. Last thing you want is a lot of sweaty vineyard workers and trailers piled high with grapes invading party central.'

'Totes. Thanks so much for sorting. You better send out some save-the-dates or something. By the way, have you got an address for Angus? I mean, it's not like he could still be in your — albeit sparklingly clean — hobbit hole of a flat any more.' Jenna's throat burned and she found it hard to swallow at the mention of her ex-boyfriend.

'Is. . . is he invited?' she stammered down the phone line.

'Obvs, sweetie. Just because you and he aren't mano-a-womano any more doesn't mean the guy should be socially ostracised. Plus, I heard he'd hooked up with the glamorous Diane again in Hong Kong, so it looks like you might have snost and lost, sweetie, soz.'

Jenna was silenced. Diane Blane — a stunning half-Ugandan, half-American model — had been Angus's girlfriend while he was Singapore, but she'd left him after the ambush he'd had to fight his way out of — the same one that had left him with the jagged scar across his cheek. Apparently, she had been appalled when Angus had admitted to her that his part in the fight wasn't all self-defence that he'd hit out at one of the triad fighters who had threatened the life of his boss and mentor Pei Ling, as well as his own. But with Jenna's forgiveness of his act, her caresses and even slight hero-worship, he'd got over the loathing he had of his scar and all it represented. Perhaps enough to forgive Diane and accept her back into his life?

'You still there, babes? Sorry for the bombshell,' Bertie did at least sound a little contrite, 'but you know what it's like, sticking plaster and all that — best to know quickly so you can get over it. You are over him, aren't you? Surely you've found a little froggy lover over there in Château Lurve?'

'Yeah, yeah, of course.' Jenna was trying not to let the sound of her tears hitting the ledger undermine the Oscar-worthy act she was putting on. 'So they're both on the list, eh?'

'Oh God, yah. I mean she is so hot right now. All the major brands are begging for her to be in their campaigns and she's been on the front of *Vogue* and is walking for Victoria's Secret. I mean, don't take this the wrong way, sweetie, I'm not throwing shade in your direction but if I were Angus I would be giving her one hell of a second chance.'

Ouch, thought Jenna. Trying to be as professional as possible — and thinking to herself that if all else fails she could probably get herself job as a party planner after all of this — she ran through diary dates with Bertie and struck upon the last Saturday in July as the perfect summer night for the big bash.

'Isn't this all getting quite tight, time-wise I mean?' Jenna asked, realising that there was barely now a fort-night before the party.

'Jenna, people kill to come to my parties. They will clear their diaries. Just get those invos out stat.'

'Right. Will do.' Once the painful conversation was finally over, Jenna held her head in her hands and wept. She still loved Angus, of course she did. But she hated him too, not just for the fight they had and the things he had said, but for totally ignoring her and then running off to China without a word and now this. Jonty was right, he'd been an absolute shit and she deserved better. Wiping her tears away with her sleeve she clumsily pushed back her chair and bumped along the desk edge in order to put the ledger away. Sniffing as hard as she could to stop the first real blub coming, Jenna dashed out of the office and into the kitchen, which for once was empty, ran to the large old ceramic butler's sink and splashed cold water on her face. Realising at that moment that she had, for once, bothered to put mascara on this morning, she quickly wiped under her eyes with a tea towel to de-panda herself and hoped that would get her through the rest of the afternoon. Menou did look a bit oddly at her when he came in from the little kitchen garden clutching a bunch of freshly picked herbs, but he just broke into one of his wide smiles and then gently shooed her away as he started prepping the herbs for the bubbling pot on the stove. The warmth and calm domesticity of the kitchen calmed Jenna down a bit and she stood for a moment, pretending to examine the napkins that Madame Lefort had laid out earlier on the dresser, before deciding she was composed enough to enter the fray again.

'Ah, here you are.' Jonty bumped into her in the corridor and then looked at her, the intensity back in his grey eyes. Jenna almost wanted him to cup her face in his hands again and tell her that everything would be okay and that she in no way resembled an endangered bear, but instead he said, 'Look, why don't you pop upstairs quickly? I'll start walking the merchants down to the winery and you can follow on − I'll tell them you needed to change your shoes.'

His understanding and kindness almost felled her so she blurted out a quick 'thank you' before hitting the stairs at a run, worried that the newly falling tears might trip her up at any moment.

32

'So, young Jenna,' Spike was leaning in closer and closer and Jenna was finding it hard not to recoil further and further from him, 'you do have the most lovely pair of. . . eyes, by the way.'

Jenna smiled wanly. It wasn't like she was wearing anything revealing, in fact she had The Blouse on, and although she wore a relatively short skirt, which had helped glam it up, it wasn't exactly Playboy Bunny material. She'd ended up next to Spike again at dinner, something she'd really tried to avoid, but as the household — Jenna, Jonty and Philippe — and the guests had filed through to the dining room Spike had cornered her by the door, holding them both back. He'd asked some inane question about the wood carving around the door and how much she thought it would cost as someone he knew back in Cheshire had 'one of them footballer's houses and wanted it bling, but you know, classy bling'. After that they had to take the last two seats around the table and she found herself with him on one side and Ginevra, who although fancied herself as achingly cool was actually just boring, on the other.

'How are you finding the wine with the food, Spike?' she patiently asked halfway through the meal, hoping that tipping the conversation over into wine geekery would stop him from making any more lewd comments. The 'I'd have you alongside my *tarte au tomate* any day' during the starter had almost led to him having his fricking tart all over his face, along with her glass of the rather nice Château Montmorency rosé. Never one to waste good wine, she'd gulped it down instead, and now here she was, one more course in, trying to fend him off again.

'Actually this 2005 is rather good.' Richard Sitwell, who was sitting opposite her saved her by swilling his glass around, inhaling deeply of the wine and then rhapsodising to the table about that particular year and how even compared to the highly acclaimed wines of the 2000 vintage it was a stand-out year in his mind. 'In fact,' he continued after a fashion, 'I had a bloody good lunch at a club in Pall Mall where they served us some corkers from '05 and by God we weren't unhappy with our lot in life!'

Fergus chipped in with a story about Château d'Yquem, a deliciously sweet dessert wine from the same area — and the most expensive white wine in the world. 'I'll top your '05 clarets, Richard, with some '01 sauternes — and I'd wager anyone around this table would agree.'

'Not me,' Ginevra interrupted Fergus, halting his victorious glass raise with a sour-faced rebuttal. 'Personally I think it's all overrated and over priced. I try to champion less well known growers, especially female winemakers. . .'

Jenna sat back and let the wine merchants argue about their favourite wines. Just as she was about to fork a piece of beef into her mouth she felt a nudge against her thigh. Glancing down she saw that Spike had spread his legs so wide that his knee was now rubbing up against her. Horrified, she swivelled her legs away from him, accidentally doing the same knee-bump to Ginevra. What surprised Jenna more than Spike's move was the hand that Ginevra now placed on her knee. *Oh fuck*, Jenna thought, as she realised she'd gone from the frying pan straight into the lesbian fire. *That* was what Jonty had been too reserved to talk about earlier and she glared at him across the table, even though he was obviously unaware of her current predicament. She didn't know what to do about Ginevra's hand that was now sitting heavily on her knee and she prayed to God that the woman would use it to pick up her knife and eat properly. Being an east London foodie, she was of course vegan, and didn't Jenna know it from her constant barracking earlier about how meat rotted your guts and animals shouldn't have to suffer for human needs. Jenna had desperately wanted to point out her hypocrisy over her woollen shift dress and leather Birkenstocks but kept schtum on the chateau's behalf. Anyway, this meant she was only, if rather rudely in such sublime surrounds as the formal dining room, using her fork to eat the lentil curry that Menou had happily whipped up for her. Finally, after possibly the most awkward few minutes of Jenna's life, where her knee had become practically welded it seemed to Ginevra's hand, Madame Lefort came in to clear away the plates and Ginevra finally saw fit to move her perving paw.

Pudding was almost as farcical as the main course as Jenna did her best to cross her legs under the table so she couldn't be pushed against either of her wannabe lovers – oh, if only it had been this easy to pick up potentials when she'd been at perfectly nice dinner parties in her early twenties; all the boring bankers and awful accountants come back, all is forgiven! However, Spike had other ideas and pretended (Jenna was sure of it) to find eating his strawberries and blueberries, which crowned the enormous pavlova that Menou brought in, oddly difficult. With one particular berry finding its way onto her lap, Jenna had to get physical to stop him from reaching between her legs to retrieve it.

'Here you go, Spike, no need for you to go rummaging down there,' she said through gritted teeth as she plopped it back on his plate and shook out her napkin. She didn't know whether to laugh or cry as she witnessed Ginevra give Spike the biggest stink eye she'd ever seen and then begin a tirade on how the north of the country wasn't pulling its weight when it came to hand-selling interesting bottles from obscure countries.

'For every one of these supposed fine wines,' she battled on, glaring at Spike across Jenna all the time, 'I will easily hand-sell four or five bottles from truly artisan makers. In fact there's a little place in Georgia that I found after hiking through the Caucasian mountains that now sends me his entire UK allocation of the local wine made from the saperavi grape — all eighteen bottles of it. We call it Crimean Claret and it flies.'

'Well, we're not all blessed with your open-minded customers, Ginny, old girl.' Fergus felt he needed to reassert himself after she'd cut him off mid flow before. 'Blow me if I can't get anyone off the bordeaux and burgundy.'

'I just don't think you're trying hard enough to be honest,' Ginevra sighed and ran her fingers through her aggressively short hair.

'I can try all I like, my dear girl.' Jenna could see Ginevra getting more and more irked by Fergus's *pater familias* posturing. 'But it remains the same year in, year out. Who wants Georgian plonk that's so heavy it'll leave your teeth black when you can get damn fine stuff like this?' He indicated the glass in his hand and then raised it to Philippe, who had been very gracefully staying out of the conversation.

Jonty took control of the situation and calmed the rival merchants down. 'I think what we have here is a happy compromise. At Château Montmorency we take huge pains to make our wine biodynamic and as eco-friendly as possible, so we do stand out to the more eclectic market, like yours, Ginevra, but at the end of the day we're one of the oldest wine-producing estates in Bordeaux and have the heritage to match, which keeps your customers happy, Fergus.'

'And our pockets nicely lined,' Spike had to chime in with a bit of vulgarity, albeit financial, rather than sexual. 'Cheers, Phil, damn fine plonk. I'll take my usual amount and enjoy foisting it off onto the label-loving *nouveau riche* nobs of Cheshire. Nothing makes a grand profit like a *grand vin*!' He also raised his glass to Philippe, who bowed his head to him, impressing Jenna again with his almost limitless bounds of grace and composure.

The dinner party finally broke up and as it was still such a beautiful evening outside the company made their way out onto the terrace. By now Jenna was itching to be away from the clumsy fumblings of both her dinner neighbours and made a beeline for the relative safety of Fergus and Richard, who were deep in conversation about the fall of sterling and the problems with foreign currency exchange. So dull! So safe! Bliss. Although even Jenna could only keep up with them so far and it was clear that the 'marketing fluffy' wasn't really needed in their conversation so she made her excuses and left them to it. She saw Jonty talking earnestly with Ginevra and clocked that Spike was puffing on a fat cigar while leaning against the balustrade of the terrace. She paused for a second, remembering how she and Angus had leant against that very stone and kissed. Before the familiar fizzing in her nose and burning in her throat, which heralded tears, could take hold Jenna slipped back inside the French windows to the dining room and found a half-empty bottle of rather nice red wine still sitting on the table. *Why not*, she thought, reaching over to help herself to a little top up. Suddenly the stench of cigar smoke filled the room and Jenna turned around to see Spike leering at her from the large French windows. He brushed the floating voile curtain aside and came into the room.

'Now that was a sight worth savouring.' He took a long puff on his fat cigar and very slowly let the smoke out in large, pulsating rings. Jenna felt very vulnerable all of a sudden, wondering how far up her legs her skirt had risen as she'd bent over the wide dining table. No words came to her, nothing witty or sharp that would have put him back in his place. It had gone beyond a joke and, as much as she respected Philippe and adored the chateau, she wasn't willing to put herself on the line for it any more. Spike backed her up against the table and took another long drag on his cigar while one of his hands reached out and stroked down the side of her arm. Pinned where she was she could do nothing except strain her neck as far from him as possible as he blew his smoke straight at her face.

'Stop it! Get off me!' she yelled, pushing him away. He flew back from her touch and landed squarely on the floor, spluttering and grimacing. Unless she'd developed superhuman strength, there was some other force at work. That other, rather Superman-ly, force had been Jonty.

'You'll pay for that, you upstart shit.' Spike brushed himself off and retrieved his cigar from the floor where it had burnt a neat little black mark on the centuries-old parquet.

Looking at it, Jonty replied, 'And you'll pay for that, Spike. I'll get Philippe to add the restoration fee to your exceedingly large order from the chateau.'

'Whatever — try getting me to order any more of your fine wine bollocks now, mate.'

'I think you'll find you will, or Miss Jenkins here will be phoning the gendarmes and the UK police and lodging a serious sexual assault against you.'

'It was hardly serious, I didn't even want the girl, just a bit of fun.'

Jenna had regained her composure and spoke out at last. 'Jonty's right. I'm this close,' she pinched her fingers together, 'to calling the police. And bullshit you didn't want me. You've been perving on me all day and I've had enough.' At that she straightened her skirt and left the room, hoping Jonty would work out a suitable retribution for the sleazy merchant from Cheshire.

33

Jenna slammed the door of her bedroom and paced the room — she was frustrated that she hadn't stood up for herself more during the day and furious that Spike had taken advantage of her. She was also a little bit pissed off at Jonty, as although he'd done the whole knight on a white charger thing and rather heroically vanquished her foe, he'd taken his bloody time to notice how pervy Spike had been all night and hadn't exacted much revenge on the douchebag except selling him rather a lot of nice wine. And let's face it, Spike would have ordered that pre-fiasco anyway, and sell on at a decent margin — fan-bloody-tastic. Oh and the bill for a small burn. Yeah, like that'll show him that being inappropriate with women is wrong, thought Jenna as she finally came to a stop and stood, looking out of her window at the twinkling lights of the village in the distance. She had the overwhelming urge to put on her trainers and run, run, run through that bloody vineyard and escape this house and its occupants and just be free.

She was just about to grab her Nikes from under the bed when there was a soft knocking at her door. Jenna froze and thought for a split second about what to do. If it was Spike then should she stay quiet or lunge out of the door and clobber him with her trainers? Whoever was out there would have seen the light shining from under the door, so she armed herself with a very heavy copy of some French philosopher's tome (it had obviously been left in her room by some previous and more erudite tenant) and called out, 'Who's there?'

'It's me, Jonty.'

Jenna was still annoyed at him for letting Spike get as far as he had, but her urge to talk more about the drama downstairs overcame her and she let him in.

'Are you okay?' He looked genuinely worried, his eyes roving over her face and body as if he was checking for injury.

'Yes. I'm just angry.' Jenna stood aside to let Jonty into her room.

'I'm not surprised. It looks like you were about to bash me with the Barthes.' He indicated the book and she put it down as he continued. 'Spike has had a taxi called for him and he'll be leaving here in a matter of minutes. I wasn't going to have him in same house as you any longer.'

Jenna softened towards Jonty. 'Thank you. That means a lot to me. I was a bit, well, I mean, thank you for pulling him off me, but I rather hoped I might get more revenge than just being able to send him a hefty wine bill.'

Jonty laughed, rested his hands lightly on her shoulders and pulled her into a hug. She wrapped her arms around him and rested her head against his chest listening to his voice.

'Don't worry, he's got more to come. Don't forget, it's not the 1980s any more and men can't get away with that sort of behaviour — especially not when a militant lesbian is on the same trip. And especially not when that same militant lesbian is a contributor to one of the main trade rags and is well known for her scathing articles of the machismo normally associated with this trade. She'll be all over this. Plus Richard and Fergus might seem like boring old farts who wouldn't care a jot about someone else, but they're influencers, plus they won't risk tarnishing their reputations. They'll be distancing themselves and spreading the word that they're doing so as fast as a champagne cork travels so I wouldn't be surprised if Spike ends up with very few buying partners or friends in the trade soon.'

'Whoop-di-do.' Jenna pulled away from Jonty, but didn't want their closeness to end altogether. 'I mean, that's great and everything, and thank you again for banishing him. It's just, well I guess it's just annoying how these men feel they can get away with it.'

'I know, but I don't know what else we could have done tonight?'

'Without bringing the chateau into disrepute, I know. And I understand, really I do. I'm just annoyed at myself for letting it happen.'

'Hey.' Jonty pulled back from her and looked her straight in the eye. 'Never blame yourself. Never. He was a perv and you were nothing but professional.'

Even with his words buzzing in her ear, Jenna started to feel like there was something incredibly *unprofessional* starting to happen between her and Jonty and she quizzed herself a little as to whether she really minded. No, she didn't, was the answer and after the shock of hearing about Angus's reignited romance this afternoon (with a bloody supermodel, for God's sake) she felt like she needed those strong arms around her more than ever.

'You *can* blame me now though.' She pulled him back towards her, her hands spreading out across his broad back.

'What for, Miss Jenkins?' He smiled down at her and lowered his head closer to hers.

'This. . .' she reached up and kissed him and in a moment he was kissing her back, his hands cupping her face as his passion intensified. Jenna felt alive again, as tingles spread through her body as his hands started caressing her and stroking her. She slipped her hands down his back to grab his butt and then back up again to feel his taut muscles through the thin cotton of his shirt. Without thinking, she pulled at the cloth, untucking it from his trousers and slid her hands underneath it to feel his smooth skin. Taking that as the invitation it was, he did the same and started unbuttoning the beautiful silk blouse, kissing her collarbone and chest as each new inch of skin was revealed. Jenna reached up and arched her back to let him nuzzle her in between her breasts and slipped the silk off her as he reached the final button. Fiddling with his shirt buttons took too much time, so she lifted it up and Jonty pulled it off and over his head, revealing his bare chest. Jenna ran her hands over it and kissed it and let Jonty slowly move her towards the little single bed. He stopped her just before they both fell onto it and kissed her again, this time his hands expertly tackling the clasp of her bra. Jenna helped him slide the straps down her bare arms, before dropping it to the floor.

'You are so beautiful.' His voice was husky and Jenna felt so amazingly free — freer than any amount of running away through the vines could have given her.

'I want you,' she whispered as she slipped off her skirt and climbed onto the bed, with only her knickers protecting the last of her modesty. Jonty did not need asking twice and his trousers were off in seconds, revealing a rather large and very erect cock that only got bigger as Jenna giggled in happiness at the thought of the delights to come. And come she did as Jonty moved down her body, teasing her and kissing her until she could bear the expectation no longer. He entered her slowly at first, having reached into the pocket of his trousers on the floor and sheathed himself, while she kicked her knickers off and flung them to the other side of the room, but his thrusts became harder and more urgent the more she gasped and grabbed his back in pleasure. He waited for her to climax then shuddered into her before kissing her again and lying down next to her, their sweaty bodies tightly curled into a hug that neither of them wanted to loosen.

'As your line manager,' he teased her, 'I have to say that you have very successfully passed your probation period and have been promoted from marketing fluffy to five-star shag.'

'With an extra bonus for having great tits?'

'Oh God, yes.' He caressed them again, playing with her nipples until they hardened between his deft fingertips. Jenna moaned a little and arched her back again which led to Jonty finding his way down between her legs and kissing her and licking her until her moans crescendoed with her body as waves of orgasm came over her again.

'Thank you,' she whispered, amazed at how easily he had brought her to such an exquisite climax.

'Well, Miss Jenkins, you are more than welcome — bonus delivered.' They both giggled and lay for a while longer in each other's arms before Jonty got up and slowly started to clear his clothes off the bedroom floor.

'As romantic as these little single beds are, I think it's time for me to retire to my own little monkish cell.' Jenna had been almost dropping off to sleep so didn't argue. Instead she stretched a naked arm up towards the crucifix on the wall and murmured, 'Forgive me, Father, for I have sinned.'

'Amen,' said Jonty, as he tucked her in under the eiderdown and kissed her before heading for the door, switching her light off as he left.

34

Brrrring.

Jonty put his foot on the accelerator and Jenna felt the wind rush around her and through her hair. She flung her arms up and felt the coolness of the rushing air, the freedom of speed.

Brrrring.

The car took off from the dusty track and as they soared she saw the chateau and the vines beneath her. But the clouds that they headed towards became faces. . . Sally, Picasso faces abstractly grotesque, Angus. . .

Brrrrring.

Jenna came-to from her dream and flailed her arms around trying to locate the intrusive sound. Her phone was vibrating itself across her bedside table and she caught it just before it fell over the edge and onto the hard wooden planks below.

'Hello?' She hadn't clocked the time but judging by the weak light outside it was early. Far too early. 'Hello?' she said a little louder, but there was nothing except static. The crackly white noise filled her ear as she pressed the phone a little harder to her cheek and called out again. Still nothing. Jenna held her phone in front of her and squinted at the screen. Blocked number. She huffed at the intrusion from this unknown caller and was about to slide her thumb across the screen and cancel the call when she heard a tinny voice coming from the phone. But when she put it hard against her ear again it was gone. 'Hello! Hello!. . .' She faintly heard some tinkling music through the ether — hold music, perhaps? But it was too distant to make out so Jenna gave up and hung up on the unknown caller.

She felt a bit unsettled though and couldn't fall back asleep, even though, now she'd checked the phone clock, it was only 5.40 a.m. She curled herself up in her eiderdown and snuggled into her pillow. Remembering who had also been in her bed last night filled her with all sorts of conflicting feelings. She had really, really wanted Jonty last night, there was no question about that. Her body had ached for his touch in a way that made her far more frisky than usual. Like, really frisky. Like frisktastic. But there had a been a nagging doubt, somewhere in her mind, that she was cheating on Angus. That fuzzy phone call. It couldn't have been him, could it? From the middle of nowhere, rural China, the other side of the world. And if it was, what was he trying to say? And to be honest with herself, what would she have been willing to listen to?

As the minutes ticked by, she went over in her head everything that had happened last night. Ginevra, Richard and Fergus would all still be in the chateau and she'd need to be super professional with them and see them off with all due sycophancy. And then she'd have the rest of day with Jonty. . . She couldn't help but remember the rather heroic way he saved her last night, throwing Spike to the ground before he could blow any more of that disgusting smoke at her. And then, oh and then. . . the sex had been amazing. Perhaps, just perhaps, because it had been just a little bit naughty and oh so incredibly liberating. . .

Jenna scrunched herself into her pillow once more before finally getting up and facing the day. A quick shower and rough blow dry later and she was ready for heading downstairs and grabbing a quick breakfast before seeing off the other wine merchants. Good riddance, she thought to herself, they'd been nothing but trouble and even if the loathsome Spike was no longer down there, she'd keep a beady eye on Ginevra and her wandering hands and she couldn't care less if she ever saw Richard or Fergus again. Heading down the stairs from the servants' quarters she looked towards Jonty's door. It was firmly shut and she couldn't make out if her lover was in there or not.

Having not seen a soul on her way down the stairs she was confronted with quite a sight in the beautifully decorated hallway. Stacks and stacks of open crates, marked '*Propriété d'Opera Paris*' each filled with the most elaborate masks. Madame Lefort was fretting about the hallway looking so cluttered and exclaimed to Jenna when she saw her coming down the stairs.

'*Mon dieu!* Jenna! Your friend, she is crazy!' She twirled her finger around her temple to make her point. 'I cannot move for boxes and in *dix minutes les merchants* will come downstairs for their breakfast and the dining-room door, it is blocked!'

'I'll move them!' Jenna was still in shock herself as she helped Madame Lefort drag the grey crates down the hall and into one of the storage rooms next to the kitchen. Jenna wanted to rummage through them and admire the masks — she spotted everything from feathered faces to old-fashioned plague masks, some glittery and sequinned, others matt black and dark as night — but she knew she had to go and be polite to the guests, so she gritted her teeth and followed Madame Lefort back into the dining room where Ginevra, the first one down, was helping herself to a grapefruit half from the laden buffet table. Jenna greeted her, but kept her distance, waiting for the other woman to find a seat around the dining table before choosing one herself.

'So, you rather did for Spike last night.' Ginevra attacked her grapefruit and seemed to Jenna to be her usual acidic self. If there was ever a woman who needed a spoonful of sugar. . .

'I think *he* rather did for himself.' Jenna helped herself to some scrambled eggs that had just been carried through from the kitchen. She didn't feel up to accusing the militant vegan lesbian of sexual assault too, and so instead placed her plate of eggs and cold meats down with a satisfying clunk on the table in her direct view.

'Your gut will rot.' Ginevra sighed, a look of disdain and pity playing across her pallid face. Jenna smiled at her and then ate a huge forkful of the creamy eggs, followed by an entire piece of ham. Before she could finish chewing, the men entered the room, at least Richard and Fergus and Philippe did — there was no sign of Jonty. Philippe came over and gently rested a hand on Jenna's shoulder and leant down to speak to her.

'How are you feeling, my dear? I was worried that perhaps Spike's terrible actions would scare you away from us?'

'No, don't worry, Philippe. And thank you for banishing him from your house.'

'*De rien*, my dear, but of course. He was a scoundrel and did not deserve to be treated as anything more for a moment longer.'

Jenna loved the way Philippe said 'scoundrel' as if the Scarlet Pimpernel himself had been seen fleeing across the ramparts. Philippe squeezed her shoulder again and rose up, his joints clicking as he did so. Jenna noticed how old he seemed this morning, as if the visits of the Bradstocks and these merchants had taken it out of him. At least there were no more overnight stays — until Bertie's party, at least — just day trips from French merchants and the odd tourist coachload who could easily be dealt with by her and Jonty. She promised herself she would do more to look after this kind older man who seemed to have the weight of the world on his shoulders.

As the merchants tucked in — Richard and Fergus taking no notice of Ginevra's steely stares as they too piled their plates full with ham and cheese along with eggs and buttered bread — Jenna kept looking towards the door, hoping Jonty might make an appearance. She obviously did it one too many times as Ginevra accused her of having a tick and questioned why she kept 'nodding at the damn door'? Jenna mumbled something about helping Madame Lefort and made her excuses, but instead of heading to the kitchen, once safely out of the dining room she followed her intuition and gently opened the door of the cellar.

Jenna tiptoed down the stairs and once she was down and out of earshot of the hallway upstairs she softly called out Jonty's name .

'Hello there,' he answered back, moving through the gloom into the circle of light of the single bulb that hung near the stairs.

'Hello.' Jenna suddenly felt a bit silly and shivered. What if he regretted last night?

'What brings you down to my dark domain?' Jonty came nearer, so near in fact that Jenna realised that no part of Jonty regretted last night at all as his hands skirted around her waist and he pulled her into a passionate kiss.

'Well, this for one. . .' Jenna said once she'd been released from his embrace. 'And secondly, well, this again, really. . .' She stretched up and kissed him, and this time she let him pull her in tighter to his chest and she melted into him as he wrapped his arms around her. Finally, he softened his arms and she pulled away and looked up at him. 'And I needed a tonic for that Gin woman. You missed breakfast.'

'God, sorry. I lost track of time. I've been down here for hours, getting a bit ahead of myself so, well, so perhaps we can spend a bit of time later?'

Jenna's heart leapt at his suggestion. Right now she couldn't think of anything better than mucking around with this handsome man for the whole day, and if Carstairs & Co wanted to pay her for it, whoooopeee!

'Still, I guess I better come back up for air.'

'And see off the merchants — the wicked witch and the two ugly sisters.'

Jonty laughed at her and Jenna caught his hand and began to lead him upstairs. He released her grasp halfway up the stairs so that when they emerged into the light of the hall no one would have guessed the hanky panky of a few seconds ago.

'Ah Jonty!' Richard and Fergus were ready to put the assembled suitcases in his car and Jenna said her goodbyes as sweetly as she could muster, especially to the caustic Ginevra.

'How good to meet you, Ginevra,' she held her hand out for the other woman to take, but Ginevra ignored her and merely wafted past with her case and coat. 'Fine, sod you then,' Jenna mumbled under her breath as she followed Ginevra out of the hall and stood on the top step just outside the front door. The three merchants got into Jonty's car and once the doors were closed it slowly pulled away from the chateau. 'You lot can cork right off,' Jenna whispered through her stuck-on smile as she waved them off.

35

While Jonty took a couple of hours to get back from the airport, Jenna sorted the crates full of masquerade masks and stacked them neatly away. She'd been on the phone to various swan sanctuaries and was firming up plans for the inflatable gold elephant — all thirty feet of it — which would be the centrepiece of the terrace for Bertie's party. She'd phoned a local modelling agency and was waiting for their portfolio to come through — she remembered Bertie had asked for 'shit hot' guys 'because they will be the only ones with their actual faces on show' and Jenna had to admit, this part of the party organising hadn't been too bad. Gustave and Emmanuel had been especially pleasing to peruse online and Jenna chuckled to herself that perhaps the benefit to Bertie stealing Max away from her earlier this year was at least she knew what Bertie's type was. As she zoomed in on Gustave's chest she did wonder whose type he *wouldn't* be, but had prepared a presentation for Bertie just in case. The last chore of the morning was to phone Izzy. It had been Sally's idea, texted through earlier that morning, to get their old chalet girl back to help Jenna out. She'd done a great job of organising the kitchen for Sally and Hugo's wedding and she spoke perfect French, which would certainly help when it came to talking about caviar blinis and gold-leaf flaked truffle cups — both firmly requested by the birthday girl.

'Yah?' the ex-public school girl's voice monotoned over the line.

'Oh hi, Izzy, it's Jenna here from Château Montmorency.'

'Oh right, yah. You're there now. Ridic sitch you got into back in Mayfs.'

'How do you know about that?'

'Props to my pal Mungo whose sis knows Belbel from lax, so first-hand info straight from the horse's, so to speak.'

Jenna was finding it harder than ever to understand the younger woman. She herself had been to an okay private school, but none of her friends had ever sounded — or had nicknames — like this. She strained her ears to catch the words, translating them into 'normal' as she went.

'Um, yes, well, luckily I found something else, so back to the question in hand. . . can you come and help me here with Bertie's birthday party? You would be an awful help, especially with your excellent French, and I know Sally and Hugo will be thrilled to see you.'

'Yah, whatevs.'

'It really would be an enormous help.' Jenna didn't want to beg, but Sally had been right, trying to manage additional caterers as well as Menou in the kitchen would be nigh on impossible with her limited French. Finally, though, Izzy agreed and after they'd negotiated a tidy sum for her, thankfully all covered by Bertie's extreme budget, Jenna left her to book her flights for a couple of weeks' time and said she'd send Jonty to pick her up from the airport.

'Oh, awesome. That'd be lit.'

'Send me through your arrival time and I'll make sure Jonty's there.'

'Sick.'

Jenna scribbled Izzy's arrival in the diary for the day before the party. She was just about to check her emails again when Philippe popped his head around the door of her office.

'Jenna, are you busy?'

'Not for you,' Jenna knew the correct answer to that question — you should never say 'no', otherwise a boss might think you don't have enough work to do, but say 'yes' and you end up sounding hoity-toity. Still, she did wonder if her answer had come out sounding a little more flirty than it had when she'd used it on Martin Roach countless times before.

'Wonderful, wonderful. I have a small favour to ask.'

'Anything.' Again, the cringe-ness of it, what was up with her today? *Anything*... Perhaps last night's lovemaking had turned her into a one-track-minded sex-bot.

'Thank you, dear girl.' He came fully into the room and sat himself down on the corner of her desk. 'Now I remember you saying that you are fond of art?'

Jenna's face coloured at the memory of her old life, and more specifically, the (if not priceless, then incredibly pricey) Picasso prints that had spelled the end of her much-loved career in the art world.

'Yes, I, er,' she stammered, but recovered herself enough to nod and carry on. 'I know a bit about contemporary artists, more than perhaps I let on to Tessa Bradstock.'

'Ha, yes, our very own muse, *magnifique*.'

Jenna looked expectantly at Philippe as he gathered his thoughts. His barely accented English was superb, but perhaps some of his poise was just the fact that he took a little longer to form his sentences in his mind.

'Is there something I can help you with, with the chateau's art collection?' she prompted him, wishing in a way that she hadn't as surely going anywhere near her old profession could prompt him to enquire more over how and why she left it.

'*Oui*, in a way, yes, you can,' Philippe continued. 'I have invited an old friend of mine to come here tonight. She's an art dealer from Paris. I want her to look over some of the paintings, not to sell, you understand.' He shuffled some of Jenna's papers on her desk while he carried on talking. 'But for insurance reasons, you know how it is. It is as well to know their value, just in case.'

'I understand,' said Jenna, who thought she actually understood all too well. The times she'd glimpsed him in his study with his head in his hands, the peeling paint of the front door — there was obviously some chink in the armour of the Montmorency finances and maybe auctioning off a couple of the lesser known paintings might just weld that chink together for another season or two while Carstairs & Co helped the brand make its mark on the international scene.

'My friend is called Lakshmi Kapoor, she runs the Galleries Kapoor in rue St Honoré in Paris, but she's coming with her new English lover who is in the business too. Anyway,' Philippe raised himself off the corner of the desk and made to leave, 'I hope that you will join us — and Jonty too, of course — at dinner *ce soir*.'

Jenna's heart raced a little at the mention of Jonty's name and she tried to suppress a smile.

'It'll be my pleasure, Philippe.'

'Excellent, so let's say drinks on the terrace at seven o'clock? I shall order dinner for eight.'

Jenna smiled up at him and nodded in affirmation. Philippe leant over the desk and gave her shoulder a gentle squeeze and nodded back, before leaving her alone in the office with her thoughts. She would have to be careful not to talk too much about her art gallery experience — or how she came to leave it. At least Roach & Hartley had never really traded on the Continent, sticking to the English-speaking markets of the UK and the US. As far as she knew the theft had been kept out of the press, but being out here, away from the gossipy private views and drinks parties she had no idea how much anyone else in the art world actually knew. Jenna shivered, even though the room was warm with summer sun pouring in through the high-level window of the old butler's pantry. *Where were those Picassos now*? She tried to block the familiar feelings of shame and self-recrimination that swept over her whenever she was reminded of them and prayed that tonight wouldn't be the night that Philippe or anyone else here at the chateau found out about her secret.

36

Even though the promised time together hadn't happened, thoughts of Jonty hadn't been far from Jenna's mind all afternoon. He'd phoned from the airport and apologised in advance for being back late; he was going to go and 'sniff around' some of the other chateaux on Carstairs & Co's books — and a few rivals — while he was out and about. Jenna hadn't minded really, and had cracked on with the afternoon's work, filing away invoices and responding to emails from wine geeks and journalists. At 6 p.m. she'd shut down her computer and stretched herself out — raising her hands up as high as they could go. Click. Crunch. God, sitting down all day was not good for the old bones, *but at least*, she thought, *in this business not every day is an office day*. . . in fact as she walked out into the corridor, and then crossed the hall and went upstairs, she thought about the pros and cons of staying in the wine trade. She was so used to the art world and its characters — plus the perks of paid-for parties when your gallery (and those of your friends in the same business) put on a private view. There had been several rather large Mayfair nights out that had been ably abetted by the free wine at a private view. Why they always had to be on school nights had always flummoxed her and she was sure there were times when Martin Roach was about to breathalyse her on a Wednesday morning. Still, it had been fun. But then. . . well, here she was in a glorious chateau with a job that involved *drinking for a living* — the dream, surely? Plus, it was sunny outside, the view was to die for, she was invited to an elegant *soiree* tonight and the people, well, the people. . .

As she pushed open the door to her bedroom her mind flashed back to this morning's phone call. The muffled beeps and static line that had been from no one. Or from someone. She tried to push thoughts of Angus from her mind as she brushed her hair and generally freshened up, but it wasn't until she heard Jonty's door open and close just down the corridor that she managed to banish Angus completely from her thoughts.

Jonty must be home from his adventures, she thought, and as she rummaged around in her suitcase for something suitable to wear (white jeans again — hey ho) she held in her heart more than a little anticipation at hearing him tell her — and the other guests — all about it.

Jonty counted out the notes as he sat in his room. He'd done his tour of the neighbouring chateaux this afternoon, sure, but soon after he'd left the wine merchants at the departures gate at the airport — with pleasing promises of orders to come from them — he'd driven into the centre of Bordeaux and found a branch of his, luckily quite international, bank. Withdrawing four and half thousand euros had been a painful experience. The English-speaking clerk had quizzed him lightly over his reasons — a new car perhaps, *monsieur*, or possibly a building project? 'Something like that,' he'd nodded and shoved the notes into a jute bag that he'd bought just before he popped into the bank. He hoped Whitey would appreciate the sentiment of 'I heart Bordeaux' emblazoned on the side of it — a heck of a lot more than he did anyway. Now sitting on his bed he double-checked the fifty-euro notes and sorted them into piles. Done. That was enough. He glanced at his watch and his signet ring caught his eye — he had been careful to leave it out of the bargaining as he'd be damned if that signifier of quiet class was taken away from him. He had a few minutes spare to make his drop. He placed the notes into the bag and then went over to his chest of drawers and opened his sock drawer. Scrabbling around at the back he found what he was looking for and slid it under the notes and the reinforced base in the very bottom of the bag. *God*, he thought, *it's like something out of a cop drama*. This really is ridiculous. But still, he carefully opened his door and checked that Jenna, or any of the other staff, weren't in the little corridor then slipped down the stairs and out to find Whitey.

Hearing his door click once more, Jenna knew that Jonty was heading downstairs, ready for the pre-dinner drinks on the terrace. She peeked out of her window as she fixed a bangle onto her wrist and saw one of the vineyard workers, a rough-looking sort, loitering by the edge of the vines. She carried on dressing, careful to make sure her curtains were tightly drawn. However, she hadn't seen a car out there so Lakshmi and her friend must have been dropped off while she had been working that afternoon − with perhaps the radio on a little too loud. She would never have been allowed that at Roach & Hartley − another tick in 'pro' column for the wine world − and wondered if anyone else in the chateau had heard the euro pop, with occasional UK chart hit thrown in? Jenna gave her hair a final brush, and then undid all her good work by running her fingers through it and giving it a 'Sloane flick', as she and Sally called it. She checked herself in the mirror above the basin and applied another slick of lip balm. She was oddly nervous − maybe it was because she was happier when there weren't 'strangers' in the house, and let's face it, last night had hardly been uneventful. . .

'Right,' she said to her reflection. 'You've got this.'

And with that she headed out of her room, closing the door softly behind her, and down the flights of stairs to the guests on the terrace.

37

'Ah, my dear girl!' Philippe stretched out his arm to her as she slipped from between the voile curtains of the dining room and onto the terrace. Jonty was leaning over the balustrade talking to an older gentleman. Both of them had their backs to her, but she couldn't help but let her eyes linger on the way Jonty's chinos pulled taut across his bottom as he leant over. Philippe guided her towards a chic woman in a scarlet salwar kameez with gold edging and gently wafting silk scarf. She nodded hellos with Lakshmi who seemed to her to be the paragon of Indian elegance. She was holding a champagne flute by the stem with one bejewelled hand, while the other held a thin cigar. Jenna graciously took a champagne-filled flute from Philippe (and mimicked Lakshmi's way of holding it so elegantly) and wondered if perhaps Philippe was slightly in love with Lakshmi himself. *Poor Madame Lefort*, she thought, *if I were her I'd be over-salting Lakshmi's food and spitting in the gravy*.

'Jenna, this is my old friend, Lakshmi Kapoor.'

'*Bonsoir*, Jenna, please, call me Mimi.' She made no attempt to shake hands, but merely shrugged her shoulders to indicate that both of her hands were full. None of the clumsy Englishness of trying to hold both glass and fag in one hand like Jenna would have done. She added 'is also like attending finishing school' to the list in her head of the pros to working here, which was growing longer by the hour.

The sound of a glass smashing against stone broke the spell that Lakshmi, and her wafts of jasmine-filled perfume, was weaving over Jenna.

'Bloody hell!'

It was a voice Jenna knew the moment the expletive sounded. *Oh God. . .*

'Clive?' Jenna turned to face the balustrade where Lakshmi's guest had been standing. The puddle of champagne seeped larger around the broken flute, yet Jenna barely noticed as she locked eyes with her old boss. Jonty looked at Jenna by way of explanation, and she said a few more silent swears to herself as her brain kicked into action, whizzing through thoughts such as: 'Will he tell Philippe about the Picassos?' 'Will he call me out right now about it?' 'What the actual fuck is he doing here. . .' and finally. . . '. . .with a woman!'

Her brain caught up with her express train thoughts and applied the brakes. Clive was always the nice one, and he'd be far too worried, she was sure, about being seen here himself — and not with Pablo — to start yelling at her.

'Jenna,' he began as he started crossing the terrace towards her, then he paused, 'Oh, Philippe, I must apologise for your glass, I'm so sorry, a little slip.' His eyes darted from Philippe to Lakshmi and then back to Jenna. He took another couple of paces towards her and reached out his arms. Jenna had to concentrate very hard to stay upright as her legs suddenly felt like eels, jellied ones at that, as the shock of seeing her old boss ricocheted through her body.

'Clive! I mean,' she stammered, remembering to be polite, 'it's so good to see you.'

'Darling Jenna.' His voice was at its camp best and Jenna was finding it harder and harder to process what was happening. As he hugged her he whispered in her ear, 'Shhh, later.'

As they released each other, Jenna was relieved that Clive took the lead.

'Mimi, this young woman used to work with me in Mayfair. A while ago now.' He winked at her. 'Philippe, again I'm sorry for spilling such delightful bubbles.'

Jenna stood back as the tableau reformed around her. Madame Lefort had taken time out, no doubt from lacing Lakshmi's food with arsenic, to fetch a dustpan and brush and she was scooping up the smaller pieces of glass while Jonty helped pick up the larger ones from the dusty gravel of the terrace. Philippe reassured his guest that the broken glass was but a trifle and poured Clive another one. Now Lakshmi was standing next to Clive, looking at him with girlish adoration as he told Philippe all about Roach & Hartley and the on-going investigation into some stolen art work. The hairs on Jenna's arms prickled, her heart raced and her throat felt dry and she slugged back the champagne, worried at any instant she might become the punchline. But Clive skirted around it and the older folks' conversation soon turned to life in London and Paris respectively and how Clive and Lakshmi had met.

'He was also in New York, at the big art fair, you know, I go each year?' Lakshmi told Philippe.

'Ah, I see — you were "eyes meeting across the room", as you English say, Clive?'

'More like eyes meeting the beautiful necklace my assistant was wearing,' Clive chipped in and Jenna's ears perked up again. *She* had accompanied Clive — and unfortunately Martin too — to the New York Art Fair last year, and indeed she had been loaned, for one afternoon only, a particularly stunning gold-and-ruby necklace by one of the London jewellers, also exhibiting there. It had long ago belonged to some empress or another, and she'd been so proud to wear it as she fielded questions about Roach & Hartley from the American art investors and critics — and of course telling anyone who was interested where the necklace was from as part of the quid pro quo. Lakshmi must have been one of the attendees milling through the crowd, pausing to stop and look at the paintings that Roach & Hartley had shipped over for the event. Jenna subconsciously raised her hand and laid it flat against her now blushing neckline. Lakshmi noticed and winked at her, and released the scarlet scarf that had been elegantly draped around her neck. To Philippe's gasp, and Jenna's wide-eyed astonishment, there it was: the gold-and-ruby necklace that she had once worn. So precious it had been that she'd been sure the jeweller's minder had had half an eye on her all the time she was wearing it — and now, here it was again, worn so elegantly, but casually, by Clive's. . . well, his *lover*.

'Bravo!' Philippe applauded. But Clive looked if anything a little sheepish and glanced over to Jenna.

'It's beautiful,' Jenna whispered.

'Hey up, what's this?' Jonty had re-emerged from picking up broken glass and had rejoined the group.

Lakshmi gently stroked her necklace while Philippe filled him in, all the while Jenna could feel Clive's eyes boring into the side of her head. . . *there's more to this than meets the eye*, she thought, *and it's not just Clive's sudden change of sexual orientation*. . .

At the sound of the dinner gong, Philippe led his guests into the dining room and assigned them seats. To Jenna's relief — and in some ways horror — Philippe pulled out a chair for her next to where he'd just placed Clive, with Jonty on her other side. Of course, Philippe had asked her to join them because of the English friend of Lakshmi's. . . never in a thousand years would she have guessed it would be Clive Hartley she'd be sitting next to.

'Well, this is a surprise,' Clive whispered.

'I just can't. . .' Jenna dug her fingernails into her clenched palm, so worried that Clive was going to ruin everything right here, right now. A quick bit of diplomacy was needed and she whispered back, 'It is nice to see you, though. I feel like, well like it was rather left a bit, you know. . .' She was worried that her hushed tones might draw attention to them, but she couldn't risk Jonty or Philippe overhearing her conversation.

'Rushed?' Clive could have picked one of many much worse words. 'Yes, I know and I am sorry I couldn't rein Martin in any more. He was rampaging for days afterwards.'

Jenna cringed, the memories of the shouting, the shame, the spittle at the side of Martin's mouth as he told her to *fuck right off* — the whole episode had been a nightmare, a living nightmare.

'I'm so sorry, Clive, I really am. Especially to you. I, well, I—'

'I know, I know.'

'And have you found them? Did the police find out who it was? You've kept it out of the news.'

'Yes, that's one relief.'

Jenna paled as she suddenly expected the worst. Now Clive knew where she was, could he perform a citizen's arrest?

'Look, I'll tell you more about it later.' He paused as bowls of chilled gazpacho soup were placed in front of them and Jenna couldn't help glancing at Lakshmi to see if she had indeed incurred the wrath of Madame Lefort. . . that Tabasco bottle can so easily slip. . .

'So will you get anything back for them? For the client?' The real problem, Jenna had realised almost as soon as the prints had been stolen was that Roach & Hartley would have to reimburse the client who they were exhibiting them for.

'A fair chunk. But let's leave it there.' He patted the sides of his mouth with the linen napkin and continued with his soup.

*

Talk naturally moved on to the chateau's own art collection. Jenna noticed how wistful Philippe looked at times as he spoke of the past masters that were once on show — some lost in the fire of 1759, others bought and sold or stolen during the tumultuous revolution years just thirty years later.

'Win some, you lose some,' he said, describing the Bouchers and Watteaus that were lost, 'but better to swap a painting for a few francs than to lose your head!'

'Makes the London art market seem positively tame by comparison!' joked Clive.

'Heads don't roll quite so frequently?' added in Jonty, while Jenna blushed as pink as the peppercorns in the curried lamb she was now eating. *Could he have found out how she left Roach & Hartley?* Her thoughts were curtailed, as Philippe continued.

'We were lucky. It wasn't just art that our family had to bargain with — we had wine too. . .'

'And nothing stops a revolutionary force quite so quickly as a magnum of bordeaux?'

'Exactly, Mimi, a head winemaker can't make his blend, well, without his head!'

Once chat had changed from art and heads rolling, Jenna realised that she really was quite enjoying herself. The atmosphere in the room was convivial and Lakshmi turned out to be a wonderful orator, telling the table in near perfect English about her gallery and various exhibitions that she'd hosted. Jenna wanted desperately to join in the conversation and show off her knowledge of the art world, but knew that keeping schtum was probably best. To take her mind off the conversation that she'd barred herself from, she turned to Jonty, keen to find out about his afternoon.

'Definitely worth doing,' he replied, 'even if it meant I did miss spending an afternoon with you.' He winked at her and took a sip of his wine. Once he'd placed the glass back down on the table he carried on. 'Margaux itself I couldn't get into.' He was referring to the chateau of the same name — the most notable one in the area — notorious for being appointment only and not open to visitors unless you applied weeks in advance. 'But I snuck on a tour going around d'Angludet and Giscours was interesting too and I had a good chat with the winemaker at Monbrison. Yeah, so, all in all, a good day's stalking.'

'Stalking?'

Jonty changed the subject. 'So, tell me, how do you know Clive?'

'Clive was my old boss.'

'Ah, so it's him I should have got some references from?'

'Er. . .'

Jonty laughed. 'Don't worry. How or why you left is your business. Isn't it extraordinary that he's here, though?' He raised his glass again and Jenna subconsciously mimicked him, or was it that she felt she really, really needed a drink — or ten — to get through tonight?

'Jonty, it's not just extraordinary.' She lowered her voice to a conspiratorial whisper. 'He's. . .. *gay!*'

Jonty almost spat out his wine and had to apologise to the others while turning it into a strained cough. Jenna slapped a fake smile on her face and they both waited until the other three were absorbed back into their own conversation.

'A little camp, maybe. . .?' Jonty ventured.

'A little? Camper than a Kylie concert. And with a *boyfriend* back home to prove it.'

'Ooh, now you're getting interesting. So this here really is a clandestine hook up.'

Jenna coughed to cover his words as she thought Clive might be listening in and waited until the meal was finished, and she and Jonty could natter in private out on the terrace. However, as they downed napkins and unanimously thanked Madame Lefort, and via her Menou, for the wonderful supper, it was Clive who took Jenna's arm and steered her out between the voiles of the dining-room doors to have a chat.

'But Clive, what about Pablo?' she said once they'd got to the edge of the balustrade.

Clive had picked up two glasses of cognac on his way past the drinks tray and as he took a sip he looked at Jenna so sincerely, so piteously almost, that she wondered what revelation he was going to give up next. 'And how long has it been going on with Mimi? I mean the New York art fair was, what, last March?'

'Oh, don't tell me off, Jenna, I know I've been naughty.'

'Naughty?' Jenna couldn't decide if she was more shocked at Clive's admissions or just the tiniest bit pissed off that he hadn't confided in her over the last fifteen months. 'Leading a double life is, yeah, well, it's definitely naughty.'

Clive sighed. 'Oh, Jenna, you don't understand. Pablo and I were having so much trouble. He's not always the darling you see at the private views, you know. There was a. . .' he lowered his voice, '. . .dark side to him.'

Jenna was entranced. This was prime gossip and she had a pang for the old days at Roach & Hartley where chats like this would have been discussed around the ancient coffee percolator.

'He was always off with other boys, young ones too, not, you know, illegally young, but I just felt that, well, I mean why would he want to be with old, grey me when he could have any young spunk he wanted?'

Jenna couldn't help but wrinkle up her nose at the word 'spunk'.

'But he loved you. Cheating aside. . .'

'Oh cheating, Snapchatting, Grindr. . . you name it, sugar, and he was on it. Then, when I met Mimi, well, something happened.'

'You fell for her?'

'Yes. But I had to come out all over again.' He took a restorative sip of the brandy and clenched his eyes shut before opening them and carrying on. 'I don't think you can comprehend, Jenna, how hard it is for a proud gay man to come to terms with the fact that he, I, am not actually one hundred per cent gay. It was like the Frankie Says Relax T-shirts in my wardrobe were suddenly mocking me! And the warm embrace of the Vauxhall saunas no longer soothed my aching muscles and worst of all. . .'

'Yes?'

'Pablo found out. And told all of our friends. I was ostracised.'

'Oh Clive. Clive.' Jenna wrapped her old boss up in a bear hug.

'Thank you, darling, thank you. I mean, don't get me wrong, it blew over in a trice once Pablo proved himself a total dick and started getting *emotionally* involved with a bell boy from the Savoy.'

'I was going to say,' Jenna had pulled back away from him and was cradling her glass again, 'I don't remember you being terribly upset at work, I mean, no more than usual.'

'Oh, this all happened since you've been gone, darling!'

'In the last month?'

'Yes. I mean, not the affair with Mimi, but the show downs with Pablo. It's quite put the whole drama about those pissy Picassos to the back of my mind!'

His words brought them very much to the forefront of Jenna's mind, but right now she was more intrigued about Clive's love life. 'Does Lakshmi, you know, *know*?'

'That I am, for want of a better term, bi-sexual?'

'Yes!'

Clive paused for dramatic effect. 'I don't know, darling, to be honest. I mean, here we are in France and, let's face it, all the men are quite camp, aren't they? Well, except your Jonty over there. He's one hundred per cent hetero sausage, isn't he?' Jenna smiled. 'But what happened to your nice skiing boyfriend?'

'Don't change the subject,' Jenna frowned at him. 'Tell me all about the necklace.'

'Well, when I realised I adored Mimi — oh, Jenna, the things she can do with a chapatti, I mean, you have read the Kama Sutra, haven't you? I knew I had to buy her that necklace. It's your fault, you know. If you hadn't worn it so splendidly. . .'

'Oh, Clive, flattery will get you nowhere.'

'Well, it got me into a lot of trouble. After the art fair that necklace came back to London and I walked past the bloody jeweller's bloody shop almost every day. I'd started my *affair d'amour* with Mimi and I knew she would love it.'

'Not to be rude, Clive, but how did you afford it? It cost tens of thousands of pounds.'

'Let's just say I came into a little windfall. . .' He winked at her and then turned around to face the others who had all now come out onto the terrace. He gave the campest little wave to Lakshmi who came over to join them and as she and Clive giggled and whispered, Jenna couldn't help but notice the facets of the antique ruby and the exquisite gold mount catch the light from the chateau's windows. *A windfall. . . Tens of thousands of pounds. . .* Somewhere in her wine and cognac-addled brain some more of those ever-needed pennies were dropping but she couldn't quite catch hold of them as they fell.

'Boo.'

'Oh, Jonty!' Jenna jumped a little bit; she'd obviously been deeper in concentration than she thought.

'Will you?' He took her brandy glass off her and placed it on the balustrade. While she'd been talking to Clive, Philippe had laid his hands on a very old gramophone and had found some old vinyls of Edith Piaf and other 1940s *chanteuses*. He and Madame Lefort, who'd taken her apron off and repinned her hair, were already dancing on the terrace and Jenna smiled up at Jonty as he led her across the gravel with Lakshmi and Clive following suit. By the first twirl she had lost her train of thought regarding the necklace and she let the warm night air, the warming cognac and especially the warmth of Jonty's arms comfort her on the dance floor as they spun and shimmied, swayed and waltzed until the moon was high and the comfort of all their beds beckoned.

38

'How strange,' Lakshmi began as she ran her hand over Clive's chest, 'that you knew the English girl here tonight.'

'Small world.' Clive took a long drag from Lakshmi's cigarillo before handing it back to her. They'd been making love for several hours now, and Clive was ready to fall asleep. But Mimi seemed intent on conversation.

'Small indeed, *trop petit*.' She inhaled deeply and blew out the smoke before rolling over and leaving the little cigar to rest on an ashtray on the bedside table. 'Was she the one who let the Picassos get stolen?'

Clive pushed himself up on his elbows and looked at his beautiful lover. She may be in her fifties — like him — but her skin was soft and smooth and the light from the bedside lamp illuminated the curve of her shoulder and slim upper arms, washing them in a golden light. The ruby in its gold mount was nestled in her cleavage and Clive reached out and stroked it, letting his fingers linger close to her breasts, the urge to touch them and stroke them almost overwhelming. Since he'd met Lakshmi he'd found himself fantasising about her questioning his own sexuality — although he couldn't call a twenty-year relationship with Pablo 'just a phase'. Bi-sexual seemed so commonplace a term for how he was feeling. What had Oscar Wilde once said? There was no such thing as good or evil in people, just those who were charming or tedious. Well, he felt like the sexual version — there was no gay or straight, just times when he was wildly in love or miserably unhappy.

'Clive? You are very quiet, and how do you say, contemplative, today. Is it that girl?'

He blinked out of his reverie. 'Yes, that was the girl who let the paintings be stolen. I do feel sorry for her though.'

'Why? She has fallen on her feet and she seems very much at home here in the chateau with my old friend.'

Clive rested his eyes on the ruby pendant that was slowly falling and rising with Lakshmi's breath. She looked every inch the Indian Maharani and he felt that the ruby, like Wilkie Collins' moonstone, was finally back where it belonged. He didn't want to say much more about Jenna and the trouble she had got herself into to Mimi as it really hadn't been the poor girl's fault, but he also didn't want to incriminate himself and Martin. *Christ*. Martin had been persuasive, and what with his own debts and the recession having knocked the bottom out of the art market, well, he had found it far too tempting a scheme. Having those prints stolen to order had fixed so many problems. Not only had he and Martin been bunged a huge wodge of cash from the new owner, but he wasn't lying when he said the insurers had paid a lump sum too. All he'd had to do was make sure that both he and Martin were out of the gallery with fool-proof alibis — that auction and his clumsy attempts at bidding had given them both that — and then let the hired heavy do the rest. He'd very much hoped that the insipid intern-of-the-month would have been on the front desk — a debutante with barely a brain cell between her pearl earrings — and she would have let the masked man take the prints with barely any resistance, but as it happened it had been on Jenna's watch and she had left her post, making the steal so very much easier. . . though harder to claim against the insurance, hence Martin's apoplexy when it had happened. Clive felt guilty, of course, but how else was the generations-old gallery meant to pay the new rent hikes? Or indeed, how was he to afford such a beautiful gem for the new love of his life? He hadn't banked on seeing Jenna again, that was for sure. And he wasn't certain if he'd almost given too much away during the evening, subconsciously letting the cat — or cat burglar, in this case — out of the bag, just for the sake of their old friendship.

Oh Jenna, Jenna — Clive pulled Lakshmi into another embrace as he tried to put his wronged employee out of his mind. Mutually assured destruction, he decided — if she cottoned onto him, he could just as easily turn on her and tell her new employers all about her gross negligence. And with that he explored Lakshmi's body again, delighting in her giggles that soon turned to something more guttural as she gave herself to him over and over.

Clive needn't have worried, as Jenna, true to form, hadn't let the penny drop properly (it was like the annoying 2p in the arcade push machine — so close to tipping over but not quite ever getting there). She nuzzled down into her pillow and let waves of drunkenness wash over her. To be fair to her brain, it was somewhat occupied with replaying the long, lingering kiss Jonty had just given her at the top of the stairs. They'd danced the evening to a close on the terrace, the gentle summer breeze wafting scents of lavender and jasmine over them as they all tried jiving and doing the Charleston before resorting to a romantic slow dance. Jenna, much to her genuine joy, had noticed Philippe tenderly caress Madame Lefort's back and play with a loose curl from her chignon as they danced. When the needle had jumped over the last groove, the couples had unpeeled themselves and Jenna had helped Madame Lefort carry the empty wine glasses through to the kitchen while Jonty and Philippe said goodnight to their guests and started putting the gramophone and old vinyl records away. Once the table was cleared and Madame Lefort had ushered Jenna out of the kitchen with a goodnight kiss and a flick of her tea towel, she had met Jonty in the hallway and he'd guided her up the majestic staircase, and then again up the smaller servants' staircase to their garret rooms. He'd not once suggested coming to join her in her room, which made Jenna fancy him that little bit more, and as he'd gently laid his hands on her shoulders, moving them slowly down her arms to pull her close to him, she'd closed her eyes and let him kiss her goodnight.

Rustling around under her eiderdown, she finally found the comfy spot and drifted off to sleep; for once not thinking of Angus or the painful way she left her old life in London. Seeing Clive again had given her closure on the whole horrible business of being fired and Jonty's gentlemanly — and oh so romantic — ways were helping her get over Angus, one lingering kiss at a time.

39

'I'll see what I can do.' Clive shook hands with Philippe and then shuffled through the bits of paper he'd been making notes on. Three paintings by a lesser-known eighteenth-century French artist might not cause a sell-out, one-in-one-out exhibition at the Tate, but would help the social standing of Roach & Hartley no end. To be honest, Clive thought to himself, Philippe seemed a little disinclined to let go of the set — and he couldn't blame him. The paintings showed bucolic frolickers, their milky, dewy skin barely covered in pastel silks as they laughed and danced in the woodland scenes. A perfect trio of pre-romantic, verging into the neo-classical style, paintings, and taking them on consignment for the gallery was a no-brainer for Clive, still high from the financial gain of the pinched Picassos.

'Do you think they'll sell?' Philippe had asked Clive. The early morning light had illuminated them — diffused through the voiles of the drawing-room doors. Clive thought Philippe had sounded like a client at a pawn shop — dreading, rather than hoping, that his items would be sold — so he had been careful to manage his new client's expectations. Of course, he wanted to secure the paintings for their next exhibition, so with the correct balance of English restraint and genuine praise he'd nodded and explained to Philippe the allure of these paintings to the London market.

'I guess it's like fine wine. Russians, Chinese: they're the core buyers now and these paintings are just what they're after. I mean, look at them.' He'd gestured towards the pretty paintings. 'They're glorious in their portrayal of aristocratic fun and games. And although they're not by well-known masters, well, I think we can drum up some excitement.'

'And when is the exhibition?'

'Not until the early autumn, Philippe.' Clive could see Philippe's shoulders relax a little. It didn't take a master sleuth to work out that if the chateau's fortunes fared better in the next few weeks, these paintings would stay right where they were.

'And you would take good care of them? I heard you had a little problem a month or so ago?'

'A blip.' Clive pressed his lips together — *mutually assured destruction*, he reminded himself. 'We have improved our security and your paintings will be as revered and respected in our hands as they are here.'

And so Philippe had signed some contractual paperwork, and Clive said he'd arrange the transport back to England, and by 10 a.m. the business was adjourned and the two men were sitting at the breakfast table when the ladies arrived to join them.

'Morning, all,' Jenna chirruped as she poked her head round the dining-room door. Lakshmi had arrived downstairs just before her and offered her a coffee as she poured herself one from a steaming cafétière on the sideboard. 'Ooh, yes please.'

When Jenna had woken up she realised that it was a Saturday — and although it had never been stipulated she guessed it might mean a day off for her. If so, she planned to use it to its full and explore the local village and stretch her legs, once Clive and Lakshmi were gone of course.

'Ah, *le weekend*,' Philippe smiled at her when she suggested her plan to him amid mouthfuls of flaky croissant.

'I'll need a walk to work off all this buttery yumminess.' She laughed and patted her stomach. She'd put all of last night's intrigue to the back of her mind and was genuinely happy to be in such a beautiful place with a day to herself. She'd all but forgotten about the horrors of her initial realisation that Clive — who could drop her in it in an instant — was here at the chateau. After breakfast, he took her to one side in the hallway and she had to remind herself that far from the actual sunbeam in which she stood, the metaphorical ice on which she found herself was actually rather thin.

'Jenna, dear.' Clive popped a kiss on each cheek and gently gave her shoulders a goodbye squeeze.

'Lovely to see you, Clive, really.'

'And you, sugar, and thank you for not blurting out anything about my, well, my more colourful past, last night.'

'Oh, of course.' Jenna stammered and clutched her hands in front of her as she tried to think of what to say. 'I mean, what goes on tour, stays on tour — or sort of the other way around. . . oh, whatever! You know what I mean!'

'I do.'

'And ditto,' she continued, 'thank you for not ratting me out to these guys.'

Clive reached inside his jacket pocket and pulled out a brown envelope. 'Take this, quickly.' He nudged it into her hand and wouldn't carry on until she'd rammed into her back pocket and showed him that her loose shirt covered any sticking out bits. 'Just a little severance pay.'

'Oh, Clive, I don't deserve this, really.' All the feelings of shame poured over her again as she mentally recounted how much to blame for the theft she was.

'No really, Jenna, I think it's only fair. One minute of carelessness after years of hard work with us. Just don't tell Martin.'

'I won't. I mean, I doubt I'll ever see him again.' She tried to sound wistful, but even Jenna could see that the obvious upside of her firing had been that she'd never have to work with Martin Roach again.

'Well, treat yourself to something.' He winked and then within minutes Lakshmi was there and hugs were being had and cars arrived and goodbyes said, and Jenna found herself once again alone in the large circular hallway. She checked down the corridor and there was no sight or sound of anyone and Philippe's study door was firmly closed. She pulled the envelope out of her back pocket and ripped it open. Packed inside were lots of twenty-euro notes — there had to be about five hundred euros in all — and a little note in Clive's spidery handwriting. *It wasn't your fault.*

A tear fell from her eye as she read the words. And a weight that seemed to have followed her from London suddenly lifted from her back and she looked up and out the door into the bright sunshine of the day and felt the power of the rays lift her spirits further as she skipped down the steps and off along the drive to go exploring.

40

Things quietened down at Château Montmorency after Clive and Lakshmi's visit and Jenna settled into her daily life. Her mind — and pulse — raced every time she saw Jonty, and bearing in mind they shared the same little office that was quite a lot — so much so, she thought she might need an echocardiogram by the end of the summer.

To add to her raised blood pressure, if being asked to help plan Bertie's party had meant being thrown in at the deep end, the fact it was brought forward by two weeks was the equivalent of Jenna diving into the Mariana Trench. *Was she waving or drowning?* Who knew, but the fountain was ordered and Coco had been put in charge of finding suitable hosing to plumb it in. Bertie hadn't really thought out the details when it came to how the champagne would be pumped around the fountain ('Don't ask me, sweet cheeks, I'm the muse, you're the woman what dos'), so Jenna had had to push her French to the limit, explaining to Coco with a variety of diagrams and hand signals quite what she thought could happen. She'd also failed to find any swans and had resorted at times to staring blindly at the presentation she'd made of the male models — their hairless, gleaming torsos a visual break from the spreadsheets and table plans that otherwise occupied her time.

She also caught herself daydreaming, more than she cared to admit, about the night Jonty had saved her from Spike and their rather passionate session afterwards, not to mention the lingering kiss of the other night. *Had it been better than her love-making with Angus?* She chewed on a pen lid and absent-mindedly clicked through a link to the male model's profile. No, not better, but different. Freeing in a way. Rebound-ish perhaps.

One of her daydreams was interrupted by the protagonist himself. Jenna accidentally dropped her pen as she saw in the flesh what she'd just been imagining, only this one had slightly more clothes on.

'Fancy getting out of here tonight?' As soon as he said it Jenna realised she'd been feeling incredibly cooped up over the last week, even in a house the size of Château Montmorency. 'Just somewhere local, I know a little place, if you'd like?'

Jenna *did* like and with the thought of a night out ahead, charged through her afternoon's work of sending out press releases. They were in umpteen different languages and Jenna really hoped that Google translate hadn't let her down and 'slips down a treat' really did have the same connation worldwide – the last thing she needed was PR drama to add to her summer of disasters. Once upstairs she delighted in the ritual of getting ready. It felt like a proper date this time and the excitement that filled her helped to replace the emptiness that she felt when her mind wandered back to Angus and what he might be up to now. No doubt living it up with Diane and her Victoria's Secret friends. Jenna wiped the day's dust off her scuffed shoes, hoping the pair would last her until she could hit the shops back in London – Clive's 'severance pay' was burning a hole in her pocket and although paying off her credit card bill might be wiser, she'd decided she was going to treat herself to some amazing designer heels – Jimmy Choos no less. The only bum note came from Madame Lefort, who seemed oddly uneasy at the thought of Jenna going out with Jonty.

'Do be careful, my dear,' she'd said, when Jenna had asked her if she had some spare cotton wool. 'I know it is exciting to be, how you say, *romanced* by a young man, but this work and pleasure thing, it is so easy to mix up the two, yes?'

Jenna had responded uncharacteristically rudely. 'Same could be said for you and Philippe, madame,' and then instantly regretted it as Madame Lefort's face fell and she silently handed over a few fluffy white balls. Jenna had been wondering why Madame Lefort had felt the need to warn her off Jonty, and more importantly how she could make amends for hurting her feelings, when Jonty knocked at her door.

'Ready?'

'Ready.' Madame Lefort's words, however, were still ringing in her ears, but wasn't it a bit too late to worry about muddying the waters of the chateau pond now? Let's face it, literally, physically and also metaphorically, she'd already been there and done that.

'You look absolutely gorgeous, Jenna.' Jonty took her hand and led her down the stairs. They hadn't touched like this for days and Jenna sensed the chemistry between them start to build. By the time they were at the front door she felt like she might explode with sexual tension, like a Second World War bomb that had lain silently for decades, sparked into reaction by the simplest of touches. Unexploded ordnance, or in her case, a sex bomb waiting to happen.

Jonty opened the door to his car for her and she got in. The sun was still high in the sky and there was warmth in the summer evening. As Jonty slipped the car into gear Jenna saw Madame Lefort and Philippe standing on the steps, not exactly waving them off, but looking on and waiting for the car to disappear out of view.

*

The restaurant Jonty took her to was a world away from the village bistro she had found in the little local village the day she'd gone exploring and she was grateful to the gods of fate that she'd upped the stakes and delved into the not-quite-bottomless suitcase for something a bit sexy. Her black skinny jeans seemed to fit her better these days and they skimmed over her thighs, looking pretty chic teamed with a black camisole top. The thin straps exposed her moderately tanned back (she had snuck off after lunch every now and again for a bit of nudey sun-bathing in the walled garden) but she had a trusty cardie for later once the sun went down. She felt like an English version of Sandy from *Grease*, all dressed in black, and as they'd whizzed along in the smart hire car she felt like Jonty in his best peacock blue trousers and a white linen shirt, was very much right now the one that she wanted.

The restaurant stood at the end of a typical French village. Heralded by large detached properties built of the warm stone of the area, the village then slowly started to build up. The road narrowed as the stone houses crept in on it, the plots becoming smaller and closer together, the front doors opening right onto the pavement. Some houses were deceptively large and had double gates mounted on intricate iron posts hiding tree-lined courtyards beyond. One of these courtyards — or at least the building surrounding it — contained the bistro restaurant and Jonty parked the car in the road just outside. There was a buzz about the little place and as they entered the courtyard from the street the maître d' welcomed them in and showed them to a table in the corner, next to a weathered stone fireplace. The whole place had the feel of faded grandeur. It had once been an internal great hall — the roof now long caved in and removed and the old fireplace, stone carvings and smoothed hearth stones left open to the gentle southern French elements. The terrace they were sitting on along with a few other diners, whose chatter competed with the sound of classical music, was decorated with cascading garlands of fairy lights strung among the boughs of trees that had long ago started to grow in the courtyard. Jonty ordered a bottle of champagne and the waiter brought it over to them. Instead of addressing Jonty, the waiter threw his white tea-towel over his shoulder and said to Jenna, 'How would madame like it opened?'

Jenna looked quizzically at Jonty who laughed.

'What he means, Jenna, is how loudly would you like him to go?'

'*Oui*, would madame like a, how you say, gentle *pffffst* or a pop *magnifique*?'

'Oh I see!' Jenna laughed. 'I really don't have any *grape expectations* as long as it ends up in my glass!'

Jonty chuckled at her and nodded to the waiter who opened the bottle with the barest of *pfffsts* and poured them both a glass.

'I'm a fan of the gentle *pffffst*, or as one Carstairs chum calls it, the Duchess's fart.' He raised his glass to toast Jenna and she clinked him back.

'Oh, I don't know, I think I'm more of a *pop magnifique* type of girl.'

'Or an explosive thrust?'

'Rocket-fuelled release?'

'Too much! Too much!' Jonty had laughed at her and seeing him look so relaxed and so handsome in the evening light, the tiny fairy lights illuminating him against the dying of the sunlight, she felt as if she could possibly be ready to take things further emotionally, as well as sexually with this charming man.

Their meal had been sublime, too. The scallop starter had led to a steak and frites so deliciously simple that they'd barely paused to talk while they'd set about it hungrily.

Instead they'd just locked eyes and clinked glasses and let the chemistry between them flow. Pudding had been a chocolate soufflé, so light, yet rich that Jenna had been rendered speechless. Even Menou and his kitchen wizardry had never come up with something so magically decadent.

Once the bill was paid and the temperature had dropped on the sheltered terrace, Jonty had taken Jenna's cardigan and draped it around her shoulders, then took her arm in his and led her to the car. Thinking about it later, Jenna couldn't remember if it had been his hand on her thigh or her arm snaking up to pull his head towards her that had started it, but they'd both known that a repeat of the other night was very much on the cards. The drive home had been tantalisingly long and they had barely closed the large front door of the chateau behind them before Jonty's hands were all over Jenna's body, ruching up the silky camisole, his kisses feathering her neck as she arched into his body and let him bring her back to sexual life. Two flights of stairs couldn't be tolerated so they'd let themselves into the drawing room. Jonty managed to take his hands off her for long enough to find some matches by the ornate fireplace and he set about lighting a few of the candles that were dotted around the room. Their light flickered on his naked torso as he undid his shirt buttons and Jenna followed suit, until she was down to her underwear and lying on a silk upholstered chaise-longue. Candlelight and moonlight were a heady mix and before she had been able to analyse how she was feeling or what she was doing, she was being pleasured by a very dextrous Jonty, who helped her forget all her heartache again and again as the waves of pleasure crashed through her body.

41

'It's really rather exciting,' Jenna gushed to Sally one morning about a week later, stealing another quick phone call while she was alone in the office. Jonty had driven into the local town to stock up on printer paper and ink cartridges and although Jenna would have loved to have gone with him, she had far too much to do. And anyway, she and Jonty had been into the town together on Wednesday when it was market day. Brightly coloured stalls with striped awnings and trestles piled high with cheeses, meats and bread had lined the main square and while Jonty had spoken his really rather good French to the grocers and butchers, ticking items off Madame Lefort's shopping list, Jenna had meandered through the rows of artisan stalls, touching the smooth leather of hand-made bags and smelling the fresh lavender picked from the fields of Provence. She'd found an amazing floppy hat that she'd fallen for, and decided to raid the Jimmy Choo fund and splash out twenty euros on it. It was pink and huge, and when she put it on she felt fabulous and chic. . . Even Jonty hadn't recognised her as she snuck up behind him, her sunglasses and hat obscuring her face completely.

Back in the present, Sally was a little more cautious about Jenna's dalliance than she thought she might be.

'I know it must be, darling, but do be careful of this work romance. It's all very well Jonty dipping his quill in the office ink, but you don't know how many other ink wells he's been dipping in too.'

'I am being careful — well, sort of.'

'I'm not talking about safe sex, sweetie, I'm talking about looking after your heart. I'd hate to see you rush into anything, JJ.'

'I know, I know.' Sally's words echoed those of Madame Lefort's from the other night and it reminded Jenna that she really should do more to make up to her for her rudeness. She felt slightly deflated, too, now and changed the subject. 'Bertie told me the other day that Angus was seeing Diane again. . .'

'Really? First I've heard, although I must say we haven't really had a peep from him since we saw him at the airport.'

'I think she might be coming to Bertie's party with him.'

'Oh, sweetie. No wonder you're rebounding like squash ball with Jonty then.'

'I think it might be more than that though now. I'm, well, I'm starting to really like him.'

'Well, if that's the case then it should be easier when you see Gus.'

'*Should* being the operative word.'

'Well,' continued Sally, 'I know Hugo and I are both bursting to see you, sweetie. His tux is dry-cleaned and my dress is pressed – we're all ready for the party of the century! See you in a few days! Got to dash, mwah.'

Jenna had air kissed her friend down the line in return and turned back to her notepad. She'd been jotting down notes such as 'don't forget to buy body oil for the male models', 'check new fountain plumbing for leaks – do not want to waste champagne!' and 'WHAT TO WEAR?!!!' when she heard the crunch of gravel under tyre.

She sprang up from her chair and ran along the corridor and caught Jonty just as he was coming into the hallway.

'Well, hello, Miss Jenkins,' he bowed at her

'Mr Palmer-Johnston, I do declare!' Jenna dropping a curtsey, all reservations about her chateau romance, fleeting as they were, gone.

He swept her up into a twirl and she almost pirouetted into the centre table with its large stone urn.

'Oops. And I promise I haven't even been drinking!'

'Occupational hazard around here. I wouldn't blame you if you had!'

'Did you get everything you need in town?' Jenna felt like she should appease her inner Sally and get things vaguely back to a professional relationship.

'Yup, all done.' Jonty indicated the reams of paper under his arm and plastic carrier full of various coloured inks for the printer. 'Let me dump these in the office and then,' Jonty checked his watch, 'yeah I think we have time before lunch. I have something much more interesting to show you.'

Jenna squeezed the firm little grapes between her fingers. She and Jonty were standing at the very southern edge of the main vineyard, the one that she looked over every morning from her bedroom window. There was, for once, a gentle breeze and Jenna felt it ripple through the skirt of her dress. Perhaps a white summery dress was overkill for a normal day, as was the amazingly large and floppy sun hat, but now, out here with Jonty in the glorious sunshine, she felt fabulous. This wasn't just any dress after all, it was the summer version of the The Glad-Rag-Iator — it flared out at just the right place to make her standard-issue waist look tiny and it was slightly risqué with its low back and sexy halter-neck top. She relished the hot sun on her back as she admired the ripening grapes in front of her.

'These are looking plump and juicy.' Jonty rolled a grape around his palm, squeezing it gently and testing its resistance to his touch.

'Just how you like them?' Jenna took the grape from his hand and studied it, trying to look knowledgeable but finding it hard not to smile.

'But of course it's not all about juiciness.' He took it back off her. 'We have to make sure we have enough sugar in there too.' He gently raised his hand and moved the grape slowly across Jenna's lips, tempting her to eat it. Under his spell, she let him pop it in her mouth. Unlike the cask sample of wine she'd tried with him, this grape tasted ripe and utterly delicious.

'It's so sweet.'

Jonty plucked another one from the vine and popped it into his own mouth. 'Hard to imagine this being turned into a wine, isn't it?' He spat the pips out and then took Jenna's hand and led her deeper into the vines.

'Are we still in the *clos*?' Jenna wondered as they ducked under a leafy bush, the tendrils of the vines tickling her bare back.

'We're in the most special part.' Jonty replied as he brought them to a halt. Again he tested the grapes that were hanging on the vine and bit into one as Jenna looked on. As he looked back to her again he said, 'Perfect.'

'Should I be honoured to be in this special part of yours?'

Jonty laughed. 'Everything you say sounds so dirty, Jenna, I love it. And I can't resist. . . it's I who should be honoured to be in your special parts, surely?'

'Jonty!' Jenna biffed him on the chest but did not resist when he wrapped his arms around her and started kissing her neck, moving down her shoulders and kissing her arms as she let her head roll back in pleasure. 'I like getting close in the *clos*, Jonty.'

'And perhaps entwined in the vines?'

'Oh, you're good. You *pipped* me to that one.'

Jonty laughed and stopped Jenna from coming up with any more terrible puns by kissing her — at first softly, the taste of the grapes still lingering in both their mouths, then deeper as they lost themselves in the vines.

'Should have brought our picnic blanket. . .' Jenna giggled as Jonty lay down. 'I would, darling, but this is my last clean dress. . .'

'Well, you better use me as your picnic blanket then.' Jonty pulled her down on top of him, and in a very slick move had released the clasp of her halter neck dress so her hair and dress and breasts cascaded in front of him.

'Now these are the ripest berries I've seen all day.' Jonty caressed her as she giggled at him again and it wasn't long before clean dress or not, they really were entwined in the vines and the closest a couple could possibly get in a *clos*.

Dusting themselves off, they slowly made their way back to the chateau where Jenna nipped upstairs to change out of her dress into something more casual, ready for a quick lunch and another afternoon of party planning.

If Madame Lefort noticed the flush in Jenna's cheeks or the ruffled nature of her hastily rebrushed hair, she said nothing about it, and chatted away to the pair as they ate tapenade on toast at the large kitchen table. Menou had been fretting over the party caterers coming in and taking over his kitchen so had decided to take a few days off before the party and had left Madame in charge of feeding the household until he got back. With far too much to do already they were down to cupboard basics and the baguettes that Jonty had just brought back from the market, but Jenna barely noticed as she and Jonty made eyes at each other and shared in-jokes as they ate.

After lunch, Jenna expected him to go back into the coolness of the cellar and she herself needed to keep an eye out for the new fountain — the faux fountain as she called it — which was to arrive at any moment. But instead Jonty followed her into the office and switched on his own laptop and tapped away. Before long the familiar sound of the printer kicking itself into action was heard and Jonty stood up to watch the pages being spat out into the tray.

'Little bit of housekeeping, I'm afraid,' he said to Jenna and she looked up at him over her screen.

'Oh yes?'

'Just a signature for the pallets of wine that left the country this week and went over to Carstairs & Co. I thought as Carstairs' newest employee you might like the honour of signing off on the wines you've been helping to sell.'

'Oh, how exciting, yes!' Jenna picked up a pen from her desk and met Jonty at the printer. 'Where do I sign?'

The paperwork looked complicated and mentioned various acronyms and jargon she didn't understand, but the Carstairs & Co crest was at the top and the language looked like the sort that would send you to sleep if you bothered to read it, so she skimmed through it, noticing there was a line or so where it mentioned pallet rates and in-bond pricing — all very much the sort of thing she'd heard him talking about to Philippe over the last few weeks — and signed where Jonty pointed. She felt that buzz of belonging. She was signing on behalf of Carstairs & Co, Britain's most prestigious wine merchants and that felt pretty bloody good. She really was starting to believe that this had been the best enforced career move ever and she happily slipped back into her seat and smiled up at Jonty as he folded the paperwork and slid it into an envelope. His goodbye kiss turned into quite a frisky smooch as Jonty hoisted her onto the desk — sending her pen pot flying dramatically to the floor in the process — and then he kissed her, at first on her lips, then moving his kisses down the front of her shirt as he unbuttoned it and pulled it out from the waistband of her pleated skirt.

'I wish you still had that dirty little white dress on,' he whispered as he pulled her forward on the desk and sat himself down in her chair.

'Or off?' Jenna edged her legs apart and let him bury his head between them, pushing up her skirt and grabbing her arse as he kissed her around her knicker line while she arched her back in pure pleasure. Keeping her moans to a minimum just in case anyone heard them was Jenna's hardest task and she clasped the edge of the desk in pure ecstatic spasm as he gave her such exquisite pleasure for the second time that day.

Jonty kissed Jenna goodbye and headed towards the kitchen for a drink. He thought a little stubby bottle of *biere d'Alsace* would do the trick and was just helping himself to one from the fridge when a cough alerted him to someone's presence. Jonty turned to see who it was and almost dropped his beer when he saw Whitey standing at the open door to the kitchen garden.

'Don't mind if I do,' Whitey said, heading towards Jonty, who was temporarily stricken into paralysis at the sight of his blackmailer.

Gathering his thoughts he shielded the fridge door with his body and hissed, 'What are you doing here, Dave?'

'Shooting the breeze with my old mate Jon Boy.' Whitey raised his eyebrows daring Jonty to challenge him. 'Having a beer it seems.'

'I thought the deal,' Jonty passed Whitey his own bottle of beer as a compromise, 'was that you would leave me alone now.'

'Ah no, you see,' Whitey paused as he pulled the cap off the beer bottle with his teeth and spat it to the floor. 'I remember very clearly saying that I would be very much around for the foreseeable. Just keeping an eye on you.'

At that Whitey took a long glug of the beer then left back through the kitchen garden door, whistling a tuneless ditty to himself.

42

As dusk fell Jenna leaned against the stone parapet of the terrace and watched the light fade from the sky. She thought about the gentle touches and caresses she'd received that morning in the vines. Bliss. Who knew nibbling on a few *premier terroir* grapes could make a couple do such things! Not to mention the 'desk job' Jonty had given her just after lunch.

Jenna sipped the chilled white wine from her glass and turned to face the monstrosity that dominated the upper terrace of the chateau. It was a fountain so ostentatious, with its alabaster swans and stone cherubs, that Jenna didn't know where to look first. Bertie had called about an hour ago to check that it had been delivered and plumbed in okay today.

'Is it there, Jenna? Is it absolutely fabulous?'

'It's absolutely something.'

'I chose the biggest they had, which reminds me, the champagne will be arriving tomorrow. The unhelpful man said something about pallets being needed so I assume you have a forklift or something to unload it.'

'Yes, Bertie, don't worry. I'll take time off from treading the grapes to woman the forklift myself.'

Bertie blithely ignored Jenna's joke. 'Great. And did you test it?'

Not with champagne she hadn't, but even Jonty had been tempted out of his cellar to see how the ghastly fountain worked and they had spent a hilarious twenty minutes with Coco the gardener, who had been scratching his head and muttering French obscenities for an hour before as he attempted to link the fountain up to the water tank that would be filled with fizz for the party. Jonty had been the first to catch a squirt of water from the nipple of a water nymph, whereas Jenna had been more ladylike and just filled a glass from the tinkling penis of a plump seraphim.

Alongside the fountain fiasco — the lorry that delivered it had knocked over two stone urns and almost run over the grey-and-white cat that had been sunbathing on the driveway — Jenna had taken delivery of at least five miles' worth of fairy lights that came with the delivery note to 'Harrods-up the house'. This was another of Bertie's ways of communicating with her, which was almost more desirable in its succinctness to the drawling phone conversations at all hours of the day. She'd also had a delivery of about £10,000 of fireworks with the simple note 'don't get wet, midnight set off, big bangs, darling' and the thirty-foot-high inflatable gold elephant had arrived, deflated of course, and looking rather sadly limp, but it came with the instruction 'pump me up well — no one likes a flaccid pachyderm'. What the elephant, gold or not, had to do with a masquerade ball Jenna had no idea; but looking at the fountain she could sense the style Bertie was going for. Blingtastic.

Jenna walked over to it, and took another swig of her wine. She ran her hand over the crude stone base, its rustication giving way to finer marble and stone work. Some of the nymphs were finished with silver and gold and the cherubs had glittering loin cloths and wings. 'If only I had something half as glamorous as you have to wear to this bloody party,' she said to one particularly glittery cherub before taking another swig from her glass.

'You'll be the belle of the ball, whatever you're in.' Jonty had appeared from the French windows that led out from the dining room.

'It'll be vine leaves and a well-positioned glass at this rate,' Jenna let him kiss her hello and he slipped an arm around her waist. They both looked at the fountain again, almost speechless at its size and total brashness.

'It's going to be one hell of a party.' Jonty broke the silence and Jenna laughed. He squeezed her tighter into him and she rested her head on his shoulder. 'Madame Lefort has scraped together some cold pie and salad for supper, coming in?'

Jenna nodded and slipped her hand in his as he led them both from the terrorised terrace and through the house into the kitchen. Madame Lefort wasn't there but joined them a few moments later, puffing with a little exertion, but encouraging the young couple to eat up as soon as she saw them.

'Is Philippe joining us?' Jenna asked.

'*Mais non*, he takes his supper at his desk tonight. I am worried about him, he seems so, how you say, stressed. But I am sure he will work out what is wrong with those books. Jonty,' she turned to him, 'you will help him a little, yes? He seems so unlike himself, so withdrawn.' She looked so crestfallen that Jenna felt doubly terrible for saying what she did the other night. It was clear that far from a workplace fling, Philippe's darling housekeeper was utterly in love with him. Jenna reached out and placed her hand over Madame Lefort's. The older woman took it gratefully.

'We'll look after him, Madame. And once this party is over, Bertie will pay her final balance and he'll be swimming in cash.'

'*Bof*! This party! He needs to concentrate on making wine!'

'Don't worry, that's what I'm here for.' Jenna squeezed her hand. 'Not an ounce of Philippe's puff will be needed to fill that giant elephant.' Madame Lefort looked at her quizzically but squeezed her back all the same.

238

'As the youth say, "hashtag" things I never thought I'd hear you say,' chuckled Jonty. Jenna released Madame Lefort's hand, pleased that there seemed to be no long-lasting grudge being held for the other night, and laughed at him too, and together with Coco who appeared through the kitchen garden door at the sound of their voices, they all tucked in to the scratched-together spread.

'I better go and see to the old boy.' Jonty stood at the bottom of the grand staircase. Standing one step above him, Jenna had made their heights slightly more even.

'Well, I'm off to bed,' she kissed him goodnight.

'Good night then, JJ.' Jonty held her face in his hands and kissed her again.

'Won't you come up and wish me one yourself later?'

'Are you sure?'

'Jonty, you've ravished me among the vines, devoured me on a desk and fondled me by a fountain already today, I think I'm okay with a little late-night visiting too.'

'Okay then. . . get that dirty sexy dress of yours back on and I'll be up there as soon as I've calmed Philippe's fevered brow.'

And true to his word, barely an hour later there was a soft knock at Jenna's door and her floaty white dress barely lasted a minute before it was crumpled on the floor again, its wearer transported to pleasurable places where no dress code was required.

43

Jenna woke the next morning to the now-familiar blue sky and morning sounds of the vineyard — the gentle buzz of a bumble bee bouncing along her half open window mixed in with the doodle-doos of the village cockerels. She'd stopped doing her morning ritual, and instead of seeing the dawn mists rise from the vineyard before gradually stretching and yawning herself to full wakefulness, these days Jenna was more of a 'shit, it's 8 a.m' type person who dashed to the bathroom. One more tick in the 'pro' column for working in the wine trade, though, was that the near constant, but low level, drinking had really built up her resistance to alcohol, and even after quite a few glasses of the rather nice white wine last night — not to mention the brandy Jonty had brought her when he came to undress her before bed — she didn't feel in the least hungover. Or no 'grape depression' as she'd heard the dreaded h-word be called.

Jenna showered and dressed and headed down to breakfast where Madame Lefort was already serving up fresh pastries to a hungry Jonty. Jenna pulled up a chair at the long kitchen table and tried not to catch his eye, fearing that she might explode into giggles if she did and Madame Lefort would then have good reason to suspect — and disapprove of — the inter staff relations that went on last night. Luckily Jonty kept a straight face and after he'd swallowed his mouthful of croissant and washed it down with a gulp of his steaming coffee he announced that he needed to head back to London for a quick overnighter.

'Why?' Jenna asked, trying to hide her disappointment and wondering why he hadn't mentioned it before.

'Woke up to a text this morning. You know the pallets we exported? Some mess up at the docks, which is then affecting the bonded warehouse. Someone's screwed up and I need to go and fix it.' Jonty seemed very serious and it reminded Jenna of the morning of the wine merchants' visit. She didn't mean to sulk, but Jonty obviously noticed and smiled at her. 'I'll be back before you know it.'

'I hope so.' Jenna couldn't hide how glum the prospect of a day and night without him here in the chateau made her. Not just because she was starting to really quite like him, but because he was still doing an awfully good job of distracting her from the pain of the Angus split. Without him there — and let's face it, easy access to a lot of wine — would she relapse back into tears and sniffles?

As if to prove her point, thoughts of Angus were banished again from her mind when Jonty kissed her goodbye on the steps of the chateau a little while later.

'When I'm back from dealing with whichever cock screwed things up,' he lowered his voice and whispered into her ear, 'I'll give you a good cock-screw too.'

And while Jonty spent his time back in the UK sorting out pallets of wine at the bonded warehouse, Jenna's days had been filled with more party organising and deliveries coming in — and of course umpteen calls from an increasingly irritating Bertie.

Jenna was in the little office, checking off the spreadsheet she'd made up of the male model waiters who would be mask-less and pretty much topless too — save for bow ties and glittery mini waistcoats — when another call came in.

'Darling, final numbers, promise promise. A couple of last-minute RSVPs including your boyfriend, or ex, or whatever he is to you. Honestly, I know he's been in rural China but like, manners.'

'Is he, is he definitely coming then?' Jenna had tried to put the fact that Bertie had invited Angus, and rather insensitively his new, or perhaps old, girlfriend, the runway model Diane Blane, to the party.

'Yes, finally got a ditty from him. Sent from arse-end of bloody nowhere, no doubt, but he is indeed on his way back to civilisation as we speak. Will be so nice for Maxie to see him, I always thought Angus was a rather good influence, you know?'

Jenna sighed. 'Yes, I know. I'll make sure they get a nice room in the chateau. I assume they're staying?'

Bertie had invited over a hundred people and of course not all of them could stay at Chateau Montmorency. Part of Jenna's job over the last few weeks had been to find as many hotels, taxis, Air BnBs, gîtes, chambres and anywhere else that would be suitable for London's A-list to stay. Only the very lucky few — old friends — were assigned rooms in the chateau itself, and included in that number was Max's old best friend, Angus.

'Not "they", sweetie, just him. *Toute seule* as they say, mano-a-on-his-own-o. Zero girlfriend-o.'

'Oh, I thought he had Diane in tow?'

'Yah, soz. Shame, actually, as *Hello!* would have loved to have taken her pic. I did tell you that their nice photographer was coming, didn't I? Hilarious as they're doing a shoot down in Monaco so it's just a short heli-hop up to Bordeaux really and the darling editor said they couldn't possibly miss the party of the season, obvs.'

Jenna 'ummed' and 'ahhed' at Bertie, who was prattling on about 'darling so-and-so' and 'simply divine whoever', while her mind was racing. Angus would be here, at the chateau, in two days' time. She'd been having such a nice time getting to know Jonty, practically living with him (oh the daydreams about chateau life together!) but the basis of it all had been that a) as discussed Angus had

242

been a douche to dump her and b) he was now happily shacked up with someone else, which would have given her leave to do exactly the same thing. Now Angus was single — perhaps he'd never even got back together with Diane — well, it made Jenna feel just the tiniest bit guilty. Enough to take the gloss off anyway.

She ended the call and felt drained — as per usual after being Bertied. But she had also made up her mind. Like her literary hero Jane Bennet (far too much drama in Elizabeth's life and Jenna shuddered to think how terrifyingly hectic life as Lydia would get) she would meet Angus as nothing more than 'a common and indifferent acquaintance'. Or in more modern parlance, as just somebody that she used to know.

Jenna had barely got up from her seat when she heard voices in the hallway. The cut-glass accent was unmistakable and its slight judginess whooshed back memories from earlier on in the year when Jenna and her friends had been waited on by Izzy the chalet girl, who obviously thought she was several rungs higher than all of them on life's ladder.

'Izzy, hello.' She met her out in the hallway and had to do a double take when she took in what Izzy was wearing. The most micro of shorts showed off her lean, tanned legs and a barely there blouse was pulled tight across a push-up bra. Jenna caught sight of Jonty unloading her bags from the back of his car. When he'd texted her earlier to say he'd rather cleverly timed his flight home to pick her up at the airport he'd failed to add 'and she's dressed like a hooker'.

'Oh, hiya.'

'Um, right, well. Get yourself settled in and then I'll show you around.'

'Durr. No need to Jensplain things to me, I totes remember — I was only here, like, a few weeks ago, right?'

'Right. Anyway, get yourself settled in — and maybe think about wearing something slightly more work appropriate,' Jenna paused as Izzy glared at her. 'And I'll chat you through the itinerary for the next few days afterwards. It's going to be party central here and like it or not, we're going to give Bertie the best damn party she could have.'

'Fine. See you in a bit.'

'Jonty will show you up.' Jenna rolled her eyes at Jonty who had just come in, a bag held in each hand. He blew a kiss to her and raised his eyebrows, which made Jenna giggle. Despite her guilt over Angus, she was pleased to see Jonty again and breathed a sigh of relief that he was back from his travels in one piece.

Jonty followed the scantily dressed girl up the stone staircase. She'd stayed in one of the top-floor rooms last time so she let herself up through the hidden door from the landing and held it open for him as he came up behind her with her bags. This could get awkward. Jenna was his primary focus right now, but he'd found Izzy impossible to resist when she was at the chateau last time and little Jonty in his pants was finding the sight of her toned, tanned legs going upstairs in front of him, fairly hard to resist again. He reminded himself of the gentlemanly code of the upper classes — the set he was so desperate to join — and he didn't think shagging two girls at once counted as *noblesse oblige*, unless you could roughly translate that as nobbing obligingly. No, he had to stick to one girl at a time and not. . . oh God. Izzy had walked straight up to *his* room and opened the door. Before he could put her bags down and mention that she might have jumped the gun, she was unbuttoning her blouse, revealing her push-up bra underneath. Jonty was lost to lust and with one quick kick he closed the door behind him.

*

Jenna was relieved that when Izzy came downstairs she was wearing something slightly more appropriate for chateau life. The tiny Daisy Dukes were replaced with some neat white linen trousers and a smart black T-shirt which made Jenna feel that her own slap-dash outfit of jeans and a scruffy old floral shirt didn't pass muster. It wasn't like she hadn't been able to wash her clothes, even if she always felt slightly embarrassed hanging her knickers up on the line in the kitchen garden in full view of everyone. Still, she had packed thinking she'd mostly be hard at it in the vines, and although she had had something hard in the vines, it really hadn't been work related. She smiled to herself and then got back to running through everything with Izzy and then left her with the list of names to write out neatly onto the table plan.

'Don't forget the titles. I think some of those hons might get testy if you neglect their heritage.'

'Jenna, chill, I know my earls from my elbow you know. *Some* of us just know these things.'

Well, some of us aren't stuck up little madams, Jenna almost said out loud, but instead just gritted her teeth and smiled at the girl and left her to wield the gold Sharpie pen of power over the table plan.

44

In only a few hours the chateau had gone from relative calm to full on Piccadilly Circus, if Piccadilly Circus was populated by stubborn French deliverymen bearing hampers full of live doves. The delivery note this time just read 'Don't kill them. To be released during the speeches.' *Fuck me*, sighed Jenna to herself and made sure the birds were stored in the relative cool of the garages with enough food and water to get them through the night and then the day of the party.

By the time the day came to an end and she, Jonty, Izzy, Madame Lefort and this time Philippe too, gathered round the kitchen table to eat, Jenna was knackered. Izzy was practising her already excellent French and Jenna was only mildly jealous at the happy response she was getting from Philippe. He seemed more relaxed than he had in days — which was odd bearing in mind it was his ancestral home that was, for the first time in its history, now also the home of two slightly grumpy alpacas, which had been delivered to the old stable block, luckily just after the dove hampers had been moved out of the way. Bertie had texted Jenna this time with the simple instruction 'Alpacas might spit, but make sure they're in their cutest outfits for when guests arrive.' The alpacas, obviously a bit stressed out from their journey across rural France, had indeed spat and Jenna was still sporting a *Something About Mary*-style quiff in her hair that she couldn't really do anything about. Madame Lefort looked more relaxed too, which again was odd when you thought about the amount of work she'd been putting in to making all the guest bedrooms as lovely as possible, including changing over all the toiletries to Bertie's signature scent. Apparently, her aroma-consultant had told Bertie that if the whole house — down to the shower gel in each room — was 'attuned to Bertie's own personalised perfume' then the party would be a harmonising success. And duly, boxes and boxes of Chanel body creams, hand soaps and shower gels had arrived. *Someone very clever must be making Bertie a lot of money for her to be spending it quite so stupidly*, thought Jenna as she semi-guiltily pocketed a mini shower gel or three for herself from the box. Still, Philippe and Madame Lefort were definitely looking perkier and as the evening meal broke up and the household went their separate ways she noticed Madame Lefort follow Philippe into his study and close the door behind them.

Jenna decided that she could do no more Izzy-sitting and once Jonty had left them to go back down to the cellar — he had, to be fair, been awfully good all afternoon helping her with the deliveries of livestock and whatnot — she headed up to bed. As she opened the door to her little garret room a sudden wave of déjà vu hit her. She could have been standing looking at the four-poster bed downstairs all those weeks ago as the feelings of shock and gratitude were just the same. This time, instead of a new blouse to replace the one she had ruined in the luggage carousel, there was hanging up the most exquisite evening dress. It was in a soft dusky pink, floor length, with full and swishy chiffon skirts. The top had a plunging neckline and silvery sparkly epaulettes graced the shoulders in a beautiful vine leaf pattern. Beneath it a fabulous pair of satin shoes peeped out and Jenna gasped when she saw that they were Jimmy Choos — her dream shoe! — and this pair were the most wonderful she'd ever seen, with crystal sparkles up the heel and covering the very end of the toe. Jenna could barely tear her eyes away from the stunning outfit yet something on her pillow caught her eye. It was one of the Venetian masks from the Paris opera — a plain one compared to some of them, but elegant in its simplicity with just cat's eyes styled in black sequins and a long black feather strikingly fitted to one side. There was a note next to it: *The belle of the ball needs something a little more special than a blouse. . . J xxx*

Jenna ran her finger over the words. He'd obviously heard her last night talking to the fountain cherub. She was stunned though. A blouse was one thing, but designer shoes! And this dress — it must have come from Paris, or at least Bordeaux — it was so beautiful. She stripped off her clothes and slipped it on over her head. The fabric fell in soft waves around her as it gently moulded itself to her body. The skirts pooled on the floor and she tip-toed over to the Jimmy Choos and slipped them on. She looked down and saw the perfect princessy toes peeking out from under the swirling skirts and then readjusted the top around her bra. Realising that her slightly greying 'day' bra was doing nothing to aid this fairy-tale moment she quickly unhooked it and slid the straps down and off her arms, and then she pulled it out from the front of the dress. She rearranged the material around her breasts and saw how the plunging neckline made her cleavage look absolutely amazing. If only there was a long mirror in her room. Could she dare slink downstairs back to her old room and then gaze at herself in this glorious dress? Just as she was about to open the door there was a soft knock and Jonty entered.

'Wow.'

'Jonty, I don't know what to say, it's, well, this whole. . . I mean. . .'

'Shh.' Jonty stepped towards her and took her hands in his. 'There's no need to thank me.'

'Yes, there bloody well is.' She leaned up and kissed him. 'It's beautiful. I just hope I'm doing it justice.'

'Justice, or just tits?' Jonty laughed as Jenna pulled her hands away from him and readjusted herself again.

Jonty stopped her fiddling and gently pushed the dress off her shoulders so that the bodice fell down around her waist.

'Just tits then?' she said and looked up into his face as he kissed her and wrapped his arms around her naked torso. Jenna let him kiss her, moving his lips down her neck to her chest, but something felt a little different now. Perhaps it was having Izzy back in the house — and all she reminded Jenna of; the ski trip where she fell in love with Angus, not to mention quite how minxy she'd been with Max — or maybe it was knowing that in a matter of hours she'd be masked-face-to-masked-face with Angus again. She shivered a little and Jonty stopped kissing her.

'You OK, Jenna?'

'Yes, I'm fine. I just think I should maybe save this pristine dress for tomorrow.'

She used his arms to balance herself as she stepped out of the high-heeled Choos and suddenly she felt very small and vulnerable. Jonty was nothing but gentlemanly though and reached across to the chair by her door and picked up her old cashmere cardigan. He wrapped it around her shoulders and let her take the rest of the dress off and hang it up.

'It really is so amazing, Jonty. When does it have to go back?'

He let out a little snort laugh and placed his hands on her shoulders. 'It doesn't need to go back. It's yours. From me to you — just a little gift to say thank you.'

'What for?'

'For helping me more than you could ever know.'

All thoughts of Angus disappeared from her mind and she let Jonty slide his arms inside her cashmere and start stroking her back as she arched herself into him and then together onto her little single bed.

Jonty had done his usual moonlight flit from her bed after they'd made love last night and she couldn't blame him, the rickety single beds were designed for more chaste night-time activities, like sleeping or reading French philosophy (she really should read that Barthes tract rather than just threatening intruders with it). It was now morning and Jenna was wide awake and had slipped into the shared bathroom, only slightly horrified to find that it had been bombed by someone in the night. The shelf above the basin, once home to just her washbag and Jonty's razor and shaving soap was now strewn with face creams, toners, cheek highlighters and exfoliating rubs. The bath that had been almost monkishly austere with just one bar of Imperial Leather on the side was now home to no fewer than four different hair conditioners and a rainbow of different bath puffs and body washes. As Jenna ran her own bath — a little luxury as a reward for getting up so early — steam filled the room. Fetching her own shampoo and conditioner from her washbag she noticed that the bathroom mirror had steamed up, but it revealed a message that had obviously been drawn onto it by the last steamy inhabitant. An 'I' then a heart, then a 'J'. I heart J. *I love Jenna*. . . Jonty. . . he must have been up early again and already shaved. She checked his razor blade and it was indeed wet. Jenna smiled at the mirror. He really couldn't make her feel any more special — and although some girls would find the whole lavish gifts and sweet messages a bit full-on, she relished it. Jenna had never really had much luck with guys — her massive unrequited crush on Max had lasted from university right into her late twenties and then Angus had come into her life, and although he had filled it up, he had also then broken her heart, so to suddenly be living the stuff of fantasy romance – well, it was too good and it *was* true and she loved it. If only she could shake the worry that she would, in a matter of hours, be seeing Angus – the man up until a few weeks ago she thought she would be with for the rest of her life.

Smoothing the nourishing cream into her tanned legs Izzy thought back to what her father had said to her just before she left. He was still bitterly disappointed that she didn't want to go to his old university and then follow in his footsteps into banking. 'Don't waste this opportunity, Isabella.' He'd wagged his finger at her. 'I know banking's not for you, but you have to prove to yourself and your mother and I that you can make this "portfolio" career thing of yours work. Network, network, network.'

And she did intend to do just that and prove to her darling daddy, who she really didn't like letting down, that no one needed a useless degree these days and she could indeed create a very lucrative career out of catering for the rich and famous. And if that didn't work out, then this morning's frolics in the bath tub with Jonty had pretty much secured her back-up plan of marrying someone rich and classy. Izzy hearts Jonty. . . he'd laughed when she'd written that in the steamed-up bathroom mirror before blowing more soap suds across the room at her.

'Darling!' A couple of hours later, Sals rushed down the corridor and caught Jenna by surprise as she was gluing some Swarovski crystals to the table plan that Izzy had written up the day before.

'Sals!' The two old friends hugged each other before Jenna then tried to extricate her sticky fingers from her friend's hair.

'All gone a bit Blue Peter in here, has it?' Sally giggled at the amount of craft paper and glue and sparkly bits that Jenna seemed to be juggling on her desk.

'Sals, you won't believe some of the things she's asked for. . .' Jenna pointed out the sparkling table plan and then held up signs for the loos which read *Phantoms of the Poopera*. 'Okay, so that was my own touch. To be honest though, she's done most of the ordering herself, it's just these last-minute things and all the deliveries. It's been mad!'

Sally was listening but the glittering table plan had caught her eye. 'Oooh, so who's coming? Anyone we know? Anyone we *should* know?'

'You mean among the models, marchionesses and media fiends? Well, there's the Blake-Howards, do you remember Monty from university? And I think Bertie debbed with the Honourable Emma. Plus there's models Carly, Cara and Cate; there's a table of "influencers", whoever they may be, over there,' Jenna pointed up into the top corner of the table plan but was interrupted by Sally pointing down to the bottom left.

'And Angus. . . sweetie, how do you feel about seeing him again?'

'Oh, Sals, I just don't know. One minute I'm swooning around thinking about mine and Jonty's future, and the next minute I just remember how incredibly in love I was, or at least thought I was, with Angus and how completely and utterly terrified I am of seeing him again. But once I've seen him, well, I'm sure it'll be fine after that and I'll be so occupied running the party I'm sure I can ignore him, you know, without being rude.'

Sally nodded and thought for a little bit. 'So are you and Jonty a bona fide item now?'

'Well, we haven't had The Chat, and I don't think he's on Facebook so we can't go official on there. . . but

Sals, last night he gave me the most amazing dress. And Jimmy Choos!'

'He what?' Sally was stunned and demanded to see this fairy-tale ensemble as soon as possible. 'He sounds like a keeper, sweetie. I'm so truly sorry that it hasn't worked out with Gus, it just seems so bizarre that it didn't, but I'm so happy for you that you've fallen very much on your new designer-clad feet, darling. I do miss you in London, though!'

'Don't worry, I'll be back soon. Jonty is needed for the autumn tastings back at Carstairs & Co and our little summer secondment out here in paradise will be over soon enough. I'm not sure how I'll cope with real work again!' Jenna waved a glittery glue stick in the air, and after Sally had recovered from another giggle fit she went with her to find Hugo and see them up to their room. Other guests were arriving and Madame Lefort was armed with a clipboard and smile and was describing each room to the guests so they could find it.

'Aha, let me see, ah, *oui*, Madame et Monsieur Hugo Portman, you are in the Artois bedroom, it is up the stairs, second door *a la droit*, I mean on the right, next to the painting of the pregnant Madonna with the, well with the ample pomegranates.'

Sally giggled again and took Hugo's hand as they made their way up the stone staircase to find their room. A buzz in Jenna's pocket just a few minutes later was a text from Sally: 'Chanel in the bathroom!!! Hope you nicked some?' Jenna sent a winky face back and then helped Madame Lefort as she greeted more overnight guests, some arriving in the smartest of limousines, others dusting themselves off from old Land Rovers that seemed to have limped their way down through rural France all the way from the Cotswolds.

46

There was no mistaking Bertie's arrival. A buzz filled the air as the helicopter's blades cut through it. The trees shook and the drive once more gave up its dust in huge billowing clouds as the chopper slowly lowered itself down to the small patch of grass the other side of the drive, just before the vines started. Once down, the helicopter's blades gradually came to a halt and Jenna, who like several other guests and staff had gathered on the chateau's steps to watch the spectacle, witnessed Bertie making her entrance. First the co-pilot got out and slid open the side door of the luxurious machine, revealing cream leather and walnut trimmings. . . and its occupants; Bertie was the first to descend, shielding her face from the dust and whipped up air of the still rotating blades, but gradually standing upright. There were one or two audible gasps. Her hair was magnificent, a mane of golden highlights that seemed to defy gravity and bounce around her shoulders and down her back. Her face was obscured by a massive pair of aviator sunglasses that matched the military-style leather jacket she was wearing over a tight black top and black skinny jeans. She was managing to saunter across the lawn in heels so vertiginous that Jenna winced as she watched. *She* had fallen into a luggage carousel while wearing flats. . . think what travelling in those babies would do to her? Jenna, however, was the first to admit that her style of travelling (economy class, last-minute dash to the airport, coins scraped together for a shuttle bus) was very different to Bertie's. Following Bertie out of the chopper was Max. Jenna's heart — as if it needed any more beats being skipped at the moment, did just that when she saw him, although she thought it was mostly now out of habit rather than any latent desire for her old friend. In fact, he'd been even nicer to her since the whole ski trip travesty when he'd got together with Bertie; genuinely listening to her and enjoying her company on their occasional nights out. Jenna fretted over what he might think about the whole Angus thing, he was, after all, his best mate, but she was keen to chat to him about it too. He might have an inkling over what was going on in his old friend's mind.

'A welcome committee! How adorbs! Thank you, Jenna, such a sweet touch.' Bertie obviously had no clue that the 'committee' was merely a few gawping caterers and Jenna, Madame Lefort and her clipboard and by this time Jonty and Philippe too.

'Yes of course, you are after all the woman of the hour.' Jenna reached out her arms to her old university friend, in welcome, of course, but also as a subconscious support to seeing anyone walking in such shoes.

'Hour?' She pronounced it with just the one syllable. 'Woman of the *day*, of the *night*, of the *year*, I should hope, dolls!' she laughed and climbed the stairs kissing Philippe and Jonty before entering the chateau. Max came up the steps behind her and wrapped Jenna in a large bear hug before launching a raspberry on her neck.

'Ew.'

'All right, Jenksie?' The familiarity of Max's greeting and her old nickname flooded her with emotion — how long did it feel since she'd last seen him, and all her old friends, before these last few weeks of upheaval and change?

'Hello, Maximilian,' she teased him. 'How was your flight?'

'Which one? Honestly, it's been crazy.' Jenna laughed as he rolled his eyes at his own girlfriend's retreating back. 'We took a chopper from Battersea to somewhere in Surrey where a private jet flew us to some obscure Bordeaux airport and then another heli from there to here. I feel like I'm in the special forces or something.'

'Don't even try to make me feel sorry for you.' Jenna laughed and then realised that Jonty was still standing next to her. Her two different worlds suddenly very much colliding. 'Max, do you remember Jonty from the Carstairs tasting?' The two men shook hands and Max thanked him — and Jenna profusely — for all their help organising Bertie's party.

'Honestly, she's been a nightmare. It's been the only thing we've talked about on every night out and night in since Hugo's bloody wedding!'

'Don't worry, mate.' Jonty seemed to bond with Max instantly. 'It'll be brilliant. Your friend Jenna here has made sure of that.'

'Thanks, Jenks, you really are a star.'

Madame Lefort was being as nice as she could bring herself to be to Bertie — especially as the older woman partly blamed Bertie for Philippe's summer stresses — and was telling her where their room was. She and Max were in the grand bridal suite that Sally and Hugo had had last time.

'It is at the very end of the passage, ah *je pense* alongside it is a painting of Venus covering her modesty with some grapes while cupid fires some, how do you say, *flèche*, um, arrows over the door.'

Bertie looked at her blankly and just said, 'I'm sure some little man will show us, yes?'

'*Oui, bien sûr. . .* Coco!' Madame Lefort hollered down the corridor as Bertie winced, but her expression changed as she caught sight of some of her London friends coming down the stairs.

'Ems! Monty! Amazing! Mwah, mwah. . .' and so the guests kept arriving and more air kisses were given out than at the Oscars and Jenna found herself running backwards and forwards checking on things between welcoming guests and sorting out the caterers — with Izzy's and Menou's help now he had finally returned from his mini-sabbatical — and finally she came to a natural pause (having moved the doves into position for later and met the pyrotechnic specialist in the gardens) amid the chaos.

47

Jenna's pocket buzzed with a message from Bertie, sent out to all the party guests by the looks of it:

Party Countdown!!!! FIVE hours and counting till we get the part-tay started. Commence personal preps now, people. xoxox

God, thought Jenna, who wouldn't dream of spending five hours getting ready for her own wedding, let alone a party. But it did remind her that she'd promised herself a little Jenna-time today — call it burn-out prevention — and she decided now was as good a time as any to retreat to her little garret room and gird her loins for whatever the rest of the day and evening threw at her. Most of the house guests must be here now, she assumed. She hadn't seen Angus yet, although admittedly she had been occupying herself at the far reaches of the estate in order to avoid him.

She crept up the stairs and just before she pushed the hidden door that opened up to the staff quarters an urge took over her. Just one more glance at the beautiful room that had been hers — theirs — as long as no one was in it. She trod softly along the corridor, careful to stay on the central carpet runner so as not to creak any floorboards as she went. The whole end of the corridor was quiet, the other bedroom suite doors closed, their residents perhaps catching a quick disco nap before the party began. She moved closer to the door of her — and Angus's — old room. Would Madame Lefort have put him back in there again? Oh, the irony! She peered in through the crack. Not a sound, so she pushed the door open a little further and again didn't see much sign of occupation. On a whim she walked into the room and looked at herself in the full-length mirror that had taken up one of the doors of the antique armoire. It was the first time she'd seen herself properly in weeks and she was happily surprised at how she seemed to have lost some weight — quite a feat with all this wine and food around — and her hair looked longer and blonder, scruffier perhaps, but then she had been overdue a trip to the hairdresser by several months even before she came out to France. She was tanned too, not just around her face and neck, but her arms and legs as well (hurrah for the walled garden nudey sessions!). She'd put on a semi-smart but reasonably practical outfit today of a sleeveless floaty top and skinny jeans — nothing compared to Bertie's glamorous attire but still. . .

'Jenna.' The familiar voice behind her made her go rigid. She turned away from the mirror and saw Angus framed by the bathroom doorway, a cloud of steam behind him, giving the impression of a celestial entity, or something from the classical myths, his white towel slung low around his hips, the muscles of his abdomen clenched into a six pack. She stared at him, his face lightly tanned but for the white scar that jagged its line from his mouth almost to his left ear.

'Angus, I. . . I. . .' she was stuck like a rabbit in extremely sexy headlights. Still rigid with shock she could do nothing but stare at him — in all his semi-naked glory — until her legs suddenly began to give way and she fled from the room. Hearing his shouts behind her, like a child she covered her ears and made a dash for the servants' staircase and the sanctum of her own little room. Flinging herself into it and pushing her back against the door she let out a long breath. And then a sob. And then another until she was crying with such force it was like nothing had changed since the first moment he'd left her in her little flat in London. The sadness was as raw now, perhaps even more so, as she caught sight, around her room, of the gifts Jonty had given her — the dress and shoes, a little flower picked from beside the vines, an interesting stone they found outside the winery — each gift acting like a little sticking plaster over the wound in her heart caused by Angus leaving her.

She tried to rein in her sobs but they got caught in her throat and only made her blubber more. She heaved herself away from the door and fell onto her bed. Her only hope at this very minute was that no one else on this floor was around — surely all too busy party prepping — so she could weep all she needed to let it all out.

As she calmed down a bit she started to analyse how she felt. Was she still angry at him? A little. Did she feel as indifferent towards him as Jane Bennet had taught her to be? No, not really. Seeing him there looking so damn sexy was killing her. All she'd wanted to do was touch him and hold him and kiss him and pretend that everything was normal and it was the day after Sally's wedding and could they please just go back to that day?

But then she glanced at the Jimmy Choos that poked out from under the hem of the hanging dress. She remembered how free and fun things had been with Jonty over the last few weeks. He'd patiently waited for her, he'd rescued her from sleazy guys, he'd given her gifts of such beautiful things. . . Jenna sniffed a bit and wiped her face with a tissue. Building Jonty back up in her head was becoming easier and yes Jane Bennet, I can now face Angus as 'a common and indifferent acquaintance', especially if the next time I see him I'm wearing that gorgeous dress. She got up and left her room and went into the bathroom to wash her face, trying very hard to ignore the fact that Jane Bennet never really did master that indifferent thing and became Jane Bingley before very long.

48

Jenna braced herself to go back downstairs. Luckily, she encountered no ex-boyfriends or lovers on the way. Letting herself into the busy kitchen she caught up with Izzy, who rather annoyingly impressively seemed to have everything under control. Canapés were being prepped and the non-residential guests were due in four hours. Izzy had a way of making Jenna feel inferior at the best of times, but she was at her patronising best when she looked at Jenna, and her red-rimmed eyes, and just said: 'Seriously, you may want some time to yourself before everyone gets here.'

Fat lot of good the 'me time' was when I last tried, thought Jenna testily to herself, but thanked the younger woman for her advice and decided to leave her to it in the hot kitchen. As she was leaving, she bumped into Jonty in the corridor who gave her a quick kiss on the cheek.

'Very chaste,' she whispered at him.

'Better be on best behaviour from now on.' He winked at her. 'But I can't wait to see you looking so sexy later in that dress.'

Jonty's adoration was like a talisman that kept her from falling into the abyss of despair that seeing Angus again had brought on and she squeezed his arm in thanks and left him to go and check up on the kitchen staff for himself while she headed back into the office and busied herself with collecting up all the signs and the table plan she'd made. Heading back out into the sunshine she passed the fountain on the terrace, now happily tinkling champagne from its many orifices. She wasn't sure if Coco, who had been jealously guarding it from the approaches of other thirsty workers, hadn't had one too many tries from the nymph's nipple himself, but she left him to it as it was hot work making sure the ice that was needed to cool the tank of fizz was constantly topped up.

In the orangery the fairy lights were definitely Harrods-ing up the place and every architectural detail was picked out with tiny LEDs. The tables were laid with starched white cloths, each laced with silver thread and the hot model waiters were polishing the crystal glasses and dishing out the table favours, one for each place. Jenna pitched the table plan on a large easel and then wandered over to where she was sitting. She'd designed the plan, so knew she was next to Hugo on one side and a film producer on the other. Angus had been put on a table with Bertie and Max themselves, a hangover from the original plan when Bertie had insisted 'darling Diane' be honoured by such a seating arrangement. Now at least it meant that Max had one true old friend near him on the night. Jenna picked up the little red and gold box that was on her place setting. Cartier. She creaked the stiff lid open and saw the little charm — a heart with a tiny red ruby set in it. Jenna hadn't been responsible for ordering these; she couldn't as she'd had nowhere near the budget for it or the ability to sign off on such an amount, and what with everything else going on, she'd forgotten all about the favours. Bertie must have brought them all herself from London. Jenna was almost overcome by Bertie's generosity. She knew it wasn't personal, but she also knew she would treasure that little golden heart as a symbol of how she could overcome any heartbreak. *Couldn't she?*

Bertie admired the cherub-strewn ceiling as she lay naked in the gold rococo bed in the Louis XIV suite. Max was demonstrating quite how much he loved her as he slowly and carefully brought her to an astonishing climax, each deft little lick of his tongue sending an electric pulse through her perfectly toned and tanned body. She'd been preparing for weeks for this party — not the boring sort of prep, no, sweet little Jenna had really proved quite useful doing that — but she had been back to celebrity trainer Tracy Anderson who had helped her sculpt her already bloody amazing figure into a svelte, honed, glowing example of womanhood. Flashes of almost excruciating pleasure punctuated her thoughts as she reached down and stroked Max's dark, thick hair as his head bobbed between her legs. Turning thirty wasn't so bad after all.

'Thank you, darling,' she purred at Max as he came up and joined her, resting his head on the pillow next to her.

'One of many little birthday treats, darling.'

Bertie kissed him as he lay back, panting slightly and slowly moved her own mouth, kiss by kiss, down his torso, until she found his very erect cock waiting for her. Rather than go down on him, she instead raised her body over his and lowered herself onto him, and rhythmically brought them both to a fabulous climax.

'Fuck, that was amazing.' Max pulled his girlfriend down on top of him as they both caught their breath.

'A little Bertie benefit for you, darling.'

And a beauty one for me, she thought as she peeled herself off him and dropped her legs over the side of the bed. Pulling on her silk dressing gown she swept into the wonderful en-suite bathroom and peered intently at her complexion in the mirror. Her therapist had been right — sex did give you a fantastic glow. As she stepped into the pre-drawn bath, filled with bath oil in her signature scent she decided that Max never needed to know that she'd only instigated their little lovemaking to achieve the perfect pre-party facial.

49

The chateau had been transformed, not just by the glittering lights that fought against the mellow light of the evening sun, but by the super-glamorous people who now decorated the terrace in their sparkling dresses and eye-catching masks. Flashes from cameras went off and the sunlight caught on sequins and glitter so that the terrace rippled like the sea at sunset, reflecting glorious colours back into the sky.

Jenna looked down at them all from her window as she fixed a rather modest pair of pearl earrings into her ears. She had only started to get ready as the first guests had arrived — before that she was careering around the estate checking that everyone and everything was in position for the important events of the evening. The vineyard worker who was more used to de-stemming grapes was now, she hoped, a mini mastermind in bird care and ready to launch the doves into the air at the appropriate signal. Izzy in the kitchen had maintained a moderate degree of level-headedness as the canapé mini soufflés had all collapsed and had to be made again. Jenna had been begrudgingly impressed at the calmness of the young chef, and more so at Menou's seemingly limitless patience. The calmness and patience, however, had come at the cost of the language, and anyone listening at the kitchen door could be mistaken for thinking the poor guests were about to be served 'cockwombles' and 'fuckpuffins' alongside their caviar blinis and smoked salmon roulade.

Jenna had finally escaped up the stone staircase as Bertie — resplendent in a silver fishtail-style gown with a mask of such splendour that its feathers almost touched the chandelier above her — had started the official greeting line. Madame Lefort, herself in a beautiful green velvet gown, accepted the invitations, without which you would most certainly not get in — although Bertie had waved her own forgetful parents through.

'Mummy, you are the limit,' she'd chastised her mother while air kissing her and accepting a hug from her father, dapper in a purple dinner jacket and rather loud bow tie. 'Daddy you look divine.' Bertie straightened her father's tie while her mother kissed Max hello.

'Just had it dry-cleaned after old Bunty Moorhead spilled his champers over me at Glyndebourne — couldn't come here with it tatty from Taittinger for you, darling girl.'

'Oh, Daddy,' Bertie sighed as her father pumped Max's hand before moving out through to the terrace to join the throng of Bertie's friends.

Jenna, now dressed and trying to do her make-up in a hurry, looked out of her bedroom window and saw that the fountain was in fact a huge success with guests milling around it refilling their glasses with the champagne that tinkled out from nymphs and cherubs. The huge inflatable elephant, far from seeming incongruous, was the most amazing selfie foil, and pouting girls posed next to the gentle-looking creature before Instagram-ing the hell out of the photos — #bertiesbirthdaybash. The previously not-so-gentle creatures — Jenna had renamed them the Attacka Alpacas — were somehow now as docile as beachfront donkeys and were happily being led along the lower terrace by 'stressed out' execs and partygoers who felt aligned with their spirit animals or whatever bollocks Bertie had told them to believe. The 'cute' outfits that Bertie had insisted on were made up from mini top hats and waistcoat-style rugs emblazoned with a sparkly, sequinned 'B' on each side. Jenna thought it all looked so fantastical she snapped a few pics before slipping her phone into a little evening bag she'd borrowed off Madame Lefort, and then stepped into her heels. One last look in her rust-spotted over-basin mirror to check her make-up and she headed downstairs, wishing she could risk a look in the full-length mirror in Angus's room one more time. She was saved by Sally, who had also been running late, and when she bumped into Jenna on the landing she whisked her into her room.

'Jenna, thank God, love. I need your help with this pesky zip. Hugo's gone downstairs already, the arse, and left me here with this impossible thing.' She tugged behind her back as if to make a point. Jenna twirled her friend round and with a couple of stiff little pulls the zip was done up.

'Ta da!' Jenna looked over her friend's shoulder and into the full-length mirror. Sally looked lovely, a vision in peacock blue silk. The dress was floor-length and the blue silk was shot through with petrol-green and teal, depending on how the light shone on it. Edging both the very bottom of the maxi skirt and the top of the bodice was an intricate gold brocade that echoed the simple, yet stylish gold necklace and earrings that Sally was wearing. 'You look glorious, Sals. I love that dress!'

'Oh, thank you, sweetie. I had it made while we were on honeymoon — and thank God I did otherwise I'd have nothing to wear to this shindig! Couldn't let Hugo have all the tailoring fun in Honkers! But. . .' she stepped aside and let Jenna look in the mirror, 'you, darling, you are looking absolutely frigging fabulous.'

Jenna smiled at her friend. Even she had to admit that she had scrubbed up rather well. The dusky pink chiffon fell in folds around her sparkly toed shoes and the daringly low-cut top of the dress was kept in place with the help of a few safety pins she'd luckily found in her washbag. With her boobs now not about to make their own dramatic entrance, she felt a little more secure in the dress and admired herself in the mirror. 'Like Cinderella,' she murmured.

'And you shall go to the ball.' Sally put her arm around her and rested her head on her shoulder.

'But which Prince Charming will I leave with? That's the question.'

'Well, darling, for heaven's sake don't go losing *those* shoes as the clock strikes twelve!'

Jenna laughed. 'For once in my life I do feel more princess than pumpkin. Come on, let's go and join this party and see how the other half live.'

They headed downstairs together and before long, glasses of freshly fountained champagne were in their hands and the sea of decadent masks had swallowed them into its glittering midst.

50

'Excuse me, sorry, excuse me. . .' Jenna pushed her way through the partygoers on the terrace. She needed to check that the alpaca handler knew that the fireworks were due at midnight and she couldn't remember if she'd told him or not. A pair of frightened stampeding South American spitters would be the last thing Bertie would want, and although Jenna felt like she owed Bertie no favours, she couldn't do it to the poor animals. 'Oops, just squeezing past, sorry, oops. . .' she accidentally nudged the elbow of a man standing just at the top of the steps that led down to the lower terrace. His champagne flew out of his glass and splashed onto the stone balustrade of the terrace. 'Oh I'm so terribly sorry!'

'Jenna?'

She looked up and realised that the masked gentleman was Angus. With his face — and its tell-tale scar — disguised by a plain white theatrical mask she hadn't noticed him, but of course his height should have been a giveaway. Even among the wealthy and exceptionally high- (as well as well-) heeled here tonight, Angus was a good few inches taller than most, but since she'd last been with him he'd bulked up slightly, so that his lean frame was now padded out with extra muscle. Extra muscle she hadn't failed to notice when he'd come upon her in his bedroom earlier. In fact, his dinner jacket was slightly tight and he pulled at his cuffs as they both stammered a greeting.

'Jenna, please don't run off this time, we need to talk.'

'I'm so sorry I broke into your room.' She let the apology flow out, knowing full well that it was by far the easiest of the things she wanted to say to him.

'That doesn't matter.' Angus slid his mask up onto his sandy-coloured hair and Jenna looked up into his piercing blue eyes. He was looking at her so intently, and with such focus, that she blushed under her own mask. Her heartbeat raced as Angus gently put his hands each side of her face and pulled the mask away. 'It's so nice to see you, JJ. I. . .'

But Jenna interrupted him, 'I have to go, the alpacas need me.' She turned to continue her way down the steps but Angus reached out and held her arm.

'Jenna. . .'

'Angus, let go of me!' She wriggled her arm free but the action unsettled her and she teetered dangerously in her heels, completely losing her balance. *Oh God*, she thought, as time slowed and she saw the unforgiving stone steps ready to take their first victim of the night. At once, Angus's arms were around her and she was suddenly crushed against his chest, safe from the steps, but with thoughts hurtling so fast through her head she wasn't sure if she had been saved or captured.

'Jenna, I need to talk to you.'

'Angus.' She had pulled back from his chest now but had let him steady her against the stone balustrade. She had tried desperately not to inhale his familiar scent, but being pressed so close into him it had been impossible and the aroma filled her with memories of them lying together, dancing together, making love to each other. 'Let me go, Angus.' The fight had gone out of her voice. 'You did it before without looking back, so you can do it now, I'm sure.'

'I never wanted to let you go.' His words shot through her heart like a poison-tipped arrow. The initial pain was instant but the lingering effects took a while to seep through before crippling her in front of him.

'But you did.' She almost whispered her answer and it took all her strength not to crumple into the stone.

'I was so confused that night. You were angry at everything I said—'

A new fire burned through Jenna. 'Don't turn this on me. You were the one who said things were never permanent between us and walked out on our home together.' She started jabbing her finger to his chest. 'It was you who never apologised, or phoned me and. . .' she paused to take a breath before issuing the final attack in her arsenal, 'it was you that skipped the country without a by your leave.'

'Hey, hang on a minute. Look where you've been working for the last few weeks. Not exactly Bognor Regis, is it?' Jenna looked up at him as he fought his corner. 'And I did try and call. You never told me you were heading off here, or working with that Palmer-Johnston guy. I wouldn't trust him as far as I could throw him.'

At the mention of Jonty's name, and said with such loathing and derision by her ex-boyfriend, Jenna really got angry. 'Don't you dare bring Jonty into this. He has been nothing but kind and generous to me. He gave me my dignity back when I needed it most. Not to mention a bloody good time recently!' She knew, deep down, that those last few words would be like the sting of a whip to Angus.

'Jenna, have you and he. . .' Angus looked crushed and Jenna noticed his shoulders sag slightly.

'I don't think it's any of your business now.' She'd lost some of the anger that had fuelled the last few moments of their fight.

'Please tell me that you're not involved with him,' Angus pleaded with her, his eyes imploring her to give him the answer he needed to hear. He reached out for her but stopped just shy of touching her, his hands hovering just inches from her arms before he dropped them again.

'I. . . I can't. . .' Jenna looked down, not being able to bear the hurt in Angus's face as she delivered the words.

'He's been very nice to me. I'm sorry.' She slipped away from him and down the stairs, lowering her mask so that the other party goers couldn't see the tears springing up in her eyes. If she'd looked back she would have seen the blue eyes she loved so much start to water, too, as he stood, still and silent, framed by revellers on each side of the terrace's stone steps.

'Don't forget to get the elephant in the background,' Bertie snapped at the photographer as she posed on the terrace with Max. 'And that doesn't mean you, Sally, shoo!' she added as a very put-out Sally side-stepped her way out of the lens and accidentally into a semi-naked male model carrying a tray of canapés.

'Oops, but oh hell, yes please,' she said to the handsome model as she helped herself to not one but three of the delicious little nibbles. 'If her Royal Bitchy Bertiness says I'm an elephant I might as well eat like one!'

'Steady on, Mrs P,' a familiar voice said behind her. 'Leave some for the rest of the herd.'

Sally spun round and was about to clout Hugo when she realised it was actually Max, his voice distorted through the ludicrous black velveteen mask Bertie had made him wear. He'd been let off from photo duty but was on his way to round up Carly, Cara and Cate, Bertie's friendly supermodels, so she could pose with them in the fountain. 'Wish me luck,' he whispered to Sally who was still chewing the last of the little blinis that she'd swiped, 'I can barely tell them apart in real life, let alone when they're masked.'

'Oh, get off with you, Maximilian,' Sally chided and swiped him on the bum with her evening bag. 'You love it and don't pretend otherwise.'

Just as he was leaving Sally felt a hand on her bum that then gave her a playful little squeeze.

'Hello, pickle,' she said lovingly, turning round to see that to her horror once again it still wasn't her husband who had just caressed her bum, but Monty Blake-Howard, who had now taken off Hugo's mask, which the real Hugo thought was absolutely hilarious.

'Mr P!' Sally steamed at him, spotting him over by the fountain. She gave Monty B-H, who was still creased over with laughing, a good biff and carried on. 'Mind you keep that safe distance you, you. . .' but the real Hugo had dashed forward and picked up his frustrated wife and twirled her around, plonking her down next to one of the better endowed of the little champagne-tinkling cherubs.

'Hello, pickle.' He winked at her through his mask and she pulled it off his face to play-fight with him properly.

'Oh, Hugo Portman, I really don't know what to do with you sometimes!'

'Just don't do anything to my pickle!'

Sally let out an exasperated sigh and held out her glass for a refill.

'And don't get any ideas,' she wagged her finger at Hugo, 'I do not expect any naked penises to be *de rigueur* in our house when we get back, fizz-flowing ones or not!'

'It would be the talk of Putney.'

'Penisney, more like,' she collapsed into giggles as Hugo took his turn to shake his head in wonder at the workings of his wife's mind.

'Guys!' Bertie's tone was unmistakable. 'Move, scram — you're in the way again!'

'Oops.' Hugo led Sally by the hand away from the fountain and let Bertie dominate their vacated spot, posing in a variety of ways with some very leggy blondes.

Jonty wasn't having half so much fun. He had kept a wary eye open all evening for Whitey, knowing that he was very much still around. At least when Bertie's party had been scheduled for the autumn the harvest might have been over and Jonty's nemesis — yes, that was the word for him — would have been gone, cap in hand, to the next manual labouring job. But here now, at the chateau, his two worlds could quite easily collide and if they did. . ..

Jonty had bumped into Jenna just moments earlier. She'd seemed in a bit of a hurry so he'd let her go and check on the alpacas or whatever it was she'd said, saving him the job and he used this spare few minutes this gave him to survey the kaleidoscope of colourful masks, picking each one off in his mind and eliminating any of them from being Whitey. . . until, there — damn, is that him? Jonty made his way through the crowd, skirting around chattering groups and smooching couples to get to where he thought he'd seen a bald head standing alone by the dining room French windows. Damn. No one. Jonty kept his guard up though. Everything hinged on him never being found out, and if Whitey went back on his promise and exposed Jonty tonight he'd be. . . well it didn't bear thinking about.

51

Clink clink. The knife hit clear as a bell against the crystal glass. The guests chattered on around the tables eagerly opening the Cartier boxes and hanging their masks on the backs of their chairs.

'Ahem!' Clink clink.

The chattering was overcome by shhh-ing and gradually the whole orangery was silent. A room that had housed fifty or so guests for Sally and Hugo's wedding was now filled with over a hundred, all sitting around the perfectly laid round tables that Jenna had supervised the male model waiters prepping earlier. The tables were packed in together and Jenna was squeezed in next to Hugo in the far corner. Still, she heard every word of what was to come.

'Thank you all for coming here tonight,' Bertie started, welcoming her guests and then carrying on with various thank yous, especially to Philippe and her darling parents and to the 'team' of helpers, which Jenna took to mean her. She'd never much thought about what thanks she might get on the night, but now she had been completely overlooked it slightly smarted. Jonty looked at her over the table and mouthed a 'thank you' to her and she smiled back and shook the red leather jewellery box at him — she couldn't really be put-out while she had such a stunning party favour to take home with her, even if every other female guest had one, too.

Jenna, however much as she tried to listen to Bertie, was still addled from her run-in with Angus and chewed their encounter over in her mind. 'I never meant to let you go. . .' What did that mean? She'd escaped down the steps from him and had run straight into Jonty who was also on his way to double check that the alpacas would be safely away before the fireworks were due. His thoughtfulness made her almost despise Angus and his insistence that Jonty was untrustworthy. It tickled her slightly, as she peered between the well-coiffed heads towards the top table, that Angus's reaction towards Jonty must stem from some sort of jealousy. *Well good*, she thought, *be jealous*.

Bertie prattled on and then introduced her father who said a few words about how he and his wife were very proud of Bertie and all she had achieved. 'Her Instagram followers, whatever they may be, have reached the one million mark, which I'm told is better than average,' he winked at his daughter, 'but I still remember thirty years ago when she arrived into this world and her mother and I became the first two followers of this extraordinary girl — super-fans, you could say.' The guests rippled a collective 'awww' at the lovely speech and Jenna was left wondering what Mr Mason-Hoare would have left to say if he was ever a father of the bride.

'Before I let you all carry on with your feasting and revelry, let me pass you over to the other important man in my Roberta's life, Max Finch.'

Robert Mason-Hoare sat down and passed the microphone over to Max.

'Thank you, Robert, and don't look so surprised, Bertie.' Bertie was indeed looking quite surprised. This had not been scheduled in her party plan. She looked quizzically up at him as he continued. 'In fact, Robert and I had a little chat the other day, Bertie, and we came to the same conclusion. That you are one hell of a woman. We're already such a fantastic team. We've just had an offer accepted on our first house together and I'm truly excited to be having absolutely nothing to do with designing the interior.' Again, a ripple of laughter spread through the guests. Jenna, who had tuned out of Bertie's speech was now giving Max her full attention. He carried on. 'So I hope you forgive me for springing this on you, but here, in front of your family, our friends and in this beautiful setting, I want to ask you, Roberta Mason-Hoare,' at this point Max got down on one knee next to her, 'will you do me the utmost honour of agreeing to be my wife?'

Silence.

'Yes, oh Maxie, yes!'

The room was on its feet in a heartbeat, the romance of the shock proposal eliciting whoops and whistles and a thunder of clapping hands and stamping feet. Jenna watched through the crowd as Max gave a triumphant fist punch in the air and then produced from another, if slightly larger, red Cartier box a ring with a diamond the size of a pebble in it and placed it on Bertie's finger.

Jenna felt a little numb. The conversation now around her table was of nothing but The Wedding To Come and bets were laid on the style and type of do Bertie would go for and whether Max would have any say in it. Jenna nodded and smiled at the rest of the table and did manage to have a semi-serious chat to Hugo about the pros and cons of a Monaco wedding (pro, how much he could win in the casino; con, how much he could lose in the casino) and she ate a few mouthfuls of Izzy's really quite delicious food. But she'd lost her appetite really and spent the last few minutes of the meal pushing some whipped cream around her plate, hoping no one had noticed that Hugo had snaffled her meringue and strawberries.

'Not good for the old tum tum,' he'd winked at her as he 'helped her out' and then just said, 'yum yum' which raised a half-hearted smile from Jenna. Sally, misconstruing this as Jenna being upset over the engagement, nudged Hugo out of his chair and sat down next to her best friend.

'Darling, are you okay? Ever since The Announcement you've looked as glum as a Victorian urchin. You're not, after all this, still in love with *Max* are you?'

'Shh, keep your voice down!' Jenna was only far too well aware of how many gossipy bloggers and journalists there were here tonight, all of whom would show no loyalty to the birthday girl in releasing a hot story. 'And no, it's nothing to do with Max. Well, not him — but them.'

'And?'

'And. . . I just thought it might be me getting engaged soon, you know? And then this summer happened. . .'

'Oh cheer up, sweetie.' Sally nodded over to where Jonty had been sitting just a moment ago. 'Mr Wine-Me-Dine-Me-Sixty-Nine-Me might be showering you in diamonds next — his first few pressies have been rather spot on and rather *lurve*-ly you have to admit.'

Jenna was about to tell Sally all about her most recent fight with Angus when Hugo galumphed back to his seat with a coffee and a plate of petit fours and swept his wife up in conversation about the Z-list celeb he just accidentally bumped into.

'She was not amused when one of my truffles fell down the front of her dress.'

'Oh, Hugo, honestly!'

Sally reproached him as she popped one of the remaining chocolates in her mouth and then was rather glad she was rendered speechless when Hugo continued, 'at least I didn't try and retrieve it.'

The master of ceremonies — a nearly naked male model again, but this one had aspirations of being an actor — announced that the party would continue outside and as the guests left the orangery the doves, which had been moved into position during the meal, were released giving the assembled photographers their dream shot — a stunning power couple, a glamorous array of guests, a gorgeous setting and a birthday party turned engagement do. Among the flashes and smiles they didn't catch the girl in the dusky pink dress, clutching her shoes and skirts up in one hand and a refilled glass of champagne in the other, slinking off into the trees by herself.

52

Jenna hiccoughed and took another slug from the glass. She'd found herself back in the walled garden. There were a few shrieks of delight as other partygoers obviously had discovered the same privacy that she and Angus had once enjoyed, and there were rather more doves skitting around and pecking at the ground than usual. But it was almost dark now and candles lit the narrow pathways through the herb and vegetable gardens and alcoves were easy enough to be found. Jenna just needed some time on her own to work out her confused feelings.

So Max and Bertie were getting married. Let's process that one first, she told herself as she swigged back the champagne again. She had spent about ten years of her life in unrequited love with Max. . . still, he'd then gone off with Bertie and in turn Angus had swept her off her feet. Oh Angus. Real and very much requited love — but he left her with no word after just a few months together and that really, really hurt. She had been broken when they'd split and it had only just started to heal with the careful attention of Jonty; Jonty who had given her a job, had flirted with her and then been patient enough to wait for her to be ready to go any further, who had rescued her from a sexual predator and who had given her so many lovely presents right from the start. . . Jonty who. . . who she now saw entering the walled garden, the light from the chateau terrace filtering through the gated archway enough just to illuminate his features. Jenna sat upright and sucked her tummy in. A lovely little tête-a-tête with Jonty would set her right. To her growing horror, though, he wasn't alone and Jenna saw him lead another person through the gate. She gripped her champagne glass tighter and peered out of the alcove to see who he was with. Izzy. Jenna stifled another hiccough and cowered further back into the protective darkness of her hidey-hole as the pair crossed the walled garden in front of her. Hidden as she was they didn't see her, but lit by the hundreds of candles that she herself had put in place earlier in the day, Jenna saw Jonty twirl Izzy round as she squealed in flirty excitement until they hit the brick wall at the back of the garden, whereupon he pushed her up against it, in between the espalier fruit trees, and started kissing her. Jenna slammed her palm across her mouth to stop herself from yelling out. Her Jonty! And Izzy. She couldn't bear it, but she couldn't move either and she tried to close her eyes so as not to see the treachery in front of her. Forced to listen to Izzy's yelps of delight reverberate around the garden's walls, Jenna opened her eyes just in time to see Jonty thrust into the younger woman, her legs wrapped around him and his trousers around his ankles. The sight was both horrifying and comical — Jonty's naked bum illuminated by candles and moonlight, bobbing back and forth. Jenna closed her eyes again and waited for the squeals and groans to stop. But they didn't (God, the stamina of youth!) and Jenna couldn't bear it any more. Hoping they would be pretty much as preoccupied as two people could be, she decided to make a dash for it, but she couldn't get to the safety of being beyond the walled garden's gate without having to cross the candlelit garden. Trying to tip-toe as elegantly as possible along the gravel path, she held her breath until she made it. One last glance behind her showed her that her escape had been good, and Jonty's moonlit bum had been the only thing to see her leave.

*

Trying to keep the tears at bay, Jenna silently thanked Bertie one more time for choosing a masquerade ball as the theme and pulled her mask down over her face. She tripped and stumbled away from the walled garden and up towards the terrace where by a stroke of luck she saw Sally, who was uncharacteristically taking a massive, if surreptitious, puff of someone's fat cigar. She was leaning against the balustrade of the terrace and seemed to be flicking away her companion as much as the lingering cigar smoke. As Jenna climbed the steps the smell of it reminded her of that night with Spike — the night Jonty and she had first made love. Her chest started to heave and she reached Sally just in time to grab her arm and then almost explode in a snot-filled blub.

'Jenna, Jenna, God's teeth, sweetie, whatever is the matter?' Sally wrapped her arms around her friend and rubbed her back. 'Jenna, tell me, what's wrong?'

'Everything,' Jenna sobbed as she hung onto Sally and hugged her back so hard that Sally finally had to pull herself away.

'Come, sit down.' Sally led Jenna over to the edge of the champagne fountain, which was finally starting to run out of fizz. 'Now tell me, is it Angus?'

'Yes. . . and. . .' Sally had one arm around Jenna and was gently squeezing her. The warm affection was too much for Jenna who shoved her mask off her face and wiped her hand across her eyes, smearing what was left of her mascara and eyeliner across her temples.

'And what?'

'. . . And Jonty. I've just seen him fuck *fucking* Izzy in the *fucking* walled garden. I thought. . . stupid, stupid me. . . well, I thought he might love me.' Jenna dissolved into sobs again as Sally sat in slight shock.

'The total git.'

'I heart J. . .' Jenna mused out loud between blubs.

'Do you really, sweetie, oh dear, I did warn you. . .'

'No,' Jenna explained. 'I heart J — Izzy loves Jonty. Steamed up in the bathroom mirror — I thought *he* was writing it to *me*. Oh, how stupid of me!'

'Oh petal, how were you to know?'

'Why did he buy me all these beautiful things if he didn't like me?' Jenna blurted out.

'I should imagine he likes you very much, sweetie, and still does. It just seems that he's not one for keeping his dick in his pants. And you can do better than that.'

Jenna stifled a hiccough and then a yawn; crying always made her so tired. 'That's what you said last time. When I was crying over Max. And look what happened!'

'Tell me about Angus.' Sally wasn't quite ready to admit defeat on that one — she was still totally bemused that the couple she had nicknamed 'Jengus' (well, it was better than 'Anga') hadn't made the distance.

'He said he never wanted to let me go. But he just blamed it all on me. Said I had made no sense the night we broke up.'

'Had you?'

'Sally! Whose side are you on?'

'Yours of course, sweetie, but just playing devil's advocate here, I mean you did say that you were quite a bit tipsy that night. Chardonnay and coherency are not usual bedfellows. Perhaps Angus has a point?' Jenna hung her head and bit her lip. Sally placed her free hand over Jenna's in her lap and in the softest of voices said, 'In light of what's just happened with Jonty, well, is it worth hearing Gus out? He might just be able to explain himself.'

'Perhaps. I felt so confused when I saw him. Did I tell you I accidentally caught him unawares. . .'

Sally perked up, 'Ooh no? When?'

Jenna told her about Angus emerging like a near-naked god from the steamy bathroom. 'I felt weak at the knees just seeing him again and I had to go and have a good cry before convincing myself that life was okay, I had Jonty now. . . Oh God. . . first Angus, then Max getting *bloody* engaged and now this! I just don't think my life could get any worse.' Jenna burst into tears again and sobbed onto her friend's shoulder.

'Jenna Jenkins?' the voice was stern and sharp. Jenna looked up from Sally's tear-soaked shoulder.

'Yes, sorry. . . I mean, hello.' Flustered, Jenna wiped her eyes again and then realised that she was being addressed by some sort of policeman as a warrant card was flipped out of a wallet just in front of her.

'Miss Jenkins, I'm Senior Preventive Officer Malcolm Fisher from Her Majesty's Customs and Excise and I have authorisation from both the French and British police to place you under arrest for the illegal export of counterfeit wine into the UK from France, more specifically from this chateau and others in the surrounding area. You do not have to say anything, but it may harm your defence if you do not mention when questioned something which that you later rely on in court. Anything you do say may be given in evidence. Please come with me.'

'I. . . I. . .' Jenna stammered at the British officer who reached down and lifted her up under her armpit. Two sturdy — and worryingly quite heavily armed — gendarmes stood behind him, giving him even more authority and creating quite a threatening presence.

'Hang on a minute,' Sally's usual authoritive tone didn't seem to work on the Customs Officer who was now hauling Jenna to her wobbly, Jimmy Choo'd feet and putting a pair of handcuffs on her. One of the gendarmes stepped closer to Sally. 'Is that really necessary, officer?' Sally said.

Jenna was aware that the tableau they had created was drawing quite a crowd of onlookers. 'I'll come quietly,' she whispered, shocked out of her sobs.

'I'm afraid it's protocol to cuff the suspect in all arrests, madam,' Fisher replied.

'Bloody silly protocol if it means your victim can't bloody walk!' Sally was getting frantic now, looking around her to see if any of their friends were behind the masks that were looking on, grim and grotesque in the flickering light of the terrace's candles.

'Help me, Sals, I haven't done anything!' Jenna pleaded with her friend, who for once was completely out of her depth.

Fisher marched Jenna, her head hung in shame, in front of the staring crowd of wealthy partygoers, all of whom were whispering and pointing at her as she went towards the waiting police car parked alongside one or two others in the front drive. She saw its blue lights flashing — silently, thank God — as she and Fisher crossed through the hallway and down the stone steps. Jenna's mind raced — how could this be happening to her? *What* on earth had she done? The policeman — or customs officer or whatever — had mentioned wine, so it couldn't be Clive snitching on her about the Picassos — and even then, it was hardly her *fault* they were stolen, not in a 'red-handed, it's me guv' type way anyway.

She'd just resigned herself to years in jail for a crime she couldn't see how she could possibly have committed and was getting into the car, her head guided down by Fisher's hand, when there was a commotion from the hallway and Angus burst out of the chateau door. He ran so fast down the stone steps that he practically fell into the car with her, and in so doing managed to stop Fisher from closing the door. . . but also had two submachine guns pointed at him from the over-protective gendarmes.

'Whoa,' he steadied himself and put his hands up. 'Sorry, sorry — but please,' he addressed a less than impressed Fisher, 'you have to hear me out.'

'I do not have to do anything, *sir*,' he replied as he gestured for Angus to move out of the way — a gesture emphasised by the nozzles of the two guns. 'You, however have to stop obstructing the police and let us get this suspect back to the station for questioning.'

'But you have the wrong—'

'Sir! Please desist from your badgering and let me pass!' Fisher pushed Angus out of the way. Once he was in the front of the car, he buzzed down the window and leaned out. 'Look, anything you have to say, come down to the station tomorrow morning at nine.'

At that the window slid up and the police car left the chateau driveway. Jenna turned around in the back seat and could see Angus running after them, his face glowing red in the car's tail lights.

Angus was halfway down the drive, his hands resting on his knees and his head hung low as he caught his breath. He'd tried running after the police car and all he'd seen was Jenna's face, turned to look back at him through the barred rear windscreen of the car. He could barely make out her expression but he could guess at it. She needed his help, now more than ever, and if he could get her out of this mess, then maybe she'd believe him when he told her he missed her and loved her more than anything in the world.

'Gus!' Sally yelled at him from the front door of the chateau. Hugo held her arm — as much for his own balance as hers — and they met Angus at the bottom of the stone steps.

'Fuck,' Angus swore. 'This was not supposed to happen.'

'The old knight on a white charger thing not quite working out for you?' Hugo said.

'Oh, Hugo!' Sally rounded on him, and then looked back to Angus. 'I hope that wasn't some stunt that went horribly wrong? I mean. . . what did just happen? How did you know the police would be here?'

'I didn't!' Angus held his hands up. 'Honest to God. I just saw the lights and then saw Jenna being manhandled down the steps. But. . .'

'What?' Sally was fuming.

'But I did alert the authorities to a fraud going on.'

'You what?' Sally was less cross now, and more confused.

'What on earth?' Hugo chipped in too, although he'd had to seat himself on the steps as he really had indulged a little too much at the fountain of fizz. Angus squatted down next to him and Sally checked how clean the step was before sitting down too

'Look, there's just a few more things I need to check out, guys. But I have a sneaking suspicion that someone round here hasn't been playing with a totally straight bat for the last few weeks.'

'Really? Carry on. . .' Sally was naturally intrigued.

'Well — I need to check something with Madame Lefort, then. . . well, then, I probably need a taxi.'

'Ugh, you would keep it all mysterious.' Sally let Hugo pull her up off the step and then crossed her arms and frowned at Angus. 'But if you even vaguely started this, you better rescue our girl, Gus.'

'Yes, ma'am.' He saluted and then bounded up the steps into the chateau.

'I'm confused of Clapham.' Hugo looked at his wife.

'I know, darling. Me too.'

'Ah, Angus.' Philippe was sitting at his desk. Angus had found him relatively easily. The older man had not struck Angus as being a party animal at heart, so when he left Sally and Hugo on the steps he'd started his search inside the house.

'Monsieur Montmorency. . .'

286

'Please, just Philippe.'

'Philippe. They've arrested Jenna.'

'What?' Philippe looked troubled and Angus saw him run his hands through his thick, grey hair. '*Non, non, non. . .*'

'I know. They wouldn't give me a chance to explain, but if we can get some evidence together here, now, I'll follow them to the police station. The English officer in charge – a customs guy I think – did say I could make an appointment at nine tomorrow morning, but. . .' Angus hesitated. He just didn't want Jenna to spend a moment longer than necessary in a police cell, but he also knew rushing now could have an effect on the whole sting.

'Poor girl. I understand, Angus. But I'm sorry – I don't know what we can do until morning.'

'By morning,' Angus pointed out towards the hallway in the direction of the chateau in general, 'all the evidence could be cleared away. We need to get going now. Where's Madame Lefort?'

'I see, *oui, oui*, you are right.' He stood up and ushered Angus out of his study and along the corridor to find Madame Lefort, and if they were lucky, the proof Angus needed to prove Jenna's innocence.

53

'Right, young lady.' Fisher wasn't nasty, but his authoritarian tone scared Jenna right to her core. She wasn't used to being shouted out, or framed for crimes, or being arrested for that matter, and any warmth that had been in the night air seemed denied to her now as she was left in the cool, cement-walled cell of the local gendarmerie. She shivered as she stood next to the low bunk with its scratchy wool blanket and one slightly dirty pillow. The French officers had removed her shoes from her, not without a bit of a fight on her side, and also her jewellery, which she felt was a step too far. She was thankful that she'd slipped her Cartier charm and its box into her evening bag, which she remembered being stashed somewhere in the orangery. At least they couldn't take that away from her. Everything else, including her dignity, seemed to have been stripped away, and she stood, gently shaking in her dusky pink dress, barefoot and alone in the cell as Fisher closed the door on her. For how long she just stood there, she didn't know, but slowly her faculties seemed to return and she blinked a few times to wash away the hypnotic spell the back of the grey cell door had spun on her. She shook out her arms and grabbed the fusty old blanket and swept it around her, then plonked herself on the bunk. She had some serious thinking to do.

Fisher was about to turn the lights off in the small office he'd requisitioned for his investigation and head back to the local B&B when he saw a car's headlights pull up outside the police station. For a relatively small town, he'd already had to fight for space in the gendarmerie as the cells seemed full of drunken grape pickers and randy Frenchmen sent to cool off from the heat of the *eau de vie*. He reckoned there would be a few sore heads and hurt egos tomorrow morning, but they'd all be easily processed and released, not like his prize catch. Anyway, he hoped the lights didn't belong to another patrol coming in with another drunk vineyard worker. As criminal as she obviously was, he felt sorry for the young woman he'd just left in cell four, alone and scared, no doubt, and probably naively unaware of quite how much trouble she'd be in. The headlights turned off and he heard a commotion in the reception.

'Bloody hell,' he sighed as he went out to find out what all the fuss was about.

Jenna sat very still and put her best thinking head on. So. What had the officer said? She was being arrested for fraudulently importing wine into the UK. Or was it importing fraudulent wine into the UK? Well, she hadn't been back to the UK since the start of the summer. . . and the only paperwork she'd had anything to do with was Carstairs & Co's documents, which were prepared for her to sign. She'd helped sell the wine, and of course she'd been bunged that cash by Clive. . . but no, backtrack, backtrack. . . *she* hadn't been back to the UK, *she* hadn't prepared the paperwork, but. . .

'Mr Fisher, I implore you!' Philippe was standing in the reception area, flanked by Angus and Madame Lefort. Fisher had come out of his little office to find the three partygoers trying to schmooze their way past the officer in charge of the reception and was now holding his hands out in front of him, almost physically stopping them from leaping over the desk and hunting down their friend.

'This is not police protocol. You sir,' he pointed at Angus, 'were told to come back tomorrow morning if you had anything to say — not at half past bloody eleven at night!'

'But, officer, please, please hear us out. It's important, and not just for Jenna in the cell, but because if we leave it any longer, the person you do need to arrest could be getting away. And you don't want to have made a career-busting mistake for the sake of a few more minutes of overtime, do you?'

Fisher wasn't totally sure he liked the arrogance of the younger man but he could see that he made a point. And if he, plus these two quite respectable Frenchies, was so adamant then he could at least hear them out. He looked pointedly at his watch. 'You have five minutes. This way.'

Leading them into his office he'd barely sat down when Angus started talking at him.

'Officer, you've got the wrong person.'

'I'm sorry, sir, who are you?'

'Angus Linklater. I'm the one who alerted you to the problem from China.'

'And I am Philippe Montmorency, the owner of Château Montmorency and this is my,' he paused, 'partner, Madame Lefort.'

'Ah.' Fisher opened his notebook and started making notes as Philippe continued.

'Officer, this gentleman is correct. He was a guest here, along with the young lady you have arrested, at the start of the summer.'

'Which is when we believe she made her first contacts here.' Fisher wasn't giving up on his arrest.

'If you knew Jenna. . .' Angus was going to make a joke, but the seriousness of the occasion pulled him up sharp. 'Mr Fisher, I alerted you to the problem because I had cause to believe that some serious fraud was going on, but I'm absolutely sure it doesn't involve Jenna.'

Fisher paused. 'Mr, er, Linklater, was it? I'm sorry, sir, but after your tip-off we investigated the imported wine and all the evidence points towards Ms Jenkins. She's the signatory on the export papers for the pallet that included the forged bottles. We looked into her background and it seems she was party to a suspicious theft in her last job. . .' he licked his finger and found the page in his notebook, 'ah yes, a collection of valuable Picasso prints that are still to be located. Plus Carstairs & Co, when they checked their records at my request, could find no references for her or a proper recruitment process. She seems to have ingratiated her way into the very workings of the company and in turn your winery, sir,' he acknowledged Philippe, 'in order to perpetrate her crime.' He seemed to be ticking the weighty evidence off a list. 'When we requisitioned the pallets at the bonded warehouse in the UK we checked through them and the wooden cases that contained the forged bottles — hidden in among your bona fide Château Montmorency wooden cases on the pallet — were all clearly marked with her initials "JJ" on them.'

'You've made a mistake, it's not her.' Angus placed his hands palm down on the desk. 'The art theft was a terrible mistake — she was on the loo when the thief nicked them. You can hardly arrest her for needing a pee!'

'It is not her.' Philippe had more authority and Fisher turned his scowl away from Angus and looked up at him as he continued. 'Angus here phoned me several weeks ago from his office in Hong Kong. He told me what he told you I think, that there was indeed a fraudster in my home, but it is not her, it's. . .'

Philippe was interrupted by a fairly indistinct but loud and echoing holler that was coming from the other end of the corridor. Fisher shushed them all with a finger and they listened collectively as the shouting and banging came into focus. As it became more obvious to them all what was happening, Fisher relented and pushed back his chair as he stood up. Opening a drawer of his desk he pulled out a bunch of keys and made for the door.

'Wait here,' he told the others. 'I think we have another witness wanting to make herself heard.'

'Jonty!' Jenna banged on the door of her cell and shouted out that bastard's name again and again. 'It's not me! It's Jonty Palmer-Johnston! He's been doing me over all summer!' *And doing me too*, she thought wretchedly to herself. All those days he spent in the cellar 'cataloguing' — he must have been bloody counterfeiting! She wanted to shout at him, to swear at him, to shake off all the feelings she'd been developing for him. Jonathan *Palmer*-Johnston — JJ — no wonder she'd been accused! He'd asked her to sign all that paperwork and she stupidly hadn't read it.

She was about to hammer her fist against the raw metal of the door another time as it suddenly opened.

'Oh, officer! Thank God, look, you have to help me. Oh!'

As Fisher had unlocked the door, Angus had taken his chance to skirt around the officer and face Jenna.

'Angus!'

'Excuse me, sir, *really*?' Fisher wasn't blessed with a barrel load of patience, and this was starting to get farcical. As if to make a point, he handcuffed Jenna again, much to both her and Angus's dismay. 'Both of you, now, into my office!'

Jenna didn't need asking twice to leave the poky little cell and guided by Angus she swept down the hallway in her now rather bedraggled dress, and almost fell into Madame Lefort's arms when she saw her and Philippe in the shabby office. But it was Angus who took her back into his arms when Fisher walked in and Jenna didn't resist as he kept her close while he carried on with his explanation to Fisher.

'When we were here earlier this summer I happened to pop down to Philippe's cellar and I didn't think anything of it at the time but once I'd got to China and started work on one of their new mega-wineries, well, I realised what a bottling plant looks like — even a small one. I knew something was up, so I called Philippe who agreed to observe things a little bit. He and Madame Lefort kept an eye on Jonty and monitored his "cellar cataloguing" time.'

'It struck me as odd too,' Philippe chimed in. 'I had asked him to catalogue my private collection, but *oh la la*, the time he spent down there for such a modest amount of bottles. . .'

At this Madame Lefort, still in her lovely green velvet gown, handed some rather blurry-looking Polaroid photos over to Fisher.

'I'm sorry, monsieur officer, but these are the best I could get, but I'm sure the bottling. . .' she waved her hand as she couldn't find the word, 'stuff is down there still so you can see for yourself. This one,' she pointed at one of the pictures that Fisher was now rifling through, 'this one shows the labels, the glue, the old corks. . . and here, this one is the bottles collected after *la marriage* where very nice wines were drunk, but now see. . . same bottles, now full again. Also here,' she pulled a stash of faked labels out of her evening bag. 'I found these in his desk drawer just now. They are fake labels — he has even soaked them in,' she sniffed them, 'Earl Grey tea, I think, to make them look older. Château Margaux down the road, it is a much more expensive wine than ours, so putting our wine into these faked bottles, he could make a fortune!'

Fisher took the labels from Madame Lefort and slipped them into an evidence bag. 'Hmm. You shouldn't have moved these, but I'll take your word for it where you found them. You'll have to sign a statement.' He placed the evidence bag down on the desk and took a deep breath before carrying on. 'When we requisitioned the pallets at the docks we found forty two cases of forged bottles, fourteen hidden in each pallet.'

'With Margaux labels?' asked Philippe, trying not to be upset that his own wine was obviously not deemed flashy enough for the fraudster.

'Yes, most of them. Some from your previous vintages too, monsieur.'

'Aha.' He did a mental tally. 'So if Jonty sold them on at five hundred pounds a bottle, he would stand to make. . .'

'About two hundred and fifty grand.' Fisher filled in the blank.

The sharp intake of breath from almost everyone silently spoke volumes about what they were thinking.

'And with my own wine, from this vintage, being syphoned off and used for these fakes and all of those bottles disappearing,' Philippe continued, 'it's no wonder my books haven't been tallying.' He rubbed a hand over his tired eyes and forehead and accepted the caring hand of Madame Lefort on his arm.

'Please, Mr Fisher, can you let Jenna out of those cuffs now?' Angus brought the conversation back to his wrongly accused girlfriend. 'It's clear she's not the one who's been orchestrating this whole thing.'

'I was too bloody busy planning that party for one thing,' Jenna sighed, but optimistically raised her cuffed wrists up to the officer in the hope they would be undone.

54

Jonty took a deep puff of a fat cigar and gently blew out the smoke in large, satisfying clouds. Izzy had just given him one of the best blow jobs he had ever had and had now gone back to the party to get them both another glass of champagne. Young, beautiful and blood as blue as Elvis's suede shoes, *she'll make an excellent partner in crime*, he thought as he inhaled another puff and looked up into the starry sky, its natural twinkliness obscured by the laser beams criss-crossing it from the DJ decks on the terrace. The party was very much in full swing and he noticed coloured lights being projected across the back wall of the house as he sat in the walled garden recovering slightly from his efforts at pleasuring — and indeed being very pleasured by — Izzy. Green zig-zags and red hearts whizzed across the ancient stone facade, followed by yellow stars and a flashing blue that seemed to come from inside the house. *What a fucking amazing party.*

And what a summer too. He'd smuggled an immense amount of Château Montmorency wine disguised as Margaux out in the pallets all signed off by Jenna. It was faultless. And she had played her part, and served her purpose perfectly. Still, he couldn't shake the feeling that he'd been just a bit of a cad and although he doubted he — or to be more exact, she — would ever get caught, he probably hadn't needed to lead her so far down the garden path to make sure she would obliviously sign anything he put in front of her and he felt like she was owed a proper goodbye. Then he and Izzy could start the autumn off in style — with a little help financially from her daddy, who, by the sounds of it, could afford to keep both his darling daughter and her plus one in quite some comfort. A couple of afternoons shooting and one or two good dinners should be enough to fool the old boy into thinking that Jonty's family could be traced back to The Conquest too and old moneybags would soon be dishing it out, hand over fist. Add that to his not insubstantial profit from this summer and it was boom times a go-go. But, first things first, he better finish it with Jenna before Izzy got wind of his summer indiscretions — rich daddy aside, he wasn't going to let that former head girl (or indeed head-giving girl) get away.

Just as he was getting up to see how she was getting on with the fizz, Jonty spotted the bald head and unmistakable double denim workwear of Dave White.

'Fuck,' Jonty swore under his breath. There was nowhere he could hide in the walled garden, not now Whitey was making a beeline for him through the ornate herb garden. *Play it cool,* Jonty thought to himself, *we're almost home and dry.*

''Ello, 'ello, 'ello,' Whitey mimicked the traditional greeting of the London copper and it rankled in Jonty's ears.

'What do you want, Whitey?'

'Just coming to say goodbye, me old mucker.'

Relief flooded through Jonty. It had been an expensive reunion with Whitey and news that he was off was music to Jonty's ears. He thought better of trying for a gentlemanly handshake this time though.

'When are you off?'

'Keen to see me go?'

'Send my love to the sink estate.'

Whitey's face turned into a nasty scowl. 'I ain't going back there. Not now I've found myself a nice little earner in the shape of you, sunshine.'

'I was afraid this would happen.' Jonty didn't sound afraid though, which led Whitey to cock his head slightly to one side.

'Eh?'

'I said I was afraid something like this would happen, so I took out an insurance policy.'

'What you on about?'

'The money I gave you. First, total and final payment. If you demand any more I'll alert the authorities to the stash of cocaine that you keep buried in a silly I heart Bordeaux bag. Try and dump that bag and you'll find mysterious packages follow you wherever you go — extort from me, I incriminate you. Simple.'

'You try that and I'll just go to yer fancy bosses and tell them all about you.'

'Who'd believe a coke-addled chav like you?'

There was silence between the two men, broken only by the persistent beat of the music.

'What's he saying?' Sally pulled at Hugo's sleeve as he spoke to Angus, one ear stuck tight to the phone while he tried to block out the sounds of the party, and his wife's queries, from the other. 'Hugo. . . what's happening?'

'Right. Okay. Shit a brick, really?' Hugo was concentrating on what Angus was relaying from the police station and shushed Sally down as he listened. Finally, much to a very frustrated Sally's relief, he finished the call and filled her in.

'Well, you'll never believe this.'

'What?'

'It's extraordinary.'

'What?' Sally was growing increasingly annoyed at Hugo's unwitting obfuscation.

'Jenna's in the clear.'

'Oh, thank God.' Sally's happiness was multiplied by the knowledge that it was Angus who had obviously sorted everything out. 'I knew he'd win her back.'

'Thing is, old girl, we're on a mission.' Hugo slipped his phone into his dinner jacket pocket and then placed both of his hands on his wife's shoulders.

'Oh, right. What?' Sally was all ears, although nothing quite prepared her for what Hugo was about to tell her.

Jonty stubbed out the end of the cigar on a stone lion that stood sentry to the walled garden. Whitey had rather satisfyingly fled from the scene, no doubt off to check his caravan from top to bottom in case anything else had been planted. Jonty had taken a gamble that Whitey would be too shocked by any sort of retaliation to really think things through and luckily he'd been right.

Still, one loose end down, one still to go. Dumping someone was never fun, but at least Jenna would have her best friends — and former boyfriend — around to comfort her. He scanned the partygoers for the pink dress and was more than a little peeved when he couldn't see her. Most of the guests had lost their masks by now — it was getting on for midnight — but a few were still reeling and dancing on the terrace, scooping up the last of the champagne from the depths of the fountain and braying and shouting their way to massive hangovers tomorrow. Tomorrow. . . he should probably prepare to leave — best to lay low back in London for a few days while Jenna licked her wounds and the dust settled — in fact, a nice layer of genuine dust wouldn't harm the newly labelled bottles in Philippe's cellar either — a head start for the next shipment. *Plus*, he thought to himself, *probably time to shift some of those counterfeit wines from the bonded warehouse and get them sent up to Spike*. Jonty wove his way through the dancing toffs — noticing Bertie and her new best friends, a trio of rather hot blond model types, looking on in disdain at their drunken friends while they flicked their hair and held onto the same glass of champagne they'd probably been nursing all night. Jonty congratulated himself for never setting his sights on Bertie — fuckable she may be, but God, she must be a nightmare to live with. He flicked apart the voile curtains that hung over the doors of the dining room and darted in, crossing the empty room in a few seconds before entering the hallway, intent on just checking on his cellar one more time.

'Ah Jonty!' Hugo accosted him.

'Mate, hi.' Jonty turned up the rah-dial and clapped the larger bloke on the back and was about to make an excuse about heading down towards the office, when he remembered he still hadn't found Jenna. 'Hugo, you'll know. Seen Jenna anywhere? With Sally, perhaps?'

'Actually, I was going to ask you the same question.'

Jonty noticed that his voice had a slight edge to it and lacked its usual bonhomie.

'Haven't seen her, mate.' Jonty was suddenly feeling very much on the back foot and wondered where this change of tone from one of the most laid-back men he knew had come from.

'Yeah. . . that's probably because at this very moment, she's languishing in a French jail, accused of a crime she didn't commit. One in fact that you did. . .'

Jonty didn't waste any time hanging around to explain himself and pegged it as fast as he could away from Hugo and out towards the front door of the chateau. He could hear Hugo hollering after him, but making a plan as he ran, Jonty instinctively thought *garage, car, go, go, go*.

He didn't get as far as he wanted to, though, as just as he was darting through the old front door of the chateau a small, but exceptionally effective, foot was stuck right out in front of him.

'Fuuuuck,' he exhaled as he flew forward and grabbed onto the stone balustrade to try to stop himself from sprawling all the way down the steps. An unholy screech accompanied him as the grey-and-white cat made its feelings quite clear on how little it liked its sleeping spot on the steps being disturbed, and as Jonty's not inconsiderable frame rammed against the stone balustrade, knocking the air out of him as he bounced against it and down the steps, he was also treated to a dagger-like claw ripping its way through his trousers.

'Ha!' Sally looked on with quite some pride at her footwork, but wasn't quite ready to sit on her laurels, not until her husband was sitting on something else. 'Squash him down good and proper, darling!' she called over in encouragement as all sixteen stone of Hugo followed Jonty down the stairs and sat on him before he could get his breath back.

'Gerrofff.' Jonty struggled to breathe, let alone speak, as Hugo pinned him to the ground at the bottom of the steps.

'One bonus,' Hugo mentioned, as if he was just having a casual conversation with his quarry. 'At least you had the decency to have your trousers on.' Hugo studied his finger nails as he carried on. 'Heard you'd just been rather, well shall we say, *well catered for*, in the walled garden.'

'Da. . .fuck?' a muffled voice came from under Hugo's arse.

'Just saying, we wouldn't want to add indecent exposure to the list of crimes against you too.'

'Oh Huggsie.' Sally had come to squat down on the bottom step, next to her reclining husband on his prisoner pillow on the gravel drive. 'You are the limit.'

55

Blue lights lit the scene just as Hugo was getting a bit of pins and needles in his leg.

'About bloody time.'

'Aha! The cavalry!' Sally stood up and straightened out her skirt. 'Whooo! Over here!' she called and waved to the approaching police car.

Moments later, aided by the armed gendarmes, Jonty was up and on his feet, wholly unimpressed at not only his capture but also the fart Hugo had managed to squeeze out just before he was released from under him. The cuffs went on and Fisher read him his rights, as another car came up the driveway and out bundled Angus, Philippe, Madame Lefort and a barefoot Jenna, sparkly shoes in hand, having wrestled them back from the gendarmes on her release.

'You utter, fucking, piece of shit!' Jenna yelled at him as soon as she saw him standing there between the gendarmes, needing Angus to hold her back as she almost spat the words out.

'Oh come on.' Jonty had recovered his breath enough to force out the words. 'Don't say you didn't enjoy it, just a bit. I know I did.' His smirk made Jenna want to lash out at him, but not being naturally violent or argumentative she found it hard to retaliate.

Jonty timed his next verbal punch terribly, though. 'And you can think of me when you wear your Choos.'

Jenna instinctively hurled the pair of designer heels at him. Even in cuffs he ducked and they flew across the bonnet of the police car and skidded to a stop on the driveway.

'Please, Miss Jenkins,' Fisher implored her, 'I don't want to see these gendarmes arrest you for assault and damaging police property now I've let you go for fraud.'

'Sorry, officer, I just. . . oh, I'm just so angry at him!' Jenna clenched and unclenched her hands, each fist driving her nails further into the palms — a painful distraction to stop her from crumbling into the tears that would no doubt follow soon. She barely noticed Angus's hand on her shoulder.

'To be fair,' Fisher whispered to her, 'I wouldn't blame you.'

'Thank you.' Jenna felt quieter now, waking up as it were to the new reality around her — one where, on the positive side, she was once again a free woman and respectable citizen, but on the bummy-bumface side of things she'd been lied to and cheated on. 'Please just take him away.' Her voice was barely audible and she felt herself crumpling down onto the steps of the chateau where she sat and rested her head on her knees, wrapped her arms around herself and cried — tears of hurt, of relief, of shock and of sheer exhaustion. Angus sat down next to her and tentatively put his arm around her. Jenna willed him to keep it there, a lifeline of support as she felt like her world was falling apart for the second time this summer.

'I'm sorry they got the wrong end of the stick and arrested you first. I suppose I forgot that Philippe and I hadn't told the customs guys everything we were suspicious of after the first tip off. I never accused you, I promise. I always thought it was Jonty.'

'A few hours ago I would have bitten your head off for implying he was involved in anything.' She flared her skirt out around her a bit and rested her chin in her hands. 'I guess I've been pretty blind to a few things recently.'

'So have I.'

Jenna sat upright and clasped her hands together in her lap. 'Angus, I—'

'No, me first.' He reached over and held both of her hands in one of his. 'I'm so sorry I hurt you. I can't forgive myself.'

Jenna looked up at him, sitting there next to her, his face pale now the adrenalin had stopped coursing through his body. She instinctively reached her hand up and traced the line of the scar on his left cheek.

'Of course you should, I mean, I forgive you, of course I do. You've been a hero again, saving another female in need.' She laid her hand flat against his cheek and stroked his scar with her thumb. She let another tear escape her eye and run down her cheek, only to have Angus wipe it away for her. Looking into his eyes she saw all the love and affection he had for her. Angus was no summer fling, no rebound distraction — this was the real deal, she knew it. The love she'd known — not imagined! — when they'd been together flowed through her as he leaned in closer and gently kissed her.

Angus and Jenna weren't the only couple sealing the end of the night's events with a romantic kiss. Madame Lefort hadn't been expecting such a show of affection from her long-standing employer — but when Philippe had realised that not only would his accounts start to look a bit healthier once all of his wine was properly credited to his account, but he was probably also due a heavy compensatory pay out from Carstairs & Co — and totting that up with the cash that Bertie had just paid him for the party. . . well, his much-loved paintings were saved, and he swept Madame Lefort up into a Clark Gable-esque kiss, bending her over backwards much to her delight and feigned anguish.

'Oh, Philippe!' she exclaimed when he had pulled her back up to standing. '*Sacre bleu!* You take me for a much younger woman, *je pense!*'

'*Bien sûr*, my Angelique, just so long as you let me take you, I care nothing for your age!'

'Oh, Philippe!' Their kiss somehow expressed the suppression and longing that living together — but apart — in the household for so long had made them feel. Philippe nearly crushed his housekeeper as he hugged her to him and whispered words of love into her ears before he twirled her around again out of excitement and joy.

Suffice to say, the birthday girl herself caught wind of what had been going on out on the front steps of the chateau as one or two of her guests had reported back about 'some fracas' happening as they left the party. Max wasn't far behind her as she appeared, still looking pristine and glorious in her stunning fishtail gown, at the door.

'Oh.' She dismissed the scene in front of her as being of no consequence. 'Just a bit of tonsil tennis from the olds, yuk, and Jenna and Angus — boringville. At least those two aren't at it,' she nodded towards Sally and Hugo. 'Not sure my stomach could take it.' She winked at Max who had the decency to give her a withering look — as close to a reprimand as he ever dared.

As if to taunt Bertie, or perhaps just caught up in the romance all around them, Sally and Hugo fell into each other's arms and snogged like teenagers. Bertie made a face like she had just smelt the inner workings of a dung beetle and turned around and headed back into the party, snaring Max with one long fingernail in his cummerbund as she went.

Izzy ran, tears streaming from her eyes into the kitchen. Menou and the other catering staff had cleared out, thank God and she flopped down on one of the kitchen chairs. She'd just seen — unobserved by the party on the steps of the chateau — her lover being borne away by two burly gendarmes. She'd hidden just the other side of an ornamental stone vase and heard the officer read Jonty his rights — not to mention the revealing fracas with Jenna — before he was shoved into the police car and driven away. Slamming her fists down on the kitchen table she let out a guttural scream of annoyance before finding some kitchen roll to wipe away her tears. She'd wasted so much time mooning after Jonty, time she could have been spending setting her sights on someone much more worthy. What was it with her and men? And what, oh what, would Daddy say when she went home and told him that far from making contacts at the highest level at Carstairs & Co — Daddy's own wine merchant — she'd been fucking a fraudster? She scrunched up the kitchen roll in her fist. Even this bloody table reminded her of what a fool she'd been. She sniffed and then slipped her phone out of her pocket. Her finger swiped through a few of her emails before she found what she was looking for. Admissions secretary, Jesus College, Oxford. Sod social climbing and canapé soirées, she was going back to school.

56

'Ooh, look at this.' Sally passed the international edition of *The Times* over to Jenna as they sat in the village café drinking indecently good coffee and wolfing down croissants and pains au raisin. A few days had passed since the drama of Bertie's party and life had certainly been different since. Angus and Jenna had spent the day after the party at the police station, making statements and leaving contact addresses among other administrative things. And with the evidence mounting against him, Jonty had finally admitted it all. Fisher wouldn't release any more details to Jenna, but obviously a mole in the gendarme had leaked the story to the press and there it was, in black and white, on page four of *The Times*.

'Mr Palmer-Johnston of Hammersmith, London, was charged with several counts of wine fraud under the Forgery and Counterfeiting Act 1981, and for smuggling alcohol into the UK without paying the correct duty or VAT. He was arrested at the source of the crime, the top-end Château Montmorency in Bordeaux, France, which exports fine wine into the UK via its UK agents, Carstairs & Co, who were the employers of Mr Palmer-Johnston and his previously falsely accused assistant.'

'That's you, sweetie!' Sally raised her coffee cup in acknowledgement as Jenna kept reading.

'Although sentencing for these crimes is usually light, a source reports that Mr Palmer-Johnston was also in possession of several hundred grams of cocaine and a witness has come forward with evidence of past misdemeanours that could lead to several cold cases being reopened.'

'Blimey.'

Jenna carried on reading, 'Mr Palmer-Johnston declined to comment to the press, however our sources say that he had smuggled over five hundred bottles of forged wine into the UK via his official employer Carstairs & Co's shipping company, and was then relying on, among others, an independent wine merchant in Cheshire, Spike Spooner of Life, Cork & Spoon in Alderley Edge, to fence the forged bottles.' Jenna dropped the paper in a rage. 'That bastard! So he was in cahoots with Spike all along!'

'Was he the sleazy one that Jonty rescued you from, before, you know. . .?'

Blushing in embarrassment remembering her summer fling, Jenna replied, 'Yes that's him. So he must have been receiving the forged bottles from Jonty and then foisting them off on his "more money than sense" customers.'

'But didn't Jonty rather blot his copy book with him when he attacked him for you?'

Jenna thought for a bit before the light-bulb moment struck her. 'Or. . . was it that having "rescued" me, he had something to hold over Spike in case he ever wanted to end their nefarious partnership? Far from issuing some sort of retribution for sleazing on me, he was going to blackmail the bugger!'

'The total shit!'

'Yes, and to think I was seriously starting to fall for him. You know, not in an Angus way, but in a sort of rebound way. God, and he was cheating on me the whole time with bloody Izzy!'

'Oh yes. Rest assured, darling, Hugo and I will not be seeking the services of that little madam again, no matter how scrummy her gougères were.'

'But I guess I do have to thank him in a way, for you know, getting me in trouble, as if he hadn't then Angus and I would never have got back together.'

Sally lowered her cup and leaned into her friend. 'It was rather wonderful, wasn't it, I mean the way he rescued you from the police cell. Although I must say, I think Hugo and I played our parts quite well too!'

'Oh you did, you did, thanks, Sals. Did Hugo really fart on him?'

'Yes. He called it his trump card.'

Jenna laughed at her friend as she shook her head. 'Back to Angus, though. So he'd been keeping tabs on Jonty's movements all the way from China, apparently. A proper Interpol sting operation!' Jenna idly pulled apart one of the pastries in front of them and mused on, 'Madame Lefort had been so worried about Philippe before then, his blood pressure must have been through the roof trying to trace where all his stock and money was going. How horrid of Jonty to have used him so badly for his own gains. Ugh, he was like a parasite wearing down his host but needing him alive so he could keep feeding.'

'Oh, poor Philippe,' Sally agreed. 'Para-shite, more like!'

The girls giggled and just before she popped another piece of buttery pastry into her mouth Jenna changed the subject. 'I just can't believe I let matters get so bad between me and Angus in the first place — what was I thinking?'

'Well, I did try to tell you, sweetie. . .'

Jenna heaved a sigh and took another sip from her coffee. She and Angus had clasped each other so tightly sitting on those steps after the police car had gone. Guests leaving the party and getting cabs had slowly filed past them and the evening had come to an end by the time they had let each other go and, even then, they were always touching some part of each other as they wordlessly and in total mutual agreement climbed the stone staircase and headed along the opulent corridor to Angus's — and now her — room. The fervent and passionate kissing had started almost as soon as the door had closed and Angus had undressed Jenna, not realising the significance of flinging the bejewelled dress to the floor and accidentally standing on it as he ran his hands down Jenna's naked body, stroking every inch of her before the need became too much and they both fell helplessly and deliciously onto the four-poster bed.

The next morning had seen a blissful re-enactment of the lovemaking from the night before and again, after they were home from the police station they had snuck back upstairs and made love hungrily and lovingly. It was only that evening when Philippe had invited Jenna and Angus, and Hugo and Sally, to stay on for a few days that they had finally become more social and joined their friends in dissecting every bit of what had happened. And so it was that Jenna and Sally were sitting in the little café in the village next to the chateau reading the paper while waiting for Hugo and Angus to finalise their new flight plans and come and join them.

'Oh London, London,' Sally sang to herself as she stretched out her legs into a sunbeam. 'I just don't feel like going back.'

'You and me both. Lord knows what I'm going to do with myself back there. I am done with the art world. I'm definitely done with the wine trade and, even after a summer here in the vineyards, I think I need a holiday!'

Acknowledgements

My thanks as ever to my agent Emily Sweet, my editor at Orion Clare Hey, and my copy editor Justine Taylor — you've teased the best out of me yet again. Also to the owners of the many chateaux I've visited over the years — your golden-stone walls, elegant shuttered windows and gravelled terraces have provided so much inspiration for Château Montmorency. Weddings, holidays or wine-buying trips — you never know when inspiration will hit! Thanks also to Sofa.com for my 10-year-old sofa, which has quite literally 'supported' me as I tip-tap-type away — with the cat vying with my laptop for attention, but usually settling comfortably, like me, into the feathered cushions. My love and gratitude as always to my friends and family for putting up with me while I go into boring writer mode and my darling husband, Rupert, who makes sure my glass is always topped up.

If you loved *Summer at the Vineyard*,
then get ready to jet down to the
Côte d'Azur for Fliss Chester's next novel

Meet Me at the Riviera

Coming Summer 2019

It's all about millionaires, Manolos and mega-yachts as
Jenna Jenkins starts her new job as a party planner on
the French Riviera. Not always a fan of the fabulously
wealthy — Jenna surprises herself and finds she has a
real knack of helping the super rich go overboard as
event after glittering event is held on the decks — and
dinghies — of the amazing yachts, not to mention in
the ballroom of the luxurious Hotel Metropole.

Little does Jenna know, however, that behind her
back there's a tussle going on for her affections and
her loyalty to her darling boyfriend, gorgeous Angus
Linklater, is about to be tested by the mysterious
millionaire who keeps flirting with her over the caviar
and canapés.

With Max and Bertie's wedding to plan, old friends
Hugo and Sally bursting with news of their own and
a lot of champagne to drink, it's going to be a very
interesting summer. Just meet me at the Riviera. . .